THE HIDDEN

SARAH PINBOROUGH

LEISURE BOOKS   NEW YORK CITY

To Martin, with love

LEISURE BOOKS ®

November 2004

Published by

Dorchester Publishing Co., Inc.
200 Madison Avenue
New York, NY 10016

ISBN 0-8439-5480-9

Visit us on the web at www.dorchesterpub.com.

ACKNOWLEDGMENT

I'd like to thank my agent Steve Calcutt and editor Don D'Auria for liking my words, and a special thanks to Tim Lebbon for his help, support, and general fabulousness.

ACKNOWLEDGMENTS

THE HIDDEN

PROLOGUE

It was four o'clock in the morning when the dreams woke her again. Her heart was thumping rapidly against her chest as she leapt upward in her bed, lungs gasping for air. Still clinging to the sheets she rolled over, falling to the floor where she crouched, retching for what felt like an eternity as the cool sweat dried against her skin. Fumbling frantically above her, she found the bedside lamp and with shaking hands managed to turn it on. As light flooded into every corner of the small room, the sudden change making her eyes cringe, she leaned back against the built-in wardrobes, and breathed deeply. She was still shivering, but as she focused on the familiar surroundings, her body slowly calmed down. Hauling herself to her feet, she made her way into the bathroom to splash her face with cool water.

God, she looked like shit. Sure, the mirror was old and a bit cracked, but it was still reflecting faithfully enough. Her gray eyes were a little too pink around the edges, and the rings underneath were getting blacker daily. She'd also lost weight. Hah. No wonder she hadn't been getting laid lately. She forced a smile. Soaking her hands first, she ran them through her hair, the only part of her that still looked healthy, and sighed deeply. Maybe it was time to go back to the doctor and get some Valium or whatever the latest version was. The shrink certainly didn't do any good, but then, that could hardly be classed as his fault. How can you analyze someone who's being ripped apart by terrible nightmares when they can never remember the details from the moment they wake up? God, she was fucked up. The last five months had seemed like an eternity, every night worse than its predecessor, dreams emerging from nowhere, for no real reason.

Her head was starting to throb, like the onset of a bruiser of a migraine. Great. Perfect. Maybe it was a tumor growing insidiously inside the shelter of her skull. She pushed that comforting thought out of the way and reached for the handle on the cabinet above the sink, sure that there was aspirin waiting within to rescue her.

She stopped halfway, her hand hovering uncertainly in the air, for the moment completely abandoned by her brain. Something was happening in the mirror. Something small, but something that was growing fast. There were colors, shapes, things moving. She looked closer, confused, her head really thumping now, her heart rapidly catching up with it. What the fuck was that? Something she almost recognized was trying to pull itself into form, but was getting all messed up with her reflected face, distorting it, stretching her lips and eyelids. It wasn't nice. She wanted it to stop now, oh yes, stopping now would be good. Her stomach knotted with dread as the world around her drained away, leaving only the mirror and the headache. Her heart was trying to escape her chest and her legs were like water as she felt the heat rush to her face. She was starting to panic, and dimly, beneath the haze of pain her bladder gave way and she heard the rush of liquid as it hit the tiles beneath her. The pain was engulfing her completely and she slid down the wall behind her, coming to rest in the warm puddle of pee she had so recently released. Please God, I don't want a brain tumor, please God, I don't want to die in my bathroom, please God, make whatever's happening in the mirror go away, please somebody help me, please. She was moaning gently, indistinct sounds, slipping away uselessly.

The surface of the mirror was stretching out toward her, whatever thing that was in there, eager to be released. This was it, she was dying, she knew that now. She could see what was happening in the bathroom but knew that none of it was real, none of it could ever be real. It was in her mind. None of it mattered, except she was dying and she didn't want to. She was dying in her own piss, alone and terrified. She could feel consciousness wresting itself away from her desperate grasp and just when she thought terror would overcome her, she glanced back up to see the writhing shape before her smashing the mirror, as it emerged new-born.

It was then that it all became clear, the dreams flooding back in a flash, images piercing the pain. She realized with terrible clarity that there were some things that were worse than death, some things that were much much worse, and as the figure leaned over her smiling, she screamed and screamed with the last of her breath; not for help, because she knew that would be futile, but she screamed for what she knew was to come.

For what the dreams had shown her.

CHAPTER ONE

It was so peaceful in the dark, in that blackness that exists only somewhere between unconsciousness and death, with no light or sound or sense of existence to fear the loss of. It seemed that she had lain there forever, entombed inside this body, her body, before, from nowhere, the humming started. At first it was only a tentative invader, like the buzz of a distant fly on a quiet summer's day, but slowly, bringing time and dimension with it, it grew closer, drawing her out from the tranquillity of nothingness, refusing to be ignored. Eons later, the droning formed shapes that somewhere in the depths of her subconscious she knew she recognized. Her awakening mind grasped at them quizzically, that fly now darting around her head, in her ears, too close to swat away. Four minutes later, her eyes opened.

"Ah, you're awake."

The sound was gentle and she turned her head to see who had spoken, whose voice it was that had brought her out of the void. The answer was sitting on the edge of the bed leaning toward her, holding one of her hands, the touch almost intimate, but lacking something. She sensed instantly that it was a caress full of concern but no personal affection. The expression on the mildly handsome face looking back at her evoked the same feeling. A doctor then. She tried to focus her dulled mind on the room around her, separating each off-white shape from the one next to it, allocating each to its correct noun: cupboard, chair, sink, lamp, savoring the way the images and sounds slotted together so perfectly. Nothing too wrong with the brain then. The clinical blandness of the decor, combined with her companion, brought her swiftly to the right conclusion.

"Am I in a hospital?" Jesus, she was thirsty. Her voice was nothing more than a dry rasp. How long had she been out? Could you get this dehydrated overnight? She eased herself upright in the bed, ignoring the giddiness that attacked and reached carefully for the water beside her.

Smiling, the doctor watched as she drank greedily from the glass. He nodded. "You certainly are. We've been a bit worried about you. You've been out cold since the ambulance boys brought you in, and that's about thirty-six hours ago. All I can say is you must have really needed a good sleep, because we've run some tests and we can't find anything physically wrong with you." He paused to refill her glass. "Not that I mind having beautiful damsels in distress delivered to my door! I'm Dr. Hanson by the way." Watching as she started to gulp down the second glassful, he pulled her hand away from her mouth slightly and laughed.

"Take your time with that, there's plenty more in the tap. Take a breath, and if you feel up to it, why not try telling me what happened. Do you remember what made you collapse? Did you feel particularly ill at all?" Still holding the glass she leaned back against the pillows without responding. The doctor looked concerned.

"If you're too tired to answer, don't worry, this can wait, but sometimes the patient can help us see something we might have overlooked, especially in cases like this where the police have been involved." He raised one eyebrow and waved a mocking finger at her. "Anyway, it can damage my professional reputation when patients manage to heal themselves with no help from me at all." The attempt at light humor passed her by.

Police? She slowed down to sipping. "I don't remember anything."

The doctor tried to jog her memory. "Well, apparently your neighbor heard glass smashing and screams coming from your flat in the early hours of the morning. He thought you were being attacked and called the police. They arrived and broke in to find you curled up on your bathroom floor surrounded by pieces of broken mirror from the cabinet above your sink." He left out the detail that she had wet herself. Who needs to know something like that? "Anyhow, they couldn't find any sign of an intruder, nor could they wake you up, so the sergeant called an ambulance and here you are. Is any of this ringing bells?"

There was no impatience in his voice or smile but that didn't bring the woman much comfort. She was listening to his words, but this time she could find no images to match up with them. Flat, neighbor, bathroom, mirror. They were just floating abandoned in her mind, no anchor to give them solidity.

"No, you don't understand." Her voice was a whisper as she tried to squeeze the words out before the chill that was running up her body froze her throat. "You don't understand. I don't remember anything. Anything at all. I don't even know who I am. I don't even know my own name." It sounded like an ocean was rushing through her ears as her flesh tried to pull inward away from her skin in panic. What was happening to her? The room was getting watery and she fixed her wide-eyed attention on the doctor as if he were her personal messiah. She grabbed his arm tightly. "Can you help me? You've got to help me!" The voice sounded disembodied, as if it wasn't hers at all, but then, she reasoned, suppressing the urge to giggle hysterically, how would she know? She didn't even know who *she* was.

Dr. Hanson mentally examined the pale young woman in the bed. She wasn't joking or faking. He recognized the look. She really couldn't recall anything. Sometimes that could happen after a blow to the head or a shock of some kind, but it normally didn't last long, maybe a couple days or so. This was different though. The girl didn't have a bruise or a scratch on her when she came in, nothing to indicate a trauma of any kind, not externally anyway. He sighed inwardly. Then again, it could just be a case of the brain protecting itself. She was pretty but obviously drained and underweight. Maybe she'd been having a breakdown, not exactly uncommon in these changing times. He saw more and more of that kind of thing, a by-product of people forced to the edge living in a world that was developing faster than they ever could. What was it called? Future Shock? Something like that. She seemed an unlikely candidate; according to the neighbor she edited children's fiction for a successful publishing house. But you couldn't tell these days, he'd seen weirder things. Mostly he was too tired to think about it. With his caseload, every night he went home and found his wife still there was a blessing. Bringing himself back to the problem before him he noticed that her hand was as cold as ice and clammy.

"Your name is Rachel Wright, you're twenty-nine and single." He paused for her to absorb the morsel of information, testing it for recognition, finding none.

"I understand that this must be very unsettling and frightening for you, but I want you to keep a firm hold of one thing." She noticed that he had kind, tired wrinkles around his eyes as she focussed on him; this stranger who at this moment was the only person in the world she knew, her closest acquaintance. He was rubbing warmth into her hands as he spoke. She liked the feeling of security it imbued. "This is probably a very temporary affliction. Amnesia is common after suffering a shock or trauma of some kind. You still have control of all your movement facilities. You know how to speak, and if I'm correct, you could recognize Piccadilly Circus if you saw it." Rachel ran a quick mental check, avoiding the dark empty spaces and found with relief that he was right.

"Therefore, what you have is partial amnesia, a version of memory loss that only pertains to the details of your personal experiences. For example, you'll know what kind of shop Safeway is, but won't know whether you liked to buy there or not. Are you with me?" He paused again before continuing, slowly but firmly.

"It's highly likely, as it is with about ninety-nine percent of similar cases, that once you're back in your own home, surrounded by things that have personal significance, these memories will find their way back to you. Sometimes this can be a gradual process, occurring over the space of a few months, but it can also hit you in a flash. Just try not to push too hard and let your brain deal with it in its own time."

He could see that she was calmer, settled back on the pillows. In this case he was fully confident in what he was saying, but watching her relax, purely a reaction to him, he was reminded of the power in a doctor's bedside manner. It always surprised him. A good doctor had to be a good actor; no two ways about it, it was all part of the service. How many times had he smiled at people, some younger than the woman in front of him, a few probably in this very bed, smiled when he could smell death's whispers already upon them? Too many to think about. But then, every job has its downside, and with the upside as high as it was in his chosen profession, you had to expect the low to be low. As he always said to the junior doctors and nurses when faced with their first trolley downstairs, the price for being able to save lives for a living is that, however hard you try, you can never save them all.

Blood was pumping warmly through the young woman's

hand. Her immediate shock was over. "Think of this as your body protecting you. Your brain is a very clever instrument. It will only give you access to information it thinks you can deal with and I guess that this is its way of saying it thinks you could do with having a few days off from being you. When it decides you're ready, then you'll find all those doors in your head unlocked. I'm sure of it."

She nodded, his reassurances slowly seeping into her, too exhausted to maintain her panic for long. Besides, she felt healthy enough, and as he said, they'd done all the tests and there was nothing wrong with her. Her eyelids began to droop downward and she yawned. Maybe if she had some more sleep her brain would sort itself out. The room dimmed as she drifted off. *Que sera, sera.* How bad could it be anyway?

CHAPTER TWO

Opening the door of the mini-cab and stepping out onto the pavement, Rachel wrapped her coat around her to keep out the chill. Gazing up at the red brick building in front of her, she waited for Mike to finish paying the driver. Mike Flynn had turned out to be something of a knight in shining armor. Not only was he the neighbor who called the police after trying to get into her flat and save her himself, but he had also undertaken to keep an eye on her until she regained her memory, a commitment without which—and combined with his incessant visiting—Dr. Hanson would probably not have let her out of the hospital so soon. It seemed that the small matter of a loss of memory turned the men around her overprotective.

She glanced at the man getting out of the car, his slightly long, light-brown hair blowing in the gusts of wind that were attacking the London afternoon. He was about five foot eleven, and beneath his cream jumper she could make out the lines of a body that had muscles in all the right places, without having been worked too hard. This was not a man who spent hours at the gym examining himself. He was unconsciously fit, not vainly sculpted. Pushing his hair out of his eyes, he smiled at her. It was an open friendly smile and she couldn't help but smile back. The best thing that she'd figured out about Mike over the past few days was there was nothing deceptive about him. What you saw was what you got. He was a gentle man, anyone could see that. But then he was a schoolteacher, for Christ's sake! And she had a feeling that he had a bit of a crush on her, and that was doing her ego no harm, but cute though he may have been, what she needed now was a friend and her gut was telling her that this man would be a good one.

Standing next to her outside the mansion block on Luxborough Street, he thrust his hands in his pockets to ward off the chill. "Well, this is it, home sweet home! Ringing any bells yet?"

He looked at her expectantly and she tried not to feel disappointed. Shrugging, she followed him across the road. "Nope. Not a thing." He took the small flight of stone stairs leading to the impressive, darkly glossed front door two at a time. "Well, that's not really a surpise, most of the flats in Marylebone look pretty much the same from the outside. And anyway, remember what the doctor said. This whole memory thing could take months." He pushed the door and then held it open for her from the inside, bowing as she stepped into the warm hallway. "If madam would like to follow me, I will show her to her flat."

She smiled and shook her head at him. Yes, he was definitely cute. "Tell me," she said as they walked up the narrow staircase leading to the two flats on the second floor. "Do I rent or own?" He finally brought her to a halt outside a white solid-looking door whose paint was somewhat fresher than the one opposite. She remembered that the police had had to break in to get to her. Had Mike made sure that the door was repaired quickly? From what she'd seen so far, she wouldn't put it past him. He unlocked the door and then handed her the set of keys. "You most definitely own. It's the rest of us common people that rent." She liked the creases that formed in his cheeks when he grinned at her. Raising one eyebrow teasingly, she stepped over the threshold. "So I'm a rich bitch. Good. I like that."

He followed her in and put the small overnight bag down in the compact hallway, suddenly awkward now that they were back in familiar territory. Familiar to him at any rate. Considering the way Rachel glanced uncertainly through each of the doors, she may as well be in a hotel as her own home. "Look," he said, not moving any farther into the apartment, "I know you're going to want to spend some time settling back in so I'll get going. Do you want me to go down to Waitrose and pick you up some stuff? There's a pint of milk in the fridge and some bread in the cupboard but that's about it. I didn't know whether Dr. Hanson was going to give you the all clear or not today, so I didn't go crazy in the supermarket."

She looked at him from the lounge doorway and smiled. Something about him made her smile a lot. She shook her head. "Thanks but no thanks. I could probably do with the fresh air. Waitrose is on High Street, isn't it?"

Nodding back at her, he pulled open the front door to leave. "Okay. Well, I'll leave you to get on. If you need me, I'm just across the corridor."

He stepped back out into the communal hallway before she had time to thank him properly for everything he'd done, and then her door clicked shut between them, leaving her in silence. Staring into the sitting room filled with strange belongings, she felt her heart sink. She had a feeling that by the time she'd trawled her way through her life's evidence, she was going to need some company and a nice bottle of wine. After checking the lock on the front door so that she wouldn't lock herself out, she quickly moved to the opposite flat, knocking loudly. She flicked her hair out of her face and drew herself up to her full five foot eight before Mike opened the door looking concerned. "Everything okay?"

"Yes, fine. I was just wondering if you'd like to have din-

ner with me tonight." Why did she feel so nervous about
asking? It was hardly a date. Now that she'd started she
didn't give him time to reply. "I'll cook. It'll be my way of
saying thank you. Could you make it at about eight-thirty?
That'll give me plenty of time to trawl the flat looking for interesting secrets about myself." The air coming from his flat
had a warm stale smell of cigarette smoke and she suddenly felt a sharp craving. Well, there was one secret uncovered. She was a smoker.

After having some kind of mental tussle with himself,
Mike grinned. "You're on. It'll save me from A-level Shakespeare essays. I'll bring the wine. I've got a couple of good
bottles of Burgundy I've been saving for a special occasion.
This may as well be it!"

"Good." Rachel knew that the smile dancing on her face
was flirtatious but she couldn't control it. Maybe she was a
man-eater. Maybe she had a different lover every night of
the week, now there was something to think about! She
smiled to herself as she shut the front door behind her.
Given the distinct lack of visitors at the hospital that hardly
seemed likely. Mike was the only person who had come to
see her apart from a brief visit from her boss, Suzy Jenner,
so judging from that it would be safe to say she was hardly
a social animal.

Taking the long cashmere coat off and hanging it on the
five-hooked coat rack on the wall, she picked up the overnight bag and took it through the second door on the left
leading to the bedroom. Well, at least she'd got that right.
Hooray! She knew where her own bedroom was! Throwing
the bag on the double bed with the flowery duvet cover,
she sighed. Okay no more putting it off, let's see what kind
of a girl I am. She pulled open the sliding doors of the
white built-in wardrobe and started to examine the contents. There were dresses and suits hanging from the rail
and then jeans and T-shirts folded neatly on the shelves inside on the right. A lot of jeans; she could count at least
four pairs just at a glance.

Pulling a pair out, she held them against her slim frame. Well, they were definitely her size, but the cut was baggy. She didn't like them at all. Throwing them untidily back from whence they came, she turned her attention to the dresses and skirts, neatly arranged in color order working from black up through the colors to white. Maybe she'd find something to wear tonight tucked away amongst the bland long-skirted suits and full-cut trousers, something short and sexy. After a few minutes of searching, the best she could come up with was a knee-length Laura Ashley number. Hardly the stuff fantasies were made of. A quick search of her shoes and underwear drawer did little to raise her spirits. Among the sensible shoes, ankle boots, and sneakers she found one pair of barely worn black high heels, but they looked out of place, as if bought on a whim, as if they didn't belong here.

She sat down heavily on the bed, still holding a pair of sensible white Marks and Spencer's minis. High-cut leg, but hardly daring. God, she wanted to cry. She hadn't expected the memories to flood back to her once she was home, but she'd at least expected to feel comfortable, she'd at least expected to *like* her things. Looking forlornly at the pair of black high heels she'd dragged out to wear tonight, she spoke aloud. "I know how you feel. I don't think I belong here either." She tried to shrug the feeling off, knowing it was ridiculous. Of course she belonged here, she owned the fucking flat. How much more could she belong than that? It was just that she couldn't shake the feeling that she was different from the girl who lived here. Looking at the clothes and the furniture, and even the large tomes that she'd noticed filling up the wall-to-wall bookshelves in the lounge, she had the depressing feeling she'd been living the life of someone much older. Twenty-nine going on forty-five, that was her.

She flopped back on the bed and lay staring at the ceiling. Well, this is it, girl, she thought, trying to raise a smile. You're a boring old bag without one pair of lacy knickers to your

name. Why didn't she feel like that, then? Why did she feel
that all this was alien? It wasn't as if she wanted a wardobe
full of mini-dresses and g-strings, but she thought she'd have
found a few items that were chic and fun. What had happened to her in life to turn her into this stranger? A thought
came to her. Maybe by losing her memory she'd somehow
got rid of her emotional baggage and had now become the
person she might have been if life with all its cares and worries hadn't taken over? Finding the theory comforting, she
turned her head to the right and looked at the neatly ordered
dressing table by the window. There was a small bag of
makeup on it and a photograph in a silver teddy bear frame.

Rolling onto her back and swinging her legs around so
that she was on the other side of the bed, she stood up and
retrieved the picture, studying it carefully. The middle-aged
couple had their faces close together and were beaming
broadly, skin a little overwhite in the glare of the flash from
a camera held slightly too close. So this was mum and dad.
She felt an ache inside her at having lost her memories of
them. The plump woman trapped in the shiny paper could
have been a stranger as far as Rachel knew, and the same
went for the bespectacled man. All she knew about them
were the tiny morsels of information Dr. Hanson had
gleaned for her from her files: Peggy and Doug Wright, who
had adopted her when she was the unwanted result of a
teenage pregnancy and loved her as their own until they
were killed in a car accident a year ago. The thought that
she might have lost them completely and forever made her
heart contract. They were dead and she had misplaced all
remembrances of them, every loving word and deed. It felt
to her like the worst kind of betrayal. They had taken her
into their home and cherished her and she couldn't even
be bothered to treasure their memory.

Her eyes were stinging with the promise of tears and she
bit down angrily into her bottom lip. She wasn't making
any sense and she knew it. It wasn't her fault she couldn't
remember anything, and everyone at the hospital had reas-

sured her over and over again that it was all going to come back to her in time. She just had to be patient. She glanced down again at the couple in the photo. But what if the memories never came back? What if they were gone for good? She paused for a second and then put the picture back on the dressing table. Shaking off her fear, she wiped her eyes and turned to face the wardrobe.

Well, she reflected, putting her hands on her hips, if the memories never come back, then I've got a good chance of not reverting back to frumpiness. There was always an upside to everything. Her vague stab at humor didn't really help and after the initial shock of the sound, she was pleased to hear the sharp ringing tone of the telephone breaking the silence.

Even though there was an extension by the bed, she left the room to take the call in the lounge, hoping to leave her miserable mood behind her. Sitting down in the small beige two-seater sofa, sinking into the comfort of its deep cushions, she picked up the receiver from the low side table and held it to her ear. "Hello?" She wished she sounded more confident but was filled with dread that she was about to have a conversation with someone she didn't know at all.

"Hi Rachel, it's Suzy here." The woman sounded distant and crackly, she was probably on a mobile, but Rachel was just relieved that she recognized the voice. Thank heaven for small mercies. "I was just checking that you got home safely. Is everything okay?"

There was the heavy rumble of traffic in the background. "Yeah, I'm fine. It's just nice to get out of the hospital." She felt awkward talking to Suzy and knew that the other woman felt the same. Apparently they were pretty close, went out for a few drinks once a week, but when she'd come to visit in the ward, Rachel had thought she was nice enough, but there was no spark between them, no shared jokes or sense of humor. She guessed the situation must seem pretty weird to Suzy Jenner as well. There was a clumsy pause before the other woman spoke.

"Good, good. Look, I didn't know how you felt about work right at the moment, and there's no pressure, you know you can take as much time as you want, but I didn't want you getting bored, so I've forwarded a manuscript to your flat to look at if you want to. You should get it tomorrow. Is that all right?"

"Great!" Rachel said, hoping she wasn't overcompensating with her enthusiastic tone. "I'll make sure I check the post." Suddenly she wanted this conversation to be over. "I hate to cut it short, Suzy, but I've got the bath running so I'm going to have to go. I'll give you a call in a couple days and let you know how I'm getting on."

The voice on the other end didn't hide its disappointment very well as it said its farewells, and Rachel felt like a complete bitch as she put the phone down. Relieved, but a bitch all the same.

Flopping back against the sofa, she sucked in a deep breath. "Shit, shit, shit, shit, shit." She muttered while glancing round the room at all the neatly organized shelves and surfaces. The sudden nicotine craving she'd felt at the door to Mike's flat hadn't left her, but so far she'd found no trace of cigarettes or even an ashtray in any of the rooms. Maybe she'd quit or something just before her accident. Another great mystery in the unremembered past of Rachel Wright comes along to piss her off! Well, she knew what was top of her shopping list for this afternoon. Giving up had plenty to recommend it but now really wasn't the time.

Gazing across the room, her eyes fell on the bottom shelf of the enormous wooden wall unit filled with books. There stood all the childrens novels that she had edited so far in her career and there were at least twenty or thirty of them. She must have enjoyed her work and been delighted with the outcomes to have given the little collection pride of place among the myriad of other works of literature, some of which Rachel was sure would be eminently more interesting. Looking at the larger first editions on the higher shelves she knew instantly that she enjoyed reading, but the stumbling block came when her vision dropped once again to the bottom shelf and she felt her heart sink. Nothing in any of the titles caused her to smile or have even the vaguest interest in picking up the slim, brightly colored volumes. If anything, they had the opposite effect. This Rachel, this *post-memory* Rachel as she was beginning to think of herself, rightly or wrongly thought that being a children's book editor had to be one of the most boring jobs she could imagine. She couldn't contemplate spending endless days removing and adding to saccharin-infested pages of simple-mindedness. And that was the crux of it. One more thing that seemed to be jarringly wrong, and definitely the cause of the awkwardness with Suzy Jenner. How was she going to explain that one to her boss and her erstwhile friend? *Sorry, but I really don't think that this is the job for the new and improved me, have you got any openings in the erotic section? I think that's more my style, I really do.*

God, she thought, hauling herself to her feet and rubbing the tension away from her face with her hands. Why did everything have to be so goddamn weird? If all the doctors at the hospital hadn't been so thorough with their tests, she'd be pretty convinced that there was something wrong with her. Some awful brain disease you always think is going to get somebody else. Her stomach was tying itself in knots and she tried some of the deep breathing exercises that Dr. Hanson had recommended should she succumb to any bouts of anxiety. In through the nose, fill up your chest and stomach, empty your mind and then exhale slowly through your mouth. Repeat until calm.

All that was fine but emptying your mind was never as easy as emptying your lungs. She was starting to wonder if perhaps she was suffering from a mental illness, some form of schizophrenia perhaps? That thought didn't help her racing heart to slow down. *What I need is to get out of this flat,* she decided quickly. *Fresh air and a brisk walk should calm me down. In fact, just being out of this fucking flat should calm me down.*

Retrieving her wallet and pulling her coat on in the hallway she found herself relieved that she'd invited Mike Flynn over for dinner. Apart from not really wanting to spend her first evening home in front of the television feeling sorry for herself, there was something very reassuring about Mike. He had an aura about him that made her feel safe, as if everthing was going to be all right no matter what. Maybe it was because he was a teacher, used to dealing with all those young things full of hormones racing out of control. Who knows?

There was more to it than that, but she wasn't in the mood to think about those other feelings she seemed to be developing for him at an alarming rate, the way her heart beat slightly faster when he aimed that cheeky grin at her and the disappointment she felt when he left the room. Right now, all she wanted was comfort. That was all that was on the menu for this evening, except maybe a couple of big juicy steaks and salad.

Making sure she had her door keys in her bag, she pulled open the front door and then slammed it behind her as if making a point to that old Rachel whose ghost seemed to lurk within. She felt better after her little act of rebellion and, hands stuffed deep into her pockets, she contemplated the white wood that separated her from her old life.

I'm not scared of you, you boring book editor, she realized with a moment of elation, I'm scared of turning back into you! She stuck her tongue out at the white door and almost laughed out loud. Okay, so it wasn't the best way to deal with her fears, but it certainly made her feel better. Maybe she was different now, she thought as she strode down Paddington Street, ignoring the bustle of people heading home as rush hour approached, but why panic about it? The doctors all said there was nothing physically wrong with her, so who was she to disagree? And as for her mental health, well, she felt fine.

She was starting to feel a bit silly about her whole moment of panic. Everything was bound to feel weird, she rea-

soned for the thousandth time, and maybe it was just possible she hadn't loved her job as much as everyone had
thought. All she knew about herself was what little other
people had told her. Maybe her work had brought on a
breakdown, letting this Rachel, the one that had always
been lurking within, escape. Her nose was starting to run in
the chilly air as she turned into Marylebone High Street,
the dusk broken up by the warm light escaping from the
shops and boutiques that lined it invitingly.

No, she told herself firmly and finally, if you have to feel
anything about that flat, don't feel afraid at how alien it
feels, just feel sorry for your old self that you'd been living a
lie for such a long time you didn't know how to stop.

Seeing the Waitrose logo calling out to her from a hundred yards she walked purposefully forward until something caught her attention out of the corner of her eye.
Stopping so suddenly she almost caused a cursing someone to collide into the back of her, she gazed through the
small window at the three manniquins standing arrogantly
on the cream silk dais. It was the middle one wearing the
black dress that she focused on. It really was absolutely
gorgeous and she knew it was something the old her would
never have bought. Especially when she looked at the
small handwritten price tag on the floor at the dummy's
feet. It was over two hundred pounds, but whereas most
tight black minidresses veered toward tacky, this one was
elegantly sexy. Stylish and chic; just the kind of thing she'd
been hoping to find in her cupboards.

The cold had wormed its way into her boots and she
moved from one foot to the other to keep feeling in her toes
while she contemplated the price. Sod it, she thought,
thrusting open the door, enjoying the heat that rushed at
her as the tiny bell jangled above, Rachel Wright had credit
cards she never used coming out of her ears. What was the
point of having all that plastic if you didn't make the most of
it? After all, it was time things changed a little around here.

CHAPTER THREE

Callum felt tiny splinters tearing into the soft flesh of his cheek as he dragged his face along the rough wooden floorboards of the attic as he tried to raise his heavy head. The room was blurred in the dim moonlight coming from the small window above him as his head swum and his eyes battled to regain their focus. Pulling himself into an upright sitting position, he lowered his face into his hands for a few moments concentrating only on keeping down the bile that was burning in his chest. His body shook relentlessly and the fingers that were resting on his thinning hair were cold against his milky scalp. Had it happened? Had it finally happened? His rising excitement overwhelmed his nausea and he raised his head to look eagerly across the room. Shining fanatically in the gloom, his eyes searched for the outline of the dusty loft's second occupant. Oh yes, something had happened. Even in this empty light he could see that something had definitely happened.

Letting out a childish giggle, a sound out of place coming from within the angular confines of his bland, middle-aged face, he scrambled to his feet and his large hand engulfed the light switch. The yellow glare from the unshaded 100-watt bulb burned the back of his eyes and made them water, but oblivious to the pain, a smile spread across his face that made him appear almost beautiful as he gazed with wonder at the body still tied to the chair but no longer in need of the restraints. Shuffling toward the center of the room, he let out a small moan and fell to his knees, taking hold of the undamaged left hand and kissing it.

"Oh Helen," he breathed in awe, "We did it. You did it." Shutting his eyes he rubbed the blue fingers against his cheek, ignoring the tiny pricking of wood, as if expecting to get some response. There was none. For the first time in five months, Callum didn't feel her pulse speed up through the warm flesh as he touched her. He knew that no longer would her head turn toward him, eyes stretched wide with terror, face flushed with sweat, breathing hard behind her brown tape gag. The thought made him sad and he sighed heavily. He had grown fond of Helen. He would miss her.

Sitting back on his heels he looked at the body on the chair. It was amazing how little it resembled the plump, plain girl that he had first met. But then it was barely recognizable as the woman who had sat there yesterday. Her body seemed hollow as if somehow sucked dry, which maybe it had been, he reflected as his detached examination came to rest on her lower abdomen. Her stomach had split open, most of her innards now sitting in a slovenly lethargic heap on her lap, but there was very little blood. Surely there should have been more blood from such a violent wound? He looked closer, fascinated, lowering his face to within inches of her cold intestines, savoring the stale and sticky aroma. He fought the urge to run his tongue over the slimy surface. He couldn't do that, not with Helen. Helen's body was special. Sacred.

Kneeling upward he took her slumped head and lifted it gently so that he could look at her face. The skin had started to sag, the muscles relaxed forever, and color would never return to that blue-gray visage. Sadly he noted that her eyeballs had exploded, leaving clear gel splattered on her cheeks. He wiped them clean wishing that he could have seen the final, frozen expression in the windows of her soul. "Thank you." He knelt before the silenced woman as if in supplication, his head bowed. "You have given me back my Elizabeth. I will never forget you." He licked her face, tasting the last remains of salty tears. The small gold crucifix that hung around her neck glinted beneath the light. Callum ignored it. There was no power there, it was an empty symbol. Anyway, he had a feeling that Helen had given up believing in the power of God as her salvation quite some time ago.

He stood up, ignoring the clicking in his joints. Now all he had to do was wait. Wait for Elizabeth to come and find him and then everything would be as it was. Life would have meaning again. He smiled in anticipation. Oh, how he had missed her. Her love. Her understanding.

He turned the attic light out without glancing back at Helen. He was tired and his body ached. How long he had been unconscious he didn't know, but he thought that Helen had probably been through her initial rigor mortis and back again. Fifteen hours? Maybe more, maybe less. The terrible dryness in his throat made him think it might even have been days.

Elizabeth wouldn't come here, it would be too dangerous so he should go to his flat and wait for her to call. He walked down the three flights of stairs to the hallway where he picked up his thin gray waterproof jacket, glancing at himself in the ornate silver-trimmed mirror as he put it on. Despite the weight he had lost and the tiredness that was visible in the creases in his face, he still looked like the bank administrator he had been until a couple weeks ago when he could no longer stand the strain of the rituals in the attic and trying to maintain the veneer of normalcy. Respectable. Bland. No distinguishing features. He smiled to himself as he opened the front door. Not on the outside, anyway. And Elizabeth had seen through all that, had recognized a kindred spirit, had understood his secrets.

The dark green Mondeo was where he had left it on the drive and he slid the key into the lock, opened the door, and got in. He looked at the house as he pulled the seatbelt across his shoulder. The ivy-clad walls that rose elegantly upward from the foundations of the detached four-bedroom residence betrayed nothing of the macabre events that had occurred within; it's Georgian front a veneer of suburban respectability. Urban detachment in every sense. The next time he saw it, she would be with him. They could clean it up together. He could show her the things he had done for her. Exactly as she had told him to. He could show her Helen.

Reversing on the gravel, he turned the car around and then drove up the narrow lane to emerge from behind the safety barrier of leafy oaks that lined the perimeter of Elizabeth's property and out into the relative rush of London's evening traffic, leaving Hampstead behind and heading to his somewhat more modest flat on Finchley Road.

Forty-five minutes later, he was back at Mother's and about to slide into a hot bath. He still called his home "Mother's" even though the sour woman had been dead for over ten years now. Apart from those terrible four days of escape when he was twenty that he no longer cared to think about, this was the only place he had ever lived. His sanctuary against the cruelty of the outside world. He remembered the look of gloating on his mother's face, when he had come back a broken man, a humiliated man, and her laugh when he had asked her, begged her, why she had never told him he wasn't *normal*. Why she had let him find out *that* way? What kind of mother was she?

She had regarded his misery with contempt and spat at him, her black eyes glittering feverishly out of her too thin face. She had leaned over him and beneath her buttoned-up blouse he could see the outline of a bra that was cutting into her, the bra was obviously too small, as if she were try-

ing to flatten her chest, deny her femininity. Wisps of gray-
ing hair had escaped from her bun and curled around her
cheeks. She had never been a pretty woman, and when
she had stood over him that day, his face clasped firmly in
both her hands, her eyes wide, her whole body shaking, he
had a moment of clarity and could see she was wearing
the face of madness. She was as purely mad as a person
could be.

"That'll teach you to want to be a dirty little boy like all
the others, won't it?" She spoke through clenched teeth, the
force of her words spraying warm, odorous liquid at him.
"Did she laugh at your thing when you tried to put it in her?
Did she, Callum? Did she laugh?"

He had shut his eyes and let the tears flow. Oh yes, she
had laughed. Laughed through the red lips he had until
that moment adored. She had laughed and laughed until
he had taken his clothes and run from her. Run home to
mother. He could still see those sharp, white teeth flashing
against the moist lips. *Is that it? Is that all you've got? But
that's hardly an inch! Oh my God, I don't believe it, you wait
till I tell the girls, they'll never believe it!* He sat on the bed
watching her beautiful head thrown back laughing uncontrollably, sniggering at him, the sound mean and harsh. He
had loved her, he had fallen hopelessly, romantically in
love with her two months previously when he first saw her
in the bar, red dress cut low, so proud of her sexuality, so
different from Mother, so free. Her sense of freedom had
made his breath catch in his throat.

It took him a week before he could bring himself to
speak to her. A week of shaking at the bar of that God-awful
pub surrounded by big burly men with foul mouths that
made him feel so uncomfortable. But in the end, it was at
the bank that they finally came face-to-face and it was she
who took the initiative, drawing him into conversation. She
seemed amused by him, but he didn't care. She suggested
going out and he took her to the most expensive restaurant
in the local area. He bought her champagne. Her name

was Gloria. It was she who suggested he move in with her, he could help her with the bills, he could get away from *that terrible woman,* it was time for him to be a man, get out from behind the apron strings. He thought that all his dreams had come true. He and Gloria would live happily ever after. They would have a beautiful family. She would love him forever. What became glaringly obvious to Callum as he watched her turn to ugliness, laughing gleefully in her bed, was that all Gloria had wanted was his money and his *thing.* She never wanted *him* at all. What kind of fool had he been?

He had sobbed openly and shamelessly at his mother's kitchen table, snot running down his face. Why, why had he been born that way? Why hadn't she told him? His mother filled her old metal kettle up with water from the tap and put it on the gas ring, lighting it with a long match. When she turned around the aggression had gone from her face and she was wearing an odd, twisted smile, as if he had said something funny.

She tucked a loose strand of hair behind her left ear and tilted her head to one side. When she spoke, her voice was back to normal. "Don't be so ridiculous, Callum. Nobody's *born* like that. I did it to you when you were a baby. I saved you from yourself." He looked up at her in shocked horror, the tears drying instantly with the impact of what she had said. Her mouth frowned a little with disgust. "I couldn't let you grow up to be like your father. I couldn't let that happen." She shivered, as if shaking away an unpleasant memory, and then smiled. "What about a nice cup of tea?"

Callum watched in silence as she filled the pot, her back to him. Oh yes, his mother was mad. Stark, raving mad. But still it took him ten years before he could bring himself to kill her. Some bonds are hard to break. Gloria, however, wasn't so lucky. He allowed her an interval of three or four lovers, not long by Gloria's standards, and then disposed of her. Out of sight, out of mind as the old saying goes. Her body was never recovered and it always gave him great satisfaction to know that she wasn't laughing at him at the end. Oh no. She definitely wasn't laughing.

Peeling off his shirt, trousers, and socks, dropping them into a small heap on the stone floor, and stepped into the warm water with his blue underpants still on. He would soap himself beneath the fabric and then remove the wet shorts when he had a towel firmly secured around his waist. To look at his body naked made him cringe and if he could avoid it at all, then he would.

Sighing, he slid down the enamel until the water was lapping at his chin. Even beneath the steam he shivered. For some reason the cold and ache in his muscles hadn't dissipated since he came to on the attic floor, if anything it had grown worse. Maybe he was getting the flu. Maybe it was just shock, who knows. Using his left foot as a lever he opened the tap and added some hot water until the temperature was near scalding. God, that felt good. He splashed some on his face and then shut his eyes, surprised at how calm he felt.

Perhaps it was just sheer exhaustion after the past few months or maybe it was just so hard to believe, that finally, it had happened. He had brought Elizabeth back. Somewhere in this city she was breathing, eating, drinking, living. A different-looking Elizabeth, a younger version, but Elizabeth all the same. And he was sure she would be thinking of him, thinking of a way to contact him. Elizabeth would come for him, he thought in a bubble of excited happiness. They loved each other. He had been as a disciple to her, and he had brought her back. Him and Helen.

Rubbing the bar of coal tar soap absently over his pale, thin chest he felt a pang of sorrow thinking of Helen. Poor, cold Helen. She had been a gentle soul, so different from the all-consuming, grasping demands of Elizabeth. In many secret ways he had begun to look forward to his evenings with her. She had looked at him as if he were something special. She had been so pathetically grateful for his attention.

Of course it could never have progressed, even without Elizabeth's plans for her. She could never have understood his little secret, his problem. She would have become Gloria all over again, and that he could never have borne. No. It was better this way, even though he would miss her. This way she would always be pure, always be special, having sacrificed herself for something so much bigger than the both of them. And whatever feelings he may have had for her they were mundane and colorless next to the excruciating agony of loving Elizabeth Ray. The romanticism of it all made him want to cry. He felt a slight itch in his stomach and chased it round his small flabby belly for a moment, seeking relief.

Helen Holmes had been coming into the Finchley branch of the bank for as long as Callum could remember. Not that he'd paid much attention to her. After Gloria and before Elizabeth, the only woman who had his attention was Mother and eventually he'd plucked up the guts to get rid of her, *say thank you and good night, Mother,* leaving himself at last in peace.

In many ways their situations had not been that different. Helen was chained to her own mother by the elder woman's invalidity and she too had never found the inner strength to break free. Once a week she would come in to deposit her mother's pension and her own benefits allowances and pay whatever bills she had outstanding, taking the money out of the blue leather clip purse with careful hands. Never anything large. There was nothing extravagant about Helen's life. Even the cash withdrawals she occasionally made, no doubt for personal spending, clothes, or toiletries, were lower than the average teenage girl was capable of spending on a Saturday afternoon. No, there were no expensive face creams or lipsticks for Helen. Until she had unwittingly become central to his life, Callum had given her no thought whatsoever. She was just another bland existence eking itself out, waiting for death, not even interesting enough to kill. In the end though, it was the very emptiness of her life that led to her fate. And of course her choice of bank. How easy is it to find a suitably isolated virgin these days? Helen had been walking into his domain for years as if waiting for him, waiting for her destiny to take hold.

He had tried to explain all this to her terrified eyes as she choked on the beaker of Elizabeth's blood, that first night, when it was still warm, and the scent of the very essence of her being made him light-headed. Helen choked on the liquid and he had to tape her mouth closed quickly to stop her vomiting up her precious cargo. It hurt him to think she hadn't understood. He expected more from her.

He had gone for the clichéd approach, watching her through the brown tinted glass that made up the branch wall, timing his entrance perfectly with her exit. He later told her it felt like that INXS song, the one that sang about two worlds colliding. She had liked that. Elizabeth had been right. Plain, fat girls were all romantics at heart.

He bent down to pick up her bag, ignoring her flustered attempts to do it herself, holding his cheese-and-onion-chutney sandwich under one arm. He held her belongings out to her. "I'm so sorry, I really should learn to look where I'm going." It was hard to catch her eye as she kept her head low, just making furtive glimpses up at him. She shook her head as if annoyed at herself.

"No, it was my fault. I was in a world of my own." She was blushing and her voice was low and soft. Callum wondered briefly what other kind of world this pathetic creature could possibly inhabit. She started to move away but he stopped her gently with one hand on her arm. "Helen, isn't it?"

She looked directly at him now, surprised, and he saw that her eyes were really quite a vivid blue. He smiled his best engaging smile and nodded in the direction of the bank. "I work in there for my sins. I've seen you come in. How's your mother?" As if he cared.

Her brown hair was pulled back in an untidy ponytail

and she fiddled with it with her free hand either out of embarrassment at her untended appearance or awkwardness from being in a conversation with a member of the opposite sex, he couldn't tell which.

"She's fine, thanks." Again her eyes slid from his face and she glanced around the busy street as if looking for an escape.

Having seen her account details he knew that she was thirty-two, ten years younger than him, but time had been kind to her and there was no signs of lines or aging around her eyes and forehead. She had the complexion of a sixteen-year-old. But then she had never really done any living, had she? Oh, how delicious it would feel to take a paring knife and delicately peel that pale, peachy skin away. To hear her scream beneath his fingertips. Hmmm. She most have noticed something intense in his gaze, because smiling slightly, the edges of her mouth twitching nervously, she started to move away.

"Helen, wait!"

Used to doing as she was told, she stopped instantly and turned to him. He shuffled from foot to foot and was surprised at how naturally the blush he was trying to force came to his cheeks. "I was wondering, well, I was wondering," he coughed and paused, easing into his role as the nervous suitor, "I was wondering if maybe you'd like to go out for dinner with me one evening." He smiled nervously. "There, I've said it. I've been trying to get myself to ask you that for weeks."

From a few feet away, with her childlike face and middle-aged woman's demeanor, she looked at him incredulously. She didn't say a word. Just as she was about to decline, to run back to the safety of her empty world, he played his trump card, letting his face and head fall, although not quite low enough to show where his mousy hair was thinning.

"Of course. How silly of me. Of course you wouldn't be interested. I should never have presumed to ask. I suppose it was just, you know, meeting like this, out of a formal situation, it made me braver than usual." He kept his face averted, as if he couldn't bring himself to look at her. "Please forget I ever asked." He turned away and headed toward the automatic door. He could almost feel the indecision emanating from her. She chewed her lip. "Mr. Burnett." Her voice was so quiet it was as if she herself couldn't believe she was speaking. He turned around. "Call me Callum, please." She swallowed hard, and then smiled. "I'd love to have dinner with you."

He thought the grin that he allowed to spread across his cheeks was likely to split his face. If you applied the right quantity of guilt you could make a woman agree to just about anything. "Great! That's great! What night suits you?"

She beamed back at him, now that she had committed herself to this adventure she was eager to continue before losing her nerve. "What about Wednesday? The vicar usually calls in on Mother for a couple of hours, and then I can arrange for home help to come and put her to bed." She shrugged apologetically, and suddenly he realized how he must appear to Elizabeth; just like this lonely woman, like a puppy, eager to please. To suddenly be on the other foot of the power balance made adrenaline pump through his system giving him a surge of energy, filling him with urges that would have to wait until later to be released. He maintained his sheepish grin, pushing back the dark images that threatened to overwhelm him. "Wednesday's great! Shall I pick you up?"

Again the awkwardness flitted across her face. "No, if it's okay with you, I'll meet you here at about six-thirty. Mother can be a little difficult about guests."

He nodded, as if that was the most natural thing in the world for a thirtysomething woman to say. But then, he knew all about unusual mothers. He'd had the queen of unusual mothers. Who was he to comment?

When she walked away, glancing shyly back over her shoulder, he thought he could detect a slight spring in her

step. She was proud of herself. She had opened herself up
for an adventure, maybe even romance. She'd given herself
something to look forward to. It would be a few weeks before she realized she'd picked the wrong person to start ad-
venturing with. Before she realized that she'd let herself in
for so much more adventure than she wanted. Before she
realized she'd made a really, really bad mistake. But by
then it was horribly too late to change her mind.

Looking at the chipped paint on the ceiling of the bathroom, he thought of all the remains rotting away in Elizabeth's cellar. The two of them had accomplished so much
in the year since they first met at her bookshop. Since she'd
brought them all together, all her best customers, brought
them together to form their own secret sect, dabbling in the
forbidden. Most of the others had thought it something of a
game, but Callum knew different. He hadn't even wanted
to come, his interest in Elizabeth until that point had been
for rather more unsavory purposes, feigning curiosity in
her bookshop to stalk her, to get a taste of his prey, brows-
ing the pages to find perhaps a new and novel way to make
her scream.

He had placed the small pile of texts on the wooden
counter and taken two twenty-pound notes out of his wallet. He knew better than to ever pay for anything out of his
normal routine with a credit card. Try and avoid a link with
the victim, however tenuous it may be. Unlike others he
had read about, he had a healthy respect for the abilities of
the police.

Their hands had touched for a moment as she took the
money from him and before she opened the old-fashioned
shop till to get his change, she watched him thoughtfully.
He looked away from her penetrating gaze, never happy to
be the focus of female attention, wondering if they could
see through him to his failings, wondering how close to a
smirk their smiles were. Elizabeth wasn't smiling. She held
both his money and the books in her hands, not allowing

him the freedom to leave without it seeming strange. He figeted from one foot to the other, his anxiety rising. Now she did smile.

"I'm having a little gathering here tonight. Nothing big, just a private meeting of a few like-minded people, a secret affair." She raised one eyebrow at him. "I wondered if you might like to come." She had the arrogance of all attractive women, never expecting to be refused.

"No thank you, I'm afraid I have other plans for the evening." He whispered toward his feet, just wanting to be away from here quickly. Conversation had never been on his agenda for the day. *Yes, I have plans, and so do you, you pissing little bitch, I'm going to be peeling off your face and wearing it while I eat your motherfucking liver,* was what he wanted to scream at her, *our own little private meeting, most definitely a secret affair, how do you think you're going to like that?*

She put his purchases in a brown paper bag and held them out to him with his change. This time she grabbed his wrist tightly and pulled him in so that the wooden edge of the counter was cutting into his thin hips. *Oh God, he felt trapped. Oh God, he didn't like this, he didn't like it one bit.*

She smiled and relaxed her grip slightly and he knew she could feel his pulse hammering through the thin layer of skin. He tried to breathe. "I'm your friend, Callum." Her voice was like poisoned honey, soft and sweet, her mouth so close he could feel the warm breath trickling into his ear. *How did she know his name? What was going on here? This did not happen to him, this FEAR did not happen to him.* She pulled back slightly so that he could see her face.

She was everything that disgusted him in a woman. Her top was cut too low for a woman of her age, showing too much flesh, and her face was covered in makeup beneath her loose, dark hair, a painted beauty, Gloria at forty. Her eyes though, they were different. There was so much strength in those gray eyes he couldn't bring himself to look away, like a rabbit caught in the glare of the oncoming headlights. What she said next turned his legs to water.

"You see, I know all about you, Callum. I know all your dirty secrets. I know what you did to Mother and I know what Mother did to poor you." She paused and Callum thought he was going to throw up. She smiled at him affectionately. "The bitch deserved it. Just the same as Gloria. Come to the meeting, Callum. I think you and I can help each other. I've been looking for someone like you." She kissed him lightly on the cheek and then let him go. Standing there, his world reeling, he couldn't bring himself to move. *How could she know? How could she possibly know?*

Elizabeth was looking down at some stock sheets. She didn't look up. "Eight-thirty to nine. I'll provide the wine of course. Don't be late."

He couldn't remember getting home. And later on, he went to the meeting.

The itch in his stomach was getting worse and he looked down to see that he'd been scratching his skin raw. What was going on? Shuddering, he wondered if some kind of dust parasite had burrowed under his skin while he lay unconscious on the dirty attic floor, and was now happily laying its eggs under his epidermis. He scratched some more, and letting the bathwater out told himself not to be so ridiculous. It was probably just a touch of nervous eczema. The baby lotion in the bathroom cabinet would sort it out. He stood up and wrapped a towel around his waist before removing his wet pants and putting them in the laundry basket along with the rest of his clothes. His body still ached, every movement accentuating the pain. He was too old to be sleeping on wooden floors. Perhaps a few hours in bed would do him good.

Taking the lotion from the small cupboard he padded barefoot and dripping across the the small landing and into his bedroom where he pulled on some clean y-fronts before dropping the towel. Squeezing a generous amount of lotion onto his hand, he began to rub it into his belly. The itch had spread to his lower back and he smoothed the cream there too. The relief he expected to feel didn't come, if anything the irritation was intensifying. The aches in his muscles were worse too. He sat on the bed trying to quell his unease, to squash the rising panic. *Everything's fine, everything's normal.* That became somewhat harder to do when he saw the first tiny movement under the skin of his midriff. Tiny, but definitely there, and definitely *NOT NORMAL*. Suddenly, as he felt something dislodge at the very core of him, he wasn't so sure that Elizabeth was going to call. He wasn't so sure at all.

CHAPTER FOUR

Mike tapped gently on the front door with his free hand and waited. Nothing happened, the seconds dragging into minutes. He wondered if she would answer at all. Maybe she'd fallen asleep or changed her mind since this afternoon. Blowing his fringe out of his eyes he took a deep breath to calm himself down.

He'd finished marking the lower sixth English essays at about quarter to seven and there were several students who'd be getting better grades than expected when they got their papers back. Somehow the analysis of Macbeth as the epitome of the tragic hero hadn't held his attention and instead, like most of his pupils, he'd put more effort into watching the clock than reading the words in front of him.

It's just dinner, he told himself in the voice normally reserved solely for James Patterson in year three. Stop getting wound up. She was never interested in you before, so why should a knock on the head change that? Somehow the rational part of him wasn't having much effect, and when he heard the sound of the lock clicking, he seriously thought he might be sick.

The door opened and the two bottles of red wine that were tucked under his left arm almost slipped forgotten to the floor. For a moment he couldn't say anything at all. She looked fantastic, there really were no other words to describe it. The black dress with the shoelace thin straps hugged her figure perfectly, revealing that although toned and slim, she still definitely had curves. Oh yes, she was rounded in all the right places. Not that that should have been a surprise to him, after all, he'd seen them up close once before, even if she couldn't remember it, but he'd never seen her like this, so unabashedly, so blatantly sexy. Some small part of his brain tried to prevent him from doing the typical male thing, but he couldn't help himself and his eyes slowly worked their way from the top of her curled and styled head to her stillettoed feet and back up again. Inwardly he groaned. Jesus Christ, this was going to be a harder evening than he'd originally thought.

"What do you think?" she asked while taking the bottles and ushering him into the lounge. As she moved into the light he could see the outline of her erect nipples beneath the sheer material, and quickly brought his eyes up to meet hers. There was no need to put himself through more than he had to. Doing his best to pull himself together, he smiled. "What can I say? I think 'wow' just about covers it." His voice was slightly higher than normal but hopefully she wouldn't notice.

She beamed back, obviously pleased with the compliment and then opened the burgundy, pouring them each a large glass. Her eyes confidently met his as she handed him one. "I wasn't too impressed with what I found in my wardrobe, so I decided a change was in order. No more Laura Ashley classics for me, thank you very much!"

Taking a much-needed large swallow of wine he offered her his best cheeky Irish grin. "Well, I have to say that I always thought you looked pretty good whatever you were wearing, but you're right, this look is definitely a change."

There was something else that was different about her

and he couldn't quite put his finger on it. Sure, she seemed much more confident than she'd come across on the few conversations they'd shared outside of that one romantic interlude, but hey, he could hardly claim to know her that well, and after the embarrassing morning after the night before he was hardly going to have been seeing the best of her. Still, she'd always been so *serious* and that somehow had changed. Even when she'd been drunk that night it was as if she was taking getting drunk very seriously. She seemed to get very little fun out of it. If he was honest, the same could be said for the sex. This Rachel, however, seemed more frivolous. Definitely more flirtatious. How could that have happened?

He laughed wryly at himself as she went into the kitchen to check on the dinner. What am I doing? I'm a teacher not a psychologist. Why can't I learn to just enjoy an evening with a beautiful woman without having to analyze it? He wondered if maybe he had a dose of seriousness himself.

Topping off his glass, he took his place on one side of the small pull-out dining table. She'd lit two candles and dimmed the lights, and between the glow of the small flames and the warmth of the wine he started to relax. Well, whatever this changeable woman was, she was certainly pretty remarkable. Gone was the vulnerable, frightened girl he'd encountered in the hospital a week ago. She might not have gotten her memory back, but she was definitely recovering in other areas. You had to give her ten out of ten for bravery. He had to admit she seemed pretty amazing all around. Listening to himself eulogizing her, he shook his head. Get a grip on yourself, he thought as she came into the room carrying two plates. It took you about six months to get over your last infatuation with her, if you're not careful you'll be starting a whole new one. And that is something you can happily do without.

She put his plate in front of him and then pulled out her own chair and sat down, tucking a stray dark curl behind one ear. "I hope you weren't expecting anything fancy. I haven't decided if I'm a good cook or not yet." She raised her glass. "Cheers! Tuck in."

Mike looked up from his meal, confused. "Rachel, this is steak."

She swallowed her first mouthful and her brow furrowed. "Oh God, don't tell me you're a vegetarian. You should have said."

She moved to take his plate away but he shook his head. "No, you don't understand. I'm not the vegetarian. You are." As soon as he said it, he realized what had been bugging him before. When she'd opened the door, she'd been smoking. Rachel had always hated cigarettes, that he definitely knew about her.

Looking up at her, he saw the flash of fear in her eyes before she covered it with a smile. She raised one eyebrow at him. "Not any more apparently." She cut herself another mouthful and after she'd swallowed it, drank some wine. He put down his knife and fork, his concern making it impossible to let the matter rest. "While we're on the subject," he spoke as gently as he could, "you don't smoke either."

She stared at him, and he could see a touch of anger there. Fear disguised as anger at any rate. Her voice was defiant. "Maybe I used to smoke the same way as maybe I used to eat meat. Who knows? I certainly don't, but I'm not going to spend my time worrying about everything that's different about me now compared to then okay, so why should you? Things are fucking weird enough for me at the moment as it is. How well did you know me anyway?"

She glared at him after her outburst as if challenging him to respond. For a moment he said nothing while his internal voice lectured him. Well done Mike, he thought. Now you've really pissed her off. Good work, mate. You always did have a special way with the ladies.

She had a point, after all. He didn't really know her very well, so who was he to comment on what was normal for her? Still, what was niggling at him and what he couldn't let go was that he was pretty sure she'd told him she'd never smoked. In fact, he was positive, but there was no way he was going to say that now. And anyway, what did it matter? Maybe the shock she'd suffered had activated different parts of her brain or something. He'd give the good doctor a call in the morning just to check that everything really was all right, but in the meantime there was no gain to be had in worrying her. He raised his hands upward in surrender.

"You're right. I hardly know anything about you or your past. I'm sorry." She stared back at him, sulkily. He tilted his head. "But hey, I'm not complaining, I love steak. And does this mean that I can smoke in your flat, because I am really dying for a cigarette."

The dancing smile began to return to her red lips. She'd certainly chosen a dramatic shade of lipstick. In the pale yellow light it looked like she'd been drinking blood. Sitting back in her chair, she wiggled a finger at him. "Okay, you're forgiven. For now." She looked down at their full plates. "Now come on, let's eat. I'm starving!"

It wasn't until they'd opened the second bottle of wine that his conscience got the better of him. He'd been meaning to tell her all evening, but they'd been getting on so well he hadn't wanted to spoil it. Looking at this laughing, vital woman though, he knew he had to come clean. After all, she might get her memory back at any moment and he'd seem pretty low then. He took a deep breath. There was no time like the present. He found it hard to look her in the eye.

"Rachel, there's something I've been meaning to tell you all week, but there hasn't really been the right moment and it's a bit of an awkward one." He chewed the side of his mouth, while she raised one eyebrow above a slightly glazed eye.

"That sounds interesting. What about?"

He could feel the blush creeping up beneath the collar of his cream shirt. Oh God, this wasn't easy. "About you and me. Something I should have told you earlier, but I guess I didn't have the guts."

Regarding him cautiously, her lips a deeper purple now, stained by the wine, she spoke slowly. "Go on then. Spit it out."

He drained his glass before speaking. If he was going to get kicked out of this flat for the second time in his life then he was going to do it drunk, or as close to drunk as possible. He ran his hand through his hair. "Okay, it's like this. About eighteen months ago one of the tenants downstairs had a leaving party and we were all invited. You and I had had the odd conversation before, you know, in the hallway, etcetera, nothing special, but at the party we got talking and then we got drunk." He could hear himself waffling. "Well, to cut a long story short, we ended up sleeping together." He paused to see her reaction.

She watched him, coolly, and he shrugged. "Well that's it, nothing to tell after that. Two consenting adults passing like ships in the night as the old saying goes. I guess I just felt weird being the only one of the two of us to remember it."

"Yes, that certainly gives you the advantage." She said dryly, staring at her wineglass. Looking up at him, she forced a smile. "So what happened? Wasn't I very good, or could you just not be bothered to call?"

He laughed before he could stop himself and then explained quickly before she blew up at him again. "God no, it wasn't me! If you must know I was over the moon. It was you. You made it very clear to me that you considered the whole thing a mistake you'd like to put behind you. Since then you haven't really spoken to me at all."

She looked shocked. "Oh. Right." There was a moment's silence before she started to giggle, snorting into her wine. This time it was Mike's turn to look confused. This definitely wasn't the reaction he'd been expecting. He let her amuse herself for a few more moments before speaking. "What's so funny?"

Pushing her hair out of her face, she exhaled, fighting back another laugh. "Well, it must have been you that was a

lousy lay then and that's a relief. I've found out enough boring facts about myself today without adding that one to the
list!" She smiled at him happily and he frowned back.

"You're really not very funny," he said in a mock stern
voice. "As a matter of fact, amazing though you may have
been, I was very proud of my performance on that particular evening."

She raised an eyebrow teasingly, enjoying the game. "Is
that a fact? Well obviously you just didn't meet with my ex-
acting standards. Judging by the lack of men in my life, not
very many do!"

There was a moment of awkwardness and then she
smiled softly. "Thanks for telling me, Mike." She stood up,
moved to where he was sitting and leaned over, her hair
brushing his face. "I just can't believe I let you walk out of
here, though. I really can't." She whispered before kissing
him, her tongue pressing gently into his mouth, parting his
surprised lips.

Taken unawares, Mike couldn't stop himself from responding, unable to believe the heat that was coming from
her and he pushed the chair away, standing up without
breaking the kiss, pulling her toward him, taking control.
He didn't know what was going on here, but his body was
on fire from just touching her, smelling her, feeling the soft-
ness of her skin. He groaned quietly as she ran her fingertips expertly down his spine and pressed her hips into his
erection. Her free hand followed, touching him through his
trousers and his mind exploded in a thousand colors. Jesus, it had been good before, but this was something else.
She had no shyness at all. He could hear her panting as he
slid one hand down from her hair, lightly touching her
neck before cupping her breast and teasing her nipple
through the thin material. He dropped his head and
sucked it through her dress, teasing it with his teeth until it
was so hard he thought it would explode. Her panting
turned to soft moaning as she pressed herself toward him,

trying to undo his zipper, and raise her dress at the same time, and he knew that if he didn't stop now, he'd be here all night.

His arms shaking, he slowly but firmly pushed her backward. Her face was flushed and her lips slightly swollen and seeing her so aroused he had to look away to keep his resolve. This was more than should be asked of any man and he wondered whether he was being noble or just the craziest man alive. His body was screaming at him that the latter was more likely.

"What?" She said, her breath still out of control, "What's the matter?"

Mike lit a cigarette and inhaled deeply. Christ, doing the right thing was a pain in the arse sometimes. He smiled and rubbed his face. "I would love to stay tonight. I mean, I would really, really love to stay," he smiled, trying to lighten the moment, "but I can't." Rachel frowned.

"Why not? Is it me?" She sat on the sofa looking hurt.

Mike couldn't believe she could think like that. Hadn't she felt him? What more proof of her own attractiveness did she need? He laughed gently. "God no, it's not you. You're great, you're perfect, you're fucking amazing." He smiled at her raised eyebrow. "It's just that I think you should spend your first night back here on your own." He paused. "So did Dr. Hanson, and I don't want to be the one to break the good doctor's trust." He picked up his jacket. "So as much as I would love to stay, I think it's time for me to say good night and thank you for a wonderful evening." Suddenly he did feel tired, exhausted by fighting his desire. Tossing his coat over his shoulder he went out into the corridor. Her voice followed him and he could hear the merriment in it.

"What about tomorrow night?"

Smiling, he turned the snib releasing the latch. "Oh, tomorrow night's a different kettle of fish completely. No rules apply." Rachel still hadn't left the sitting room but called through. "Good. Thank the Lord for that! I'll see you tomorrow then, you great big party pooper!"

"It's a date!" He closed the door quietly behind him and pulled out his door keys. A cold shower and then bed, that's what he needed. It had been one hell of a week.

CHAPTER FIVE

When things really started jumping in Callum's stomach, he had recovered a hazy state of consciousness and fallen off the bed to crawl to the telephone in the hallway. He hadn't made it very far, his body drained of energy, limbs lifeless, all strength concentrated on his flesh that was on fire with an itchiness he couldn't alleviate. His skin was itching from the inside, that warm, damp underbelly he knew only too well, had tasted and licked clean, *but not his own, dear Lord, not his own*, itching like nothing he could imagine and if he looked down at himself he could see, *Oh God, oh God, there are things inside of me, what things inside of me, how the fucking hell did these things get inside of me?*, the tiny squirming bodies that were multiplying too rapidly, far too rapidly to contemplate.

He hauled himself to the wall, pulled his body into an upright sitting position and slumped there, thin, pale legs spread naked in front of him, eyes staring unfocused down the beige carpeted stairs to the front door. His breath was harsh in his chest and he moaned as he felt an itch separating and start working its way upward from his belly. *What's happening to me, why to me? THIS Can't BE HAP- PENING, NOT TO ME!* A tear slipped down his cheek as he sobbed, moaning quietly.

Down the stairs and a world away he saw a shadow pass in front of the door activating the night light above that Mother had installed years ago to ward away *the bad men*. He let out a small hysterical giggle. As if she had to worry about the bad men. How much badder could anyone be than he and his mad, mad mother? How much more bad- ness could this house hold? Oh, but he was paying the price now, and he had a feeling that the price was going to be much higher than he had ever anticipated.

Whatever had been crawling up his intestine had reached his neck and he began to cough, a dry rasping, choking cough as if his throat was being licked by the rough skin from a thousand cats tongues. The squirming, wriggling mass had stretched up to his chest now, far be- yond the pathetic boundary of his underpants, and as he leaned to one side heaving, retching to bring up the tick- ling blockage, he couldn't help but look at his distorted body. *What have you done to me, Elizabeth? What have you done to me?*

Suddenly he felt the lump in his throat dislodge itself and he spat the offending object out of his mouth, cringing with revulsion. The black bug was covered in slime and was so fat it could hardly hold itself up on its thin spiky legs. Callum looked in disbelief. Although damp and hard shelled, there was no shine on it's armored outer coating, the black of its wings so matte it was as if the creature didn't abide by the laws of the natural world, absorbing the light instead of reflecting it. As it tried to haul its obese body away he could hear the large mandibles clacking, searching for more food. Eyes wide with horror, he lowered his head to look at his unrecognizable torso. Food. Dear Christ, how many were in there, eating away at him? Hun- dreds? Thousands? What were they eating in there, his liver, his kidneys, his lungs? Why didn't it hurt instead of this motherfucking itching?

A sickening crunch came from his left and he turned his exhausted head to see the cause. The blue slipper had crushed the beetle *thing* and a foul-smelling thick yellow pus was oozing from beneath it. How could something so small give off so much stench, he thought idly while his brain slowly tried to grasp the reality, *the unreality* of the situation. He ignored the slipper. Despite the madness that was surrounding him, he knew it was impossible for the slipper to be there. Impossible. He had dealt with the slipper. The slipper was gone. Still, he didn't dare raise his head and look farther up. He didn't dare, because he really didn't know how much more he could take.

"I raised a fool, that's what I did, isn't it Callum? Despite everything I did for you, you're still a fool. You trusted her. You thought she loved you, didn't you?" The thin, harsh voice crackled with laughter, the scorn so familiar.

Callum shut his eyes, sweat beading at the edges of his thinning hair, and muttered to himself under his breath, whispering his sanity mantra. "You can't be here, Mother, you can't be here, she can't be here, I took care of her, you can't fucking be here, none of this is real, none of this is fucking happening, please, God, please make it stop."

"LOOK AT ME WHEN I'M SPEAKING TO YOU, YOU LITTLE SACK OF SHIT!" She screeched from the doorway of the bedroom, and suddenly he was four years old again and she was going to lock him in the cupboard in the dark where the monsters lived, only this time the monsters really were going to eat him, he couldn't hide from that, no way, because he had a sneaky suspicion *they were already eating him*.

Turning his head back to the slipper he slowly dragged his eyes upward, up past the saggy thick brown tights that covered her thin, veiny legs, trying to ignore the maggots that were dripping unnoticed by their host from beneath the A-line polyester green skirt. Slowly, slowly, unable to stop himself, conditioned by a lifetime of her domination, he lifted his vision until her glorious face came into view, her head resting awkwardly on the scrawny neck. Her hair had escaped from the tight bun, falling unkempt down one side, matted with the coagulated blood that brightly decorated the large dent in that half of her skull, and Callum noticed that her pale, greenish face was still caked with dried vegetable soup. Oh, the relief he'd felt all those years ago when he'd watched her crumple forward into that bowl, beaten to death from behind. Silent at fucking last.

Finally his eyes met hers stretched wide in defiance of death, the madness blazing at him, screaming out at him from the sunken sockets. He should have known, he really should have known then, he could never kill Mother. How could he ever have thought that he could kill Mother?

He could feel the bugs in his shoulders now, some working their way up to base of his neck, others scrabbling downward, in his thing, scratching at his anus. He watched the corpse of the woman who'd given him life wipe the dried soup from her face and lick it from her fingers with a black and rotting tongue.

"What's happening to me, Mother?" He whispered, trying to squeeze the tears back, not wanting to go in the cupboard for being a *pansy boy,* not able to take *his rightful punishment.*

She smiled back at him, sucking her fingers in sick suggestiveness, eyes glowing with mad entertainment. One of her teeth fell to the floor, and she followed it down, crouching by her son, watching the movements beneath his skin. Leaning forward, she whispered into his ear, engulfing him in her stench. "She never let you read the book, did she, that little whore of yours?" Her voice was like the rustle of dried autumn leaves in the wind. "Oh, she told you what you had to do to Helen, yesss, and you liked that, didn't you?" He felt the pressure of one, cold finger running down his cheek, tracing his tears. "But didn't you wonder what would happen to foolish, dumb Callum? Didn't you wonder that? Wasn't your stupid head just a little bit curious about that?"

From behind his squeezed shut eyes the tears were flowing freely now. "She's coming back to me. She loves me. She loves me." The words he whined sounded empty, even to him.

His mother's laugh was wheezy now. "You always liked to be dominated, didn't you Callum? You told her you'd give everything for her, and guess what? Surprise, surprise! She's taken you at your word!" She giggled as if this was the most amusing thing in the world.

Callum opened his eyes, the itch behind them making it impossible to lower his lids for long, and through the blur she almost looked like his mother again. Almost. And he felt the mix of love and fear that had been absent for such a long time filling the void. He nestled his head into her stagnant shoulder, seeking comfort. "Am I dying, mother? Am I dying?"

He wasn't even sure if he'd spoken the words aloud, but she heard them. Shrieking with laughter, she pulled herself away from him, and leapt to her feet, ripping his fantasy of support apart. Whirling like a banshee in front of him, she cackled, head rolling on its broken neck, maggots coming loose from inside her, body spinning faster and faster, until suddenly she stopped and paused, fixing him with her insane gaze.

She let out a small giggle, and dragged one hand playfully along the chipped banister. "Oh baby, it's worse than that. It's much much worse than that. They're eating your soul, you see. Can't you feel it? And when they finish, there'll be nothing left." He watched her snigger as she sang the words at him. "You really, really should have sneaked a peek in that book, my son. You're about to be erased. Eradicated."

Staring at her uncomprehending, he mewled, "She'll bring me back, like I did for her. That's what she'll do. She'll bring me back."

His mother shook her finger at him. "There'll be nothing left to bring back, Callum. Listen to Mother. They're eating your soul, they're taking your pathetic immortality! She would never come back for you. They're watching for h

They're smelling for her." With unbreathing nostrils flared, she sniffed the air. "She has to be careful. This way, she's hoping they'll stop looking." She laughed some more, twirling her blood-red hair between her fingers.

Callum felt more shifting inside him. *They're eating your soul.* Who was looking for Elizabeth? "Who's watching, Mother? Who's looking for Elizabeth?" He was finding it harder to breathe. He stared at his beloved mannequin of madness, and for a moment was sure he saw fear even in those eyes, before the dark mouth stretched into a grin.

"The Soulcatchers, of course, the Soulcatchers." The words scratched in his ears. She paused, and then turned and started hobbling back into the bedroom. His eyes followed her and saw that the loft door was hanging open and the ladder extended down. Pulling herself up the metal steps, back to her resting place of the past ten years, she stopped midway and let her head loll backward on its unhinged base, so that she was looking at him upside down.

"Death is just the beginning of an existence of infinitely wondrous possibilites. But you have to settle your oustanding accounts. Oh yes, and those bills can take a toll on the soul, believe me sugar pie! You have to suffer for your pleasures, don't they say? The Soulcatchers like the books to balance. You work in a bank, you get the picture. But that's her worry not yours, because for you it's all over. You're nothing. In a few minutes, you'll be gone. Forever."

Dragging her head upward, she gave him one more grin before she disappeared into the attic. Her voice danced down to him. "You should have read the book, baby, you should have read the book." And then she was gone.

Callum could hear his desperate breathing rattling in his lungs. No, it wasn't true, it couldn't be true, it had to be a mistake. "*I'LL PAY MY BILLS, DEAR GOD, I'LL PAY MY BILLS!*" he screamed at the wood-chipped walls. "*JUST MAKE IT STOP RIGHT NOW!*" A searing pain stabbed at the very core of him, and he knew Mother was right, she had always been right. He tried to imagine Elizabeth's face but all he could see was Gloria. The world started to blur and his heart frantically pounded in rebellion. *"ELIZABETH, YOU FUCKING BITCH. I HOPE YOU ROT IN HELL! ELIZA-BETH! ELIZABETH!"* He kept on shouting her name.

Rachel had abandoned the plates unwashed in the sink having come to the conclusion that they could wait until the morning. Her head was spinning slightly and it was definitely time for bed. All in all it had been a long day and if she stayed up much longer she was going to have to think about the way she'd just launched herself at Mike and that was something she wasn't too eager to do.

She slid the straps of her dress down over her shoulders, brushing her teeth with the other hand. How come she was so attracted to him now if she'd had the opportunity for a relationship with him in the past and turned it down? All joking aside she knew it couldn't be performance-related because judging by his actions tonight he certainly seemed to know what he was doing.

She wiggled her hips and the black material fell to the floor where she left it, then walked barefoot back to the bathroom to spit in the sink. She brushed vigorously for a few more moments and then rinsed, finishing by splashing the cold water over her face and a handful over her head. God, that felt good. If only it could cool down the rest of her, the parts that were still aching mildly after her earlier encounter. She studied the face that stared back from the new bathroom mirror. Who are you? Who are you really? The alert gray eyes offered no clues. "Fuck you then," she whispered to her reflection. "I'll figure it out for myself."

An hour later she was tossing and turning in the dark, mauling her covers as she whimpered slightly, her breathing erratic in the silence of the small bedroom. The window was open, and although the curtain was dancing in the cold breeze, her skin was covered with a light film of sweat. Her eyes moved wildly behind their protective lids as she dreamed.

The room, if it could be called that with its throbbing pulse and damp, soft living flesh as walls, floor, and ceiling was alive with horrors. Like a mutated womb it was devouring the figures that had become part of it, bloody bodies visible everywhere, from every angle hands digging into the meat trying to pull themselves free, some with only their heads left above the absorbing crimson quicksand that was dissolving them from their bones. Oh, how they were screaming, screaming like animals. How could they still be conscious or alive? How could it be possible? What kind of place was this?

In one corner she watched as the last fingertips of a woman's hand disappeared, tendons stretched tautly as if somewhere, lost in this insane sculpture of redness, she was still screaming. Rachel had a feeling that she probably was, that she had just moved to new and different torture, waiting for these others to catch up. In her dream she watched for what seemed like forever, unable to escape, to wake herself up, to look away.

At last, like survivors of some ancient shipwreck, there were only four left. One was only visible above the chin, his long fringe matted with blood over his young, terrified eyes; two other men with one arm and shoulder more, still desperately convinced they could break free. One of them, in his seventies, was screaming a name, screaming blame as if somehow that could get him out of here, get him a reprieve, a note from his parents excusing him from school for the day, anything.

The final person was female, most of her torso free, but the nipple of one large breast had sunk into the greedy floor and as she sobbed she used her shaking hands to try and keep the other pendulous breast as far up as possible.

Suddenly they stopped screaming, and the four looked at each other panting, their pain miraculously gone, silent for a moment. Filled with fragile hope, the woman started to giggle, a nervous laugh, and the old man joined in. But still they were trapped there, and slowly the room filled with the sound of harsh breathing. The laughter stopped as the deep, deep voice spoke, hurting their eardrums. "This is only the beginning. There is so much more for you to see and feel. You must purify your senses, purify your soul." The voice was irregular, not human at all, not accustomed to humanity, sound rather than words.

The woman who had giggled looked up at the ceiling as if the voice's owner could be found there. Some of her lank hair was caught in the wall behind her. "I can't, I can't. You have to let me go. I can't do this, I can't take this pain!" She was shrieking hysterically.

The voice barked with laughter. "You'll be surprised just how much you can suffer, how much you have to suffer, how much you come to understand pain when death is no longer an option. Oh, how surprised you'll be."

The breathing faded to nothing, leaving them alone, waiting for something, not knowing what. After about two minutes, the young man gargled out the words they were all thinking, his head frozen above his consumed neck. "What the fuck is going on? Is that it? Do we stay like this forever? Where did the others go? Why aren't they still here? Will someone tell me what the fuck is going on here!"

The answer came in a disinterested female whisper from the corner of the room. "The worms will come now. They always do. The worms come for the worst. The worst of the bad. And when they've eaten what's left of you you'll go to a new pain, and there'll be new people here. That's what happens. That's what always happens. Forever."

From her dreamer's viewpoint high above the action, Rachel stared into the dark area where the voice had come from, and when her eyes adjusted to the gloom she recoiled in shock.

The woman who looked just like her was huddled naked against the sticky red wall, dark hair falling in her face, shivering uncontrollably, her eyes gazing ahead, unfocused. Although she wasn't injured, there was blood smeared down the arms that were wrapped around her knees as if she had *been clung to by those being dissolved in their last frantic moments of being sucked in. Other than that, she seemed untouched by the room, set apart from its occupants and its occupation.*

The old man peered into the gloom, squinting with eyes used to wearing glasses to see. "Who are you? You can help me, can't you? Help me get out of here. None of it was my idea, I promise you. This is all a terrible mistake." The tone of his voice was low, but the dreaming Rachel could hear the desperation there. Her counterpart didn't even look at the man, but rocked backward and forward on her heels. "I can't help you. No one can help you. They're coming. Can't you hear them? They're coming." Still with her detached expression, she stuffed her fists into her ears.

The other woman looked around, her head moving rapidly from side to side. When she spoke she whispered too. "She's right. I can hear something. It's getting louder. Where's it coming from?"

The sound started like the flutter of butterfly wings trapped in a jar, but got louder and harder, clacking and clattering like hundreds of teeth chattering faster than any person could imagine. And then they came, just as she'd said they would; hundreds of large pale wormlike creatures oozing out of the walls, landing with a series of small damp thuds, and racing, slithering hungrily to the four trapped people who thrashed desperately, trying to flee from their fate.

The young man's scream was cut off as the first of the worms to reach him thrust itself into his mouth, biting into his tongue, pushing downward into his throat. Rachel saw his horrified agony for only seconds before two more creatures simultaneously attacked his eyes, impatient to reach his soft brain tissue. None of the others were faring any better. The woman wailed as one worm burrowed into the breast she had been so carefully protecting, now forgotten as she tried to swipe the things out of her tangled hair before they dug into her scalp.

The old man looked down at himself in confused disbelief

*as his stomach tumbled out of the hole bitten into his torso,
a worm wriggling in eagerly, leaving the warm innards for
its swarming companions following greedily behind.* It
wasn't long before he remembered how to scream.

With the distanced terror of the dreamer, Rachel watched
the scene unfold until the bodies were devoured and the
worms wriggled, fat and satiated back to their home in the
alive walls. Thankfully the screaming had stopped sometime
before the feast was over, leaving only the sickening sound
of the worms ingesting the bodies that she had the horrifying feeling were still somehow alive.

She managed to turn her attention to the other Rachel, the
one that rocked backward and forward, eyes shut, humming, hands still pressed into her ears. How could she be
dreaming about herself? How could she be in the dream in
two different places? How could her mind have invented this
nightmare? The girl's eyes opened and for a moment their
gazes met, and Rachel could see recognition dawning in the
gray eyes she could remember looking at in the mirror only
hours ago. The other girl was about to speak, when suddenly a name filled Rachel's head and she was pulled violently back from the dream. As the girl faded from her vision,
she saw the terrible hatred blazing from those eyes that had
been lifeless throughout the full horror of moments before.

Feeling herself spinning and moving through the darkness with sickening speed all she could hear was the name
screaming in her head, summoning her somehow. Who
could be calling her by this name that wasn't hers? Who
could be calling her with such force that she thought the
sound was going to make her brain explode?

As suddenly as it came, the nauseating darkness lifted
and she saw her caller. Again she was hovering above the
action of her dream, an observer. The middle-aged man was
sagging in his underpants against a mundane looking flock-
papered wall. He was halfway through shrieking the name
that had dragged her from her previous dream when the jet-
black bugs started to pour out through his mouth and ears,

one squeezing out from under his lower eyelid. The life there vanished but not before he glimpsed her, and the last expression those bloodshot orbs held was one of victory.

For some reason this scene—not the vileness of the previous one—caused mortal terror to run through her. The beetles were tumbling out of the small slit in his y-fronts, pushed out by the torrent behind, and it seemed that as they swarmed into the hallway, they could sense her, pausing, the sensitive antennae seeking her out.

For the first time in her dream it was she who screamed. Oh God, this was a BAD PLACE! She'd been tricked, he'd tricked her, he'd tricked her. She could smell the danger, and she knew that this was a place she should never have come to. Her instinct for survival overcame her and at last she could feel herself withdrawing from the nightmare, waking up.

Her body jolted in her bed and her eyes flew open. Sitting up, she frantically brushed her arms, expecting to feel thousands of tiny hard bodies skittering over her exposed flesh. She spent a few desperate shaking moments, searching for the light switch, before her conscious mind took control. Leaving the light off, her eyes now accustomed to the gloom, the threatening shapes of seconds before now just the shadows of comfortably ordinary objects, she lay back against the pillows, damp with her sweat. It was just a bad dream, that's all. Just a dream. Horrific, terrifying, but just a dream all the same. She took a few deep breaths, the detail of the nightmare dissipating, only the lingering images of blood and bugs tasting like metal in her mouth. You've got to get a grip on yourself, girl. There's enough stuff to deal with in the daytime without adding to it at night.

Contemplating getting up for a glass of water, she decided against it. The nightmare had left her exhausted and rehydration could wait until later. If she got up now she'd never get back to sleep, and she wasn't sure how well she was going to manage that as it was. Tired she may have been but her heart was still racing, and adrenaline pumping, ready to fight or flee from whatever she had been inflicting on herself in her mind. Sighing and rolling onto her side, she pulled the duvet up to her chin, feeling comforted by the normalcy of her surroundings and allowed her eyes to close. I guess bad dreams are to be expected, she thought, as she listened to her heart slowing down. I've been through a tough time, and my brains bound to be trying to put the pieces back together again. A wave of sleepiness rippled over her. I just wish it would do it in a nicer way. Willing herself to have only pleasant thoughts, during which Mike Flynn's face seemed to keep making an appearance, she slowly drifted off.

The rest of the night passed dreamlessly.

CHAPTER SIX

"I hope you haven't had breakfast, sir."

Sergeant Carter was waiting for him by the front door, his dark suit standing out amid the sea of white protective clothing that was the forensic team collectively carrying various bits of equipment in through the door of the respectable and definitely not cheap detached house. Detective Inspector Murray noticed that the ultimately professional sergeant was looking pale. Whatever had gone on inside the house wasn't going to be pretty, but then he'd known it was going to be bad before he'd even pulled his car into the busy driveway. It was no gut feeling telling him that, just plain old-fashioned police experience.

Firstly, you didn't get much crime in this neck of the woods, but when you did, it tended to be dramatic. All those acidic emotions that the wealthy upper classes were too polite to show had to gain release somehow, and people were just people, no matter what their social backgrounds. Look hard enough at any group and you'd find the full array of deviants lurking there. Some could just afford to hide it a little better than others.

Secondly, he'd seen the pack of press being held back by five boys from uniformed division at the top of the drive, and that was a lot of men to be doing door duty. When he'd impatiently waved his ID and finally driven through, he was greeted with an array of ambulances, police cars, and forensic vans parked wherever they could find space all the way down to the front door. He'd recognized a few of the cars. Not only was this a big presence, but the boss had called in the top dogs in every field. This was not going to be a cheap investigation. He'd been twenty years on the force and he couldn't remember seeing so much activity at a crime scene before. Something about it made him think of Cromwell Road in Gloucester. Maybe it was the way the front door was already tented over, protecting whatever poor sod the pathology team would be carrying out later in the day from as much public nosiness as possible.

Thirdly, and the most obvious clue to him that he was in for a busy day was that it would have to be something pretty drastic for Chief Superintendant Baker to call him in from compassionate leave. Emily had been dead for three and a half long weeks and although he was more than keen to have something else to occupy his mind, he knew Baker still thought his place was at home with the children, at least for another couple of weeks. Murray couldn't blame him really, not after the state he'd been in at the funeral.

He cringed slightly at the memory. He wasn't a man who was comfortable with open displays of extreme emotion, especially his own. It hadn't helped that he'd been blind drunk. Still, when you marry a woman fifteen years younger than you, you don't expect her to be the one to go first. And not so suddenly. Not just ripped away from you like that. For three and a half weeks he'd been systematically attacked by memories that he treasured but couldn't face just yet, and when the phone rang this morning it was like something sent from heaven. A temporary release from grief. Someone else's tragedy to help him get over his.

Luckily, his dead wife's mother had been only too eager to help with the kids and no doubt they were having much more fun by now than they would have been with their miserable daddy. He loved those twins, God, he did, but sometimes looking at them was just too damn painful.

Stuffing his hands in his pockets, partly to disguise the fact that his suit was now too big for him, he walked up the two stone steps to where his sergeant was standing. They nodded at each other. "So, what is it Carter, domestic murder?" The soft voice betrayed nothing of the cynic beneath. He attributed much of his success in the interrogation room to the gentle way he spoke. It was the kind of voice that made people trust him, open up to him. His eyes though, they were different. Always looking, always alert. They were definitely working hard now. "There seems to be an awful lot going on here for your run-of-the-mill suburban stabbing. Baker's going a bit mad with the funds, isn't he?"

Watching the younger man's face, how his eyes flickered slightly at the edges, he realised that John Carter was trying deperately hard not to throw up, and that surprised him. He may have been only twenty-nine, but they'd been to plenty of nasty crime scenes together and Murray had never seen him in this state. Being the friend he was, he didn't mention it, the same way he knew Carter wouldn't mention Emily. His young wife had been right, men were funny creatures.

Carter swallowed. "I'd better warn you sir, Baker's inside." Murray raised his eyes to the heavens and then sighed. "Well, there's no need for both of us to suffer him. You wait with the car while I go and face the music." Stepping past the young sergeant, he pretended not to see the look of relief that swallowed the man's face, and made his way into the crowded hallway.

He didn't get very far. Two men were on the ground bagging pieces of fragmented glass. Squeezing past them, watching his feet, he went into the room on the left, a large bay-windowed light and airy lounge, which was thankfully almost free of human clutter. It was also where he found

Baker. The rotund, sweaty man was gazing out of the window as if he had the weight of the world on his shoulders. Murray knew how that felt and for a moment almost felt sorry for the man.

He coughed slightly, and Baker spun around, pulling a handkerchief from his pocket and wiping his forehead with it. Murray noticed that the other man's thick black-framed glasses were tucked into the small top pocket of his pinstriped suit jacket. What was it that he'd seen enough of for one day?

Pulling himself together, Baker put the hankie away and looked Murray in the eye. His voice was almost apologetic. "Thanks for coming in, Jim. I wouldn't have called you if I had any choice. Are the kids okay?"

"Emily's mother." Murray answered shortly. Baker's intentions may have been good but the last thing he wanted to hear were more well-meaning platitudes. Baker got the hint, and was probably relieved. Grief wasn't a comfortable subject for anyone. The chief superintendant rubbed his hands together slowly before speaking. "It's a bad one. The press is going to have a field day. It's going to be like Christmas come early for them and I don't want any cock-ups. There's not going to be any room for cock-ups. Not without us getting crucified anyway."

Murray nodded, impatient to get on to the details of the case. Listening to his boss he knew why he himself would probably never rise much further. He'd never cared much for the politics of policing. All that had ever concerned him was solving the mystery and getting the bad guy. He tried to look understanding, as if he gave a shit, figuring it was the best way to get the man onto the matter at hand. He gave him a verbal prod. "So what happened, sir? What are we dealing with?"

Baker sat on the cream sofa. "Multiple murders. God only knows how many. So far there's one in the attic and seven in the basement. Various stages of decomposition. Forensics are going to be busy here for quite some time. They're

taking out the bathroom floor at the moment just in case
there's any more there. Another team's working on the garden." Murray idly wondered whether the pained look on his
superior's face was due to the extent of the horrors or the
extent of this year's budget being spent.

Baker continued. "No ID on any of the bodies yet. We're
getting a list of missing persons drawn up that fits the general ages. We'll obviously have more information when the
bodies are back in the lab. I should imagine it'll come
down to dental records for most of them." He shivered. "Especially the girl in the attic. You've got to see that one to believe it. I'll give you the guided tour in a minute once the
chaps are finished."

Murray remained standing. "Who notified the police?"
Putting his glasses back on, Baker leant forward, resting his
elbows on his knees, obviously feeling better now that he
was sharing his responsibilty. Murray was here now. He was
the officer in charge and if the investigation fouled up, he
would be the scapegoat. That was one of the wonders of
delegation. When he spoke this time, his voice had more of
its normal pompous authority. In some ways that reassured
Murray. Whatever had gone on here, the world hadn't
changed. There were still some things you could count on.
He listened carefully.

"It was the milkman, believe it or not. Apparently he'd
been a bit suspicious of goings-on here for a while. The
house is owned by a woman called Elizabeth Ray, forty-two
years old, unmarried. A bit of a fruitcake. She had a small
occult bookshop for the past six years in Belsize Park until
eight months ago when she sold it out of the blue. We think
she's probably one of the bodies in the cellar. Not sure yet,
but if I had to put money on it, I would.

"Anyway, the milkman hasn't seen her for months, only
one of her 'gentleman friends' as he puts it. One pint of full
cream every day and this man's been paying the bills. Because he'd seen them together in the past he didn't really
think anything of it, but he noticed that the man's been

looking a bit strange. Usual sort of thing, used to wear a tie, look smart, now looking pale and scruffy. Lost weight, red around the eyes, no conversation." Murray thought his boss could be describing him.

"And not a sign of this Ray woman for months. For the past few days, though, the milk's stayed on the doorstep, no note to cancel, nothing. So this morning he decided to have a peer through the letter box, shout hello or something and when he did he saw all the broken glass and called the police. Thought there might have been a burglary."

Murray glanced back at the men in the hall. "The broken glass from the mirror?"

Baker nodded. "There's three large mirrors like that in the house. All of them were smashed. God, knows why. I'm sure the psychologist could tell you but she's taken the constable that was first on the scene home with a packet of sedatives."

Murray could feel his brain dusting itself off. "So the officer found the bodies?"

Baker shook his head. "Only the one in the attic room. Luckily, he didn't disturb anything. He didn't actually go in. Just flicked the light on and then ran like hell down the stairs and outside to be sick. Our boys found the little collection in the cellar. Good job too. I think it's going to be hard enough to get that young lad back on active duty as it is." He looked at Murray, quizzically. "It never fails to surprise me. One pint of milk a day. Nice and routine. Nice and normal. With all this madness going on behind the front door, he still wanted his pint of milk a day from the milkman. Amazing. How do they do that, these men? How can they separate themselves like that?"

Murray shrugged. "Maybe he just wasn't ready to arouse suspicion. For all we know, he could have been pouring the milk straight down the sink."

For him there was very little that was amazing about madness and too many types of insanity to concern yourself with it. There was the kind of insanity that had gone on here, contained and typified, and then there was the kind that made teenage boys steal cars they couldn't drive and smash into a young woman carrying shopping bags, cutting her body in two less-than-neat halves. The kind of madness that let them walk away from the brick wall unscathed. He swallowed his bitterness. There was too much work to be done here to allow himself to get distracted by self-pity. A young woman dressed in a white plastic boiler suit appeared in the doorway.

"You can show the DI around now, sir. We're pretty much done. We'll take the bodies out when you've finished." Murray watched as she went back to the hallway and then outside for some fresh air. He figured out what was wrong here. There was no laughter. Sick as it sounded, you could normally count on the younger officers to make plenty of cruel jokes especially on a grim site. It was their way of coping, of not letting it in. But there was no joking here. People just wanted to get the job done quickly and get the hell out. He followed Baker out of the room and up the stairs.

When he eventually stepped back out into the beautiful sweet-smelling Hampstead afternoon he checked his watch. He'd only been inside for an hour but it felt like a whole lot longer than that. Feet crunching on the gravel, he made his way over to the blue Vauxhall parked halfway into the hedge. John Carter was leaning on the bonnet, smoking and looking decidedly better than he had been earlier. Outward appearances aside, Murray figured it was going to take longer than an hour to get over what he'd just seen in Elizabeth Ray's house.

The younger man offered him a cigarette which he took. Five years ago when the twins were born he'd tried to kick his thirty-a-day habit, but never quite made it. Still, he was pretty happy with the five to ten a day he was now on. Given his recent stresses he thought that the fact it hadn't risen was a miracle, and something of a testament to his willpower.

Carter offered the lit match in cupped hands. "As a first

day back, I should imagine that this one would take some beating, sir."

Puffing the cigarette alight, Murray raised his eyes and saw the sardonic smile on his friend's face. Inhaling deeply, he smiled. That's why he liked working with Carter. The man had the potential to be as cynical as himself and that was no bad thing in an officer. Or a friend, for that matter. His body buzzed with the nicotine as it flooded his system, and he pulled his car keys out of his pocket.

"Come on, get in. We need to get away from this circus. Go somewhere quiet. Somewhere we can think." Stamping the half-smoked butt out in the ashtray, he started the engine. Carter opened the passenger door and got in. "I think I know just the place you've got in mind, sir."

The pub was filling up when they got there, but the two men managed to secure themselves a secluded table by the large open fire. Murray enjoyed the heat that blazed agressively, warming his soul. Holding his hands out in front of him, he waited for Carter to get back from the bar with the two much-needed pints of bitter. They sat and sipped in silence for a few moments until Carter spoke, his pale Scottish skin glowing red in the reflection of the flames.

"So, what do you make of it? Do you think we've got another Fred West out there roaming the fair streets of Hampstead?" Part of Murray groaned inwardly. If both he and his sergeant had thought of the Cromwell Street murders, it wouldn't take too long before the press did either. That would give them an excuse to dig up the many sordid details of those killings all over again, and help sensationalize this case. Not that it was going to need sensationalizing, and not that he normally cared what the press did, as long as they didn't interfere with his work. Only this time he had a feeling that Baker was going to volunteer him as the spokesman for the case, and that made the news boys his headache. He sipped his beer and turned his mind to the question.

"No I don't. Whoever the man the milkman saw was, I don't think he intended to leave that house and never return. Murderers like that tend to leave a message for the police, some kind of clue so they can watch us bumbling around in the papers and on the TV and feel clever about themselves. I think if he could have got back to the house, he would. I think something's happened to him. Maybe you should check the hospitals. By all accounts he wasn't looking too healthy, maybe he collapsed." He paused. "Maybe he got knocked down by a bus crossing the road. Stranger things have happened." Carter let the reference of Murray's own tragedy slip by unnoticed, but Murray knew he was going to have to stop himself coming out with comments like that. It wasn't fair on the younger officer, and he didn't want anyone thinking he couldn't separate his personal problems from his work. Even if he couldn't.

"Anyway, the guy's not the most interesting bit of the jigsaw puzzle as it's laid out before us. The thing that's bugging me is one of the bodies in the basement. The woman's one. Brunette. Throat cut, no sign of torture of any kind. Carefully wrapped up in a clean, white sheet. Lovingly laid out. Rose on top. Separate from the rest." He took several gulps from the pint glass to see if his sergeant would get what he was driving at.

Carter looked at his boss, confused. "Well, that's obvious, sir. She's got to be Elizabeth Ray. They were lovers, they had a row and he killed her, became overcome with remorse, hence the romantic care with the corpse." He raised one eyebrow and drained his glass. "Maybe you're out of practice, but that seems pretty obvious to me."

Murray leaned across the table and tilted his head, the craggy wrinkles in his face accentuated by the concentrated stare. "Tell me, then, if you've got it all figured out." His voice was melodic. "Did you see a lock on that door leading down to the cellar at all?"

Fidgeting in his seat, Carter knew from experience that when James Murray's soft voice started lilting like that he was about to be made to feel like he'd said something stupid. If he was honest, it normally happened at about the same time that he'd said something stupid.

"No, sir. I didn't look."

This time it was Murray's turn to raise an eyebrow. "Well, I did, and I remember thinking how odd it was that there was no lock or padlock. Yes, there was a bolt on the outside that would stop some unfortunate person down there getting out, but nothing to stop anyone else in the house getting in, while he, whoever he was, was somewhere else. Can you see what I'm driving at yet?"

Carter shook his head.

"Okay, this'll probably all come out in the pathologist's report so it's nothing to get excited about, but the way I see it is that every officer in that house today was referring to Ms. Ray as a victim, right?" The sergeant nodded, and Murray continued, the lilting thankfully gone from his undulating tone.

"By the looks of things, ultimately she must have been. But not at the beginning." He pushed his unfinished beer to one side, forgotten, gesturing with his large hands while he spoke. "So far, we've got eight bodies. The girl in the attic, well we'll let the lab boys explain what God-awful thing happened to her, but needless to say, even to my thankfully untrained eye, she was the freshest. Dead maybe a week or so. Elizabeth Ray was already very dead indeed by the time he got around to attic girl." He saw a flicker of dawning comprehension on the young man's face, but couldn't wait for him to catch up.

"But out of the six other bodies in the cellar, I'd say that there could be only two, three at the most who were killed after her. A couple of corpses were pretty well gone." He leaned forward and spoke in a low whisper. "Don't you get it? There was no lock on the cellar door. He couldn't have killed those people without her knowing about it. *Not with no lock. Not in her house.* Why would he take the risk? He was a man in his forties, he could have found plenty of other places to get rid of the bodies. He probably had his own house somewhere. No. If those people died in that house, then it was because she wanted them to as much as he did."

He sat back on his stool, drained his pint and let Carter digest the information. The younger man nodded slowly and then picked up the glasses, readying himself for the trip back to the bar. He smiled, as he stood up. "Has anyone ever told you that with a brain like that you could be a policeman, you could?" His Scottish accent's impression of a Yorkshireman did no credit to either race and Murray laughed, waving the man away to replenish his drink. The warm glow he felt now did not come just from the fire. Something inside of him was crawling back to life, this terrible crime revitalizing him, reminding him that there was something he was good at, something he was damn good at. His job.

He felt the vibration on his chest and pulled the slim mobile phone from his inside pocket. The display told him HOME was ringing and pain tugged at his heart. He tried to push it back down inside him. You can't change things, no matter how much you want to, you've just got to try and get on with living. He pressed the green answer button. "Hi, Janet. Is everything okay?"

The woman at the other end of the line sounded tired, a reminder that he wasn't the only one whose life had been shattered by Emily's loss. "Yes, everything's fine. I've given them their tea and sat them in front of a video for half an hour. They're happy as Larry. I just thought I'd see how you were getting on. Samantha wanted to know if you'd be back in time to tuck her in. You know what she's like."

Although they were twins, Samantha and Sebastian were like chalk and cheese. She was quiet and shy where he was loud and bold. He led and she followed. Still, they adored each other, and he adored both of them.

"Yes, tell her I'll be there in about an hour. There's not a lot for me to do until the lab team get some reports in and the boys in the incident room have started following up their leads. I think I'll make the most of it and have an early night. It's going to be the last one I'm going to get for a while I should imagine."

Janet was concerned. "I know you can't talk about it, Jim, but is it bad this case? Is that why they wanted you?"

Murray knew he'd been lucky having a mother-in-law like Janet. Most women wouldn't approve of their daughters marrying someone that much older, and a policeman to boot. But Janet had never said a thing about the age gap, and on top of that she respected his job and the fact that his success rate was second to none. No, he couldn't have asked for more. He sighed, thinking of the scenes at the Ray house. "Yeah, it's bad. Pretty bad." He rubbed his face with his hands and suddenly wanted to be scrubbing himself clean in a hot bath. "I'll see you when I get in. And thanks for helping out like this at such short notice. I really appreciate it."

She came back quickly, but hesitant. "It's nothing Jim. It's not like I've got much else to do with my time. You know, I was thinking that maybe if this case was going to be keeping you busy, I could look after them for you. It wouldn't be a problem and I don't think a childminder would be much good for them at the moment, and I could stay over nights when you need me too." She paused, as if suddenly aware that she'd been talking too fast and desperately. When she spoke again, she didn't disguise her pain. "It helps, you know?"

He nodded. Yeah, he knew. He knew exactly what she meant. "That'd be great, Janet. Really great." Carter returned and placed the full glass in front of him. "Look, I've got to go. I'll see you at home." Hanging up, he look a long gulp of beer and felt better. Emily was gone, but he still had a family to care about and who cared about him. He couldn't afford to wallow in self-pity for their sakes. He looked at Carter.

"Is your car still at the scene?" The young man nodded.

"Good. After we've finished these I'll drop you back there and then head home to the kids. I want you to see how they're coming along with their excavations. They can't have found any more bodies or else we'd have heard, but there may be some other interesting stuff uncovered, you never know. Also, check with the coroner's office. See if they've started on any of the postmortems yet, and what the schedule is if they haven't. They've got a lot of work to get through and I want this case to have priority. Tell them to speak to me if they've got any objections. And check with the hospitals for a man fitting the description the milk-man gave. It's probably not typed up yet, but someone'll have the original statement."

"No problem, sir." Carter was pleased to see Murray getting back on form. After seeing him at the funeral he'd known that the only way his boss had a chance of getting over his grief was to sink his teeth into a case. He'd been right.

Murray rested his elbows on the table, observing his colleague. "Oh, and Carter. You've got my mobile and home numbers. I don't want to discover that I missed out on any developments in the night because you didn't want to disturb me at home. Whatever the reason."

Carter grinned, the dimple that appeared in one cheek suddenly making him appear nearer twenty than thirty. "I'm actually not that sensitive toward other people's feelings, sir. Surely you should know that by now?" They looked at each other for a moment and then both burst into laughter. Yes, it was good to be back in the job.

After dropping Carter back at the flood-lit scene, and fighting his way, bonnet first, through the barrage of press hungry for any morsel of information, he started his slow journey home through the rush-hour traffic. It was five forty-five and if he was lucky he'd be home by half past six, plenty of time to put the kids to bed and tell them a story. At least they'd stopped asking him when mummy was coming home every evening. Sam would ask sometimes, but he could hear the lack of hope in her voice. As much as he wanted them to heal from this loss, he hoped they wouldn't forget their mother too quickly. For their sakes as much as hers.

Bringing his thoughts back to the case, he said a silent prayer of thanks that it had been a policeman that had found the bodies. If the milkman had come across that girl in the attic, God knows what the headline in tomorrow's papers would be. This way they had a chance to keep a lid on the finer details and could release more information when they at least had an answer or two to offer. Smiling wryly, he studied the cars ahead. This wasn't a job you did for public support and understanding. He'd learned the sad truth long ago that people rarely had a good thing to say about the police. Until they needed them, of course, and then it was a different story.

Still, he countered to himself philosophically. You couldn't always blame people. Every day seemed to bring new allegations of racism and corruption in the force, and if you couldn't trust the police to stay honest, who could you trust? In the distance the lights changed to green, and he cursed as the brake lights ahead stayed firmly on and nothing moved. The blessings of living in London. He was going to be home late.

He hadn't thought he was going to be able to eat a thing but when Janet placed the dish of lasagne in front of him, he suddenly found that he was starving. She put her plate on the other side of the pine table.

"This smells great!" He smiled at her. "But you don't have to cook for me, you know. You're being good enough as it is looking after those two holy terrors upstairs." He pointed his knife upward. In fact, he hadn't seen the kids this relaxed since before that awful day, and Sebastian had been adamant that Granny Janet should stay overnight. Samantha was just as eager in her quiet way, as she hugged him tightly, almost afraid to let him go. After the scenes this morning when he'd said he had to go to work, this turn-around was nothing short of a miracle.

He couldn't blame them for their tearful tantrums. One Saturday afternoon not so long ago, their mother had told them she was going to the shops and would bring them and Daddy back a nice surprise, and they never saw her again. Mummy never came home and now they were scared the same thing was going to happen to him and nothing would reassure them. If Janet could ease that for them, then she could baby-sit whenever she wanted.

Tasting the first forkful, his stomach growled for more, the aubergine, meat, and cheese combination cooked to perfection. Janet smiled at him, sipping her wine. "I didn't do it for you, I did it for me. It's nice to have people to look after." Sometimes Murray had to remember that it had been a bad couple of years for Janet. First Emily's father, Peter, losing his battle for life after a series of crippling heart attacks, and then Emily herself.

Although Peter had been only fifty when he'd died last year, Janet felt it was a blessing that he'd gone before Emily. He wouldn't have been able to cope with losing his baby. Not like that. She could cope with losing Peter knowing he hadn't had to suffer that terrible pain. Murray wondered how often she wished she'd been spared that agony, too.

Watching her from over his dinner, he could see that the day with the kids had done her as much good as it had them. The tired, old look she'd been wearing recently had lifted slightly and her fragile beauty, the beauty Emily had inherited and enhanced could be seen trying to make a reappearance. It was times like this that Murray remembered that at forty-seven, she was only four years older than he was. Guilt kicked in over his bout of self-pity in the pub. This woman had lost her husband and the daughter she'd had at nineteen, all in the space of a few short months and now all she had left were the twins and a miserable son-in-law.

Pushing the blonde-gray hair out of her face, she carried on eating, unaware of his observation, and Murray felt a bout of impulsiveness come over him. Sod it. He was going to have to get a nanny at some point, so why not someone he knew? He put down his fork.

"I've been thinking, Janet. Maybe you should move in while I'm on this investigation. The kids love having you here, and to be honest, I'm going to be out a lot and I'm worried about the effect that's going to have on them. You'd be doing me a huge favor. I wouldn't expect you to do it for nothing, of course. We can work something out financially." He saw the flush run up her face and it was the first smile he'd seen reach her eyes in a month.

"Don't even talk about paying me, you big lump! We're family, we're supposed to help each other. I'd love to move in!" She paused. "To be honest, rattling around in that house full of memories of Peter and Emily isn't doing me any good. I don't need a doctor to tell me that."

She rolled her wineglass between her hands just the way Emily used to. Is this the way she would have looked if she'd lived? Murray hoped that he hadn't just invited a whole barrel of pain into his house in the form of a thousand genetic reminders. Nope, he decided, looking at how happy his mother-in-law had become, he'd done the right thing. He couldn't get much bigger genetic reminders than Sam and Sebastian, after all. And right at this minute, the four of them needed as much love and support as they could get.

The two lonely people united by a common grief smiled at each other across the table. "Right then. That's settled." He chewed another mouthful of the delicious dinner, and pointed his fork at her, his dark eyes dancing beneath his darker hair. "I'll leave you with the job of telling the children in the morning. I think you'll have just made them very happy indeed and they can do all the shrieking and running around that goes with that when I'm not here." She smiled back and he was sure that something had lifted inside her, and knowing that he'd made that happen warmed his soul. It was good to feel good.

*   *   *

He'd been asleep for about an hour when the ringing of his mobile dragged him back to consciousness. Squinting in the dark he saw on the red glow of the alarm clock that it was ten past one. Reaching for the phone, he didn't need to look at the face to know who was on the other end. Sitting up, shaking the sleep out of himself, he held the phone to his ear with one hand and scratched his head with the other.

"Carter, I hope this is good."

"Oh it is, sir. You're going to like this one. Get your dressing gown on and get the coffee going, I'm bringing it around. I'll be there in five minutes." John Carter sounded positively buoyant and Murray felt his curiosity taste buds getting tickled. "Bringing what around?" The young sergeant laughed in his ear.

"Don't spoil a young man's fun. Wait and see." The phone went dead, and pushing the covers away, Murray suddenly felt very awake indeed.

By the time Carter's car pulled up outside, Murray had pulled on a pair of black jeans and a sweat top and had the coffee machine grumbling as requested. The young policeman knocked quietly rather than ringing the bell, and Murray pulled open the door. He could see John's strawberry-blond hair and sparkling eyes above the large cardboard box, and he stood aside to let the man carry it into the kitchen. Neither spoke until the door was shut behind them. Carter spoke while Murray filled their mugs with steaming dark liquid and milk.

"We owe a favor to a guy called Ian McIntosh. Mac and I did our basic police training together. He's been working with the excavation team, and when I left there this evening I told him if they found anything interesting to give me a call." He took the mug and indicated the box with his other hand. "They found this lot at midnight under the floorboards of the master bedroom, and he called me straightaway. The fingerprint boys have been at them, of course, and I had a hell of a fight to get them released to me. That pratt Gillingham is in charge on the scene and you know how far up Baker's arse he is. Anyway, I preempted him by calling our Lord and Master to get his okay. I told him that if I didn't take them you'd only come down and get them for yourself. After all, the letter is addressed to you."

Murray's cup stopped halfway to his lips. "What letter's addressed to me?" Carter smiled, enjoying the moment. "It's a box of Elizabeth Ray's diaries. Taped to the one on top was a plain while envelope addressed to The Officer in Charge. And to my mind, that makes it addressed to you. Baker reluctantly agreed, but he wants this lot back in evidence by the end of tomorrow."

Murray nodded not really listening, and putting down his forgotten coffee, carefully opened the box. Ignoring the books for the moment, he pulled out the white envelope and opened it.

To Whom it may concern,

By the time you read this letter I think you're going to be in need of a little help figuring out what's been going on in my house. Interesting, isn't it? I should imagine that this is the kind of case that left unresolved could make or break a man's career. But don't worry, I'm going to give you a helping hand.

You'll be pleased to hear that the man you're looking for, the man who helped me kill my little cellar collection, and then killed myself and poor sweet Helen is no longer a menace to the society of which I am sure you are undoubtably proud. You'll find him dead in his flat above the bookmaker's on Finchley High Road. I shan't give you the street number, I think it's only fair that you should do a little bit of detective work for your money. Don't you? Oh and by the way, if you look hard enough you might just find his mother there too. The cause of death might be a bit hard to establish, if I had to hazard a guess, I'd say it was likely that he died of fright, but I'm sure the doctor will find something suitable to cover it, to make it understandable.

Anyway, why listen to me? I'll be dead before he will. In

fact. I'll be technically dead in a few hours and I'm sure he's still got a couple of months left in him.

So, there you go, I've closed your case for you. Multiple murderer found dead of a heart attack in his flat. Tragic loss of life in Hampstead home.

Still, if you have any kind of curiosity, you'll be wondering how I could possibly know that Callum is dead, how I could know what will be going on after I've taken my place in the cellar? It's tickling you, isn't it?

Well, lucky you, I'm going to tell you. I'm going to let you read my diaries and not out of any need to purge my soul (for as you'll discover I've embarked on a way to neatly bypass anything like that), but maybe so that someone will understand just how special I am, since unfortunately I will no longer remember. But hey, as they say in all those adverts for the sexually unadventurous, safety first, and not remembering will definitely be safest for the new me.

So, I'll leave you to decide whether to read on or not, and only add that if you do, I hope we'll meet one day. But you'll have to forgive me if I don't remember this little introduction. Things will have changed for me by then. Happy Hunting.

Elizabeth Ray.
P.S. Should you not wish to show your colleagues this letter now that the case is closed, there is a more appropriate one taped to the inside bottom flap of the box.

Murray handed the letter over to Carter and started to take the pile of notebooks carefully out of the box and place them on the side. The box finally empty, he ripped the bottom section upward to reveal its underside. There was the second letter, taped as she said it would be, addressed identically to the first. He held it up.

"Those boys should learn to be more thorough before releasing evidence." Carter put down the original letter and looked at his boss. "Well, there's a woman who was definitely one can short of a six-pack, if you don't mind me saying." Murray smiled wryly in agreement as he read the second note. Nothing insane coming from those pages. Just a straightforward "Should I be found dead in suspicious circumstances, the person who did it lives at etc." Carter was right, the woman was definitely crazy. She had to be to do what had been done to some of those people, never mind the rest of this stuff. He started to repack the notebooks and then picked the box up, tucking it under his arm. Being a big man had some advantages.

"I'm going to get dressed. Get on the phone, I want the address of that place on Finchley Road and I want a squad car to meet us there with a warrant in an hour." Carter nodded, moving over to the phone that hung next to the fridge on the kitchen wall. "The judge won't be happy getting woken up at two in the morning," he muttered. Murray raised an eyebrow. "He will be if it means we've closed the case on the first day."

Leaving the room, he took the diaries up to his bedroom and put them on top of the wardrobe where he knew the children wouldn't look. He'd read them later, not for the reasons in the letter but because they might quickly provide identification for the victims. And there was the depressing thought that there might be more murders recorded from years gone by. A few more tragic names to strike from the missing persons register. Pulling on his socks, he decided that Ms. Ray, if she were still alive, would be bitterly disappointed in him. It would take more than she was offering to get him to believe in anything that he couldn't see or feel. The only time Emily had managed to drag him to church was for their wedding. And her funeral, the small bitter voice that still lived inside him whispered.

He dragged his shoes out from under the bed. Whatever the crazy dead woman had convinced herself of, Murray knew there was a thousand ways she could have known about her partner's imminent demise. Maybe he had a heart condition or an illness of some kind, or maybe she'd mixed poison in with his dried porridge oats, murdering him slowly after he'd murdered her. Who knows? And who really cares, he thought, doing up his laces, as long as the bad guys have been caught one way or another.

Taking his jacket out of the wardrobe, he glanced at the box one more time, before going downstairs. Yep, he'd been right. That kind of killer always leaves a clue, a message of their own self-importance, that only served to betray how inconsequential they really were. Carter was waiting by the front door, and the two men stepped out into the crisp, black night and this time got into the young man's car. Murray watched the silent windows of the houses as they drove by, wondering what things went on within. How many dead bodies lay in cellars undiscovered. People always thought that there was something special about men who did bad things. Something that made them stand out from the crowd. But there was always one thing you could rely on in life: Stripped down to basics, evil was always mundane.

CHAPTER SEVEN

Dr. Hanson regarded her thoughtfully over the top of his glasses. Charming she may have been; but oh, so stubborn.

"So there's nothing I can say to persuade you to see the psychologist?" His tone of voice wasn't hopeful, and on the other side of the table, Rachel shook her head adamantly. "Look, I wouldn't have mentioned the dreams if Mike hadn't made me promise to, and from what you've said the shrink wasn't helping before my accident or whatever you want to call it, so why should it be any different now?'

Looking at the earnest, pretty face the doctor wasn't convinced. "But don't you think it's something of a coincidence that you were having nightmares you couldn't remember before, and now you're getting them again? Perhaps the root cause of your memory loss is tied up in your dreams. Surely you must want to try every avenue to get your life back?"

Rachel's smile was warm as she thought of her blossoming relationship with Mike Flynn. "Actually Doctor H., apart from the dreams my life is going really well. If anything I'm scared of spoiling all that by getting my memory back. So let's just let nature take its course, okay?" Glancing down at her watch she realized she had only forty minutes until she was meeting Suzy Jenner for lunch. Much as she was fond of the doctor she wished she didn't have to keep having these fortnightly appointments. If it had been up to her she wouldn't have come, but Mike was insistent and she figured that if an hour at the hospital kept him happy then it was worth it. For her part, although her tone was light what she'd said was the truth; she was scared of getting her memories back. Crazy though it sounded she was perfectly happy to let sleeping dogs lie.

Doctor Hanson leaned back in his chair and after making a final note in her file shut the brown buff folder and raised his hands in submission. "Right, I get the message, I won't push on that one, but if you change your mind, don't hesitate to call me. Just remember, fear of the unknown, of finding things out about yourself that you might not like, is perfectly natural, especially in cases like yours when the amnesia lasts a relatively long time." He lifted an eyebrow. "But I've never had a patient that wasn't much happier when the memories were back, warts and all, and that's the truth. In the meantime we'll see if there's any change over the next fortnight."

Jumping up from her seat, Rachel ran round the desk and kissed the kind and gently handsome cheek of her first friend in this new life. "That sounds like my cue to get myself out of here!" Blushing slightly, the doctor waved her away. "I'll see you in two weeks. And say hi to that charming teacher of yours. I'm glad he's looking after you so well."

Rachel had her coat on and was picking up her bag. "Yes, I think you've got yourself an ally there. Personally I think there's some kind of conspiracy going on between the two of you." Smiling, she blew him a kiss from the doorway and was gone.

Peter Hanson browsed through the folder in front of him for a few moments before putting it away. It was good that she was doing so well and was obviously fit and healthy, but there were things about her case that bothered him. Firstly, her amnesia should have been gone by now. Mysterious as the brain was, there hadn't been enough physical trauma to sustain it for this long. Correct that. There hadn't been any physical trauma. There was no reason that he could fathom for such a complete loss of memory. On top of that, from what he could gather from her file, and conversations with her GP and the psychologist she'd been seeing, this Rachel Wright was almost a completely different girl. Gone was the serious and studious bookworm with no-nonsense clothes and attitude. In her place was a woman with a real joie de vivre, flirtatious and fun-loving. Almost too fun-loving. He rubbed his face with his hands and glanced at the pile of patients notes on the right of his desk. Why is this bothering you so much, he thought, annoyed at himself and the uneasy feeling that he couldn't shift. She's obviously doing fine, so why not worry about the rest of your caseload? God knows, there's plenty there that need your help. Help you can actually give with parts of the body that respond to basic medicine, not second-guessing the psyche.

Taking his own advice he reached for the top file and buzzed his secretary for the next patient. Hopefully, the clinic wouldn't overrun today. He'd promised to take his wife out to dinner tonight, and for some reason he felt the urge to spend time with her pulsing in him stronger than ever.

Sitting in the black cab that was crawling toward her lunch-time meeting in a Soho eaterie, Rachel lit a cigarette and inhaled deeply. God, it was good to get out of that hospital, away from the smell of death, illness, and the reminder that all was not as it should be in her head, and back into the buzz of the London streets. And although she hadn't agreed to go back to the psychologist she had kept her promise to Mike and mentioned the dreams. She allocated herself an imaginary relationship brownie point. Mike actually suffered with the nightmares more than she did because although she was a bit tired in the mornings she never remembered anything. He was the one who was kept up all night with her tossing and turning.

She'd tried to make a joke of it, but she knew they must be bad because she'd caught him looking at her funny a couple times, first thing in the morning, and then today he'd told her rather reluctantly that she'd spent most of the night screaming about orgies of blood. Great. She certainly knew how to impress the boys. She smiled wryly. And the good doctor wondered why she was worried about getting her memories back. Still, from what she knew of the formative Rachel Wright, she didn't think orgies of blood were really her style.

Looking at the *Evening Standard* boards that lined the street, each asking in bold black marker, CAN YOU TRUST YOUR BANK MANAGER?, she shivered. Maybe that's where her bad dreams have come from, this gruesome story that had dominated the news for the past week or so. Mike was certainly absorbed by it, reading the daily papers for more of the horrific details as they emerged, reviled by them and titillated at the same time. From what she'd seen on the news a bank manager in North London had gone mad and killed his lover and a multitude of others in the lover's house in Hampstead. One of the victims was a customer at his branch, a young girl who'd gone missing after her mother's body had been found in their house months ago. Apparently he'd kept her alive for ages before he killed her. She couldn't help but wonder how terrible that must have been. Day after day, trapped in the clutches of a madman, hope of escape slowly slipping away from you, wondering if each breath would be your last.

Stubbing her cigarette out in the overcrowded ashtray, she turned her mind to more pleasant things. After her lunch with Suzy she planned to go to Selfridges and get some indulgently decadent foods to cook for Mike when he got in from work. She had to laugh at herself. Take it easy girl, you'll turn into a little housewife before you know it! Somehow she didn't mind doing things for him. Perhaps it was because he was such a caring person himself. Her internal voice laughed at her rationalizations. That's not the reason, and you know it. The reason you want to do things for him is because you've fallen hopelessly and madly in love with him. Admit it. You don't have to say anything to him, but at least be honest with yourself. You're as smitten as a girl can get and there's no denying it!

She frowned at her inner self as the cab pulled up outside the trendy and not inexpensive restaurant on Brewer Street. Well, that may be the case, but I'm certainly not going to be the first one to use the L word. That is most definitely his job!

An hour later and Suzy and Rachel had made polite conversation through their warm chicken salads while Rachel drank half a bottle of Chianti. When she lit up a cigarette as the waiter cleared their plates, Suzy took a sip from her sparkling mineral water and then spoke. "So what did you make of the manuscript?"

Rachel tried to meet the gaze of the cool blue eyes, and sighed. It was reading the manuscript that had brought her to her decision and now it was time to share her news with her soon to be ex-employer. Oh well, there was no time like the present. She ran her hands through her hair and sat back in her chair.

"That's why I wanted to see you. I've decided to resign. With everything that's been going on I think I need some time to re-evaluate my life." She'd rehearsed her words in her head and they came out effortlessly. Looking at

Suzy's face, she knew that the other woman wasn't surprised.

"To be honest, I've been expecting it. We've hardly spoken since you got out of the hospital." Rachel winced slightly at the hurt and reproach in her voice. It was true, she had been avoiding her erstwhile friend. She was pleased when Suzy didn't elaborate on that subject. She didn't know what she'd have said if she had. Nothing that would have made any sense anyway.

"What are you going to do? You used to go mad if you were left with no work for too long."

Rachel ignored the reference to her previous self and shrugged. "To be completely honest, I don't know. I might even come back to editing." Then again, pigs might fly, but she forgave herself the little white lie. "I've got a bit of money put by, a few investments here and there, plus my inheritance from my parents, so I don't really need to worry about cash for a while. Without meaning to sound like an aging hippy, I just want to spend some time rediscovering myself."

Suzy nodded. "That's understandable. You've had a rough ride recently. But just remember, you've always got a job with us if you feel like coming back. And more importantly, I'm always here as a friend if you need one."

Rachel could feel the atmosphere between them lifting now that she'd been honest. "No hard feelings, then?"

Suzy's smile was open and generous. "Don't be silly. Of course not." She pulled a mocking stern face. "But if you go and work for the competition then it's all-out war!" Rachel laughed and pushed her chair back.

"I don't think there's any danger of that!" She stood up. "I've just got to go to the little girl's room and then I'll get the bill. I won't be a minute."

Suzy shook her head. "No, this one's on me. I'll claim it back from expenses. You unemployed girls need to hang on to your pennies."

Rachel smiled over her shoulder as she headed toward the stairs that led down to the toilets. "Very funny!"

Her head was buzzing as she negotiated her high heels on the marble. Life was good. She'd packed in her job and the world was her oyster. Maybe she could persuade Mike to take a couple months off and they could travel a bit. Go to America or something. Who knows? Suzy had turned out to be nicer about it all than she'd expected and quite a sweet person with it. Maybe she would try to keep in touch with her. Easy tiger, she thought. That's the wine talking. She doesn't smoke and barely drinks. Hardly the girl for a good night out. Still, it was nice to have left her old life behind on a pleasant note. Yes, life was definitely on the up. Pushing the heavy door open she walked into the perfumed air of the empty ladies room and entered a cubicle, locking it behind her.

As she started to pee, she heard the outside door swing open and another pair of heels clicking into one of the other stalls. She imagined that this would probably have embarrassed the old her, this aural invasion of a most private act. But not the new and improved post-memory Rachel Wright. Peeing was one of the most natural things in the world, after all, everyone did it. What was there to get embarrassed about in the sound of water hitting water? She pushed the handle down and unlocked the door, heading toward the marble sink to wash her hands. Watching her reflection, she smiled at herself. Not a bad looking girl at all. No wonder Mike can't resist you! Young, free, and without a care in the world. And no more bloody editing. The bonuses of this new life seemed endless.

She had squeezed the liquid soap into her hands and was running the hot tap when a noise caught her attention and made her grimace. *Scratch, scratch, scratch.* It was like fingernails on a blackboard, a high-pitched screech. Exactly like fingernails on a blackboard. Leaving the tap running, she looked around quizzically, first at the locked cubicle behind her. There were no sounds there. Funnier still, she thought, as her feeling of disquiet rose, she hadn't heard any sound coming from there. Maybe the occupant was waiting for her to leave? Suddenly she heard the scraping again, and she spun round to her left, to the mirrors and sinks against the wall there. That was where the sound was coming from. *Tap, tap. Tap, tap.* Bemused, her hands still covered in soap, she slowly walked over to take a closer look. Something was happening in the mirror, some distortion that was making that horrible noise. Was it a bug or a spider of some kind stuck there somehow, trying to get itself free? What was it?

About two feet away from the mirror she stopped. *Jesus Christ, what is that?* Her heart pounded in her ears almost blocking the insistent scratching and she let out a small moan, one hand absently going to her mouth, as her eyes tried to comprehend what they were seeing. The surface of the mirror was moving, bulging as if being pushed with a finger from the other side. *Knock, knock. Who's there?* She stifled an hysterical giggle as she saw the surface being pressed out again, rippling her reflection. She watched, unaware of the taste of soap in her mouth as the pattern took shape. In the recesses of her mind her sanity screamed it's prayer that Jeremy Beadle was going to jump out from somewhere and tell her she'd just been framed. That this was Suzy Jenner's idea of a farewell joke, anything but that what she was seeing was real. Ignoring her, the patterns were staying on the surface as whatever was creating them moved relentlessly on with its terrible squeaking sound.

Oh Christ, oh Christ, whatever it is, it's writing to me, she thought with rising horror as she watched the letters forming in reverse. It's fucking writing to me, it's mirror writing, *oh you're funny, mirror writing,* as if someone, someone who hadn't written for oh such a very long time was trapped on the other side of the glass pressing out a message. The finger was still moving, and she watched absorbed and numbly terrified, like the terror felt in a dream, emotion without clarity, until it had finished its work.

THEY'RE COMING
FOR YOU

The invisible finger fell silent but the words lingered, defying Rachel's denial of them. *They're coming for you.* Fear burned her face as she saw colors forming at the edge of her vision. If she wasn't careful she was going to pass out, but still she didn't move. *No, no, this isn't happening, this just can't be happening, the doctor got it wrong, I must have a tumor, something must be wrong with me, because this just can not be happening.* Her brain was screaming at her to get away, to get out of there, but she couldn't bring her legs to move, and instead just stood there, helpless, staring at the words that couldn't be there, words that filled her with a dread that itched, that itched at her to know what they meant.

The standoff between herself and the silent mirror could only have lasted a few seconds but to Rachel it felt like hours. Slowly, slowly, she felt a coldness work its way from her very center outward to her skin leaving a trail of goosebumps in its wake. She saw her own pale reflection hiding behind the words and took strength from it. "Fuck you," she whispered. "You're not real. Fuck you." Her breath hung like an expectant mist in front of her, and she realized that the cold was everywhere, not just inside her, small icicles having formed at the mouth of the taps, and a solid lump of ice now replaced the hot water she had left running. As she looked around at the winter that had formed, her cold breath scraping her lungs, the scratching came back and this time the writing was quick and sharp, filling the mirror. *Angry. It's angry. I've pissed it off.*

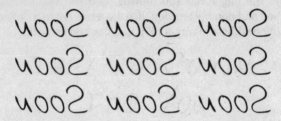

The mad repitition filled the mirror, the words stabbing at its surface so violently that Rachel stumbled backward reaching out for something, anything to use as support. Her hand thankfully grasped the ice-cold enamel of the other bay of sinks where only moments ago she had been happily washing her hands.

Soon. They're coming for you. Soon. She felt bile rising in her throat and she swallowed hard and shut her eyes. The darkness was an immediate relief. *There's nothing there. I'm going to open my eyes and everything is going to be normal. There is going to be no motherfucking message in the mirror.* But she kept her eyes shut very tight and then after about a minute she heard it. The toilet flushed. There was warmth in her cheeks. Very slowly she lifted her lids and saw only her own white, drawn face looking back at her. *Dorothy's back in Kansas*, she thought as she looked with disbelief at the hot water running into the sink.

She turned off the tap and noticed that her hands were shaking uncontrollably. The sharp sound of the cubicle unlocking made her jump and she ran the cold tap to splash water on her face. *Maybe it's time to stop drinking at lunchtime, Rachel Wright, or maybe it's time to check yourself and your lack of memory into the funny farm. You're losing it, babes, you're really losing it.*

A smartly dressed middle-aged woman had joined her

and was washing her hands. She looked at Rachel, concerned. "Are you okay, dear? You look a bit pale."

Trying to pull herself together, Rachel managed a wan
smile. "Whatever you do, don't have the prawns." *And don't
look in the mirror too long, something in there seems to like
to talk. To tell you things you think you know. Like you've
heard the words in a dream long ago. Things that cause
FEAR.*

Pulling a sheet of paper towel from the machine, she
dabbed her face dry and dropped it into the wastebasket,
before dragging her unsteady legs back into the corridor
and up the stairs. All she wanted to do was get out into the
fresh air and have a cigarette.

Suzy was signing the credit card slip as Rachel returned
into the blessed daylight. Looking at the perfectly smooth
blonde hair on top of that eminently sensible head, for a
moment she would have given anything to be her, mineral
water and all. Let her deal with frozen bathrooms and messages written from the other side of mirrors. See how well
her perfectly organized life holds together with that kind of
shit going on. As she picked up her jacket from the back of
the chair she noticed her hands were still trembling. *I'm going mad, I really am. Did that shit really just happen?* Looking at the people eating their meals around her, all
perfectly normal, she felt overwhelmed by claustrophobia.
*Jesus Christ, if I don't get out of here soon, I'm either going
to throw up or burst into hysterical laughter.*

Suzy looked up and smiled. "All done?"

Rachel nodded. "Thanks for the lunch. Sorry I've got to
run off, but I forgot I promised to pick something up for
Mike before three-thirty." She was amazed at how even her
voice sounded. Suzy raised an eyebrow. "Oh yes, Mike.
That's a bit of a turnaround, isn't it? From what you said before, you were never that interested in him."

Rachel was in no mood for small talk about her love life.
"Yeah well, things change. Anyway, I've really got to go."
Feeling the atmosphere that had come between them

again, Suzy's smile fell. "Of course. I've got to get back to the office, anyway. It was nice to see you, it really was. And remember, I'm always here if you need me."

Rachel gave a brief smile. "Thanks. I'll keep in touch." The words sounded hollow to both women.

Watching the newly stylish Rachel Wright striding purposefully out of the restaurant and onto the pavement, Suzy Jenner let out a sigh. So that was that. The end of a friendship. She watched until the woman disappeared out of sight and felt an ache in her stomach. Who are you trying to kid? It wasn't just *a* friendship. It was *the* friendship. Your little black book's hardly overflowing with the numbers of girlfriends itching to spend an evening in your scintillating company, is it? Her internal reproach voice was always that of her mother's. *You should try harder to make friends, get out more. Get your nose out of that book, for a start.* How many times had she heard those words as a child?

But growing up as a fat teenager in Surbiton, books had been a safe haven for her. She could lose herself in the pages and completely relax in some fantasy place away from the rest of the world. She'd learned only too well how cruel girls could be. *Jelly belly Jenner.* She still winced at the old nickname that had accompanied her all the way through high school. Well, she may have lost the weight and turned out not too bad looking in an ordinary kind of way, but she never lost her reserve around other women. And if she was honest, most of them bored her. Clothes, makeup, men. Clothes, makeup, men. I mean, how many times could they have the same conversation?

But Rachel, Rachel had been like her. A serious person. And she loved books. And they both made a damn good living together out of what they loved. Rachel had been a person she could talk to. About anything. It might have been a quiet friendship, but it was a strong one. And now it was gone. Rachel was gone. Just like that. She tried to shake herself out of her sense of mourning. Why was she thinking about her friend in the past tense? It wasn't like she was dead or anything. But that's what it feels like, she mused. Right or wrong, it feels like she dead. She's not the same woman anymore.

Still gazing out of the window with a heavy heart she shivered. Suddenly she was cold. They must have turned the air-conditioner up, she thought. Why on earth would they want to do that at this time of year? As she collected her things together to leave, she never noticed the dark shadow that fell from nowhere across her table.

CHAPTER EIGHT

"Well, this makes a change, spending the evening at mine. I was beginning to think you didn't like my decor."

Rachel pushed the plate of spaghetti bolognaise that she'd managed to half-eat away from her and smiled. "Yes, well I thought it was time that you had the washing-up. Anyway, by the time I'd left Suzy I didn't have time to pick up any dinner." *No you didn't did you, because you were far too busy rushing home and taking down all your mirrors, weren't you? What's he going to think when he sees that? He's going to think that his mysterious no-memory lady's finally flipped her lid, that's what he's going to think. And can you blame him?*

Mike picked up the plates to take to the kitchen and kissed her on the forehead. "I don't mind. It's nice having you here."

Looking at the cozy untidiness that surrounded her as she kicked off her shoes and curled up on the sofa, she was starting to doubt what she saw at lunchtime, or even if she saw anything at all. Maybe it was the wine, it might have been corked or something. You hear about people having funny reactions to things like that all the time. She'd put the mirrors back up tomorrow. The day after at the latest. She couldn't carry on putting her makeup on in the reflected glare of her flat lights in a window, that was for sure.

Taking a careful sip of her wine she let herself start to relax. Even if she did see something, it might have just been her brain trying to sort itself out. Maybe *They're coming for you* meant her memories were trying to come back. No doubt that's what a shrink would say. But she couldn't lose the feeling that somewhere deep inside she knew what the words meant. And it had nothing to do with her memories. Maybe she'd mention it to Dr. Hanson next time she saw him. See how things went.

Mike sat down next to her and topped off her glass. "So, how does it feel to be a lady of leisure? You know, if you get bored you could always become my charlady. I'm sure I could rustle you up one of those fetching housecoats from somewhere. And some wrinkly brown tights, of course. Hmm. I'm quivering just thinking about it."

Looking at his cheeky grin, she couldn't help but join in. She tried to keep her face serious. "Mr. Flynn. Is this some secret fantasy that you've been hiding from me? Because if so, then it's something I really feel we should discuss."

He looked at her wide-eyed. "Oh, it's only one of many. My favorite is the one where you're my naked house slave, with a collar and chain that runs between the bedroom and the kitchen. Obviously we can negotiate on the amount of time you spend in the kitchen, it's not the most important area of the house, and you might get a bit chilly with all that nakedness and everything."

Smiling, she snuggled in a bit closer so that her lips were almost touching his. "Well, that sounds a little more appealing. Why don't we give it a test run?"

Sighing, Mike playfully frowned and shook his head. "It'd never work. I haven't got the collar and chain."

Running her hand up the inside of his thigh, she purred. "Oh, I think we can probably do just fine without those, don't you?"

Groaning as she reached her target, Mike pulled her toward him. "Rachel Wright, you really are a very wicked woman."

She giggled as she kissed him. "I know, I know. I just can't help myself." Feeling the warmth of his mouth on hers as he picked her up and carried her into the bedroom, she let the worries of the mind slip away as she lost herself in the pleasures of the physical. Everything was going to be okay. It was. It had to be.

She woke up with a start in the darkness, and carefully shifted Mike's arm so that she could read the clock. Four in the morning. What could have woken her? Mike was fast asleep and snoring softly, so for once it couldn't have been the bad dreams. Those tended to wake him before they did her. She lay there for a second and then she heard it. A faint giggle. Not a nice one. Where was that coming from? Downstairs? There were a few seconds' silent pause and then she heard it again. It sounded closer this time. She listened for footsteps on the stairs but there were none. Sitting up in bed she strained her ears for noise. When it came her whole body jumped. The whisper was loud and harsh. Demanding. Female.

"Psst! Psst! I know you're up there. They're coming for you, you know. You can't hide. The Soulcatchers are coming. Can't you feel them?"

Oh God, it can't be, it can't be. It's coming from under the bed. There's someone under the bed. She looked at Mike, still sleeping peacefully. How come he couldn't hear it? *I'm still dreaming, that's what it is. It's just another fucking dream. I'll wake up and I won't remember a thing.* Shivering, she pulled the covers closer around her and started to lay down. *Long, deep breaths, remember what the doctor told you. None of it's real. It's all in your mind.*

"Don't fucking ignore me, bitch! You owe me! You fuck-ing owe me!" Rachel froze halfway to her pillow. *I know it's not real, I know it's not real, but please make it stop now, please*. There were tears stinging at the back of her eyes and her bladder was itching to burst but she couldn't get up to go to the bathroom because that would mean getting out of bed and standing on the floor and she knew, oh God she knew, that if she did that there was going to be a hand scrabbling, scraping, reaching for her, a hand just like the one on the other side of the mirror. *A hungry hand*.

Not aware of what she was doing she started to rock backward and forward, half-sitting, half laying in the bed. "It's just a dream," she whispered. "It's just a dream."

The laugh was like a bark, as if the lungs were bleeding and raw. "It's no fucking dream, it's your worst fucking night-mare." There was a pause filled with the sound of some-thing sucking in awful watery breaths. "You don't get it yet, do you? They're coming and you can't stop them. They're playing with you."

The Soulcatchers are coming.

"You thought you were so fucking clever, didn't you? But you want to hear something funny? You killed me for noth-ing. They wrote the book, sweetcheeks. You thought you could escape, but they wrote the book. They created the book for people like you and you fell for it."

It's coming from under the end of the bed. I'm sitting above it's fucking feet. I can't take much more of this, I really can't, even if it is a dream and sweet Jesus, the Soulcatchers are coming, they're coming and I can't hide and I should know what that means, I know I should but I don't and God I just want to wake up. The warm tears were hot against her frozen cheeks, running down her neck and under the cov-ers to her naked breasts. *If it's just a dream why does every-thing feel so fucking real?*

This time the voice was teasing, taunting. "If I'm not real, why don't you come and take a sneaky peak under the bed? You made me what I am, what's there to be scared of?"

Oh but I am scared, I'm so very scared.

"Go away. You're not real. It's just a dream." Her own voice was a low monotone, talking as much to herself as to whomever, *whatever* was under the bed.

"Well, if I'm not real, then I can't hurt you, can I? And aren't you the teeny-weeniest bit interested to see what you did to me? You weren't there at the end were you? I should make you proud." So much bitterness in the voice.

What have I done, I didn't do anything, I didn't do anything.

"You always thought you were so strong, didn't you? Not so strong now. Not so strong at all."

I think I'm going crazy but if I don't look under the bed then I really am going to go crazy because this is all in my mind, and I'm in Mike's flat and he's a teacher and things like this don't happen in teacher's flats and it really is JUST A DREAM AND I WILL NOT BE AFRAID.

Slowly, her own breath coming in irregular gasps, she edged, inch by inch toward the bottom of the mattress. It's my dream, she thought, as she lowered her head over the side, her heart beating so hard it was almost as if it wasn't beating at all, it's my dream and I'm in control.

Her dark hair was hanging below her forehead, trailing toward the ground and before her eyes had even followed it, something grabbed it and pulled her head harshly under the bed. Struggling frantically, Rachel's world spun in horrified disbelief.

Oh God, oh god, she's got me and she's got no eyes, how can she have no eyes, am I screaming, is that me screaming?

The woman was smiling manically, holding her thrashing head so close, *I'm going to be sick, that smell, I'm going to be sick.* Lips drawn back showing broken teeth, the woman, the thing, under the bed drew her closer. "So do you like it? Do you like what you did to me? Do I seem real now?"

The pain in her scalp seemed dim and distant compared

to the horror so terribly visible in the gloom. *Oh God yes, oh God yes, you're real and the Soulcatchers are coming, the Soulcatchers are coming, they're coming and I can't hide and how can I make this stop and am I screaming and Oh God something's got my arms, SOMETHING'S GOT MY ARMS GOT MY ARMS!*

There was an earthquake starting in Mike's dream so he was quite relieved when the alarm went off, shrieking at him, piercing his sleep. Time to get up. As he dragged himself back to the surface of consciousness the sound became less familiar, too harsh, too effective to be his alarm clock. His still dulled brain struggled to recognize it. What was that sound? His eyes opened into the darkness and he saw the writhing, screaming figure hanging over the end of the bed. Oh God no, not again. Fully awake, he lunged forward and grabbed her arms, pulling her toward him, calling her name. Still in the grip of her nightmare she fought back, struggling to break free. Jesus Christ, she was strong. For a second she seemed like a wild animal struggling in a net, desperate for release.

"Rachel! Rachel! It's me, it's Mike. Wake up!" Her hand lashed out and he felt a stinging pain where her fingernails were slicing through the skin of his shoulder. Grasping her wrist, this time tight enough that she couldn't get loose, he shook her, her hair falling over her face. Her eyes were wide open, but it took a moment before she recognized him. Her face shone with sweat as she glanced terrified around the room. "The Soulcatchers are coming. The Soulcatchers are coming." Shaking in his arms her words were barely a whisper.

Stroking her hair he slowly sat her back down on the bed. "It was just a bad dream, Rach. Just another bad dream." He felt a sob rack her slim body as she shook her head. "No, no." There was still panic in her voice. "It was real, there was a girl under the bed, a dead girl, she had no eyes. It was real, Mike, it was real."

He rocked her gently for a few seconds until he felt the tenseness in her muscles start to relax and then took his arm away to reach for the light. As he flicked the switch he saw the time glowing tauntingly at him. Four-fifteen. Now that his heart had stopped racing his exhaustion washed over him. Too many nights of broken sleep. He was too old to be living on four or five hours a night. Leaning over, he looked under the bed. Nothing. Resurfacing he looked at Rachel. "Nothing there but my smelly socks." She didn't look convinced.

"I promise. There's nothing there. It was just a bad dream." He smiled tiredly at her, but the smile was only surface deep. These aren't just any bad dreams are they? he thought to himself. These dreams are tearing through both your nights, and they're getting worse. She never normally wakes up with them, and yes, you may love her, but it's time to make her do something about it. For her own sake as well as your own.

Reaching for a cigarette he groaned with the thought of having to face 6F in five hours time. He just didn't have the energy to deal with the kids these days and he was running out of Shakespeare videos to show them. God, what he wouldn't give for a good night's sleep. Just one blissful eight hours of complete shut down. Heaven. He let out a sigh.

"Are you angry with me?" Her voice was tiny, empty of her new-found confidence, and she looked like a delicate, beautiful child sitting there with her knees drawn up under her chin. Mike felt his heart melt. He stroked her face. "Of course I'm not angry. It's not your fault, is it?" He paused and then passed her the cigarette. "But it is time you did something about it. These aren't the kind of dreams that come for no reason, you must realize that. And until we figure out what's causing them then neither of us is going to be getting any sleep."

Rachel looked as if sleep were the last of her worries. What was it that could be plaguing that locked-up mind of hers? Okay, he'd never known her that well, but she seemed to have lived such an ordinary life. She always seemed so sensible. Even when her parents had died in that car crash, she'd just got on and dealt with it, organizing the funeral, arranging flowers. What could possibly have been going on behind the scenes to cause all of this? It just didn't make sense and he was too tired to think about it. What a mess. He finally gets the girl of his dreams and it turns out she's got some pretty powerful dreams of her own. Nothing ever could go exactly smoothly, could it? That would just be too much to ask for.

"I won't see that psychologist. I'm tired of people comparing me with the old me. I don't want to see someone that knew me then. I hate the old me." Her voice was defensive and Mike knew that this wasn't the time to point out how ludicrous she sounded. He'd been doing a little research in the school library and most memory loss sufferers were desperate to find out about their old selves. Why wasn't she? *Yes but most of them probably haven't changed quite as dramatically as the gorgeous Rachel Wright, have they?* He had to admit that his inner voice had a point. Rachel wasn't the same girl any more and that was that. No wonder she didn't want reminding of it. He rubbed his face. "Okay, point taken, but there's got to be another way. Something less formal." He paused, an idea coming to him. Why hadn't he thought of it before? Because, dear boy, he answered himself, you're hardly firing on all cylinders these days, are you? You're barely getting enough sleep to get the motor started. Rolling onto his side, he propped his head up with one hand, and stroked her leg with the other. He looked at her frankly. "I do have one suggestion. I don't know what you're going to make of it though."

Sucking the cigarette down to the butt, she raised an eyebrow at him. It was still defensive but at least she was interested. Oh well, here goes nothing.

"I have an aunt, Aunt Ruby. She's a very lovely older lady and my favorite living relative. I'd like to take you to meet her."

Mike noticed with an internal smile that Rachel was losing her lost little girl look and regaining her spirits. She passed him the cigarette butt to put in the ashtray. "Well that's all very sweet and everything but what's Aunt Ruby got to do with my bad dreams?"

"Ah. I'm just getting to that. As well as being a little old lady whom you're going to adore, she also makes a healthy living helping people get over phobias and fears with hypnosis and regression. She's very well-respected." He figured that he'd got this far so he might as well tell the whole truth. She'd find out soon enough anyway. "She's actually a medium. Not that I believe in that kind of thing, but that's what she does. Anyway, the medium thing aside, the hypnosis and regression really work, she's helped a couple of friends with it."

He paused as she regarded him thoughtfully. "So basically, what you're saying is that she's a complete fruitloop. You want me to get help from the Flynn family fruitcake, is that correct?"

Slapping her playfully on the thigh, he laughed. "Do you mind! That's my most favorite aunt you're talking about!" He shrugged. "But yes, if you want to put it like that, then yes. So what do you say? She makes the best homemade biscuits."

Rachel's eyes narrowed. "Can she make those biscuit things with the layer of caramel and then the chocolate on the top?"

Mike matched her serious expression with one of his own. "The best."

Smiling, she leaned forward and kissed him. "Okay it's a deal. But only if she makes the caramel biscuit things." Reaching past him she flicked the light off. "Now why don't you send me off to sleep in the manner to which I have become accustomed?" Laughing, he pulled the duvet over their heads and tried not to think about the rapid approach of 6F. Some things were just too damned enjoyable to skip for the sake of sleep. He'd get an early night tomorrow.

*   *   *

At eleven-thirty the next morning Mike poured himself his second coffee of the half an hour break. Well, least he'd got through the morning without too many problems. That made a change. He yawned as he added cream to his mug.

"Not burning the candle at both ends, I hope? Or is it just the effects of a double lesson with 6F?" Turning around he saw the cheerful face of Steve Taylor, the head of Physical Education. Mike smiled.

He normally didn't like the sports staff too much; their minds never normally expanded past the rugby pitch. Sport was all, physical perfection the ultimate aim, and God forgive you if you ever smoked. Smokers seemed to have a path straight to hell, according to those guys. He supposed he put it down to his childhood when he became the school sports pariah after refusing a football trial for a professional club when he was fifteen. Not only had he stolen the school's moment of glory but no one seemed to understand that as much as he enjoyed a good game of footie, running around in the mud was not the way he wanted to earn his living. He ended up quitting the First Eleven because he couldn't be bothered with all the barbed remarks. Safe enough to say, he'd been left with a lifelong aversion to men who wore tracksuits and whistles in their chosen careers. But Steve was different. He loved all aspects of learning and had even been known to light up a Marlboro or two after one too many pints. And that was good enough for Mike.

He waited for Steve to get his coffee and then they found themselves a table and a couple of tatty chairs over by the window. As they sat down, Steve regarded his friend with interest. "So is the enigma lady keeping you up all night? Can't get enough of your manly body? Go on. Make me jealous."

Mike laughed. "Well yes, she is, but not in the way you think." He paused reflectively. "Well not entirely, anyway." That was another thing that was bothering him. He never thought he'd have a problem with a woman wanting a lot of sex, but she seemed to be getting more and more demanding and there was a mania about it, an urgency that didn't seem normal. It definitely wasn't the Rachel whom he used to know. But then, as he'd already ascertained he hadn't known her all that well, after all. Get over yourself, Flynn, and just enjoy it, he told himself. You've got a beautiful woman who loves you and loves having sex with you. Where's the problem there? Most men would kill to be in your shoes. Steve included. The day you start complaining about that is the day you turn into a grumpy old man and you're way too young for that.

Steve sipped his coffee under his ginger curls. "So what's keeping you up at night then?"

Mike rubbed his unshaven stubble. "Rachel's been getting these bad dreams. Really bad ones. She wakes me up screaming and shouting in her sleep most nights. I guess it's just beginning to tire me out a bit." Oh yes. Always the master of understatement. You couldn't run round the football pitch if you tried at the moment and don't kid yourself otherwise.

Steve leaned forward making sure his whistle didn't dunk itself in his drink. "What are they about? Anything interesting?"

Mike shrugged. "That's the weird bit. She's normally forgotten them from the moment she wakes up. But the stuff she shouts about is enough to stop me getting back to sleep. Really horrible stuff, like the worst gory horror film you could imagine seeing. Only in her head, while she's sleeping, it's all real. It makes my blood curdle."

Steve looked as if he was about to make a joke and then thought better of it. Mike looked genuinely concerned and stressed. "Has she got any of her memories back yet?"

Mike shook his head. "Nope. She's a complete blank. I don't think she wants to get them back. It's as if she's afraid of them or something. I just don't get it. I mean, don't get me wrong, I think she's fantastic, I'm crazy about her"—*You're more than crazy about her, you're head over heels in love with her and terrified of it*—"but she's so different. I don't know what to make of it. If it wasn't for the nightmares maybe it wouldn't worry me so much, but they're so god-damn severe, it just isn't natural. You know, her doctor says she was seeing a psychologist for nightmares before her collapse. There's got to be a link there somewhere." God it felt good to talk to someone about this. He hadn't realized how much he wanted to get it off his chest. Hah. Maybe he was the one who should go and see the psychologist. His brown eyes looked at Steve. "So now I guess you think I'm crazy, huh?"

Steve's freckled face fell into an easy grin. "I've always thought you were crazy." He put his coffee cup down. "But seriously Mike, I know it's all very romantic falling in love with a beautiful mystery lady, but are you sure you know what you're getting yourself into? It sounds like she's got some serious issues in her past to deal with, otherwise she wouldn't be having the dreams, and who knows what they could be? I know it sounds harsh, but maybe you should cool it off for a while until she's a bit more sorted out. Look after number one for a while. You've never been very good at that at the best of times."

Listening to his friend, Mike knew he was making sense but just the thought of breaking up with Rachel made his stomach tie itself in knots. It was a feeling that he hadn't had for years and he couldn't give it up now. Dreams or not, there was no way he could leave Rachel. He was in way too deep for that now. He didn't meet Steve's eyes. "I'll think about it. Really I will." He checked his watch and saw that only five minutes were left before his next lesson.

Standing up, Mike rummaged in his pocket for change. "I hate to love you and leave you but I've got to make a phone call. Thanks for the chat, Steve, I really appreciate it."

Steve still looked concerned but smiled anyway. "No problem. And if you ever fancy a beer after work just let me know. We haven't had a few pints for ages."

Mike nodded and started to walk over to the pay phone. He hadn't been out for a beer with Steve since he'd gotten

things together with Rachel, but he knew there was no reproach meant in his friend's comment. That was another
thing he liked about him. He understood things like that.
His brain had developed beyond the playground.

He lifted the receiver and tapped in the number. When
the pips sounded, he slid two fifty-pence pieces into the
slot. These things seemed to eat money these days.

"Hello?"

His heart warmed when he heard the voice. There was
always something reassuring about talking to Ruby. "Is that
my favorite woman in the whole wide world?"

The voice at the other end was full of joy. "Mike! How
lovely to hear from you? How are you?"

Mike looked at the seconds ticking away on the phone
display. "I'm great. Look, I can't talk for long, I'm on a pay
phone and my money will be gone any minute. I was wondering if you could help me with something."

"Sure, what is it?" Ruby was at least in her late sixties,
she'd been much older than his own mother whom he suspected had been a bit of an accident, but she always
sounded so full of energy.

"Well, I've met this wonderful woman called Rachel and
I'd love you to meet her, but she's got a few problems with
some bad dreams and I thought maybe you could try some
hypnosis on her or something." He kept his tone light. "What
do you say?"

Ruby came back straightaway. "Of course I will. But don't
tell me any more about her. I don't want to clutter up my
head with any preconceived ideas before I see her. I've got
quite a full diary, but if you're both okay with a weekday
why don't you come over on Tuesday and we can have
some dinner and then have a session afterward?"

It was the first time in the day that Mike felt some energy
flowing through him, as if a weight had been lifted from his
shoulders. "Thanks Ruby, you're a darling."

She laughed. "Of course I am. But tell me something,"
This time it was just the loving aunt speaking. "Is she spe-

cial, this girl? You must be very fond of her? You haven't brought a girl to meet me for years."

Mike could feel himself blushing. "Yes, she's special. She's very special. So don't embarrass me with any baby photos, okay?"

"There's just no fun in being an old woman if you can't embarass your relatives, don't you understand that, Mikey?"

The pips were demanding more money and it was time to get to his next class of little angels. "My money's run out. We'll see you on Tuesday, okay? Bye!"

The dead tone cut in just as she was saying good-bye. He hung up and checked the table where he'd been sitting to see if Steve was still there. He wasn't. Feeling better after talking to Ruby he decided to make a point of going for beer with his colleague. Maybe tomorrow or Friday. With a renewed spring in his step, he headed out into the corridor and toward the classroom.

CHAPTER NINE

Suzy Jenner shut the binder with her amendments in it and gave up on the manuscript for the night. It wasn't getting the best of her attention. Abandoning it on the sofa next to her, everything in it instantly forgotten, she reached forward and refilled her wine glass from the half-empty bottle on the table. It was only her second glass, having opened the Chardonnay the night before. She wasn't a big drinker but she did enjoy the occasional glass of wine or two, especially on nights like this when she was feeling vaguely dissatisfied with life. Well, not with life in general, more with her life in particular.

The wine was crisp and dry, just the way she liked it and she sipped it thoughtfully. So this is how she spent a Saturday night in Central London. Sitting at home, working and going wild with half a bottle of wine. Great. She really knew how to live. For some reason she felt very lonely tonight. She tried to shake off her feeling of self-pity. What was her problem? She spent every Saturday night in, and normally she was quite happy about it. She'd do some work, make herself something to eat, have a glass of wine and then maybe ring Rachel for a chat. So why did she feel so low tonight? She considered calling her mother but then realized that by half past eleven her parents had normally been in bed for a couple hours. She laughed to herself. Maybe that's where she'd got her party girl attitude from.

Kicking off her shoes, she rested her feet on the table in front of her. It was probably a good thing that it was too late to call her mother. No doubt she'd only give her a well-meaning lecture about settling down and having children, and she really wasn't in the mood for one of those tonight. They seemed to have gotten a little more frequent since she'd crossed the big thirty barrier a few months ago.

And maybe her mother had a point. What was she waiting around for anyway? Prince Charming was hardly going to come trotting up the streets of Notting Hill to whisk her away to a life of paradise. It wasn't like she didn't get her fair share of offers, maybe it was time to take some of them up. Even Rachel seemed to have settled down. Living happily ever after with Mike the schoolteacher. Now there was a turn up for the books. Although if she was honest, as far as she was concerned, it wasn't *her* Rachel that had shacked up with the teacher. If she'd wanted to do that then she could have done so after their drunken one night stand. He made it pretty obvious he was interested. It was the new and, some would probably say, improved Rachel who had made that decision.

Is that what it is? She asked herself. Are you jealous that she's got someone else now and doesn't need to play spinster games with you anymore? Are you just pissed off that she's left you with the shelf all to yourself? She examined her feelings. No. That wasn't it. If Rachel was happy then that was fine with her. She only wished it was a happiness she could share.

Standing up, she stretched and shook herself. It was time to drag herself out of the doldrums. This was her life and it was exactly the way she had chosen it. She didn't want Mr. Right just yet and there was no way she was ready for a horde of children. So okay, her friend had changed and moved on, but maybe when she got her memory back things would go back to normal. And if she didn't, well, life would just have to go on. She'd have to find herself a new friend. Feeling a bit more positive, she headed into the bathroom and turned the taps on. An indulgent candlelit aromatherapy bath with another glass of wine was what she decided was needed.

Checking that the water was running hot, she put the plug in and added bubble bath before lighting the scented candles dotted around the room. She was starting to feel better already. There was an old battery-operated radio on a shelf on the other side of the room, safely away from any water, and she flicked it on. It would soon be time for *Late Night Love* and if ever there was anything guaranteed to stop her moping for romance, then that was it. Also, it was guaranteed to make her laugh. The room filled with the gentle sound of Sade singing about a smooth operater. Perfect.

The mirrors in the bathroom were already steaming up so humming along with the lyrics, she stepped out into the hall and used the long glass mirror to pull her hair away from her face and trap it with a scrunchie in a ponytail. The mirror was about six feet wide and as high as the ceiling and was intended to give the small flat the appearance of being much larger. Suzy thought it was a relic from the eighties and had been meaning to take it down ever since she'd moved in but had never got around to it. Anyway, it had turned out to be handy. She'd never let herself get fat again when she had to walk past that every morning in just her towel or underwear.

She squeezed some baby lotion onto a small piece of cotton wool and started to rub her face with it, removing whatever traces of makeup and dirt the day had left on her. She had just started rubbing it on her eyes when Sade was interrupted by sharp static blaring from the radio. "Great," she muttered as her eyes stung from opening them in surprise. Trying to ignore the stinging, she headed back into the bathroom and turned the taps off. The water was just at the right temperature and she couldn't wait to sink into the bubbles. The radio was still blaring static, and drying her hands, she went to check it. That was odd, it was showing the right frequency, so where was Sade? She turned the old but normally reliable tuning nob slightly left and then right, but still there was no radio station. Maybe they were having a problem with the transmitter.

She tried again, this time turning the dial farther, to where some of the BBC stations should have been, but again she found nothing. "You picked a great night to die on me," she grumbled at it. Deciding to give it one more try before resigning herself to bathing in silence, she turned back to her original frequency. This time there was no static, the sound replaced with an eerie silence, an empty sound that was almost too empty. She frowned slightly, and then tapped the side, the age-old remedy for curing anything mechanical. Nothing happened. Cursing under her breath, she reached for the off switch, but just before she touched it, she heard something. She tilted her head, puzzled and listened hard. Maybe she'd just imagined it, but she thought she'd heard a woman's voice saying her name. A nervous smile twitched on her lips. You're losing it, girl, of course you didn't hear anything.

But then she heard it again, it was still distant, as if she were listening to a broadcast from the moon, someone speaking to her from thousands of miles away, but it was a voice and it was louder than the first time. What the hell was going on? Was someone playing a joke on her? Suddenly a rational thought came to her and she clung to it. Her radio was probably just picking up a local cab signal or something. They've probably got a fare called Suzy. Her walkman used to do it when she was a teenager listening in bed. She laughed aloud to dispel her nervousness and turned around pulling her dress over her head and letting the warm steam get rid of her shivers. She tossed the dress out into the hallway and followed it with her bra.

Then she heard it, and despite the heat goosebumps arose all over her body. There was sobbing coming from the radio. A woman sobbing. Almost hypnotized, Suzy walked back to the radio dressed only in her knickers. The bath was forgotten now. She listened, unable to bring herself to switch the thing off. She knew that person. Whoever it was that was crying she knew them. But she had never heard sobbing like this, so full of sadness, so full of pain. Where was this woman? Who was this woman? There was the sound of hitching breath before the woman spoke, and when she did, it was as if it took every ounce of energy in her body to part with the words. "Run Suzy, run Suzy, please run Suzy, Run Suzy, Run now, please run now Suzy, run Suzy . . ." As the words streamed out of the innocuous black front of the radio at her, Suzy's blood ran cold, and she let out a small yelp as she stepped backward. "Run Suzy, run Suzy, Run now, run now, please run Suzy . . ."

What was this? *Turn it off, Suzy, that's what you need to do, turn it off and the world will be back to normal, just you wait and see. Turn it off and get in the bath.* But as much as she wanted to listen to herself she couldn't. Who was that? She *knew* that voice.

The words were still coming at her, in that same sobbing voice that she tried to pinpoint. *I've changed my mind, don't turn it off, just run, do what it says and run, get your dress and get out of here.* Her panic was rising through the sense of unreality, but she tried to squash it, feeling the voice's identity on the tip of her tongue. And then it came to her. It was Rachel's voice. Rachel. Rachel was crying in the radio. What in heaven's name was going on here? Suddenly the voice stopped. There was a long pause before she heard it again, but this time it was weaker, moving away, being dragged back to wherever it came from. *Wherever it escaped from.* "It's too late, they're coming, they're coming Suzy, I'm sorry Suzy, they're coming and I can't stop them, I'm sorry Suzy." And then the words were gone and Suzy was left with a terror larger than any she'd felt in years. A mortal terror. *It's too late. They're coming. Rachel's in the radio and she wanted me to run and I didn't.*

She stood there, staring at the radio, her breath caught in her chest. *Nothing's going to happen. Nothing can happen. There's nobody here but me.* A sob of her own started in her throat as she heard a cracking sound behind her. Slowly, slowly, she turned around, her whole body shaking. A large zig-zag fracture had appeared in the mirror above the sink, shining like a scar through the condensated surface. She backed away, her bare feet feeling their path across the small area of carpet and out into the hall. The break seemed to be getting bigger, spreading across the surface like angry gashes as if subject to extreme pressure from the other side, pushing against the glass. She felt her dress beneath the skin of her soles, the familiar cotton so alien now, so out of place in this distorting reality. *I don't understand, I don't understand, how could Rachel be in the radio?* Sharp retorts rang in her ears and she moaned, her eyes squeezing shut over the tears that fled down her face. She ran into the lounge, past the wine bottle from minutes and a lifetime ago, until she'd reached the farthest wall, as if the solid bricks and mortar could give her some protection from whatever was happening here.

Turning around, she saw the large hallway mirror, *Why didn't I take it down, why did I never take it down?* rupturing, great fissures appearing, spreading viciously from ceiling to floor. As the surface started to bend, to push outward in angular bubbles, she clutched her naked body, clinging to herself, as if the feel of her own flesh could make this stop. *If Rachel could be in the radio then what in heaven's name could be behind the mirrors? It's too late, they're coming and I can't stop them, run Suzy run.* She looked on in horror as the face of the glass stretched as far as the bathroom door like a distended stomach ready to burst. *You should have run, Suzy, you really should have run. Tut, tut. Too late now.* As the world exploded in reflective pieces, she screamed and screamed, curling up in a ball on the floor and covering her head with her arms.

* * *

When Suzy had been six she'd nearly died. It was a warm, summer's afternoon on her grandparent's farm, one of those glorious days that comes along about once in every summer, the air filled with fresh smells of flowers and barbecues and lemonade and where the world was an adventure playground of childish opportunity. She'd left her parents sitting on the porch sipping cool, long gins with her aunt and uncle, talking and laughing the way adults do about things that seem so very dull when you are young enough to see pirate ships in trees and princesses's castles in the shapes of the drifting clouds as if it were the most natural thing in the world.

Two years older than her, cousin William was in charge, leading the way to the stream with determined concentration. Suzy followed, the long grass scratching her legs below her shorts, the feathery dryness tickling like ants, but happy to be away from her mother's smothering attentions if only for a little while. The beginnings of the fatness that would later overshadow her teenage years had created a space for itself between her shoestring stripy T-shirt and the elastic waistband of her green shorts. The small bulge was still firm and taut and Suzy carried it indifferently as she trailed behind her cousin, her young back arched as she carefully placed one flip-flip in front of the other, small blue eyes scanning the ground for signs of snakes and spiders, hands occasionally brushing stray blonde hairs out of her face.

Billy walked with his head held high, but then Billy wasn't afraid of anything very much and certainly not things that crawled and wriggled. At Christmas he and his family had gone to Australia for a month and last night after the two children escaped from dinner he'd told Suzy about the terrible bugs and insects living on the other side of the planet that could kill you with just one bite. Apparently, he'd seen quite a few and described them and the slow and painful deaths they could cause with graphic glee.

Although Suzy suspected he was making quite a lot of it up, she'd listened with wide-eyed rapt fascination to the vivid

*descriptions of colors and teeth and scales. As she struggled
to keep her toes in sight and keep up with Billy, she was beginning to wish she hadn't listened so hard. Billy had said
that sometimes these cunning creatures, some so small that
you could barely see them, snuck into people's suitcases,
people who unawares brought them back to England. For all
we knew the English countryside could be full of black
widow spiders, lurking in the branches of an unsuspecting
acorn tree. Maybe Billy had brought some back himself.
She'd smiled with Billy when he said it but now could almost
feel thousands of tiny eyes watching her, weighing up
whether she would make good prey or not. She shivered, quietly enjoying frightening herself with the thought of rampag-
ing Australian insects hunting her in the Devon countryside.*

*Billy had slowed down and was waiting for her to catch
up, a black figure outlined by the halo of bright sunlight behind him. Suzy squinted and waved, and as she got closer
she realized they'd reached the stream. Sitting on the bank
of mud and grass, his dark curls shading his pale face, Billy
was pulling off his shoes and socks. Reaching him, Suzy
kicked away her flip-flops and they both stepped into the water together. Although the air was heavy with warmth, the
water was cold, and beneath her bare feet she could feel the
cool sharpness of the pebbles and the rocks.*

*Giggling, they paddled for a while in the comfortable si-
lence that comes so easily to children, each lost in their private worlds that could never be shared. Suzy scoured the
clear water for the glittering tadpoles that darted elusively
away from her each time she thought she'd caught a
glimpse, while Billy collected twigs and built something that
might at some time and in some age have been considered
a dam.*

*Bored of frogs that couldn't be caught by her clumsy
hands, she joined her cousin and together they worked on
the tangled mesh of wood and leaves, ignoring the cold water that crept up and splashed their clothes. Suzy was carefully weaving some fragile vines together and Billy stood*

back, fists on his hips, to examine their handiwork. His small chest was thrust out and at that time Suzy thought Billy was going to grow up to be the strongest, cleverest, and most handsome man in the world. She never once considered that Billy might not grow up at all. Sometime afterward she would wonder if the leukemia that would turn him into pale, sick Billy, who smelled bad before it finally killed him less than three years later, was already silently eating away at him that day. Softly, softly, for fear of getting caught. Was there already an agitator of adulthood hiding in the midst of that most magical day? Laughing at them from within his malfunctioning blood cells?

Well, if Billy was sick, it didn't show, not on that day at any rate. And Suzy always preferred to look back and think in that week of summer when Billy was her hero then everything was fine, he was as strong and fit as an ox.

"It needs some more wood," he concluded. Suzy nodded in agreement, although she really didn't know one way or the other. Clambering up the far bank, ignoring the mud on his knees, Billy called over his shoulder. "You stay here and finish the roof, and I'll be back in a minute. Don't wander off, okay Suze?" Suzy shook her head, eager to please. If Billy had told her to sit there until teatime she would have done it without thinking.

Blowing the thunderflies that had gathered around her head out of her face, she diligently continued lacing the strips of pliable plant life into each other with a crude basketwork-style weave, her small chubby fingers holding and threading each section with the utmost care. This was going to be the roof of Billy's dam and she wanted it to be perfect. There were four more days at their grandparents' left and she didn't want to do anything that might make Billy want to stop playing with her. He was her favorite person in the whole, wide world back in the days before going to see him would scare her and mother would have to drag her screaming to the hospital where she refused to speak to the sick, wheelchair-bound boy without very much longer to

*live. She dreamed about that sometimes. They weren't nice
dreams.*

*Securing the last vine in place, she paddled through the
water and held it over the main section, imagining what it
would look like in place. To her it wasn't a dam at all, it was
a Viking fortress and the stream was a raging river on which
the fierce warriors had chosen to live, the water filled with
unimaginable creatures that were hunted for food and fun.
Maybe she'd tell Billy about it when he got back. Maybe he'd
think it was a better idea than a dam, too.*

*Whatever it was, it was going to look wonderful, and Suzy
happily laid the roof on the side of the bank, waiting for her
cousin to come back. After a few long moments with nothing to do, she decided that what the fortress really needed
was some kind of decoration. Something that would show
the world which tribe the imaginary inhabitants were from,
some kind of symbol to represent the ferocious river people.
Something that would impress Billy.*

*Happy to have a new task, she started to walk along the
edge of the bank, her feet completely accustomed to the
coolness of the water, eyes searching for anything unusual
among the shiny rocks. She hummed to herself as she
worked, a tune of her own making, but one that she thought
a Viking princess might like.*

*The water was not proving fruitful and when she reached
the base of the enormous tree she realized that she'd wandered about one hundred yards or more from where Billy
had left her. But she could still make out the tiny
dam/fortress jutting haphazardly out of the water and so
knew well enough that she'd see Billy when he came back
too. If only she could find something interesting before then.
Her small hands rested on the rough bark as she surveyed
the territory around her. A bird darted away from the tree, its
wings rustling the leaves, causing her to glance upward.
And then she saw it and her heart leapt. That was it! That
was what she needed to finish the fortress.*

The object was hanging quite low down the tree, maybe

three or four branches up and it looked like some kind of jar made out of leaves or twigs. Squinting against the onslaught of the strong sunlight she tried to see it more clearly, but no matter how she squeezed her eyes she couldn't define it. Huffing a little she climbed up the bank, wondering if a change of angle might make it easier. It didn't. Oh, but it looked so perfect suspended there; she could just imagine it sitting on top of the roof or maybe on a stick pole beside the fortress as a warning to any who came near of the Viking tribes' might.

She looked around her for Billy, but there was no sign of him. How was she supposed to get her magnificent trophy down? If she'd been a braver girl, she knew she could probably have climbed the tree and got it that way; but although it looked quite low from where she was standing, she knew that once she'd started climbing it would be a completely different story, and she didn't want Billy to have to rescue her from the second branch up. But then neither did she want him to come back and have to collect it himself. She wanted to present it to him as a fait accompli. They hadn't had a find like this in the whole holidays and he would be so impressed, she was excited just thinking about it. No, she couldn't wait. She was going to have to get it down by herself, and if she wasn't going to climb up then she was going to have to knock it down and just hope it didn't break.

Having resolved herself to her plan, she first gathered some leaves to place on the grass approximately where she thought her treasure would land. Throwing the handfuls down, she moved quickly, racing against time, knowing that Billy would be back at any second. Hoping she had collected enough padding, she returned to the water and harvested an armful of the largest stones she could find and then scrambled back up the bank.

Trying to ignore the glare from the sun that hung enormously behind the tree, as if curiosity had forced it to come in and take a closer look at what the little girl was doing, six-year-old Suzy took aim and made a silent prayer that she wouldn't miss, and if she didn't miss then she hoped God would make sure it wasn't a bird's nest with lots of baby birds inside. She didn't think it was. She'd seen birds' nests before and they didn't look like this. Also, apart from the one that had caught her attention, she hadn't seen another feathered friend come near the tree.

Holding her breath, she launched the first rock, cursing as is skipped under the branch and rebounded from the trunk, landing uselessly a few feet away. The second time, even though the bright light was making her want to sneeze, she took more careful aim before she threw her missile. The object rocked to and fro as the smooth pebble glanced its side. Suzy let out a small yelp of glee and was too busy preparing her third attack to notice that bits of her precious prize seemed to have separated and were hovering in the air around it.

As she released the final stone she knew that the throw was perfect. She could feel the rightness tingling all the way down her arm to the tips of her fingers. Smiling, she waited for contact to be made, time going in slow motion, teasing her. At last, the stone connected and she saw the jar-thing tumbling to the ground where it landed without breaking on the bed of leaves beneath it. She'd done it! She'd done it all by herself!

Eager to have it in her grasp, she rushed forward and then paused. The prize was singing, humming just as she had been earlier, only this time there was no tune, just discordant angriness buzzing at her. She stood there watching, childish indecision making it impossible to go either forward or back, as the thing that she didn't think was quite so wonderful anymore, dissolved and rose in tiny pieces into the air, each segment hovering, waiting until the air was thick and black with them and their sound. Suzy's bottom lip began to tremble as one naked foot took a hesistant step backward, her eyes never straying from the swarm in front of her. Fear settled on her like a chill, her warm summer skin cooling, blood withdrawing to her vital organs, preparing her for fight or flight and she felt the tears trickling into her mouth, salty and frequent. "Billy," she whispered, "Billy."

And then they came.

Screaming as the hundreds of angry wasps consumed her, stabbing her exposed skin with their poisoned needles, Suzy turned and ran without aim, lashing her arms around, the pain blinding her, unable to fight the tiny insects off. Never had she felt anything like this, never had she known fear like this. With her eyes squeezed shut, her feet stumbled and she fell to the soft earth, still screaming, coated with the swarm. Where was Billy? Where was her mother? Where was anyone? She was only six years old, Is this dying, is this pain dying, is this what happened to her other grandfather that everyone whispered about? Where was her mother? Her brain raced with panic as her skin burned and she was about to pass out when suddenly there were two arms pulling her up.

Squinting through the pain she saw Billy, he too now covered in furious wasps, calling her name as he dragged her into the water, the coldness causing her infected skin to rage angrily against her. She managed to grab a breath before Billy dragged her head under the water where he held her, trying to keep both of them near the bottom.

Too overcome with panic and pain to understand what he was doing, Suzy struggled against him, fear of drowning now matching her fear of the wasps, her ears filled with the sound of racing water, but he held her firm as he pulled her along the bottom of the stream, one hand thrusting the fortress out of the way, reducing it once more to leaves and twigs. Her lungs were bursting and the edges of the world exploding with color when Billy finally let them come to the surface of the shallow waters that had saved them. They were tucked under the protective branches of a weeping willow, but the wasps were still hovering only a hundred feet or so away.

Suzy was shaking in her cousin's arms. "I feel sick, Billy. I feel really sick." Her voice was low and small. Billy nodded

*his head, his face swelling almost as much as hers from the
stinging. "I know. I know Suze. But I think we should go un-
derwater a little bit farther, just to be safe. Can you manage
that?" Looking at Billy, and suddenly realizing that he'd just
saved her life, the first time that she'd ever realized that her
life could really end one day, she tried to smile and took another breath.*

*Suzy never remembered much after that about the after-
noon. She was pretty delirious by the time they got out of the
water. The doctors said that if Billy had left her there on the
bank while he got help she probably would have died. But
he didn't. Not Billy. Covered in stings himself, he picked her
up and carried her over half a mile back to the farm. Although he was eight and she, six, there was very little difference in weight and it must have been such a very long walk
for him with the poison in his skin and the sun on his back.
But he made it. He'd saved her.*

*Suzy could feel the tears welling up inside her, tears of
rage, of guilt, of fear. Why was she thinking of Billy? Why
was her head filled with that day from so long ago?*

*Because the wasps are back, aren't they, Suzy? And this
time I've got a feeling you're not going to get away. I don't
think Billy can save you now, do you?*

*She wanted to giggle as the man, the thing, stepped
through the hole where her hall mirror used to be, her sanity
cracking, fragmenting at the edges. He was tall, very tall,
and as he approached her she could smell the pus that
leaked from the boils covering every inch of skin visible beneath his clothes. His clothes. The laugh escaped amid tears
as she looked at the faded blue jeans and old-style Liverpool
football club T-shirt. The last time she'd seen that outfit she'd
been crying too. It had been on her cousin's corpse in a cas-
ket. She thought perhaps she was screaming as the man
pulled her to her feet, but she was finding it hard to tell.*

*No, Billy's not going to save you this time, is he? And he
didn't grow up to be quite as handsome as you expected either. Not exactly Tom Cruise. She felt the Billy monster's pus*

slide onto her skin and she heard herself moan. There were slithering sounds coming from the bathroom and she knew that another creature, another thing was in there, maybe coming to join her and Billy in the lounge but she didn't want to look. She couldn't bear to see what other relatives had come to visit.

This Billy's eyes were black and angry as he pulled her closer.

"I'm sorry Billy, I'm so sorry. I'm so sorry I let you die alone," she mumbled softly through her tears.

Stepping backward from her, Billy ripped open his T-shirt, and then, in front of her horrified eyes, dug his fingers into his skin along his rib cage and tore open his own torso as if it were simply velcroed down the middle. The inside walls of his bleeding flesh were covered with razor blades angled outward and where his intestines should have been were a squirming mass of snakes and spiders.

The Billy thing smiled before speaking. His voice was so deep it made her ears hurt. "Well I hate to burst your bubble Suze, but I'm afraid sorry just ain't good enough. Not good enough for me and not good enough for you. It's time to pay, wouldn't you say?"

Out of the corner of one eye, Suzy Jenner could see a huge sluglike creature with a man's face on it laughing as it hauled itself onto her sofa for a better view. She ignored it. It wasn't relevant. Billy was right. It was time to pay. He had saved her life and she abandoned him when he was dying and afraid, and now it was time to pay.

Somewhere deep inside a small sane part of her was screaming she had only been a kid, she had been so afraid and she'd paid with guilt all her adult life and WHAT THE FUCK DID THIS HAVE TO DO WITH RACHEL BEING IN THE RADIO AND BILLY WOULD NEVER EVER EVER DO THIS TO HER but the voice was lost in the part of her that didn't care any more. This time he's come to get you, to finish the job, to make you pay for abandoning him when he needed you most, even if you were just a frightened child.

The Billy man was holding his razor-laden skin open to her, inviting her in, a slim green snake escaping from his mouth as the smile stretched farther. "Yes Suzy, I think you've got the point. Guilt is hell, wouldn't you say?" As she stepped toward him, her mind a haze of numbed broken sanity, trying to ignore the stench, the foulness of him, he laughed loudly, the sound piercing her eardrums and making them bleed, a sound that she suddenly, too late, realized had never been human. As his skin folded around her, the hundreds of razor blades slicing her naked body, cutting into her eyeballs, bleeding the life out of her, she thought for a second that she could hear Rachel screaming for her again, only this time she wasn't alone, Billy was with her, his voice young and strong as it had been on that summer's day when he'd saved her life. Maybe he was trying to do it again from the other side of the grave.

But it was too late for help. Too late for help from anyone. She knew that. The wasps were back. And this time no one could stop them. Screaming, she let the pain rip through her one last time.

CHAPTER TEN

Murray put down the book of Hans Christian Andersen's *Bedtime Stories,* and then gently pulled the duvet up, careful not to wake the just sleeping small blonde occupant. Watching his daughter's soft breathing, her body completely relaxed, he knew he could probably do with an early night himself. But as much as his body was exhausted, his mind didn't seem to switch off these days until the early hours of the morning. If it wasn't Emily running through his head then it was Elizabeth Ray. Horrific as she was, in many ways he preferred the latter. At least it was only his head she affected and not his emotions.

Leaving the room, he shut the door and headed down the stairs and into the kitchen where the first thing he did was pour himself a glass of wine. He figured he deserved it. It was over two weeks now since the grim discoveries at the Ray house and it had been like a whirlwind ever since, even though Baker and just about everybody downward seemed to think the case was closed. They'd found the body of Callum Burnett at his flat just like the letter said they would, and also the rather more decayed corpse of his mother in the attic. The coroner said she'd been dead about ten years and having seen the evidence he wasn't going to argue. The milkman identified Burnett's photograph as the man he'd seen at Elizabeth's house and he worked at the bank where the ill-fated Helen Holmes was a customer. What more evidence did any half-witted policeman need? There was the case all neatly tied up for them, no need to engage the little gray cells at all.

He took two slices of thick white bread from the bread bin, and then buttered it before reaching into the fridge and getting out the leftovers of the cooked ham the kids and Janet had had for their tea. Janet had gone to the theater with a friend from the library and much as he liked having her around, he was enjoying the prospect of having the evening to himself. He covered the meat in mustard before piling it on the bread, slicing it in rough halves then taking the sandwich and his wine over to the pine table where he sat down.

That was the problem, he thought as he took the first bite, it was all far too neatly tied up for his liking. He accepted Carter's point that sometimes policemen were allowed luck too, but his twenty years on the force told him that things were never this cut and dried, and most serial murderers just weren't that cooperative, dead or not.

Take the bodies in the cellar. Apart from two, they were all customers from Elizabeth Ray's shop, the name and address of each corpse having been written on the sole of the right foot with black marker. The coroner's office had loved that and hoped that more murderers would take up the practice. It would save a whole lot of police time. The mother of one of the victims told them that she thought her son had joined some kind of club, going out every Tuesday evening, very secretive about it, and then one day he just hadn't come home. Because he wasn't a child, the police didn't seem very concerned when she reported it. They said he'd probably just turn up.

Murray could understand her bitterness, but knew the limitations in terms of police hours and resources. Weeks could be spent searching for an adult male who'd probably just run away with his secretary.

Anyway, although the victims all came from different parts of London, it turned out that the others were all members of some Tuesday club, and they all just didn't come home one day. Elizabeth Ray must have gotten them involved in a little secret society of her own. She must have been very convincing for none of the group to become slightly suspicious as their numbers started to dwindle.

The two corpses that hadn't been labeled were a couple of hookers who had gone missing two or three months ago. They'd been killed after Elizabeth Ray was dead and were definitely Callum Burnett's; their deaths almost mimicking the torture inflicted on the others, but he just didn't have Elizabeth's imagination. The hookers probably didn't see it that way, though. A separate investigation had been set up to see whether Callum was responsible for any other missing persons. If he'd killed his mother ten years ago, then no doubt he was, but getting evidence to prove it was an almost impossible task. He didn't envy that team's job.

He swallowed a mouthful of food and then sipped his wine. This labeling of the bodies bothered him. It was too cocky. Yes, a lot of killers liked to taunt the police, but this was like a catalogue for them to find. As if Elizabeth knew she was never going to get caught. As if she knew she'd be dead by then and just didn't care.

And her death was bugging him a lot too. Traces of her blood had been found in what was left of Helen Holmes's stomach and the coroner seemed adamant that the girl had been made to drink it just before she died, maybe throughout the months of her capture. Burnett must have drained Elizabeth's body and then stored the blood until it was needed for whatever reason. And there were no marks of a struggle on the Ray woman's body, as if she'd *allowed* herself to be killed. But the one thing the coroner had found were two large but benign lumps in her right breast, so maybe she thought she had cancer and instructed Callum to kill her.

Although it made some loose kind of sense, that didn't sit right with what the profilers had made of her. Yes, without doubt she had some serious mental health issues, but she wasn't unintelligent. Quite the opposite, in fact. So why hadn't she got herself checked out by a doctor before taking such extreme measures? Serial killers seemed to regain their faith in the sanctity of life when it was their own life in question. The life they took from others so easily they seemed to cling to until the last in their own case. And why this whole routine with the blood? Nope, it just didn't make any sense. And no one was left alive to answer his questions. Not that anyone else on the force seemed to give a damn. They were all pleased that for once they'd come out of a murder enquiry smelling of roses. Promotions all around by Christmas.

After putting his empty plate in the dishwasher, he refilled his wineglass and looked at the large cardboard box under the breakfast bar. He hadn't mentioned to anyone that he'd signed the box of diaries back out of evidence this morning. Let them all rest on their laurels. The case may have been closed but at least he might get some kind of answers from Elizabeth Ray's past. There may even be some more grim murders logged in there, the resolving of which might let some unfortunate families somewhere finally lay their loved ones to rest.

Sighing, he picked the box up and tucked it clumsily under one arm, leaving a hand free to carry his wine, then went back upstairs to his study. It was seven-thirty now so he could probably get three or four hours reading in before Janet got back and then he'd probably call it a night. He flicked on the desk light and sank down into the old armchair before leaning behind him to take the packet of Marlboro from the bookshelf. This was the only room in the house where he allowed himself to smoke, which was a great way to stop his habit creeping up again, and for some reason he seemed to enjoy it more now that there was a feeling of ritual to it. He pulled one cigarette and the lighter from the carton and lit it, inhaling deeply and then took a long sip of his wine. Well, there was no point in delaying what was inevitably going to be a pretty dull task. He'd never been one for reading other people's diaries or letters and figured that most of what he'd see in Elizabeth's would be just egotistical ramblings. Still, if he didn't look, he'd never know. He pulled the first tatty notebook from the box and leaned back in the chair before opening it. The writing was like that of any child, the letters written with care but still the inexpert loops betrayed the age of the writer.

My name is Elizabeth Ray and I'm 11 years old. Things have always been strange but now they're getting horrible and I'm going to write it all down so that I know I'm not going crazy. I don't want to sit on daddy's knee any more after tea, not after what I saw . . .

The cigarette burned forgotten in the ashtray as Murray turned the pages one after the other, only stopping when each notebook was finished long enough to get the next, lost in the peculiar, fascinating, and terrifying story of Elizabeth's early life.

CHAPTER ELEVEN

Annabel Ray used to complain to anyone who would listen that there was something wrong with her daughter. It wasn't normal for a girl to be so distant, to not want to be cuddled or touched like other children did. And the problem seemed to be getting worse as she got older. Lizzy would listen to this from the corner of the small sitting room of the terraced house in one of the poorer areas of North London, chewing her bottom lip and wishing her mother would just shut up. People used to say that her mother was beautiful, but she knew different. She knew what was going on underneath. She could see things that other people couldn't, she knew that for a fact, because if everyone was like her then no one would touch anyone else, *ever*.

When she'd been very young and her parents and relatives would pick her up to cuddle and kiss her, all her head would be filled with was blackness, and maybe indistinct shapes that she could never quite make out. That had been disturbing and unpleasant, although it didn't really scare her. But recently things had become worse. A lot worse. Ever since her body had started changing, since that awful Wednesday six months ago when she'd woken up with cramps in her stomach and blood in her pants, and her mother had laughed and smiled and looked affectionately at her and told her she was a little woman now. That day had changed everything.

Her mother had driven her to school late and whispered to her teacher who too had smiled gently at her as if she had joined some special female club rather than been betrayed by her small body. All day she felt as if the world could see the bulky pad under her tatty school uniform, that rubbed against the tops of her skinny thighs and made her feel as if she was walking funny, and by the time she got home she was ready to burst into tears. And it was then that she made her terrible mistake. Walking into the kitchen, she put her schoolbag on the chair and was about to get herself a glass of milk when she heard her mother calling from the sitting room.

"Lizzy honey, come in here, I've got a surprise for you!" Unsure of what to expect, wondering whether her mother had gathered a horde of aunts to come and share in the wonderful fact that she was bleeding *down there*, she went out into the hall and then hesitantly pushed open the lounge door.

The small coffee table that was normally piled high with her mother's magazines and her father's newspapers with the names of horses ringed in pencil, had been cleared and coated with one of their best tablecloths, folded in two so that it didn't drape all over the surrounding carpet. The china left to them by her grandmother that never normally came out until Christmas covered it. There was a plate with carefully prepared sandwiches with the crusts cut off, one with slices of battenburg, her favorite cake, and one piled high with her mother's homemade chocolate biscuits. The tea pot had steam coming from the spout and beside it there were two cups and saucers with the delicate handles that she was never normally allowed to touch.

"Well, come in then."

Her mother was kneeling by the table, looking pleased and anxious all at the same time. "I thought you might be feeling a bit miserable, so I thought we could have a special tea before your dad gets home. Just us two girls."

As she edged into the room and sat in the armchair usually reserved for her father, she watched her mother carefully putting a selection of food onto a plate and felt her heart constrict with love. She really was very beautiful, with her dark hair piled high in a chignon on her head, her full lips red against the paleness of her skin, and if, beneath her startling gray eyes and delicate nose, her front teeth were slightly crooked, the imperfection seemed to enhance her attractiveness rather than spoil it. Annabel was wearing her best blue dress, one that followed her curves like an adoring puppy, stopping at her knees, allowing the world to see her slender calves. To Elizabeth she looked like the most elegant woman in the world. She must love me, she thought, for once smiling happily as she took the plate, she really must. She's done all of this just for me. Not for Daddy, just for me. It must have taken hours.

Annabel held up her cup. "Cheers!"

Giggling, Lizzy raised her own. Maybe everything was going to be better from now on. Maybe the black things in her head would go away. Maybe this was the start of a whole new beginning, a whole new *normal* life. Biting into her sandwich, she listened to her mother talking, enjoying the shape and sound of the words, rather than hearing the content of what she was saying, watching her flamboyant gestures as she mimicked this shopkeeper and that neighbor, unable to restrain her laughter. And that was when she made her mistake and the world collapsed.

Feeling a sudden rush of emotion for her mother, an urge she couldn't control, she put down her plate and

moved quickly before she lost her nerve to hug the surprised woman. After Annabel's initial shock, completely
unused to acts of spontaneous affection from her young
daughter, she wrapped her arms around her tightly and
kissed her on top of her dark hair. "I do love you, Lizzy. I really do."

Hearing her mother's words somewhere in the distance,
Lizzy braced herself against the enveloping darkness that
she knew would hit her mind as soon as she'd touched
Annabel's skin. It's not that bad, she thought as she
squeezed her eyes shut tight. It's really not that bad. I can
get through it, I can get used to it. She concentrated on the
flowery scent of familiar perfume and waited for her
mother to let go. But then something happened. Something new.

The shapes that normally lingered like shadows beneath
the total darkness in her mind began to get more distinct as
the blackness lifted. She was beginning to *see* something,
something like a blurred movie in her head. Her breath
caught in her throat, and her mother hugged her tighter,
one hand stroking her head, whispering to her, but to
Lizzie this reality of tea party and motherly love had faded
and another was taking its place. She opened her eyes
slightly but still all she coud see were images of the distorting world. And there was a smell, a bad smell. As panic
rose, her mother's arms felt like claws digging into her, and
then there was a flash of white in her head that hurt her
eyes and everything was clear.

It took a couple of moments before she realized what
she was seeing. It was her mother's bedroom upstairs, but
the bed wasn't neatly made up as it was on every occasion
she'd ever been allowed in there. This time the valance that
was normally as smooth as an ironing board across the
mattress was thrown with careless abandon onto the floor
and the sheets and blankets were crumpled, forgotten at
the footboard. Her mother's blue dress, her *favorite* blue
dress, had been tossed over the back of her dressing-table

chair. She heard her mother's moaning before the vision brought her into view. *Please stop now*, Lizzy silently wished, unable to break away from her mother's grasp, the scent of perfume now seeming sickly, *please stop now, please*. But the images continued, ignorant of her pleas, as her mother gasped and moaned in her head.

Annabel was naked on the bed, her slim body covered with a film of sweat, propping herself up on her knees and elbows as she grasped a pillow, head pressing into it, her face turned sideways, her expression one of pained concentration as the naked balding man—*not daddy, that's not daddy*—who was kneeling behind her held onto her hips and pushed himself into her, groaning. The room smelt of stale sweat as if they'd been in there for hours.

Somewhere behind the vision, Elizabeth waited for her mother to scream as the man put his thing into her. She could see it, all red and purple and ugly, pumping backward and forward, going into her at the small place where she'd started bleeding today. Adrenaline pumping, she wanted to rush in there and pull him off her mother, rescue her from this terrible man. This terrible man who was hurting her. And then she heard her mother's voice although she'd never heard her sound quite like this before.

"Oh yes," she was whispering through her moans, "Oh yes, don't stop." *Her mother was enjoying this, what this stranger was doing to her in her father's bed.* The man's hands were squeezing her mother's buttocks, kneading them, pulling them apart so he could watch himself, small eyes glazed, as he moved in and out of her. His voice was rough as he panted. "Is this what you want? Is this what you want, you little slut?" He pulled his left hand back and slapped her on one firm cheek hard enough to leave a mark. Annabel squealed and pushed back onto him. The man groaned and his breath became erratic as if the sound of his words excited him. "Is this what Harry doesn't give you? Is this what you need?" He was thrusting himself into her harder now, and she pushed herself up on her hands as her body rebounded with the force of him. Her eyes were shut tight and her face flushed. "Oh, yes fuck me, fuck me." The man slapped her again, mumbling under his breath, and this time her eyes opened with surprise, her voice rising, "Oh god, I'm coming, I'm coming, Oh yes, I'm coming . . ."

Elizabeth pulled away from her mother suddenly, and as the sitting room came back into view, she stumbled to her feet and ran to the toilet to throw up. She could hear her mother's worried voice calling her name as she followed her up the stairs, so she slammed the bathroom door, bolting it before curling up around the cool enamel and letting her stomach empty itself of sandwiches and cake. Her throat burned with bile, and tears welled up, stinging her eyes. *When was that? Was it real. Was it today? Where was Daddy, how could she do that to Daddy?* She threw up some more liquid as if by emptying her insides she could purge her mind of the lingering images that she didn't quite understand.

There was a gentle knock on the door. "Lizzy? Lizzy? Are you okay?" Her mother's voice sounded small and concerned, and Elizabeth tried to shut it out but couldn't. Leaning backward against the bath she took a deep, ragged breath and tried to collect herself as her head pounded and her stomach ached, both from the bleeding and the vomiting. The knocking came again. She couldn't stay in here forever. She couldn't hide from her mother forever, however much she might want to.

Standing up on shaky legs she went to the sink and ran the cold water, revitalizing her face, before opening the door. Annabel was standing on the other side and this time, instead of seeing beauty, all Elizabeth could see was a painted mask that swam over something dirty. Her eyes slid to the floor. "My stomach hurts. I think I need to lie down." Annabel nodded, used to the unusual behavior of her young daughter even if she didn't understand it, and smiled to try and disguise her hurt. "It's been a bit of a day for you, hasn't it? Let's get you into bed then."

She put her arm round Lizzy to lead her to the bedroom and this time the images came in a clear flash, a different man, different positions, more sordid than the first vision. Elizabeth pulled away quickly. "It's all right. I'll go by myself." She didn't want to see any more. She didn't think she could take any more.

She feigned sleep for the rest of the day, only relaxing when her parents eventually turned off the lights and went to bed, *in that bedroom,* and the next morning she kept her eyes down at breakfast, relieved when she finally shut the front door behind her to go to school, getting used to the feeling of the pad when she walked.

The cold, fresh air felt good on her cheeks and her spirits lifted slightly as she made her way through the streets, even if she did glance at men's faces that she passed to see if he was *the one.* Maybe it'll stop when the bleeding, *the period* as her mother insisted she call it, finished. Maybe then it would just go back to the blackness when she touched people, she thought as she went through the school gates. That would make sense. It started with the bleeding, it should end with the bleeding. I could live with the blackness. I could even be relatively *normal* with the blackness. She allowed herself the small hope, following the other children into the classroom.

It was in the last lesson of the day that she realized that what she'd seen when she'd touched her mother might not have really happened, might just have been a dirty secret wish in Annabel's mind.

Elizabeth was the blackboard monitor for that week and at the end of the lesson it was her job to wipe it clean of Miss Layton's scribblings. This is what she was quietly doing when the teacher dismissed the class but asked Peter Craig to remain behind. Elizabeth didn't really have any friends among her classmates but Peter was among the ones that she disliked the most. He would tease the boys and bully the girls and think he was clever doing it. Lizzy often wished hard that something terrible would happen to him,

like being knocked down by a car and not getting killed
but crippled for life, just to wipe that self-satisfied smirk off
his chubby face.

He was wearing that smug look on his face now as Miss
Layton tried to tell him off for flicking ink from his pen over
the shirts of the girls in front of him. He had even got some
on her blouse as she'd strolled up the aisle between the
desks and when she'd asked him angrily what she was supposed to do about it, he'd laughed and told her to take it off.

He was still smirking now as she handed him a note to
take back to his parents. She probably knew as well as he
did that Mr. and Mrs. Craig would do nothing to reprimand
their spoiled golden child and that was making her mad-
der. Elizabeth could see the rage simmering behind her
calm exterior as Peter swaggered out of the room. Miss Layton seemed lost in an angry reverie for a few moments until she remembered Elizabeth was there. She smiled almost
apologetically behind her glasses and touched Elizabeth
on the shoulder. "If only they were all quiet students like
you, Miss Ray, wouldn't life be easier?"

Lizzy was aware that her face was trying to smile back
but her head had filled with things her eyes couldn't be
seeing. Peter Craig's chubby body was tied naked to a chair
in the middle of the classroom and he was screaming for
mercy as Miss Layton, her ink-stained blouse glued to her
body with sweat, whipped him with a thick leather belt, the
buckle cutting into his skin with the impact, again and
again, hitting his face, his arms, his belly, his legs, no part of
him able to escape. She didn't stop until he'd stopped
screaming and all that was left of his face was a bloody
pulp.

As Miss Layton lifted her hand the classroom came back
to normal and Elizabeth saw that her teacher was looking
at her quizzically. "I said you can go home now. I'll finish
the blackboard."

Nodding and muttering some sort of thank you, Lizzy
grabbed her satchel from the desk and ran out of the room,

her mind in a whirl. Stopping at a bench in the now empty school playground, she sat down to try and get her thoughts together and calm her racing heart. What was happening to her? What were these things she was seeing? She knew that Miss Layton couldn't have beaten Peter like that, it wasn't possible, was it?

No. In the vision, which was all she could think of to call it, Miss Layton's blouse had ink on it, like Peter put there today. What she'd seen was what Miss Layton had *wanted* to do to Peter. She *wanted* to beat him to within an inch of his life. Maybe what she'd seen when her mother hugged her wasn't real either. Maybe it was just something she wanted to happen as well. Somehow she found that more disturbing. Why would her mother want something like that? And why could she see it?

As she'd calmed down, she realized that there was a cold wind blowing, making her breath hurt in her lungs, so she gathered herself together and started her trek home. Would it be like this every month? Would she always get these visions? Although she was still scared of the way she was different from everyone else, for the first time in her life she felt a shiver of excitement. How much more could she see if she really concentrated, if she looked for something rather than letting the visions control her? Would she be able to see things that people had actually done as well as wanted to do? *And would there be some good things there?* a small part of her mind asked.

Shaking herself as she saw her front door looming, she pushed these thoughts away. Just hope they go away with the bleeding, just hope they stop and let you get back to normal. That's what you really want, isn't it? She turned the handle and went inside.

But the visions didn't stop when her period finished. In fact they showed no sign of stopping at all, ever, and over the next few months, while her father was away on another oil rig contract, she learned an awful lot about her mother's friends and relatives. And none of it was good.

And some of it was real. This she discovered one Sunday afternoon when Aunt Shirley came over with her children Alice and George. Alice was pretty and clever and everyone's favorite while George was slow and stumbled his words. Annabel called him "that poor retarded boy" whenever Shirley wasn't around. Shirley was ashamed of him, she felt he let down her little family and always made him sit quietly in the corner whenever they visited. As if he wasn't there at all.

Elizabeth had swallowed her fear for the sake of experimentation that particular afternoon and hugged her aunt good-bye. Pushing the instant visions aside, after noting that Shirley wanted to do to Annabel's husband what her mother seemed to want to do to every man she met, she dug deeper, ignoring the panicky urge to shove the woman away. She had to know if she could see things that were real, that had *happened*. Her head felt as if it was going to explode as she trawled throught the dirt that lived inside people, and then she found it.

When George was a baby he'd had a fit and stopped breathing. Shirley had rushed him to the doctor's where they'd given him oxygen and revived him. Elizabeth saw that over the years that followed if Shirley had been able to turn the clock back to that day she would have. And when he had his fit, she'd pick up his pillow and cover his face with it until no amount of oxygen would bring him back. Shirley imagined this scene often full of hate and bitterness, as if just wishing it could make it happen.

Pulling back from her aunt, Elizabeth steeled herself and then whispered knowingly, "You can't turn the clock back to the day George had the fit, Aunt Shirley, however much you wish him dead."

Shirley's eyes widened and her face paled under her carefully applied makeup. Elizabeth saw the fear in her eyes for those few seconds before her aunt grabbed her arms, hissing at her. "How did you know that, you little freak? How did you know that?"

Elizabeth didn't answer, her mind filled with her aunt's fear, filled with all her fears: snakes, heights, George, and most of all old age. She could feel the scream building up inside her and then the connection was broken. Shirley had let go when Annabel came to the door with Alice and poor cousin George. Her mind was once again all her own. To Elizabeth it felt like coming up for air just seconds before drowning. She didn't see much of Shirley after that. Not until the "accident," at any rate but that didn't come until a little bit later.

As soon as the door was shut, Lizzy raced to her room, throwing herself on her bed crying, crying for George and crying because she knew if she touched George she'd see bad things there, lurking inside him, just like there was inside everyone else. Black dark secrets filled with hate, eating them up from the inside like maggots. She lay there wiping the tears from the startling gray eyes she'd inherited from her mother and wished for her father to come home. Daddy who never got cross, who always had a special smile for her, who loved her better than anyone else in the whole wide world. And she would sit on his knee without being asked because the blackness had gone and there could be nothing bad hiding in such a good man. Nothing.

During the next few months Elizabeth managed to get a grip on the developments in her head by avoiding touching people whenever and wherever possible. She tried to hug her mother occasionally, not because she particularly wanted to, but because she'd overheard her telling a friend that she was thinking of taking her daughter to "one of those child specialists." Elizabeth knew just what they'd make of her, and anyway she was getting her visions under control. She'd realized that if she did her best to stay calm then she could keep one eye on what was *really* going on around her while the images attacked her.

The hardest part was trying to smile and pretend to like people when she knew that the real them inside was like a bloated, putrid worm, full of filth and dirty secrets. She despised them, all of them. Lying in bed at night, she would dream of her father's return, and have fantasies where she told him about her gift and he would smile and tell her he had the same and they would have to be allies against this terrible world, like the X-Men or some other all-American superheroes. And then she wouldn't feel all alone and slightly mad surrounded by strangers and life would be bearable again.

She sometimes thought back to the days of blackness when she touched people, and how it would unsettle her and she would wish it would go away so she could be normal, so her family would know she loved them rather than wanting to recoil every time they reached for her, and wonder what she would have done if she'd known what was to come. On her darker days, she thought she'd probably have killed herself.

Still, she had to admit it wasn't all bad. She'd learned there were a few advantages to be found in her new ability. School had got a lot better for one. She still didn't have any friends, not that she wanted them anymore, but now her classmates looked at her with fear and weird respect, and that was a good feeling in itself. It was reflecting in her appearance too and that had the added bonus of making her mother happy. She was developing earlier than the other girls, and until recently she'd never bothered much with her hair, and her feeling of not fitting in had made her unconsciously develop a slight stoop, as if by making herself shorter she could disappear.

But now she walked tall, enjoying the way they all looked at her, her dark hair shining from brushing, hanging loose around her shoulders, her gaze direct and fearless, a small smile playing on her clear-glossed lips. There was a moment of dawning realization that she'd inherited her mother's striking looks. The boys at school noticed too but that didn't bother her one way or another. What she did like was that she could hear them whispering around her, calling her a witch, and she liked that, it made her feel special. Special and powerful. And it was all down to Peter Craig.

Like all bullies, Peter Craig could always spot an easy target and Elizabeth Ray had been one of those, no doubt about it. He could see her shrinking away every time he came near, and he'd always taken advantage of it to impress his little crowd. They in turn were generally relieved that it wasn't their day to have their lunches stolen or their hair pulled, although there were one or two, like Michelle Miller, who enjoyed it just for the sake of cruelty. Elizabeth had seen Peter approaching, his chubbiness no hindrance to his swagger, his brown hair a tangled mess on top of his head. He was laughing. "Hey! Hey, no friends!"

She stayed where she was, sitting on the top gray stone step that led into the school from the playground, and watched him from under her fringe, one hand clenched firmly on the small tupperware box that held her sandwiches. There was a group of about ten classmates behind him, gleefully waiting for the show to begin. She knew she'd find no allies there, but she wasn't worried. No, today she wasn't worried at all. What Peter Craig didn't realize was that the world had changed quite considerably over the past month or so and Elizabeth Ray was no longer going to take shit from little boys like him. Not with the power she had.

He was standing in front of her now, hands thrust into his trouser pockets, piggy eyes gleaming. "I'm talking to you, little miss no friends!" He paused to make sure that his audience behind him were paying attention. "So, what am I having for lunch today? What have you got in that box for me?"

Elizabeth raised her eyes and there was no fear in them, only mocking sarcasm. "Some might say, Peter Craig, that you could do with skipping a lunch or two, so why don't you start by leaving mine alone?" Her voice was soft and friendly, but Peter looked as if he'd been slapped hard in the face.

"What did you say?" His voice was low and menacing. No one spoke to him like that. No one. Especially not skinny gawky girls who never said boo to a goose. No way, José. The atmosphere in the small gathering was electric, the rest of the kids having expected Elizabeth to hand over her lunch without so much of a whimper.

Elizabeth smiled sweetly. "I was calling you fat, Peter. You're a fat and stupid bully, and you're not having my lunch."

The fresh wind did nothing to cool down the red that was burning on Peter's face in that moment of stunned silence. He couldn't believe what he was hearing. What the hell was going on here? There was a feminine titter behind him and he knew without turning around that it was Michelle Miller. There was another stifled giggle, and with each sound the domination of the scene was slipping away from him. Something had to be done. He had to do something.

Lunging forward, he threw his full weight onto Elizabeth, knocking her backward, pulling her hair harshly with one hand and grabbing her lunch with the other. Aware from experience that teachers had a habit of appearing at moments like this, he elbowed her in the mouth and then quickly stood up as if nothing had happened, holding her sandwiches and laughing to the admiring group.

Elizabeth sat up, the blood tasting like metal in her mouth where she'd cut the inside of her lip on her teeth. Her face hurt and she was pretty sure it was going to be sore for days, but she didn't care. Sometimes pain was worth it. She looked at the little group in front of her. Peter had turned his back, thinking the confrontation was over and was examining the contents of her lunch, offering Michelle one of her ham sandwiches, keeping the chocolate biscuit for himself. Elizabeth's voice—loud, clear, and unafraid—made him turn around again pretty quickly.

"You're not such a tough boy at night, are you Peter? Not when mummy comes to turn out the light that your father won't let you leave on. You're not so tough when you're crying and peeing in your bedsheets 'cos you're so afraid of the dark, are you?" Her voice rang around the playground and Peter was staring at her, speechless. How could she know about that?

Elizabeth smiled at the others. "I guess you lot don't know that your fat friend Peter has a plastic sheet on his bed so he doesn't stain the mattress when he wets himself after lights-out. That's what he does best in the dark. Pisses his pants. Isn't that right Peter? Put you in the dark, or in a small space, and you sob like a baby and pee yourself empty. Your daddy's not so proud of his little boy then, is he?" Bringing her attention back to Peter she raised a teasing eyebrow at him. God this felt good, seeing fear and surprise sitting on that fat face for a change. Peter's heart was pounding with guilty fear and his eyes flickered around resting on the bemused faces that surrounded him. Licking his lips he managed a half-smile. "She's making it up. It's not true, she's just making it up."

The eyes of the others had narrowed suspiciously, and Michelle Miller's were dancing with glee. She didn't know how the skinny weird girl would know something like that, but looking at Peter's nervous face, she'd be willing to bet her pocket money that it was true. Elizabeth saw the cruel curiosity that swam across Michelle's meanly pretty features and spoke directly to her. "Well, maybe I'm making it up, and maybe I'm not. There's only one way you're going to find out." Michelle studied the girl whom she'd barely glanced at during three years of sharing the same class. She purred like a cat. "And how's that?"

This time the two girls shared their only ever smile together as Elizabeth spoke. "Lock him in the sports cupboard in the cloakroom. I'm sure there's room in there to squeeze him in. It'll be a tight fit though."

Michelle burst into laughter and jumped up and down with excitement, the blonde hair that all the other girls so admired coming loose from her neat ponytail. "Yes, yes, that's it. We'll put him in the cupboard! Come on, we'll put him in the cupboard!"

Dropping Elizabeth's forgotten lunch, Peter was looking around wildly as the children drew in around him, grabbing his arms and dragging him toward the cloakroom door. Elizabeth could hear his cries of denial above the catcalls, even after the door had swung shut behind them, leaving her still sitting on the steps. She didn't need to go with them. She knew exactly what was going to happen. Picking the tupperware box up from the tarmac, she slowly ate what was left of her lunch, ignoring the pain in her mouth as she chewed. Chewed and waited.

Ten minutes later, she heard the door opening behind her. She didn't turn around but waited until Michelle came and sat by her on the step. Her face was flushed and vibrant as she reached for Elizabeth's hand.

"How did you know?" She asked with breathless wonder and excitement. "Do you know his mum or something?" She paused for a moment and then giggled, staring ahead of her, reliving the recent memory. "You could see his pee coming out under the door, it was so disgusting. You should have seen it. He was begging me to let him out. Crying and everything. God, that was so funny." She laughed again, before turning to Elizabeth, who until this point hadn't said a word. "Do you want to sit next to me next lesson? I'm sure Pamela wouldn't mind." She looked as if Lizzy should feel that this was a privilege, as if she was being invited to join an exclusive club.

Lizzy shook her head and smiled. "No, I don't want to sit next to you. I don't want anything to do with you or your friends. I just want to be left alone."

Michelle's pretty little face suddenly looked very ugly as she prepared a response to the snub, but Lizzy interrupted her. "Oh, and just so you know, it's not just Peter I know things about. It's everyone. So if I was you, I'd make sure that no one bothered me in the future."

Michelle sneered as she stood up. "You don't know anything about me. I barely knew you existed until today, you little weirdo."

Elizabeth closed the lid on the tupperware. "Well, then. Maybe I'll tell all your admiring friends how you let your brother and cousin put their hands in your knickers in exchange for their pocket money once a month and that's how you've got all those pretty hair clips and things that they're so jealous of."

Michelle turned pale in an instant. "It's not true." She whispered.

"Oh, but it is true," Elizabeth said conversationally, as she stood up and brushed herself off. "And more than that, you like it."

Michelle ran into the building without another word. Nobody saw Peter Craig for the rest of that afternoon and when he came back the next day he was a different boy, cowed and ashamed. It didn't take long for Michelle Miller to take his place in the power ladder, but she never bothered Elizabeth. It was shortly after that day that she first heard them calling her a witch. But never to her face and she liked that. There was something reverential about it. Yes, she had concluded, there were definitely advantages to being so different. Maybe she was a witch. And maybe they should be afraid after all.

As it turned out, developments at home were soon to put her school problems into perspective. Elizabeth's father was coming home. And that was going to change everything. That would be the start of the worst period of her young life. The period of fear.

Elizabeth had spent all day getting ready. She was wearing the pink dress her mother had bought her for the school disco last week, the one she refused to go to, and she'd carefully brushed her hair until it shone and put on her lip gloss. She wanted to look her best. Daddy was coming home. Her stomach had danced with butterflies from the minute her eyes opened in the morning and by three o'clock her insides felt so tight they hurt. She paced the house, the cotton of the dress swinging just above her knees, one eye firmly fixed on the front door.

Annabel watched her from behind her glass of wine. "Don't get too excited. He'll go straight to the pub to catch up with his friends and we'll be lucky if we see him by the time you should be going to bed." Elizabeth suspected that her mother didn't give two hoots whether her husband came home or not, other than the fact that the lamb she'd been roasting all day would be ruined.

Well, as far as Lizzy was concerned her mother didn't deserve her father, who was always away working, no doubt to keep his wife in nice clothes and expensive perfume, and if Daddy didn't come home till late it was probably because he knew his wife didn't want him there. Well, she intended to show him that at least one person in the house was pleased to see him, even if she had to stay up all night.

She had a long wait. Annabel had been right. Harry had gone straight to the pub and he didn't come home until closing time. Elizabeth was sitting on the stairs, determined to stay awake, having caused such a fuss when her mother tried to send her to bed that Annabel had agreed tiredly that she could stay up. She'd barely been able to eat her roast, but had forced it down so as not give her mother any reason to send her to her room. She felt like she'd been brushing her hair all day and by nine o'clock didn't have the energy left to do it anymore, so instead sat very still in the hallway so that it wouldn't get messed up. When was he going to get here? The combination of tiredness and excitement was starting to take its toll and she was close to tears by the time she heard the sound she'd been waiting for all day. The metallic clicking of the key in the lock.

The door swung open and there he was, her beloved father, swaying slightly somewhere between the street and the house. Standing up, her tiredness for the moment dissipated by the surge of excitement that rushed through her, she intended to run to him and hug him hard, but for some reason she couldn't get her feet to move. What if she saw something, what if she saw something bad? Her fear overcame her excitement and she was stuck there, frozen in her indecision. Why was she suddenly so afraid of touching him? He shut the door behind him and leaned on it, looking at his daughter, all dressed up in her new pink outfit, unaware of her internal turmoil. His smile was a little off-kilter and his eyes were glazed from too much to drink. But to Lizzie he still looked like the most handsome man in the world.

"Well my little princess, it looks like you've been growing up a bit while I've been away. And a very pretty young lady you're turning into, too. I think you're going to grow up even better looking than your mother." His words were slightly slurred but Lizzy could hear the affection in them. She smiled and blushed and was about to say how much she'd missed him, how much she'd wished for him to come home, when the sitting-room door was pulled open and her mother stepped out into the hallway between them. She regarded her husband coolly. "Hello Harry. No need to ask where the hell you've been, I suppose." She looked over at Elizabeth. "Off you go to bed, now. You've seen him and I'm sure he'll still be here tomorrow."

She started to protest, at that moment hating her mother almost as much as she loved her father, but her father raised a weary hand and gave her a conspiratorial look from under his bushy eyebrows. "Your mother's right. You've got school tomorrow and you don't want to be tired for your lessons. Not a clever little thing like you. We'll have a nice tea tomorrow when you come home." He leaned forward to whisper loudly past his wife. "Your mother seems to want a quiet word with me. I think she's jealous that I said you were prettier than she is."

Annabel ignored the giggle that was shared between the other two and tapped Elizabeth lightly on the arm. "Bed. Now." Lizzy favored her mother with a glare and smiled almost shyly at her dad. "G'night Daddy. See you tomorrow."

Harry smiled at her as she went up the stairs. " 'Night princess. Sweet dreams."

Lying under her blankets in the small, neatly ordered

bedroom that was her escape from the world, her private sanctuary, she listened to the hum of the heated conversation that was taking place in the living room. She couldn't make out the words but she knew they were arguing. It probably didn't help that her mother had been drinking. She could understand why Harry would want to go and have a few pints after spending all those months on a rig, after all, that's what men did, but her mother had no excuse. And why did she always want to give her husband a hard time? Feeling the atmosphere that had descended on the house, her stomach had knotted itself with an anxiety she couldn't explain. Why couldn't they all just be normal?

Somewhere deep inside the caves and caverns of her memory she knew that it hadn't always been like this. Before they'd moved to London, before her father started working on the rigs, she had vague recollections of them being happy. Of them being happy together. What had happened to change that? Was it her? And when exactly had her mother turned into a heartless slut, with all her dirty thoughts of other men? Poor Daddy. Poor, poor Daddy.

She tasted the blood in her mouth before she realized she'd been chewing the inside of her cheek, the soft flesh ragged against her tongue. Rolling onto her side, she pulled the covers under her chin and watched the moon through the gap in the curtains until, with an uncertain heart, she drifted off into a dreamless sleep.

Her mother looked tired the next morning at breakfast and her father wasn't up, so Lizzy ate her cereal and toast in silence and then headed off to school. She hadn't forgiven her mother for spoiling the previous night and didn't bother to say good-bye to her, just slamming the door in lieu of words. Her feelings toward her mother confused her. Even despite the disgusting things she knew went on inside her head, she still sometimes found herself needing and loving Annabel. And that felt like a betrayal of her father, her poor innocent father who probably had no idea how depraved his wife was.

The day seemed interminably long, each lesson dragging by, the teacher's words a meaningless drone as Elizabeth watched the seconds and minutes tick by on the old clock hanging on the wall. Three times she was scolded for not paying attention, but try as she might she couldn't concentrate on her rudimentary algebra or anything else for that matter, even her favorite subject, history and all the glory of the Roman Empire, holding no interest. All she wanted to do was get home and have tea with her father. To make up for her moment of doubt yesterday when she couldn't move to hug him.

By the time the final bell went, Elizabeth had already filled her schoolbag and was out of her chair before the class had even been dismissed. Finally free of the dreary walls, she ran out into the fresh air, and would have run all the way home except that she didn't want to turn up windswept and disheveled. Instead, she walked briskly, brushing her hair with the comb she'd tucked into her blazer pocket, and finally adding a touch of gloss to her lips. She might not have been wearing her new outfit, but she didn't want her dad to think it was only the dress that had made her look pretty. She wanted him to be proud of her.

CHAPTER TWELVE

Tea was a marvelous affair, her father breaking through her shyness with jokes and laughter, laughter that she couldn't help but join in with. Her mother had made toad in the hole with creamy mashed potato and a homemade apple pie and custard for pudding, which they ate on the pullout dining table that normally stayed folded against the wall in the sitting room. Even though both her parents were drinking, her mother wine, and her father strong dark beer, it seemed that they had resolved whatever they'd been arguing about the night before or at least were trying to make an effort for their daughter's sake. Whatever the reason, the atmosphere between them had lifted and her mother even gave her dad a small kiss on the cheek when she took his empty dinner plate out into the kitchen. Elizabeth's heart was exploding with happiness. She could almost believe they were a normal family and she was a normal girl.

When they'd finished eating, her father got himself another large bottle of beer and moved to his comfortable armchair in the corner next to the gas fire while Elizabeth took the rest of the plates into the kitchen and helped her mother fold the table away. He smiled at his daughter while they worked. "Why don't you come and sit on your old dad's knee and tell me what you've been getting up to at school."

Annabel's head whipped around from putting the place mats in the sideboard drawer. Her voice was anxious. "You know she doesn't like that kind of thing Harry."

There was something Lizzy didn't understand in her mother's eyes, and wondered if maybe she was jealous of the love between father and daughter. Come to think of it, as much as Annabel would try and cuddle and touch Lizzy whenever she could, she hadn't encouraged her to be affectionate toward her father since she was a little girl. It must have been jealousy, what else was there? Having found another thing to dislike in her mother, she was more resolved than ever to show her dad how much she loved him.

Handing her mother the napkin rings to put away, she pushed her hair out of her face and smiled. "I don't mind." Annabel looked at her with disbelief as Harry slapped his thigh. "That's my girl. Come on then." Taking a deep breath, Lizzy walked over to her father's chair, the familiar smell of beer and stale cigarette smoke reassuring her as she sat down on his lap. He gave her a wet kiss on her cheek and put his arm around her, pulling her in. "There you go. That's not so bad, is it?"

Somewhere in the periphery of her vision Elizabeth could see her mother watching her, looking perplexed and she tried to keep her face normal, tried to focus on the reality around her as the world gave way. Her head was filled with the heat of her father's body, heat that was rising from his legs, from his chest, escaping from his mind, burning her skin. Harry was excited, he was so excited to have her on his knee, and she was so pretty, so young and pretty, and she loved him so much, his little girl. She tried to block out the images that filled her head, images of herself, her and Daddy naked, oh god, she was going to be sick, she had to stop this right now.

Having only sat with him for a few seconds, she stood up, careful to make sure her legs weren't swaying underneath her, and tried to smile. "I'm going to do the washing-up and then I've got to do my homework." Her voice sounded hollow in her head. Without waiting for a reply she moved quickly into the kitchen and opened a window to let the fresh air in, taking several long breaths, her mind in a whirl. It couldn't be true, it couldn't, she must have misunderstood something, maybe it was her, maybe she was going insane, her daddy couldn't have thoughts like that, he just couldn't, could he?

Mechanically, her hands ran the hot water and started to methodically wash the plates. Watching them moving, they seemed alien to her. How could they work, how could they function while the world was unraveling around her? But she knew why, because as soon as this task, this *normal task* was done, she could escape from this madness up to her room. God, she just wanted to lie down. To lie down and think. Her hands were burning in the undiluted water but she didn't mind. She needed the distraction the pain offered.

By the time she got upstairs the skin on the back of her hands and arms was red raw, but she barely noticed as she turned the light off and crawled into her bed seeking some kind of sanctuary therein. The tranquility of the darkness calmed her mind as she sought solace in the view of the moon. She couldn't be sure of what she'd seen, she couldn't be sure of it at all. She'd panicked, that much was for certain, and maybe she'd been so afraid of seeing something bad, that she'd created the images herself, blurring her father's thoughts with those of her mother's. It was possible surely? Still, as much as she'd half-convinced herself that she'd misunderstood what she'd seen, it didn't stop her shutting her eyes tightly and pretending to be asleep when he rapped on her door much later that evening. "Princess," he was whispering loudly through the small gap where the door had warped and wouldn't shut properly. "Princess, are you awake?" There was a pause in which she didn't answer, and then the door slowly opened and from behind her eyelids she could see the light from the hallway flooding into the room. He pushed the door closed behind him and she heard his footsteps coming across the carpet and then the weight of him as he sat on the edge of her bed. "Princess?"

She kept her eyes shut, although she was sure they were flickering like the actors' did in films when they were supposed to be dead, and tried to keep her breath sleepy and relaxed even though her heart was hammering in her chest. She could smell the beer strongly now and realized her father was drunk again. Where was the hero of her imagination that she believed in so strongly only yesterday?

He sat in silence and she could feel him watching her and then he lifted one hand and started to stroke her hair and whisper her name. Lying there frozen, she gripped the underneath of the pillow so tightly that the next day her knuckles ached. Her head was full of his drunken, jumbled thoughts as his thick, work-calloused hand rested on her head, gently touching her face.

She's so pretty, so pretty, who'd have thought she'd have grown up to be so beautiful, and so innocent and she loves me, she adores me, and I love her, and she wants me to think she's pretty, teasing me with that little pink dress and lip gloss making her little mouth all shiny and looking so tempting, and would it really be so wrong, isn't it natural for a father to love his daughter, who best to love her, and it wouldn't be like before, like that other time, because she's my daughter and I love her and I could never really hurt her, I'd stop myself before I went too far, I learned my lesson then, I never meant to kill her, I didn't realize, but it would be different with Elizabeth because she's older and it would be our secret and she'll like it, I'm sure she will and she's so pretty . . .

All the time she could feel his thoughts her head was full of images and smells, of her father, her father looking younger, and another little girl maybe five or six, a girl she doesn't know crying, crying and her father trying to soothe her while all the time doing *things* to her, like her mother thinks of, and they're in a wood, and Elizabeth can smell the autumn leaves that cover the ground with the little girl's abandoned clothes and shoes for company, and then the little girl isn't crying anymore and is just lying there, very, very still but her eyes are open and not moving at all like they do in the films and her father is stumbling, running away, through the trees, back to his car, to their old car that they had before they moved, she knows that because she's seen it in photographs and he's thinking of her like that little girl and then—

Suddenly the hand was gone. Her bedroom door had opened again and her mother was standing in the doorway. Her voice was sharp. "What are you doing?" She felt the pressure lift from the bed as her father stood up. "I was just kissing her good night. I can kiss my own daughter good night, can't I?" *No, No, No you can't,* she wanted to scream at him, this monster in her father's body with her father's voice. There was a pause and if she could have opened her eyes she would have seen her mother regarding her husband thoughtfully. "I don't want her disturbed if she's asleep. She doesn't sleep very well. If she wakes up it'll take her hours to get off again." Her mother stayed in the doorway for a few moments after her father had left the room and then pulled the door shut.

At last, left alone in the dark, Elizabeth opened her eyes, shiny with tears. Her father was a monster. The world was full of monsters, everybody hiding a darker face beneath the masks they wore to fool each other. She imagined that beneath their thin pale skins her parents were rippling creatures, slimy and scaly with red eyes and sharp teeth. That's what they were on the inside, that's what everyone was on the inside and she was the only one who knew. She cried and cried that night, silently into her pillow, cried from fear of her father, and the knowledge that she was all alone in the world, crying out her humanity, crying herself free of her need for anyone at all.

After that night Elizabeth would brush her hair and put her lip gloss on during her walk to school and make sure that it was rubbed off by the time she had to go home. She'd hoped and prayed that her father would be off on a new contract before long but every day passed with no news of him leaving and she would feel him watching her as she moved around the house and she started locking the bathroom door whenever she was in there and trying to jam shut her warped bedroom door.

In an effort to stay out of the house longer, she joined the after school library club which meant she didn't leave school until half-past five and after she'd quickly done her homework, she would pore over large books on the supernatural and paranormal, trying in vain to find instances of other people like her. After she'd exhausted the school's supply of those, she would go to the adult section of the town's main library and study books on witches and the occult.

She quickly became fascinated with the dark subject matter and slowly realized the power her unwanted gift gave her over other people. Maybe she could become a witch after all. But no matter how powerful she felt sitting in the quiet hush of the library, protected by the high walls of knowledge surrounding her, the moment always came when it was time to go home and dread would knot itself up in her stomach and she just became a frightened little girl again. A frightened little girl who didn't want to go home and face the monsters.

Two stagnant months passed with the atmosphere in the house becoming more oppressive as if they lived constantly in those last few silent moments before a thunderstorm, invisible electricity crackling all around them. Beneath the calm surface of smiles at teatime, Elizabeth could feel her father circling her like a shark in the undercurrent just waiting for the right moment to strike and she would watch his big hands as he ate and his dark eyes as he laughed and in her head she'd see that girl in the forest, those large handprints visible in blue on her tiny neck and she would remind herself of what he *was*, of what lived inside that deceptive flesh.

Her mother would laugh and tell people that Lizzy was turning into a proper teenager, spending all her time in her bedroom, never coming out unless ordered to. When she heard this Elizabeth would wonder if anyone else noticed that her mother's eyes seemed to be shining a little too brightly as they darted around the room beneath the mascara and eyeshadow and her smile was just a little too wide on the voluptuous twitching mouth.

Lizzy had noticed a lot about her parents recently. And she was starting to wonder if Annabel had suspicions of her own about the monster that lived inside Daddy Dearest. She thought maybe sometimes in the night Annabel would find her mind turning to that little girl from long ago who just went missing one summer's afternoon. That pretty little girl who lived in the next street and who'd always smiled happily through the front window when she'd gone by with her mother. And then she'd think of Harry. Harry who never wanted to touch her, who seemed revolted by her, even though she was about as pretty as a woman could get. Harry who had come home that day with muddy clothes and no explanation. No explanation and out of the blue plans for moving to London. She would watch him sleeping with worried eyes. Guilty, worried eyes, and she would absently chew the inside of her cheek just the way her daughter did.

Her mother was drinking more now that her father was home, and every evening it would seem that she would reach for the wine and he for his beer or whiskey, as if they had to cling to the only thing they had left in common, and while her father would pretend to watch the small black-and-white television, his mind elsewhere, in the woods or upstairs, her mother would phone Shirley and speak too loudly into the receiver. It seemed to Elizabeth that when people were drunk the monsters came closer to the surface and she could almost see them without having to touch anyone at all. At times like that she would shut her door as far as it would go and pretend to listen to music on the transistor radio her father had bought her, *a present for his special princess,* while keeping one wary eye on the small gap that refused her total privacy.

The days rolled by, her twelfth birthday here and gone and then summer finally broke through the fierce grip that winter had clung on with all through the spring. As the heat increased and the days grew longer the long school holidays arrived and although Elizabeth still spent a lot of time at the library researching the occult, or in the park looking for the plants and herbs she'd read about, it was unavoidable that she'd have to spend more time at home. There was still no sign of a new contract for Harry, and every day his drinking increased and she would feel the intensity of his gaze on her legs below her shorts and the small breasts that were developing beneath her T-shirt. She knew what he was thinking and it filled her with dread. Soon it would be too late, her flower would have bloomed and he would have missed his moment. She didn't have to touch him to know this. She could see it in his eyes. It seemed she understood her father so well now.

Sometimes she would see him standing in the garden, his beer in one hand, the small paunch that was starting to form beneath his shirt hanging slightly over his trousers, gazing glassy-eyed at nothing, sucking in the smells of the summer, and she wondered if he was remembering the way the woods smelled that day, how the little girl had struggled against him on the leaves and warm, damp earth. She wondered if the little girl was still there, now part of that sweet-smelling mulch. She wondered at what point in that last journey did the child see the monster inside the man. And then her father's misty gaze full of twisted, deformed love would fall upon her and she'd stop thinking about the other girl and start to worry about herself instead. But life couldn't go on like that forever, one day the storm was going to break, and she didn't know how she was going to stop it. Or even if she could stop it all.

On Saturdays her father normally started drinking early, often leaving for the pub as soon as opening time came and then carrying on all afternoon and evening when he got back. The Saturday of the second of August, however, was different. Elizabeth had got up early and after a quick breakfast gone to the library, her refuge from the world, where she intended to stay until they closed. By eleven-thirty though, the stifling heat in the building was starting to make her feel a little sick, and so after a careful selection process she picked the four most-interesting from the pile of books on the table, and borrowed them with her newly acquired adult library card. Looking at the subject matter, the old lady behind the counter raised an eyebrow but Elizabeth glared back defiantly and the woman had no choice but to give her the four large hardbacks. She was twelve years old and she had an adult card and these books hadn't come from the eighteen section.

Holding the heavy books in both arms her orginal intention had been to go to the park and lie on the grass in the sun, but when she reached it and saw the hordes of boys and young men playing football and mothers trying to control their overexcited toddlers demanding ice cream, she knew she had no choice but to go home to her bedroom if she wanted to read the precious literature in peace. Sighing, she turned around and headed back into town, already feeling the sweat sticking to her T-shirt from the exertion of carrying all that paper, her arms starting to ache in anticipation of the twenty-minute walk ahead of her.

The summer had turned out to be scorching, as they invariably did after a long and bitter winter, and that Saturday was the start of its hottest spell. By the time she finally turned into her street, her hair glued to her face and her eyes aching from squinting, she could think of no place better to be than in the cool air of her room. Her father would probably be out and her mother appeared thankfully to have given up on trying to spend time with her for the moment, so she should be able to relax in peace.

When she came through the front door she didn't at first realize that her father was home. She could hear her mother in the kitchen and was about to head straight up the stairs when she heard the feminine voice calling her name. Putting the books down in the hallway she opened the door. Annabel smiled at her from behind a plate of thickly cut ham sandwiches and the soft floral scent of her perfume wafted toward Elizabeth in the warm air. "You're just in time. I've made these for your father but there's plenty to go around." She pulled a small side plate out of the cupboard above her head and started to put some food on it.

Elizabeth watched her mother cautiously. She was wearing a blue two-piece suit with some elegantly heeled matching shoes and her best handbag was sitting on the small kitchen table. When she spoke Lizzy tried to sound nonchalant. "I didn't think Dad would be home yet." Her sweat had dried into a cool layer on her skin and she got out a glass to make some squash. She didn't miss the way her mother's eyes darted up at her, though. When Annabel spoke it was through a large smile so big it couldn't be natural. "Oh your father hasn't been to the pub today. I'm going over to Shirley's to play bridge this evening and I need him to babysit you, so he's not drinking."

Elizabeth felt the familiar dread knot in her stomach and her eyes strayed to the wall as if she could see through it to the sitting room where her father was no doubt reclining in front of the television. Her voice was low. "I'm not a baby, I don't need a babysitter. Why doesn't he go with you?" She realized the desperation must have been plain in her eyes, because her mother's gaze slid away from meeting hers as she handed over the now unwanted sandwich. "You're too

young to stay in the house by yourself. And anyway, it's a
ladies-only night."

Annabel sighed and rubbed her face, careful not to
smudge her makeup. "I won't be home late, and your father's promised not to drink so he'll probably just watch
telly all night. It'll be fine." Her smile was stretched so thinly
over her face Elizabeth half expected the skin to start split-
ting. *No it's not going to be all right,* she wanted to scream.
It's not going to be all right at all! But looking at her
mother's earnest face and the guilty fear hiding somewhere
at the back of those beautiful eyes, she knew that her
mother had convinced herself that everything was going to
be fine because Harry had promised not to drink and what
was she worrying about anyway because Harry would
never do anything like that and no matter what she thought
in the middle of the night she was sure he had nothing to
do with that other girl going missing and *everything was going to be just fine.*

She felt her heart growing cold inside her. There was
nothing she could do. Her mother was going to leave her
with the monster just because she wanted to play cards. As
she silently left the room carrying the tray with her lunch
on it, she idly wondered if it really was a ladies night or
whether there were going to be other men there and that
was why Annabel was so eager to feed her to her father.
Without glancing into the lounge, she balanced the books
on the tray and went up to her bedroom that suddenly
wasn't half as appealing as the overcrowded heat of the
public park.

She didn't go downstairs for the rest of the day, hiding in
the room that felt more like a cage and trying to distract
herself in her books. Maybe everything would be okay.
Maybe if her father didn't drink she'd be safe. Maybe if he
was sober he could retain whatever control he had over
himself. So many maybes and they all sounded hollow to
her as her heart beat the seconds and minutes away until
darkness.

Her mother came in at about five to say good-bye and promised to be home by about eleven. Her manner seemed overly chirpy and she didn't come all the way in but hovered in the doorway as if eager to get away. Lizzy waved her off, uncaring. Whatever trace of love she had left for her mother was gone. Oh yes, she understood that Annabel didn't really think that anything was going to happen. After all, Harry wouldn't be *that stupid*, surely, but she knew that somewhere deep inside her mother there was a tiny nagging doubt, and this whole venture out was to test him. She was going to test her husband at her daughter's expense. And that was something Lizzy couldn't forgive. Her ability to deceive herself made her as bad as Harry. They deserved each other, these beasts that lived in human skin.

She heard the front door shutting, and waited, pulse hard in her ears for the sound of shoes on the stairs. They came. Her fingers gripped the hard cover of the open book as she sat up on the bed and as her father's face appeared around the door her breath caught in her throat. He smiled his cheeky grin at her.

"Since your mother's out I thought we might as well have some fish and chips for tea, so I'll pop down the road and get them." He winked at her. "Don't tell her that I left you on your own for ten minutes or there'll be hell to pay. I think she forgets you're growing up now."

Lizzy was listening to the words, but not really hearing them, her body rushing with relief. She wanted to giggle. *Fish and chips, that's all he wants, fish and chips.* Her face was blushing with the adrenaline that until a few moments ago had been pumping through her veins, and she felt her cheeks stretch into a cautious smile. Her father looked at her, puzzled. "Come on then. You get the plates in the oven, and when I get back we'll eat on trays in front of the telly."

Getting up, she expected him to wait in the doorway so that she'd have to squeeze past him, one of his newest tricks, but he turned around and headed back down the stairs to grab his coat and wallet without giving her a second glance. Watching the door swinging shut, she allowed herself a moment of hope. Maybe things were going to be all right. For today, anyway. Maybe her father wasn't that stupid after all. She headed to the kitchen to warm the plates.

The fish supper was hot and crisp and covered with salt and vinegar, just the way she liked it. She sat on the small settee, perching on the edge, expecting her father to come and sit next to her just that little bit too close, but instead he took his normal place in the armchair, and chatted about school and other mundane matters while he ate. She kept her conversation to a minimum while she slowly chewed, and watching her father's still handsome face smiling and talking, she could almost believe that the monster was gone. But of course she knew that it wasn't. There was, after all, nowhere for it to go. It was still in there, dark and dangerous, licking its insatiable lips while it waited. The best she could hope for was that it was sleeping, scaly lids lowered, allowing her a brief respite from fear.

When they'd both finished she took their trays and washed up the small amount of crockery and threw the greasy newspaper into the bin. When she went back into the sitting room, her father was watching football.

"I'm going to go upstairs and read in bed. I'm a bit tired today." She watched for his response carefully. He didn't look up at her, watching the players chase the ball over the muddy pitch on the small square screen, and his voice was disinterested, as if he hadn't really heard what she said. "Okay princess, I'll see you in the morning. Don't fall asleep with your light on."

She quietly pulled the door closed behind her and ran up the stairs and into the bathroom half expecting him to come running up behind her. Locking the door, she quickly brushed her teeth and went to the toilet before washing her hands and face. Crossing the hallway to get to her bedroom she saw the door downstairs was still shut, the dull sound from the TV escaping from behind it. Cursing her door as she pushed it as closed as possible, she changed into her nightie and then jumped into bed with her book, her body still on red alert, ready to get up and run if needs be. Still no sounds came from downstairs. After ten minutes or so, she slowly started to relax. Maybe things were going to be okay, after all.

She read her book half-heartedly for an hour and then felt tiredness wash over her. It had been a long afternoon fraught with anxiety, and now that the panic was over, she realized she was desperately tired. Turning the light off, she lay down on her pillow, not intending to sleep, just to shut her eyes for a while to ease the drowsiness that was seeping through her bones, but within minutes of the darkness covering her she'd drifted away, lost in the night. She didn't hear the sound of the first bottle of beer being opened downstairs. Or the several that followed.

CHAPTER THIRTEEN

Something was very wrong, Very very wrong. There were bad things in her head, the little girl was back and he was so excited and this time was going to be so much better because he loved her, his little girl, his princess, and she struggled to wake up, struggled to move, why couldn't she move and why was her face damp with breath and what was that smell, was it beer, oh no, no, no—

She woke up trying to scream, and felt the salty taste of her father's skin as he pressed one hand over her mouth, his face close to hers as her eyes widened in horror, his rapid breath making her forehead wet. His expression was distracted, as if she wasn't really there and he was whispering to her, telling her he loved her, *just like the little girl*, and she couldn't breathe his weight crushing her lungs and she felt his other hot hand pushing up her nightie, feeling her, pulling her panties away, the elastic cutting into her as they tore, and she couldn't move and the monster hadn't been sleeping at all and she couldn't keep her legs closed as his big thighs opened them as easily as if they were feathers and as the blinding white pain ripped into her, she tried to scream biting down on his fingers, feeling the warm sticky liquid that she knew was blood escaping from her *down there* and oh God it hurt, he was killing her and she was so afraid and, as he pushed himself into her moaning, his head became her head, his thoughts thrusting into her mind.

Somewhere in the physical, Elizabeth could feel her father moving on top of her and it hurt so bad and she couldn't move, couldn't shake him off and she couldn't bear the smell of him, the feel of him, and his thoughts, his lust was filling her head, disjointed images, sensations, her pain, his pleasure mixed, and he really loved her and she knew she would go mad if she didn't escape somehow, somewhere, and the only place left for her was farther into his head, and so she gritted her teeth and dove deeper inside him, pushing her pain and his conscious away, hiding from them, going past the rotting corpse in the wood that she couldn't help and, oh God, was he killing her? His hand was so tight on her mouth, and then she smashed past that in a glorious burst of color, and although dimly aware of herself, of her struggle and her fear, it all seemed like far away as she examined the landscape of her father's mind, of his unconscious, and then she found something. Something that made her realize that she would survive her ordeal after all, whatever it took. She felt her body distantly stop its struggling as she smiled at the monster, causing him to pause for a second and then she felt his happiness as he continued to rip her apart.

She rode on the ripples of his unconscious, like an invisible observer, and she realized the cause of her father's drinking. And it had nothing to do with the girl in the woods. Her father had a secret from her mother. So many secrets tickling inside him. He had been offered another contract on the rigs, he was supposed to have left last month, but he couldn't bring himself to take it, he couldn't bear to go back, not yet, he couldn't bring himself to go, he was so afraid that sometimes, on his own, he couldn't breathe. What if there was another fire, another explosion, and her head exploded

with the smell of petrol and it was as if she and not her fa-
ther was standing on the metal gantry with the cold wind of
the North Sea hurting her cheeks, standing in disbelief as
men ran about her with water hoses and fire extinguishers,
trying to contain the fire and someone was screaming at her
to shut down Number One and she felt her arms but not her
arms turning the heavy wheel as her eyes watched with hor-
ror as the burning man burst through the metal doorway,
screaming, screaming not like a man at all, how could a
man scream that high, and someone threw him to the floor
with a blanket over him to put out the flames but she could
smell the burning flesh and see the sticky mess where his
clothes had melted on him, fused with him, replacing the
skin and hair that was no longer there and she thought she
was going to be sick, and the man, the thing on the ground
was shaking, shaking and dying, dying in agony, his flesh
popping and blistering, and then she saw his metal badge
and it was Joe Miller, and how could that be Joe, they'd just
had breakfast together, and he shouldn't have even been
down in Number One, and how could that mewling dying
thing be Joe, and please make him just die now, please and,
oh God, that could have been me, please don't let that hap-
pen to me. And Joe was looking desperately at her, right at
her, as if she could somehow do something to stop this, to
undo this terrible mistake, and she couldn't take her eyes
away, couldn't drag them away until she knew that Joe was
gone. And this wasn't like Ellie, Ellie had been an accident
and this wasn't like Ellie at all because this could HAPPEN
TO HER.

She pulled back, leaving the scene behind, returning the
memories to her father as she felt the weight lifting from her
chest, and she rose upward, past the dead girl, Ellie, her name
was Ellie, and back to her father's conscious and her own.
The pain came back, throbbing and raw, although her father
had lifted himself off her, and she could feel bruises forming
on the inside of her thighs.

Opening her eyes, she saw her father sitting on the side

of her bed, smiling sheepishly at her, the damp sweat on his face glowing in the darkness. "It only hurts the first time. It didn't hurt that very much did it?" She wondered why he was whispering, and biting back her tears, unable to trust her voice, shook her head. His eyes, his monster eyes, shone approvingly.

"Well, let's make it our little secret, shall we?" He stood up, looking down at her lovingly and a little awkward. "Your mother'll be home soon, so why don't you go and have a wash before she gets back. I left a clean towel in the bathroom. When you've finished, just put it in your bottom drawer and I'll sneak it in with another wash tomorrow." She nodded as he ambled to the door. "Good night princess."

She waited for the sound of the sitting room door shutting until she tried to move. The pain made her wince and she chewed her bottom lip to stop herself crying out as she walked, legs apart to the bathroom. Locking the door behind her, she picked up the pink towel that was folded neatly over the side of the bath, *Oh no, the monster hadn't been sleeping at all, he'd been planning very, very carefully, right down to the last detail, put it in your bottom drawer, keep our dirty secret safe,* and with shaking hands turned the taps on to fill the sink with lukewarm water. She could feel her fish and chips rising up in lumps of congealed fat urging her to throw up, but she resisted, fighting it back. For all she knew her father was on the other side of the door and she didn't want to do anything that would arouse his suspicions. She had to be very, very careful.

Although the water was almost cold, still it burned her as she gently sponged the blood and the other sticky white stuff that was coming out of her away with a flannel. All the way up to her stomach the hot pain seared her, and she could feel her abdomen swelling to protect the bruising. She didn't realize she was crying until she'd carefully put away the towel and crawled back into the bed that was filled with his smell, where trying to ignore the pain and the shame, she planned what she had to do, and unaware to her, the monster inside herself quietly began to grow.

The next morning she woke to the smell of frying bacon and eggs coming from downstairs, the cloying scent hanging heavy in the hot air, and she numbly dragged herself out of bed and pulled on a loose summer dress. She didn't bother with any knickers, knowing that the cotton would make her bruises hurt more than they already did, but pulled her torn ones out from under the covers and put them in the bottom drawer with the pink towel.

Trying to walk as normally as possible she went to the bathroom and brushed her teeth and then her hair. She couldn't believe how much her whole body ached from the strain of trying to fight her father off. She gazed at her pale face in the mirror. How could she look so normal? How could she look *just fine*? How could she look as if nothing had happened? She smiled at her reflection, which smiled back prettily. Why was she so surprised? She knew better than anyone how deceptive flesh could be. She pulled her thick dark hair into a tight ponytail. She had things to do today and she didn't want it getting in the way. She didn't notice that her gray eyes were cold and the lines of her mouth had grown harder. Neither did her parents when she sat down, smiled, and quietly ate her breakfast.

That Sunday was the hottest day of the year, would turn out to be the hottest on record for several years to come, and Elizabeth waited patiently for her parents to take the newspapers and go and sit in the garden relaxing and dozing in the afternoon sunshine. Her mother had her glass of wine and her father, who kept giving her secret smiles, had a beer, and Lizzy knew that very soon they wouldn't care if she was in the house or not.

From the coolness of the kitchen she watched them for about forty minutes, her eyes alert, protected from sight by the glare of the sun on the smeared windows, until she saw her father's head loll to one side and her mother's hand slip forgotten from the magazine she was supposed to be reading. The monsters were sleeping. She moved quickly, re-

moving four empty whiskey bottles from the collection under the sink, making sure that their lids still screwed on
tight. Taking a tupperware cup and lid from next to her
lunch box she made herself up some cool orange squash,
although she doubted it would be cold by the time she got
to drink it, and then picked up the empty bottles. Putting
these and the squash in her empty schoolbag, she added a
sharp knife from the drawer and went through to the
lounge and checked the drinks cabinet. There were still
three full bottles of whiskey there, and a bottle of brandy.
That should be enough. She hoped it would be enough.

Her heart was pounding and she felt slightly sick and
tearful, but every time she moved she felt the painful reminder that the mark of the beast was upon her, and he
was going to be back. Her resolve hardened with her heart,
and she slipped out of the front door and around to the
side of the house. The long hose her father used to wash
the car that was parked on the pavement lay curled up like
a dozing python on the concrete. Blowing a loose strand of
hair out her eyes she quickly took out the knife and cut a
long length from it, leaving the end looking jagged and un-
even. Shoving it and the knife back in the bag, she glanced
around her to make sure no one strolling down the pavement had been curious enough to watch and then stood
up and headed purposefully toward the school.

By the time she got there her white shoulders were burning in the sun that beat down from the cloudless sky, and
sweat was stinging her between her legs, but as she slipped
through the side gate and ran behind the row of trees that
lined the fence toward the staff car park, she smiled. Perfect.

As she'd expected there were three or four cars parked in
the secluded spot, one was probably the caretaker's and
the others belonged to teachers or administration staff who
had work to do in the long holidays. One was tucked neatly
in the shade in the far corner and she headed toward it,
keeping as much out of sight of the large building as possible. Although she was being cautious, she didn't really ex-

pect to be seen by anyone. Most of the rooms that looked
out this way were classrooms and she doubted any staff
would be in there. The main thing she had to worry about
was the owner of the car returning too quickly and so she
knew she had to work fast.

Putting her bag down beside the car, she pulled out the
hose and the three whiskey bottles, and said a silent prayer
to a god she didn't have any faith in that this was going to
work. She'd only seen it done once when a neighbor ran
out of petrol, and that had been two years ago. Removing
the lids from the bottles, she then unscrewed the petrol cap
on the side of the blue car, and the heady fumes wafted up
to her. Well, that solved one problem that she hadn't considered until then. At least there was plenty of fuel in the
tank. She fed the hose in through the hole and then placed
her mouth over the other end and sucked hard, trying to ignore the dirty rubber taste. Nothing happened, and with
her heart racing she sucked until she thought her lungs
were about to explode, and as the world started to go dark
red, finally her mouth was filled with thick, foul-tasting oil.
Gagging and spitting, she held the hose over the lip of the
empty bottle and watched at the dark, shiny liquid slowly
oozed into the glass, some escaping over the side, and she
was careful not to let any of it drip onto her dress.

Halfway filled it slowed down to a drip, and squeezing
her eyes shut and thinking of the previous night with all it's
horrors, she sucked again, pulling the reluctant petrol back
up the tube. Forty minutes later the three bottles were just
about full and she screwed the lids on tight and thrust
them and the hose back into her bag. Her head was spinning and she felt nauseous, her mouth aching, and she was
sure she was going to pass out, but she knew she had to get
out of the school before she could relax. Replacing the
petrol cap, she then gathered some leaves from under the
overhanging tree and scattered them over the small pool of
oil on the ground until it didn't look so obvious, and then

ran back behind the trees and out of the school gate.

She waited until she was in the quiet crescent two streets away before she sat down, and hung her head between her knees, trying to spit away the taste. Once her vision had stopped swimming, she pulled her orange drink from the bag that now stank of petrol, and swilled her mouth out with half of it and then drank the rest. Although feeling slightly better, she still felt sick and would have been happy to just sit there for the rest of the afternoon, enjoying the fresh air on her aching body, but she knew she had to get back before her parents decided to come back into the house. She'd been gone an hour, and she was running out of time. There was no way if they met her on the way in that they wouldn't notice the pungent smell that surrounded her. Hauling herself onto her reluctant feet, she headed home, throwing the piece of hose into a bin as she passed it.

Opening the front door she held her breath, not knowing if her mother or father would be standing on the other side, but as she stepped into the delicious coolness of the hallway, she was greeted by only the welcoming silence, and she quickly ran up the stairs to hide the bag at the bottom of her wardrobe underneath some old toys. Once that was done she went into the bathroom from where she could see her parents still dozing, unsuspecting on the lawn, and scrubbed her teeth until there was barely a trace of the horrible taste. She then pulled off her dress and washed herself with her mother's perfumed soap.

Finally clean, she got dressed and went back out into the corridor and over to her parents' bedroom at the far end. The key that was never used was sitting forgotten in the lock and she took it, enjoying the feel of the powerful metal in her hand, and tucked it into her pillowcase for later. She then slipped downstairs to replace the knife, before allowing herself a sigh of relief. She was halfway there with no hitches.

Looking at the clock, she saw it was now four o'clock,

and probably time to wake her parents. She needed them
to drink a lot more before bedtime, but first she made herself a fresh, cool drink and calmed herself down for ten
minutes, until she felt the flush of activity fade from her
face. Then she opened a bottle of wine and a beer, to
which she added a small splash of whiskey from her father's open bottle in the sitting room, and placing them on
a tray with her own glass, headed out the back door and
into the garden.

That last afternoon, as she sat smiling in the sunshine,
watching her parents drinking themselves closer to their
deaths, she noticed from her detached position that the atmosphere between them seemed to have lifted. They were
drinking together, instead of at each other, and although
she could feel her father's hot gaze on her, it seemed that
her mother didn't notice it. Or didn't want to notice. As far
as Annabel was concerned, everything was *just fine*. Well,
Elizabeth thought to herself, soon everything is going to be
just fine. Just about as fine as it can get.

She noticed that her mother was getting drunk quicker
than her father, and she wondered what would happen if
she went to bed and passed out early with her dreams and
desires of other men to keep her warm. How many minutes
would it be before Harry came to visit his little princess?
Well, tonight she would bear whatever she had to and she
steeled herself for all eventualities. After all, she thought, as
the monster inside her flexed it's rapidly developing limbs,
vengeance will be mine.

As it turned out she didn't have to worry about her father's unwanted advances as he soon caught up with
Annabel, and as she lay, wide-awake in her bed, she heard
them go to theirs together at ten. The summer days were
long, dusk having only just fallen by that time, and she
knew she was going to have to wait at least two or three
hours before she moved. But that was fine. What were a few
more hours? As the day had progressed and her plan had
taken shape, she knew that she wouldn't lose her nerve,

and as the minutes ticked by, she felt herself growing calmer, cooler, an inner peace settling on her.

Finally, retribution time came, and pulling back the covers she got out of bed and took the key from her pillowcase and then opened her sash window that looked down onto the garden, feeling the still warm breeze on her face. Creeping across the hallway in her bare feet she could hear snoring coming from the other side of her parents' door and she slid the key back into its resting place and silently turned it. She didn't know she was smiling cruelly, her old nervous smile having left her for good, disappearing into the night. She dropped the key on the carpet and went to her cupboard to get her bag, quietly taking out the bottles of petrol. This time the smell seemed pleasant as she carefully held the fuel at a distance from herself and poured a generous amount on the landing and then a trail down the stairs, as she felt her way backward, staining the tattered thick pile carpet that had once been her mother's pride and joy.

Concentrating hard, she made sure the bottom few steps were soaked, one ear listening for any change in the noises upstairs that might indicate someone waking up. She didn't think the smell alone would wake them, not with that amount of alcohol subduing them. Once the siphoned bottles were empty, she went into the lounge and took the brandy and whiskey, pouring them over the curtains and the settee, and most of all, her father's armchair.

Keeping the last half bottle of spirit in her hand she then went to the kitchen and took the large box of matches from the top of the cooker and clung onto them tightly. Looking at the clock on the wall for the last time, she saw it was ten past one. She couldn't imagine anyone else in the street being up at this time. It would have to be at least a few minutes before anyone realized what was going on, and then it would probably take the fire brigade five or ten more to get here. That should be plenty of time.

Going back into the hall she then used the last of the

liquor to run a thin line from the stairs and the sitting room to the pantry by the back door, which she unlocked, ready for her escape. Taking one long match from the box, she paused for a moment and took a deep breath, before running it firmly down the abrasive side. Her nostrils burned with the smell of sulphur, and the strong yellow flame illuminated the shadows in the familiar room. It was time to say good-bye. Carefully she stepped back and then lowered the flame to the liquid path on the floor. It burst into blue flame, running away from her into the house. She watched fascinated as the fire grew, retracing her steps in glowing color, licking everything it touched, devouring the hallway, turning it into a pillar of gold. Within a few moments she could feel the power of its heat, and it took all her strength to turn around and step through the back door into the dark of the night.

The grass felt soft beneath her feet and she moved a safe distance away from the house before throwing herself to the ground, covering her thin nightie in dirt, and ruffling her hair. Looking up at her open window, feeling a tinge of sorrow thinking of the books that would soon burn there, she knew it was unlikely that she could have jumped from that height without breaking any bones, but the bruises left on her arms and chest from her father would go some way to cover her. Anyway, she doubted anyone would suspect her of anything. She just had a lucky fall. Children's bones were resilient.

The outside of the house was not yet showing any sign of being devoured from within although Lizzy could see the red glow through the kitchen window. She wondered how far it had traveled up the stairs and whether her parents were starting to stir, the smell of smoke ringing alarm bells in their survival mechanisms.

Sitting on the grass, absently playing with her hair, she watched the light spread, until the kitchen window blew out with the heat, letting the roaring beast inside take control of the house. She didn't think Daddy would be snoring now.

Unsure of how much time had passed, she heard a shout and noises of people running into the street, someone screaming dial 9-9-9, and shaking herself out of her reverie, she got to her feet and ran down the side of the house to join them, cutting the soles of her bare feet on the shards of glass that now covered the lawn.

A woman in a dressing gown grabbed her and wrapped a blanket around her shoulders, the thick wool mercifully saving Elizabeth from seeing into her mind. That was something she really didn't need right now. The woman was looking at her concerned. "Are you okay honey? Are you burnt anywhere?"

Lizzy shook her head, and hoped she looked panicked. She spoke breathlessly as she wriggled in the woman's grasp. "My mum and dad are still in there. I jumped out of the window but my mum and dad are still in there. You've got to help them please, you've got to help them, I couldn't get to them, the fire was everywhere, you've got to get them out of there!"

She watched as the woman looked up with dismay at the house that was ablaze, and then in the distance she heard the siren as the fire brigade arrived. She read what she needed to know in that stranger's gaze. Surely no one could get out of there alive. The woman pulled her back onto the other side of the pavement to safety as the fire truck pulled up, men in uniform jumping down before the wheels had even come to a standstill, and it was then that something happened at the front of the house.

At first Lizzy thought it was just the front door giving in to the immense pressure beating at it from the other side, but as it burst open, a figure wrapped completely in fire staggered out into the street, leaving a trail of light behind it, dripping parcels of flame, and as she watched, the glare of the burning body reflected in the shine of her wide eyes, she knew it was her father. For the first time since she'd lit the match she felt a moment of true panic. He'd got out somehow, how she didn't know, maybe he had another key or in his fear he'd found the strength to break down the bedroom door, *or maybe the monster is stronger than you, Elizabeth,* but however he did it, he was out. Twisting free from the woman she ran to where he had fallen, the firemen quickly putting out the flames, and when she saw the black, bald husk that remained, she knew he would never survive.

Two strong arms held her back shouting something about an ambulance, and she screamed back, "That's my father, that's my father!" as she struggled with them. She felt the strong muscles relent and she broke away, kneeling beside the shaking remains of her monster-father.

His terrified eyes met hers and she held his gaze in silence for a few moments before smiling behind the curtain of her hair so only he could see, and whispering, "Is it as bad as you thought, Daddy? Is it just like Joe Miller?" Enjoying the shock that filled his dying gaze, she took his crisped club of a hand, ignoring the heat that burned her own. "This time it's worse isn't it? Because this time it's you and you're really dying and no one can stop it. This is for me and Ellie, Daddy. Me and Ellie. I hope you rot in hell."

Letting go of the concentration required to speak, she rode on the waves of his mind, feeling every second of his terror, his terror of dying, his terror of her, *how could she know, how could she know and how could she have done this and, oh God, I don't want to die, please God don't let me die, I'll wake up soon, please let me wake up soon* and the sensations felt sweet running through her blood, oh so sweet, as she filled with the last of his adrenaline, and she'd never felt so in control of her power, never realized quite what she could *feel* with it, how she enjoyed his desperate futile attempts to hold onto life, how she could taste his death in her mouth and never had she felt quite so alive, and she had done this, she alone, she'd cowed the monster, destroyed it, and slowly, slowly she felt him ebb away, getting weaker and weaker, until she herself could barely draw a breath, and then suddenly the connection was broken. She was alone.

Looking down, her mind and body rushing, as the monster inside her roared into life, she saw that she was still holding his mockery of a hand, but she felt nothing of his mind. It was gone, blank. He was dead. Her father was dead. For a moment she was filled with anger, like an addict, wanting, needing to feel more of his terror, his dying mental agonies, but looking around her, at all these people, all these fragile people with monsters inside them, she realized that there would be other times. There was always the potential for other times. Harry had done just what she needed him to. He'd died a conscious and painful death. She couldn't really ask any more.

The men pulled her away and covered him with a blanket, giving him the dignity in death that he hadn't deserved in life, and although people tried to take her into their homes, to get her away from the terrible scene, she insisted on waiting until her mother's body was brought out from the smoking ruin of their house. She discovered later that Annabel had never woken up, Harry hadn't even tried to rescue her, and although her body was as burnt as his, she'd died from smoke inhalation before the flames had reached her. In some ways that made Elizabeth glad. Yes, she'd wanted her mother dead, but she hadn't wanted her to suffer, not in the way that Harry did, and Harry's death had given her all she needed. Given her all she thought she'd needed and shown her so much more, so much more.

She spent the rest of the night in a speechless daze that people took for shock, which in some ways it was. Shock at the realization of what her power could give her. She had nothing to fear from people, it was they who should fear her, she could read their insides, manipulate them and feed off their emotions. God, it had been good feeling her father's last frantic minutes before death. Killing him by the method that terrified him most, orchestrating his demise. She felt like a newborn god, the nerves in her tongue and fingertips still tingling with sheer delight, and looking at the people that scurried around her like ants, their heads filled with nasty guilty secrets, she began to realize what possibilities her life afforded her. There seemed to be nothing that wasn't in her grasp. Sucking in the delicious fresh air, she wished this glorious night would be endless.

By morning, she was just an exhausted child again, the feeling of power that fueled her having dissipated as the darkness slowly turned to light, but she remembered it, how could she forget, and knew that it was in her capability to feel it again. She had changed that night, and there would be no turning back. She didn't think she could even if she wanted to.

After that fateful fire Elizabeth went to live with Aunt Shirley and her relatively invisible Uncle Roger. She could tell that Shirley had taken her in under duress and it was obvious that she'd told the children to stay out of their cousin's way and that was all fine with Lizzy. The only time she really shared with them was mealtimes, the rest she would spend locked away in the tiny box room with a door that shut properly, reading her books, ignoring the sounds of family chatter and the unwanted advances of friendship from poor hapless Georgie, who was as isolated as she, but who unlike her didn't relish his loneliness.

Sometimes she'd see her aunt watching her from the corner of eyes that had never been as beautiful as her dead mother's, and she knew there was fear and wariness lurking in them. Shirley had never forgotten what Lizzy had said about her wanting George dead, had never understood how the brat could possibly have known, and she would find herself wondering if her niece, who was becoming a cool and mysterious beauty, knew anything about starting fires. Lizzy would catch her gaze as these thoughts ran through Shirley's mind and smile sweetly. Something in that smile would send a shiver up the older woman's spine. She didn't want the strange girl in her house. She didn't want her there at all. Under her makeup Shirley's face was starting to look pinched and tired.

To Elizabeth, the strangest thing that happened after the fire was that her periods stopped. At first she didn't notice she was late with so many other changes going on around her, but as the weeks turned into months, she realized she hadn't had the usual monthly cramps since two weeks before she burnt her old life away. At first she worried that her special abilities would vanish with them, but after testing them out on her new family, she found they were stronger and more controlled than ever. She couldn't understand why the bleeding would have gone away as quickly as it came, her mother had given her the impression that the unwelcome periods were here to stay. Although she was slightly relieved, there was something about the continued lack of blood appearing in her underwear that unsettled her.

She didn't mention it to Shirley who was still annoyed at having to buy her two new school skirts because she'd put on a bit of weight, even though she had taken control of Elizabeth's inheritance and there was more than enough money to cover what she was costing. In fact, it seemed to Lizzy that since her money had come through, the insurance she'd heard her Aunt and Uncle whispering about, Shirley and Alice were spending a lot more time shopping than they had before. It didn't surprise her. Her aunt's greed always filled her head when she touched her. No, she didn't like her mother's younger sister and as much as she wanted an answer to her biological riddle there seemed to be no one she could ask. So she decided to just wait. Wait and see what happened.

What happened was that one Monday morning, about four months after her arrival, she woke up feeling decidedly unwell, and after being quietly sick in the bathroom, went downstairs to join the others at breakfast. She'd been feeling a bit off color for days, but this time she couldn't hide it. Her face was pale and her hands shook as she pushed her cereal around in her bowl, feeling the eyes of the others watching her. She managed to force a couple of mouthfuls down before she knew she was going to be sick again. Standing up, she felt the world swim away from her and before she could bring herself to move, collapsed in a faint.

She came to, her head confused and filled with other people's thoughts as George and her uncle pulled her to her feet. "I'm okay, I'm okay," she mumbled, trying to push them away and balance on her own unsteady legs, the kitchen coming back into view. Her uncle was shaking his head. "No, you're obviously not all right. I think Shirley better get you down to the doctor's. No school for you today."

As she swallowed the cereal that was still threatening to return, she could almost feel her aunt's internal groan and wished that she'd managed to stay upright. It was probably just a stomach bug that would go away by itself, there was no need for all this fuss, but looking at the for once determined expression on her uncle's face, she resigned herself to spending the day with Shirley and let out an internal groan of her own.

After examining her, the doctor asked lots of questions that she tried to answer for herself before Shirley butted in. It was when the nurse brought in the results of her urine sample that he asked quizzically if she'd started her periods. Shirley was trying to say she was too young for that, when Lizzy, bored and tired and just wanting to get out of there, interrupted her loudly, telling the doctor that yes she had started them last year but hadn't had one for four months or so and was that why she had been feeling so unwell. She stared at his blushing face and wished he would just answer her so she could go home and get on with her books. The middle-aged doctor looked down at his files and then awkwardly looked at Shirley. "I'm afraid your niece is pregnant, Mrs. Raynes. Over four months pregnant." Shirley looked at the doctor in disbelief for a long moment and Elizabeth felt the hard sting of her hand, her rings digging into the flesh below her eye, before she realized that her aunt had even moved. Dazed, *I'm pregnant, I'm having a baby, I'm having the monster's baby,* Elizabeth looked up into the twisted, angry face. "You little slut! How could you? How could you do this to me? Couldn't you just keep your legs shut!"

She felt the spit on her face and wanted to giggle. *No, I couldn't Auntie Shirley, I really couldn't because he was so much bigger than me and I thought he was going to kill me, I really really did. You see, that father of mine that you wanted in your bed liked them a little younger than you. Quite a lot younger in fact. Do you get it yet, you stupid bitch? Do you get it? Alice was probably more his style than you would ever be. Maybe you should have asked him to babysit and watched him in action.* As her head raced she could see Shirley's impatient mouth moving, questioning, and eventually as the thunder that filled her ears subsided, she could make out the words. They were asking about the father. What filthy little schoolboy had done this? What was his name. Where did he live?

The doctor was trying to calm the situation down, apparently there was no use crying over spilt milk, and Shirley snarled that a little more than milk had been spilt here and all the time Elizabeth was thinking about the father, *Our father who art in heaven,* or perhaps in hell where he belonged, and inside she felt herself breaking all over again, only this time the monster was working from the inside out and maybe she would be better off if she just went mad after all, and she thought she could hear him laughing, and then she slapped herself hard around the face, much harder than her aunt had done, and she tasted the metallic flavor of blood as it filled her mouth.

The room was silent as the doctor and Shirley stared at her as if she had truly gone insane and she smiled back at them. She wouldn't let him win. She would never let him win. The baby wouldn't be inside her forever. She could take this. She was stronger than all of them. And she was special. She could do special things. She had to remember that. Her voice was strong as she looked directly into the stern gaze of the doctor who was, after all, only a man.

"I'm afraid I don't have a clue who the father is. There were far too many to hazard a guess. I wouldn't want to blame one boy when it could just as easily be another. That just wouldn't be fair would it?" She shrugged and raised an eyebrow at him and for a blissful moment she thought her aunt was going to faint.

That night Elizabeth opened her bedroom door and listened carefully to the heated conversation that was taking place downstairs. She'd been banished to her room as soon as they'd got back from the doctor's and no one had brought her anything to eat or drink since then but she didn't care. She knew that Shirley had been busy drinking, drowning her sorrows and cursing her dead sister, until her husband came home from work early to find out what was distressing her so much, and she'd heard Alice and George being sent to their rooms over an hour ago, much earlier than there normal bedtimes. Her internal situation was obviously too shameful for them to know about.

Sitting there by the small opening in the door, Elizabeth could just make out her relatives' words and the phone call that followed, the sentences broken up with Shirley's tears. When she crept back to bed, she felt a small buzz of excitement in the pit of her filling belly. So they were going to send her away. They were going to send her to faceless strangers Doug and Peggy Wright, her mum's best friend from school who couldn't have children. Shirley was going to send her there, to their home in the far reaches of South London and when *this unfortunate business* was over, they would adopt the baby and Elizabeth could come back here and nobody would be any the wiser. Everyone would get what they want. Doug and Peggy get a baby and Shirley can keep her head held high.

So they were packing her and her father's secret away.

Good. She was glad. She was glad she was going and she was glad they were giving the baby, *not her baby it was nothing to do with her,* away. And when it was over she had no intention of coming back here or seeing any of them again. Somehow she didn't think they'd miss her too much.

CHAPTER FOURTEEN

The mobile phone sitting uncomfortably on the worn leather surface of the old desk had let out three loud rings before Murray realized it was calling him. Putting the notebook down he glanced at his watch as he reached to pick it up. Jesus, it was nearly midnight. Had he really been reading for that long? Looking at the scattered books that covered the floor, he figured he must have been. Janet would be home by now but he'd been so absorbed he hadn't even heard her come in. Trying to shake Elizabeth's weird and desperate story off he took a quick look at the caller ID and then pressed the answer button.

"What's given you the urge to call at this time of night, Sergeant? Are you missing me?"

When Carter answered, his voice sounded distant and slightly crackly. He was probably in his car using the hands-free. "You should be so lucky. I hope you're dressed, our presence is requested pronto in Notting Hill. There's a body there they want us to take a look at."

Murray frowned, his mind now firmly on the present. "That's a little bit out of our area, isn't it?" Although the various divisions that made up the London police force worked quite closely together, they normally kept their investigations in-house where they could, only calling in the expertise of other officers if the crimes were linked. So what had goosed the boys from Marylebone Central?

Carter sounded tired. "Yeah, that's what I thought, but the DI on this one thought we might want to take a look while the crime scene was intact. Maybe it'll be nothing. In fact, it'll probably be nothing, but there's only one way to find out."

Murray reached for a scrap of paper and a pen. Notting Hill was midway between their houses, so it would be pointless getting Carter to pick him up. It would waste too much time. The first few hours after a murder had been discovered were the most important and Murray never trusted other officers to take the care with the scene that he would. Who knew what evidence was being disturbed? "Give me the address and I'll meet you there in about half an hour." Jotting down the flat number and street name, he nodded. "Yep, I know that street. Nice area." Just like Hampstead, he thought to himself, thinking of the frightened little girl who grew up to live in that house, and feeling his body tingling and waking up the way it did with every new case.

Picking up the tattered old books that were all that were left of Elizabeth Ray's life, he put them back in the box, the ones he'd read to the left and the remaining ones to the right, and then slid the cardboard container into the footwell of the desk before turning out the lamp and closing the door behind him. He'd finish them later when he had the time.

Despite the fact that the woman had obviously suffered from some kind of delusional disorder from an early age, he'd still been moved by her story, compelled to read more even though he was unsure how much was fiction and how much was fact. Still, he reflected, as he gently opened Janet's door to check she was home, given the way her life had ended, he wouldn't be at all surprised if she had murdered her parents in their beds. And thinking of her story of abuse he could forgive the little girl she had been; not that much older than Sam, terrified and alone. He couldn't forgive the adult, but there was some kind of justice in the child's actions.

Seeing Janet's blonde hair decorating the pillow just above the duvet, Murray quietly pulled the door closed and went downstairs to the kitchen where he scribbled her a quick note on the blackboard on the wall, finding a space between the reassuringly ordinary reminders for the children's dentist and doctor appointments. He'd probably be home before they all got up, but if so then he wanted to be left to sleep for a couple hours. If sleep was going to be a possibility. He knew from experience that it was probably just wishful thinking. Running back upstairs to grab his jacket, he caught a glimpse of himself in the hallway mirror. The lines in his face were getting more ingrained and his brown eyes seemed darker, duller. You're looking tired, Jim, he told himself, except it wasn't his voice that spoke in his head, it was Emily's. Maybe you're not ready for all this yet. He squashed her gentle tones that felt like splinters of glass trapped inside him, and headed for the front door. Maybe he wasn't ready, but then who was ever ready for what life had to throw at them?

Although the weathermen were constantly telling the world that spring was just around the corner, it was bitterly cold by the time James Murray and John Carter stepped onto the street outside Suzy Jenner's smart and trendy Notting Hill converted house. It was two o'clock in the early hours of Monday morning and the streets were quiet; all the residents sleeping soundly, preparing for another week of London madness, blissfully unaware of the horror that had taken place on their doorstep. All, that is, except the couple living below the victim who had called in the police after listening to Suzy's blaring radio for almost twenty-four hours. They probably wouldn't sleep for a few nights at least, knowing that the polite and unassuming woman upstairs had come to a sticky end while they were out enjoying themselves, and feeling guilty relief that they had been, the niggling wonder of what might have happened to them if they'd stayed in playing on their minds.

Luckily they hadn't seen her body to know just how sticky her end was. If so, they'd probably be ringing the estate agent tomorrow, negative equity or not. It hadn't been a pleasant sight. One more image to store in a memory bank that was already overflowing with sights of people's desire to hurt their fellow man. Murray sometimes wondered if his job had turned him into a monster of sorts, able to switch off his emotions at sights that would leave other people in need of counseling for months. Sighing, he knew this wasn't the time for that internal debate. He needed to focus all his intellect on what had happened to that poor girl.

In some ways, they'd been lucky. In other parts of London it would probably have been a week or more before anyone thought that something might be wrong. In most of the estates, people were too busy trying to deal with their own problems just surviving without having to worry about someone else. And in most of those places radios that played twenty-four seven were pretty commonplace. Still, having been inside that flat, he wasn't feeling too lucky.

Carter's young brow was furrowed as he inhaled deeply on his cigarette, his other hand stuffed deep into his coat pocket for warmth. He didn't look at Murray when he spoke. "How the hell could anyone kill someone like that? It would take hours. Why didn't she scream or try to get away?" His lilting accent was devoid of emotion but looking at the way the young man's shoulders were sagging Murray knew there was plenty going on inside.

He shrugged, the image of her body rising strongly before him. Suzy's corpse was covered with thousands of tiny lacerations, none in itself long or deep enough to do any serious damage, but so many in volume that she'd bled to death, her system unable to cope. He lit a cigarette himself, needing to feel the nicotine rush through his system, reminding him that he was still alive. "We'll let forensics figure that out. Maybe she was drugged." And maybe not, he added silently, thinking of the girl who was found in Elizabeth Ray's attic. They still hadn't got to the bottom of her cause of death, and although Murray was sure they'd find something to pin it on for the sake of the report, he knew it wouldn't be anything conclusive. He had a gut feeling it was going to be the same for Suzy Jenner. Inconclusive death certificates and closed caskets were going to be shared by these women who by all accounts had never done anything to hurt a fly. And people wondered why he didn't go to church. He figured that he did his bit for whatever cruel god may or may not exist by catching the bastards who did these terrible things. Emily had understood that even though she was a confirmed Catholic. There was only so much a man could give and any god that sanctioned crimes like this had no place in his world. Anyway, he'd never been able to get his practical mind around the whole religion thing. He was far too cynical. As far as he was concerned it was all just politics, and there were too many politicians struggling for power in the world and too many wars fought over people's precious religions.

Mulling over the scene they'd just left, he let out a long sigh. He wasn't happy about it. He wasn't happy at all. The mirrors in Suzy's flat were smashed, the same way they were in the Ray house and that was a detail that definitely hadn't been released to the detail hungry press. He wondered if maybe the milkman had mentioned it to anyone and made a mental note to check. But he doubted it. If he had, it would have appeared somewhere in one of the tabloids by now. And there was the unusual method of death, like the girl in the attic. It looked like his gut feeling had been right. The Ray case wasn't quite as cut-and-dried as everyone had thought, but being right wasn't making him feel any better.

Stubbing out his cigarette, he looked over to Carter who this time returned his gaze, his blue eyes seeming almost black. Murray's voice was soft. "What are your thoughts, Sergeant?"

There was a long pause as Carter absently ran his tongue over his teeth before he spoke. It was something he did when he was deep in thought and Murray was pleased to see his colleague firing on all cylinders, even at this time of night. When he spoke, his expression was frank. "Pretty much the same as yours, I guess. We've still got a sick bastard who was involved with the Hampstead business running around loose out there. That mirror thing is too much of a coincidence. I've never seen something like that in a case before, and now there's two in one year. I don't buy it, life doesn't work like that. And the way she died was weird, just like Helen Holmes. It's got to be related." For a moment he looked slightly sheepish beneath the street lights. "I owe you an apology. You were right. It looks like it did all tie up a little too neatly."

Murray waved a hand lightly at him. "Don't worry about it, we all like a quick result, and I know how much Baker was pushing for a close on this one. Believe me, I wish I'd been wrong." Stamping his feet lightly to get the circulation going, he had no desire to give the younger officer a hard time. Carter would be kicking himself enough for the both of them. Making their way through the melee of police vehicles, they headed to Murray's car. "What else did you pick up from what you saw in there?" Arrogant as it sounded, he didn't expect Carter to have picked up on anything he hadn't but it was still good to hear the thoughts out loud, to get Carter to focus on what he was good at: police work.

Carter had lit another cigarette, obviously more disturbed by what he'd just seen than he thought, and he smoked as he spoke. "Well, whoever it was, she knew him. The door had a spyhole and wasn't damaged. So she'd obviously opened the door for them quite happily. Anyway, you can't get in there without buzzing first, so she'd have spoken to them on the intercom before they'd even come up the stairs. The couple downstairs didn't think she was seeing anyone, but my guess is that whoever it was was her lover."

Murray allowed himself a small wry smile as he unlocked his car doors and they got in away from the cold. Starting the engine but leaving it in neutral he felt the warmth start to pump out of the vents. Carter was doing well. Although he knew the answer, he still asked the question. "Why?"

The other man was rubbing his red hands together. "She only had her knickers on and her dress and bra were undamaged on the floor by the bathroom where she'd run a full bath and probably lit those candles that were all burnt out. Her clothes definitely hadn't been ripped off and she died in the far corner of the living room so he wouldn't have undressed her there anyway. So she either let him in and then got undressed or she answered the door pretty much naked. I don't know which." He looked at Murray to see how he was doing. His superior officer and friend was nodding in agreement.

"I think you've got a point, although my money's on her opening the door in just her pants."

Carter looked quizzical. "Why, sir? From what the neighbors said about her, she doesn't sound like that kind of girl."

Murray shrugged. It didn't feel right to him either, but it was the only thing that fitted the scene. "There was only one wineglass and it was in the bathroom, so it was probably hers. Now if she'd opened the door to him before she'd got undressed, surely she would have given him a glass of wine to keep him company while she leapt into the bath. If she had time after his arrival and before the attack to finish running her bath and get herself undressed then I bet she would have offered him some wine. And if he was trying to lull her into a sense of security, he would have accepted, even if he hadn't drunk any of it. I think she was literally just about to get into the water when he arrived, and he probably attacked her only seconds after she shut the door, injecting her with some kind of sedative or something. That we won't know until we get an answer from the lab. I presume they'll be checking the wine as well."

He watched as Carter lived out the scene in his head and then accepting Murray's theory. He glanced at his watch. "What now, sir?"

Murray smiled. "Well now you get to go home and grab a couple hours of sleep, but I want our team to meet up with this one in the morning and make sure we've got all the evidence noted. Then you're going to go to Suzy's office and see what you can learn from there about her mystery man. I'll go and see the parents and do the same." Luckily he'd been spared the job of breaking the news to them. That had already been done by one of the officers who was first on the scene. Two more lives ruined and turned to dust. "I'm also going to want a criminal profiler. A good one. We're going to need all the help we can get."

Carter nodded, all his instructions carefully recorded in his sharp brain. "Are you going home now?"

This time the grin that spread across Murray's face reached his eyes, which twinkled. "No. I'm going to hang around here for half an hour or so, and then I think I'll give Mr. Baker a call and tell him that the shit's really hit the fan and the quick close he's no doubt been boasting about at every police function he can get himself to isn't looking quite so closed after all." He winked at Carter who was getting ready to get out of the car, buttoning up his coat. "And when I'm sure that he's wide awake and panicking, then I'll go home and grab forty winks."

His sergeant left the car laughing. Watching his departing figure, Murray wished he could feel more positive about the case and shift the niggling doubts in his stomach that were one day going to develop into one hell of an ulcer. He knew their reasoning about the killer was logical, there really couldn't be any other explanation, but somehow it didn't sit right. The neighbors were adamant she didn't have a boyfriend and he had a feeling her parents and colleagues were going to say the same, and although it was possible she'd kept it secret, maybe he was a married man, that didn't feel right either. It was a very neat, or-dered, and eminently sensible life that was lived in that flat. Nothing was untidy, nothing out of place, nothing dramatic or flamboyant about her clothes and furnishings. She didn't seem like the kind of person that could be *bothered* with an illicit affair. He had an idea that Suzy Jenner just wouldn't be attracted to that kind of man. Also, there was a manuscript on the sofa that she must have been working on. If she'd been working then she obviously wasn't ex-pecting a visitor, and if you were a married man having an affair, surely you'd call first to check your lover was avail-able before going through the routine of lying to escape your house. You'd especially want to know she was home if you were planning to kill her. And why the hell would her lover want to kill her like that anyway? It certainly wasn't a crime of passion.

He rubbed his face with his hands, as if he could wipe these problems away. I need the link, he thought, watching as the medics brought the covered body out of the front door and swiftly deposited it in the silent ambulance. I need the link between Suzy Jenner and Elizabeth Ray or Callum Burnett. Until I've got that none of this is going to make any sense. Tiredness swept over him and suddenly, more than anything, he just wanted to get back to his warm house and Janet and the kids. Janet and the kids. It still didn't sound right. If only he could get back to Emily and the kids, to creep back into bed and feel her soft breath on him as she mumbled her hellos somewhere between wak-ing and sleeping, just the smell of her enough to wash away the filth that walked the earth.

Feeling the melancholy settling on him, he shook it away. There's no point wishing for something you can't have. She's gone. Accept it. But looking at his mobile phone and scrolling through the numbers to find Baker's he knew that his heart would ache beyond belief when he finally crawled under that cold duvet into a bed too big for one person, just as it did every night and would for many nights to come.

It took him a full half hour to convince Baker that he hadn't orchestrated the murder of Suzy Jenner himself just to sabotage his superior's chances of advancement. Calmly, he waited for the ranting on the other end of the digital stream to slow down. He felt sympathy for the long-suffering Mrs. Baker who was no doubt going to have to bear the brunt of her husband's foul mood for some days to come, but he had no pity for the man himself. If he hadn't been so concerned with closing the case quickly, Suzy Jenner might still be alive. It wasn't likely, he admitted to himself. The tragedy of these kind of cases is that you normally have to wait for the bodies to pile up before there are enough leads to find the killer, but at least if they'd still been looking she might have had a chance. His own personal guilt sat heavy in his stomach, but he doubted such a thought would cross Baker's mind. Oh, how easy life must be when you're that self-absorbed. There was a pause in the other man's speech, and Murray butted in, his normally gentle voice harder, more dominant. He didn't want to spend all night placating his boss.

"Look sir, it's bad, but it's not that bad." Tell that to Suzy Jenner, he told himself wryly. "The press aren't aware of any connection between the cases, and I doubt they'll start looking for one. Why should they? As far as they're concerned the Ray case is all nicely tied up. So that works in two ways. It keeps them off our backs and as long as we don't mention the similarities anywhere, the killer might be arrogant enough to think we haven't seen the link, so that should buy us a little time to find him." He rubbed his eyes, frustrated that he was having to waste precious time explaining all this to a man who should know it anyway. He'd heard a rumor that sometime in the dim and distant past Baker had been a reasonably good detective. He found it hard to believe.

"And you're sure the two cases are related?"

Murray felt an overwhelming urge to batter the other man's head with something very heavy and very hard and tried to swallow it. "Yes, sir. I'm positive. So is the DI who was first on the scene. He saw enough of a connection to call it in."

Baker spoke quickly, his mind already focused on damage limitation. "Well, let him remain the face of this inquiry as far as the press are concerned. If they see you taking charge they might put two and two together and we don't need that, do we?"

No, I don't suppose *we* do, Murray thought wearily. "That's fine with me. You know how I feel about the press at the best of times. Anyway sir, I'll see you first thing in the morning. I'm going to go home and try and get some sleep. There's nothing more I can do here for the moment except get in the way of forensics, and if the newsboys do turn up I don't want them to find me hanging about."

Baker was beginning to sound a little more like his odious self now that he'd been reassured. "Yes, you're absolutely right. There's no need for you to stay there. Get yourself home and I'll see you at eight."

Pressing the red cancel button, Murray shut his eyes and leaned back against the headrest. Sweet Mary mother of God, as Emily used to say. The things he had to suffer for the cause of justice. He put the car into first and started his journey home. It was amazing just how quickly you could travel on the roads at that time of night and after twenty minutes of cruising beneath the streetlamps, his mind still lingering in Suzy Jenner's flat, he was gently turning the key in the lock of his front door, trying to be as quiet as possible. Slipping off his shoes, he went into the kitchen and grabbed himself a bottle of Stella Artois from the fridge and headed up to his study to have a cigarette with it before going to bed. The small desk lamp gave off a comforting glow and he pushed the door closed, shutting himself away from the rest of the house. Only then did he stretch out his legs and allow himself to relax. The ice-cold beer tasted good as the harsh bubbles fizzed in his throat and he took several long gulps before putting the bottle down and lighting a cigarette. Now that he was home he could feel the knots in his muscles running from behind both shoulders and meeting somewhere in his neck. He slowly lowered his chin to his chest and felt the tightness stretching. Had it always been like this, or was there just something about this case that was making him so tense? The horrors of this case on top of the horror of losing Emily was probably somewhere closer to the truth.

Thinking of that cold bed on the other side of the wall, he decided this was one night he could do without facing that. If he had to sleep he'd do it right here in the armchair. What the hell, there were only a few hours until he had to be back at work anyway. Sighing, he wearily pulled the cardboard box out from under the desk. There was no time like the present to finish those diaries. If the two cases were connected, he was going to have to get the box back to evidence as soon as possible. Kissing sleep good-bye, he got on with his work.

CHAPTER FIFTEEN

Ruby turned out the rather bright overhead light, leaving the sitting room bathed in the cozy glow of the two smaller table lamps. That was better. It had been years since Mike had brought anyone to meet her and she didn't want to scare the girl away.

Although she was now in her late sixties, a fact she found hard to believe, *just where did those years go*, her fashionably short hair remained mid-brown courtesy of Clairol, and although thickening at the waist, her still-trim figure was clothed in black slacks and a cream jumper. It wasn't what people expected, but then neither were her modern semi and IKEA style furniture, all light, bright and airy, no trace of ethnic throws, dark curtains, and certainly no crystal ball. But then, she'd never needed them.

Sure, she was used to the surprised and somewhat disappointed expressions on new clients' faces who had been expecting a little gray old lady in a darkened room, as if such illusions somehow gave credibility to the title of medium, but the gifts that were a second nature to her, a sixth sense that was at times almost more powerful than her other five, also meant that none of these clients ever left with any doubt about her abilities. So as far as she was concerned, there was absolutely no need to compromise her good taste to give reassurances that were ultimately unnecessary. And although not entirely true, she believed these tools to be the instruments of charlatans, and sadly there were plenty of them about, ready to take money from unhappy people in exchange for dubious information from the other side. Still, she philosophized, that was the way of the world, always had been and always would be. Why waste your time and energy fighting a battle you could never win?

Not ever having been an enthusiastic chef, she'd opted for a buffet style meal courtesy of Marks & Spencers and the pullout pine table by the window was set with plates of cold Chinese chicken legs, Indian style nibbles, and various salads. She had, however, made some biscuits like she used to when Mike was a child and there was a large dish of them on the coffee table. It didn't matter how old he got, as far as she was concerned, he would forever remain the bright cheeky chappie he was at ten years old. The surface might change and the outlook might become more sophisticated but that's who he would remain inside. And now he was bringing a young lady to see her, she thought cheerfully. A young lady with bad dreams. Those didn't worry her too much, dreams were never as complicated as people seemed to think, and nine times out of ten, you could get to the bottom of those with some good old-fashioned common sense.

Maybe this girl would be the one for him. There was an exciting thought. It would be so nice to see him settled down and starting a family, to have children around to fuss and spoil. Children aside, it would just be nice to see him happy. He hadn't had a serious girlfriend for years. Pouring herself a glass of red wine from the bottle she'd just opened, she laughed at herself for sounding like a clucking old hen. He's only just met the poor girl and you've got them married off already. If you're not careful, you'll be asking her whether her intentions are honorable, and then telling her she's not good enough for him, and that would never do.

She had however, pulled out an old photograph album to show this Rachel. Lots of embarrassing pictures there, and she knew he'd be expecting it of her. It was her one concession to "old lady" behavior and in her heart of hearts she knew he enjoyed sharing their special memories with good people.

The doorbell rang and she almost spilled the wine that she was about to sip, her heart speeding up with anticipation. Putting the glass down she moved with an agility that belied her age and was pulling the front door open in seconds. Mike stood on the doorstep, looking pleased and embarrassed, his slightly long hair flopping over his handsome face. Next to him stood a striking woman with long dark hair tied back in a ponytail and the most startling gray eyes she had ever seen. She beamed at them. "Well, don't just stand there, come on in." She held her hand out to the woman. "You must be Elizabeth."

The girl hesitated in the doorway, looking slightly confused and Mike leaned forward and placed a kiss on his aunt's cheek. "I don't know where you got that one from, her name's Rachel. I told you that on the phone. It was about the only thing you'd let me say about her. It's not like you to get a name wrong."

Ruby knew he was right. Of course he was right, she knew the girl's name was Rachel, why on earth had she said Elizabeth? Maybe she was finally losing her marbles. Smiling apologetically, she shook her head a little. "Of course it is, I don't know what's wrong with me. Now come on in out of the cold."

Shutting the door behind them, she hung their coats on the stand and then turned to Rachel. "Well, it's very nice to meet you. And you're so pretty too. Mike's landed on his feet with you, hasn't he?"

Rachel blushed slightly and laughed, before putting out

her hand. "Well, it's nice to meet you too. Mike's told me an awful lot about you."

Smiling broadly, Ruby took the young woman's hand, completely unprepared for the darkness and icy chill that hit her with a force she'd never experienced before, exploding through her senses, invading every corner of her being, and it took all her will to bite back the scream threatening to escape from the sheer terror of what she was feeling, and slowly remove her own hand. Rachel was looking at her smiling unaware, and Ruby could feel her own mockery of a grin still perching hazardously on her face. "Why don't we go through to the sitting room?" Her voice sounded thin in her head. It's all wrong. Everything is wrong here. Everything is wrong with this girl and I don't think she even knows it. She watched as Mike gave the girl a reassuring kiss on the forehead as they sat down on the sofa, and felt the chill settle at the base of her spine. Oh Mikey honey, what have you gotten yourself into here? Not ready to face them, face her, just yet, she called through something about getting more glasses from the kitchen and took her shaking body out of sight.

Sitting close together on the sofa, Mike gave Rachel's hand a squeeze. "Are you okay?"

She smiled back happily. "Yes, I'm fine. She seems very sweet. Quite a funky dresser for an old girl." Noticing the plate of biscuits on the table she nodded in their direction. "So you weren't lying. She does like baking for her favorite boy." She wiggled an eyebrow at him and he dug her gently in the ribs.

"But am I your favorite boy? That's the million-dollar question."

Slipping her arm through his, she leaned in to whisper to him. "Of course you are. But I do have something I've got to tell you, so let's not stay too late, okay?" She noticed the slight look of alarm on his face. "Nothing bad. Well, I don't think so, anyway, but it is private. Just between us."

Watching her earnest face, he was amazed at how happy

she could make him feel, just by looking at him like that. Things were just getting better and better between them, and touch wood, it looked like the dreams had stopped at last. She hadn't had one since Friday, so he'd had three blissful nights of complete rest and boy did he feel better for it. You are one lucky bastard, he told himself so often it had almost become a personal mantra, you really are.

She'd been different over the past few days as well, but he hadn't been able to put his finger on what it was, but now he could see it. She'd seemed secretive, as if she was hiding something from him that she was bursting to share. *Maybe she's going to ask you to marry her, Flynn. Now that would be an interesting one, wouldn't it? Interesting? Hah! You'd drag her down to the registry office before she could change her mind and realize that there are probably much better propositions out there for a girl like her.* He laughed at himself. Yeah, right. You don't really think she's exactly the type that goes around proposing to men, do you? Get over yourself.

Rachel was looking down at her hands and fiddling with her fingernails. "Since the dreams have stopped why don't we skip the regression and just have something to eat and then go? There's no point in putting your aunt out unnecessarily, is there? That way we can get home early enough for me to share my surprise with you. What do you say?"

Studying her, Mike wondered if she realized how nervous she looked. It seemed as if since they'd got into the house she become subconsciously unsettled. Uncomfortable. But then, it was probably just the thought of the regression. It was bound to make her feel that way, having so many unlocked secrets kicking around inside her. His brow furrowed. "We'll see how it goes. The dreams have only been gone a couple days. They might come back, we just don't know. Anyway, this might be a good way to get your memory to wake itself up, you can't put it off forever."

She stuck her tongue out at him and he took it as a sign

of disagreement and responded maturely by poking out his own. She giggled.

"There you go. Sorry I took so long, they were a bit smeared so I gave them a quick wash."

Ruby had bustled in and was standing in front of them holding two large wine glasses. He took them from her and she filled them with wine from the bottle on the table. He noticed her hand was shaking slightly and his heart squeezed. Although she seemed like she would go on forever, he knew that couldn't be the case and hoped she wasn't developing anything like Parkinson's. He pushed the depressing thought aside and smiled up at her. Behind her smile she looked pale. She waved in the direction of the food. "Well, tuck in, then. Don't let it get cold." Rachel laughed at the small joke and he saw how Ruby flinched at the sound. What was going on here? This wasn't like her. She was normally totally relaxed around new people.

He got up and helped himself to two chicken legs and a large spoonful of potato salad and began to eat. Rachel had piled her plate high and was munching happily. Ruby pushed her food around her plate, occasionally eating a small mouthful here and there and washing it down with a large gulp of wine. Mike wondered if Rachel could feel the tension in the air. Probably not. She didn't know Ruby and wouldn't have anything to compare her present behavior with. In the silence of their eating he felt the minutes dragging by.

Having lost his appetite slightly he tried to engage his aunt in idle chitchat regarding school and his not very upwardly mobile career. She smiled absently and responded with the usual, "That's nice, dear," kind of remarks that he never expected to hear from her, and then he watched her eyes would slip away from him and back to Rachel. Or to be more precise, around Rachel.

Rachel seemed blissfully unaware, and having finally finished her food, put her empty plate on the small table beside her and smiled at her hostess. "That was delicious, thank you. You shouldn't have gone to too much trouble." She leaned forward in her seat, conspiratorially. "Now you must have lots of embarrassing stories to tell about Mike when he was young. I can't believe he's always been this respectable." Her grin was cheeky.

Ruby's eyes were glittering with the effort of smiling. "He was always a good boy. There's an essential goodness inside him, always has been, always will be. Maybe that's what attracted you to him."

Rachel was looking slightly confused now, and Mike knew why. All the way over here he been preparing her for the embarrassing stories Ruby was likely to tell, that normally she would be crying with laughter telling, and now Rachel had given her the opportunity and she'd denied her usual overpowering urge to lovingly humiliate him.

His own laugh sounded hollow. "You're going to make her think I'm boring! I don't want you to put her off!" He caught the sharp glance Ruby sent his way. He also noticed the black photo album that was sitting on the coffee table that she hadn't opened to show to Rachel. She'd obviously intended to, otherwise why would she have dug it out, so what was stopping her? It couldn't be that she didn't like Rachel. What wasn't to like?

Rachel seemed slightly wistful. "Yes, maybe it was. There couldn't be a much purer reason for being attracted to someone could there?"

Mike butted in, determined to try and lighten the atmosphere. "I thought it was my manly physique."

Rachel laughed. "Well, that too, I suppose. Any girl would find it hard to resist your assets." Standing up, she retrieved the dirty plates. "I'll just pop these into the kitchen, and then if you could tell me where the bathroom is?"

"Thank you dear," Ruby said, almost as if she meant it. "The bathroom's straight up the stairs and the last door on the left." There was a downstairs toilet just past the kitchen that visitors always used. Why hadn't she sent Rachel there?

He waited until he heard Rachel's feet vanishing up the stairs.

"What's the matter, Ruby? You don't seem yourself."

Now that Rachel was out of the room, Ruby's mask crumbled and Mike saw some of the horror and loathing she was feeling reflecting on her face. Her whisper was terrifying in it's calmness. "It's her. There's something wrong with her. Something very wrong. It's all around her, inside her. There's evil there. I want you to get rid of her. Dump her. Have nothing more to do with her."

Mike felt his anger rising as he listened incredulously. The world suddenly seemed swimmy at the edges. "What the hell are you going on about? Don't be so ridiculous and don't start any of that mumbo jumbo voodoo stuff with me. Of course she's not evil. It's Rachel for Chrissake. And no, I'm sorry if I disappoint you, but I'm not going to dump her, I bloody love her! I'm sorry if that pisses you off for some reason but that's the way it is." Of all things, he hadn't expected this. How could she say these things about Rachel? He knew his anger was just hiding his hurt. He'd wanted Ruby to love her as much as he did. "Don't you want me to be happy? Is that it?"

Ruby glanced at the doorway to check that Rachel wasn't coming back down the stairs and then leaned forward and grasped his hands with hers. God, they were cold, her aging skin feeling dry and papery as she clutched him. "She frightens me, Mike. She frightens me more than anything has in a long time. And more than anything I'm afraid for you." He tried to pull his hands free, but she held on tighter. "I know you think I'm a crazy old woman, but trust me about this. I've always had your best interests at heart, you know that, so please, please, listen to me now. You have to get yourself as far away from her as possible. You could come and stay here for a while, take a couple of weeks off work."

Almost as if she realized how desperately she was behaving, she released his hands and sat up straight in her chair. Mike let out a small humorless laugh and glared at her. His voice was cold, and he saw her flinch again, this time from hurt rather than fear. "Do you know how ludicrous you sound? This is Rachel Wright you're talking about, Rachel Wright, who until last week used to edit children's fiction for a living. How unfucking weird is that? And don't you think that if there was something"—he held his fingers up in a sarcastic inverted comma's gesture so angrily, Ruby pulled back into her chair, small tears forming at the corners of her eyes "—*evil* about her, don't you think I might just have noticed? Jesus Christ!" He sat back against the cushions and shook his head at her. There was the sound of water rushing through the pipes as the toilet was flushed upstairs.

Ruby looked at him, her eyes full of sorrow, and despite himself he felt his heart soften. She suddenly looked old. Old and terribly fragile. But when she spoke he felt a chill settle over his flesh. "The problem is *I don't think she knows*. And if *she* doesn't know, then what hope do you have?" She let out a short breath of exasperation. "If there was more time I could probably explain myself better, but there isn't." Mike's disbelief must have been shining like a beacon on his face, because Ruby's normally straight and strong shoulders sagged. "Just promise me you'll take care of yourself. Be watchful. I don't think I could bear it if anything happened to you, and I think bad things are going to happen to people around her, I really do."

Rachel appeared in the doorway and felt a moment of the silent tension between the two people in the warm room. Her smile slipped a little. "Is everything okay?"

There was an almost invisible pause before Mike stood up, his hands thrust into his pockets to hide their shaking with emotion. "It seems your prayers have been answered. You're saved from your regression today. Ruby's got a migrane and doesn't really feel up to it. It's probably best if we leave her to it." He couldn't bring himself to look at his aunt, but Rachel did, her face full of concern and sympathy, and

Mike could have sworn, a hint of relief. She leaned down and put one hand on Ruby's shoulder, and he watched the almost imperceptible shudder run down the body of the older woman. Rachel kissed her on the cheek. "You really should have said. We wouldn't have come. There's nothing worse than visitors when you're not really feeling up to it. We can do the regression another time. You should get yourself to bed with a couple of aspirin and an eye mask."

Ruby managed a watery smile as she stood up and moved away from the young couple and out to the hallway to get their coats. "Thank you for being so understanding. There's nothing worse than being the party pooper, is there?"

Rachel kissed her again on the cheek before saying farewell and stepping out onto the pavement. Mike didn't, just wanting to get away from her and let his anger abate in peace. He rarely got angry and when he did it was like a torrent inside him, almost uncontrollable, coloring his view of everything. He didn't get violent, however, much he sometimes wanted to, but it did always take him a few hours to get back to his normal self. This was going to be one of those occasions. Not bothering to put his jacket on over his thin - V-neck jumper, he joined Rachel outside without a word. Ruby waved them good-bye. "I'll call you in a few days, okay?"

Mike gave her a small tight smile for the sake of appearances and tried to ignore the weight of emotion in her words and eyes. Maybe she thought Rachel was going to skin him alive in his bed or something. God, what an evening. He found the image laughable, and pulled the woman in question closer to him as they strolled down the street to look for a cab. She slipped her arm around his waist and squeezed hard, and he could almost feel his heart tighten at the same time. It didn't matter what anyone else thought of her, Ruby included. She alone was enough for him. Leaning down slightly, he kissed the warmth of her hair. "God, I'm glad we found each other. I really am." And he was.

* * *

Ruby shut the door behind them, thankful to have them, *to have her*, out of the house, and then let the tears flow, her back sliding down against the door until she was sitting on the pale tan carpet with her knees pulled up to her chin, her head leaning on them. She sat there for about ten minutes, her breath hot on her damp face until her turmoil of emotions subsided and she was able to lift her head and think properly. She'd never seen Mike that angry, she'd never imagined that she could provoke such a reaction in him. Oh lord, what had she done, what had she done?

But she couldn't help it, how could she not say anything at all and leave him at the mercy of forces he'd always denied? She knew him, and as much as he hated her now, she knew her words would stay with him, tucked into a corner of that clever brain, and when things got bad, things happening that he might not understand, they'd surface and maybe give him some kind of protection. At least allow him a little time, time enough to get himself away.

Wiping the last tears away, she leaned her head back against the door and let out a long sigh. I'm too old for this, she thought. Too old and too afraid. Half of her wished that Mike had never brought the girl here and she could carry on in blissful ignorance, but that wasn't to be. The girl had come and that was that. She'd never been very good at burying her head in the sand. And there was Mike to think of. She had to at least try and protect him in whatever way she could. As much as she wanted to put all memory of Rachel away, she forced herself to relive their meeting, to reexamine the terrible fear she'd felt when the woman touched her, the blackness that had surrounded her. The best way she could describe what she had felt was that everything about Rachel was *unnatural*, but it was more than that, so much more. There was a sense of doom there, great tragedies, all the things that result when people interfere with the laws of nature. Ruby had seen plenty of evil in people before, they carried it with them in their auras, and as they got older it tended to carry over into their physical appearance, greedy people got fat and their eyes got smaller and meaner, you didn't have to be any kind of psychic to recognize those facts, but this was evil like she'd never experienced before. Basic evil, in it's rawest form.

Pulling herself to her feet, she went back into the sitting room and picked up her wineglass, taking a long sip. I'm not making any sense, she grumbled at herself. I'm not making any sense because I haven't got a clue about what's going on around that girl apart from that it scares me witless. It's old and it's dark and endlessly cold and it makes me more afraid than anything should a woman of my age and abilities. That's the crux of it though, isn't it? Maybe what scares me more is that I've finally realized that the forces and spirits I arrogantly thought I knew so much about, go way beyond anything I can understand? How can I help Mike? How can I possibly even think that anything I do can make a difference?

Her back complained at her for sitting on the floor too long, and suddenly, for the first time in her life, she felt old. Old and tired. God help her, she'd never been brave, not really, despite what people think, appearances can be deceptive, and she'd always had her *gifts* to give her a calm and tranquility that other people, people who had to live their whole lives completely alone, would never be allowed. That was bravery. *She'd* always known that death wasn't the end, and today, for the first time, she'd become afraid of what came after. She thought she'd understood, after all, she had a natural insight, she could *communicate*, she was special, but now she knew her understanding was like light reflecting on the surface of the ocean. It could never hope to penetrate the depths below. Oh, her arrogance had been endless. That meeting with Rachel had altered her world, destroyed her comfort zone, changed her perceptions of everything. Suddenly she envied the rest of the world, unable to see beyond the physical.

Draining the rest of the glass, she knew what she had to

do. It was time to go back to the past, to where as a young
girl in the first exciting glow of her differentness, she'd studied the occult and the ways of white witches. It didn't matter how unnatural she thought Rachel, *Elizabeth, her
name's Elizabeth, I don't care what anyone says*, was that
wasn't entirely correct. They were all bound by the laws of
nature, everything with life, whatever spiritual level they
were at, there was no escaping it. The girl was just unnatural on this plane, and if she was going to find some kind of
answer, then her best bet was in the occult archives she
kept locked away in the spare room. Feeling a little of her
old self coming back now that she had her thinking head
on, she was damned if she wasn't even going to try to solve
the puzzle. Maybe this was her destiny after all.

She refilled her wineglass and was halfway up the stairs
before she realized what else had changed. The buzz in her
head was gone. The hum of distant voices, sounds from beyond the physical, that she had carried with her for as long
as she could remember, had fallen silent. She was entirely
alone in her head, as if even those people beyond any
harm that this world could possibly inflict, wanted to keep
themselves as far away from Rachel as possible. And that
really was a terrifying thought.

"Well, thanks." She muttered to the empty void they had
left behind, as she unlocked the large oak cupboard that
filled one wall of the second bedroom, looking highly out
of place against the pale walls and pine bed. "Thanks a lot.
I'll remember this next time any of you want to console
your grieving relatives. Maybe then I'll take the day off, see
how you like it." She wasn't really expecting an answer and
she wasn't disappointed.

It's just you then, kiddo, she said to herself as she pulled
open the door to reveal, instead of clothes on hanging
rails, rows and rows of old books on sturdy wooden
shelves. Just you against the forces of evil. She felt like she
should have seen this film, "old lady saves her loved ones
from a fate worse than death and does battle with the de-

vil," and wondered what the ending was going to be. If her memory of the *Damien* films served her correctly, the odds were on that she was going to come to a sticky end somewhere before the final reel. Remembering the way she'd felt when Rachel/Elizabeth had touched her, she thought there might be some truth in that. Great, she thought, just great, and then pulled out the first book and started to read.

CHAPTER SIXTEEN

In a way Rachel was glad that Ruby had a migraine and their evening had been cut short. Not glad that the poor lady was sick, but glad that she didn't have to go through with the regression. She had far too much on her mind to deal with that today. It had been a relief when Mike had explained the problem because she'd had a weird feeling that his aunt didn't like her very much, she seemed to look at her funny, but thankfully it must have just been symptomatic of the headache. From what Mike had said about her, she wasn't the kind of woman to dislike someone without a pretty good reason. Maybe she was just a bit protective of Mike's heart. Rachel wished she could've explained to her that there was nothing to worry about on that score. *I'm head over heels in love with your nephew, Auntie Ruby. Completely smitten. And if there was ever a girl looking for commitment then it's me. Circumstances have changed in the weird and wonderful world of Rachel Wright, as I'm sure you'll hear.*

Anyway, Ruby was the last thing she was spending time

thinking about. She'd only had one issue filling her brain since Friday after she'd finally got the guts up to confirm her suspicions, and she'd decided this morning that it was time to tell Mike. Maybe if she'd gone for the alternative option, she'd have kept it to herself, but she'd made her decision and now it was time to see how he felt about it. And it wasn't as if she could hide it forever, was it? Excitement and nervousness fluttered in her stomach as she followed him up the stairs to their opposing flats. Mike stood midway on the landing and smiled at her. "Yours or mine?"

He'd looked a little tired and distracted since they'd left Ruby's and she wondered if maybe tonight wasn't the night to share, *perhaps break would be a better word, honey, you don't know how he's going to react yet*, her news with him. She caught up with him and kissed him on the nose. "Mine. Are you okay, lover? You seem a little quiet."

This time his smile almost reached his eyes. "I'm fine. Just a bit worried about Ruby, I suppose."

She swung the door open and they went into the warmth of her compact hallway. "It's just a headache. I'm sure she'll be fine in the morning. I get the impression it'd take a lot more than a migraine to knock that old lady for six." She took her jacket off and threw it over the back of the sofa. "Anyway, I require all of your attention now, so I suggest you grab yourself a beer from the kitchen before you sit down. You might need it."

He looked at her with those eyes the color of brown sugar that never failed to make her insides—and certain other areas—go weak. They were slightly wary, guarded. "Ah yes. Your mysterious secret." He paused and then looked her frankly in the eye. "Look, if you're going to ditch me or tell me we need to cool off for a bit then I think I'd rather take it standing up. I don't want to have to hang around embarrassed while I finish my beer. You might not remember the incident, but I've done that once before and I don't particularly want to relive the experience."

Rachel was stunned for a second before she threw the cushion she'd been leaning on at him with full force and laughed. "You don't get away that easy! Now go and get that beer. And get me one while you're at it." She ducked, neatly avoiding her missile that was now coming back in her direction. "Go on, shoo!" She shouted at him, poking her head up from behind the back of the sofa. Watching the relief flooding his face as he headed for the kitchen, she pulled her hair from her neat ponytail and shook it loose around her shoulders, enjoying the sensation of freedom. Mike never failed to surprise her. How could he even think like that? Didn't he realize she was crazy about him? Crossing her legs underneath her she cursed her old self. The reason he's insecure is because you were such a stupid bitch and ditched him after a one-night stand. No wonder he has his moments of doubt. A soft smile played on her lips as she thought about him. He is a truly remarkable man. Ruby was right. There was an essential goodness about him. Only a truly good person would be doing his valiant best to help her get her memory back when that could mean she'd dump him all over again.

She heard the sound of the bottles being opened, and absently stroked her presently flat stomach. Well, we don't want the memories back, do we? So he's just going to have to put up with the new and improved me, and whoever you turn out to be. And I have a feeling that the three of us are going to be just fine. And if he doesn't like the idea, then the two of us will be just fine. End of story.

Mike flopped on the sofa and handed her the second beer. She noticed he'd already drunk from his. "So go on. Don't keep me in suspense."

She took his hand and gave it a squeeze. Suddenly the speech she'd been rehearsing in her head all day vaporized into nothing, leaving a large empty space with only two words left in it. Oh shit, she thought just before she opened her mouth. Here goes nothing.

"I'm pregnant."

She watched as his face froze, his expression unreadable, and she felt the flush run up her neck as she pulled her hand back. *Okay, so maybe he's not as keen as you thought he was going to be. Move to Plan B.* "Look, I'm only telling you because I've decided to keep it. If you don't want to stick around then that's fine, well not fine exactly, but I'll understand. I mean it's not as if we've been together all that long or even had a very normal relationship so far, so you're under no obligation, I just thought you should know so . . ." *God, I'm making a complete mess of this, I'm rambling and I can't stop myself, why can't the sofa just swallow me whole and get me out of here?* She couldn't bring herself to look at Mike and it was only when she felt his hand softly touching her cheek that she finally shut up and carefully raised her eyes to his. He was gazing at her in wonder, his smile dazed. "Did you just say that we're going to have a baby?"

Rachel gave a small nod. *We. He said we. Maybe it's not going to be that bad, after all.* "I did a test on Friday night when you were at the pub with your friend. That line couldn't have got any bluer. I guess we weren't quite as careful as we thought. Sorry."

Putting his beer down on the coffee table, he moved closer to her and wrapped his arm around her. "Don't be sorry. It's fantastic. It's great." His grin was getting larger and his eyes were sparkling. "We're going to have a baby. I can't believe it. I'm going to be a dad. Shit, I better get myself in training for football in the park and all that stuff."

Rachel heart was starting to beat faster with relief. "Oh. And by the way, in case you start to wonder when all this sinks in a bit, it's definitely yours. Apparently, one of the first things they did at the hospital when I collapsed was a pregnancy test, and my womb was confirmed empty at that point." Looking for a reaction, she could see that Mike wasn't really listening. His foot had started to tap and his eyes were elsewhere, dancing. He turned to her.

"You know we'll have to give up smoking. And at least

cut down on the drinking. It's Guinness or nothing for you from now on. And plenty of fresh fruit and vegetables, and lots of early nights. Thank God those nightmares have stopped."

Rachel giggled into his shoulder. "You sound like an old nursemaid." *He's happy about it, he's really happy about it, hallelujah!* "Anyway, I think maybe the dreams were my body's way of telling me there was something going on in there that I should take notice of."

Mike wasn't convinced. "That's a pretty weird way of giving you good news, wouldn't you say?"

She shrugged. "Well, in case you hadn't noticed, I'm a pretty weird girl."

Mike nodded, laughing. "You've got a point. I can't argue with you there." .

She hit him with the cushion. "Oh, you're funny."

Mike pulled her onto him so that she was straddling his waist. "Maybe we should think about making an honest woman of you, now that the two of us are going to be three. We don't want our child thinking it's mother is a loose woman, do we?" He grimaced as she hit him again with her soft weapon. "I can't believe you're beating up the father of your unborn child. I'm going to end up on one of those daytime talk shows. Battered husbands and all that stuff."

He pulled her forward so that her hair was a dark curtain surrounding them and kissed her long and lovingly. As always, Rachel felt her passion rising and pressed herself into him. *What is it that he does to me? How can just a kiss set me on fire like this? I've turned into a sex maniac, that's what it is. But shit, that feels good.* Mike gently eased her away and she felt a twinge of something close to anger at being deprived of her pleasure. It was gone before she realized it had even been there, a quiet subversive, alien visitor. Mike ran his fingers through her hair, watching the shine follow his hand. "I'm being serious you know. I love you very much, and I'd love to marry you, baby or no baby."

Rachel looked at the handsome face in front of her with

its reflective expression and her heart went through a series of small unbelievable explosions. *He loves me, he really loves me, he wants to marry me. Baby or no baby. Oh shit, I'm in danger of really letting myself down and crying or something equally stupid.* She took a deep breath to calm herself down. "I would love to marry you, but let's just get adjusted to our news before we rush into anything. I don't want to say yes and then have you going and getting cold feet on me."

Mike laughed, and she looked at him quizzically. "What's so funny?"

He shook his head at her, as if in disbelief. "If you only knew half of what I felt for you then you'd be laughing at the idea of me changing my mind, too. I fucking love you, Rachel Wright, and I'd marry you tomorrow morning."

Her face was glowing. "Really?"

"Yes, really."

This time it was her who leaned forward and kissed him. "Well, on that note I think it's time for bed."

"Now there's a surprise. You're an insatiable woman, Ms. Wright." He rolled her onto the sofa so he could stand up. She smiled cheekily up at him.

"That's why you love me, Mr. Flynn."

Picking up the two beer bottles, he winked at her. "You could well be right." As he walked toward the kitchen to put their empties in the bin, something caught his eye. "The light on your phone is flashing. Someone must have called while we were out."

Rachel got up and approached the phone with a certain amount of apprehension. It wasn't as if she knew that many people these days, and she'd never quite shook off that dread when the phone rang that there was going to be a stranger from her old life at the other end of the line. She'd been meaning to get the number changed but hadn't got around to it yet. There'd just been too many things going on. Picking up the receiver she heard the broken dial tone indicating that there was a message waiting, and punched in the BT retrieval code 1571. Maybe it was just the good doctor checking up on her. The male voice that came through was unfamiliar. Unfamiliar, middle-aged, and awkward.

"Hi, Rachel. It's Peter Jackson here." He spoke as if Rachel should know who he was and that annoyed her. Which part of the word amnesia didn't people understand? "I, um, I really wanted to tell you this in person, someone should really have come and seen you, but since you're not at work anymore and with the shock of everything, it seems to have slipped everyone's mind, but I've just seen it in the paper and I wanted to let you know before you read about it. God, I'm not making a very good job of this, am I?" What the hell was the man talking about? Why couldn't he just get to the point. She was starting to feel impatient and jiggled slightly from leg to leg.

"I'm sorry to have to tell you like this," *Liar, you sound relieved rather than sorry*. His next words froze her. "but Suzy Jenner was found dead in her flat on Sunday morning. Murdered. Ghastly business and we're all obviously very shocked and upset." There was a pause, as if now that he had imparted the information, he didn't know how to finish and get off the phone. "I, uh, just thought you should know. There's no date for a funeral yet, but when there is, I'll be in touch. Sorry to have to tell you like this. If you want to talk about it, just give me a bell at the office. I'd be more than happy to meet up." There was a click as he hung up and then the automated female voice was asking her if she wanted to save or delete the message. She ignored the options and put down the phone. Suzy was dead. Murdered. *It's started. They're coming. The Soulcatchers are coming, and there's nowhere for me to hide.* The thought was almost subconscious, a brief blur in her mind, and was gone, leaving only a trace of dark annoyance by the time she realized Mike was standing in the doorway. His face was furrowed and she could almost see the old man he would one day become in the beginnings of the lines that formed in his expression.

"What's the matter? You look terrible."

She looked down at the phone as if to reconfirm what she'd heard. Her voice was soft and although she spoke aloud, it was almost more to herself than it was to him. "It's Suzy Jenner. She's dead." She saw her own shock reflected in his eyes.

"Jesus, what happened?" Mike had never met Suzy, but he knew a little about her from Rachel's description and knew she wasn't old. Not old enough to die from natural causes at any rate.

Rachel shrugged. "She was murdered in her flat." She glanced back down at the phone. "That was some guy from work. Talked like I should know him, which obviously I don't." She sighed. "Anyway, he didn't have any details, just said something about it being in the paper and thought I should know."

Rubbing her hands across the back of her neck, she was silent for a moment as Mike crossed the room and put his arms around her. "Are you okay?" The soft tones of his voice soothed her.

"Yeah, it just really irritates me the way people insist on talking to me or my answer phone as if I should know them, I mean, Jesus Christ, when are they going to get the message? I have no memory, it isn't that much of a brain teaser, is it?" Her voice was sharp and annoyed, and she felt Mike's body stiffen as he pulled away. He was looking at her in disbelief.

"I was talking about Suzy. Were you okay about Suzy. Not the fucking phone call."

Of course he was, she thought, snapped out of her daze by the coldness of his words. Of course he was. *What the hell was I talking about? Suzy's dead, and I'm pissed off with the poor sod who at least thought to call and let me know? What's the matter with me?* She tried to focus her attention on Suzy, to feel something, anything rather than having to think about the look on Mike's face, but it was as if something inside her kept slipping away from it, pushing it aside.

She was aware of Mike stepping away from her and wanted him back, afraid of the emptiness that was filling her.

"God, I'm sorry, I don't know where that came from, I—"

Turning around halfway to the door, Mike cut her off. "And I know this might come as a bit of a surprise to you, but perhaps your amnesia wasn't top of that man's list of priorities today. Maybe something else was playing on his mind like, ooh I don't know, finding out one of his colleagues has just been murdered in her flat. Maybe he, unlike you, seemed to find that upsetting. That sort of thing can do that to a person."

Rachel felt the tears forming at the corners of her eyes. He'd never got angry with her before and she couldn't believe how miserable his outburst was making her feel. *And* he was right and that wasn't helping. God, how could their evening be ending like this? Five minutes ago they were talking about marriage and now he was looking at her with disgust. She sniffed and swallowed.

"I didn't realize sarcasm was your style."

His face was blurring slightly but she could see his anger deflating, the heated expression fading as she wiped the wetness from her cheeks. He was still exasperated though. "You just sounded so fucking callous. I mean, don't you care? She was your best friend even if you don't remember it, and she deserves a little more respect than that. I thought you would give her that respect."

Rachel could feel the tears coming again. It had been an emotional day and now she was starting to feel exhausted. Why couldn't they just be friends again? Keeping her head down she moved toward him and wrapped her arms around his waist before he could push her away. Pressing her face into his shoulder, her voice was muffled by his jumper.

"Of course I care, I do, I don't know what came over me. I'm sorry." She paused to swallow a sob. "I think it was just the shock. I didn't want to accept such horrible news straight after telling you we were having a baby, I couldn't, so I just focused on what irritated me. I just couldn't think about it." His arms softened around her and that relief brought a small fresh wave of tears. What she said made sense, so much sense that she almost believed it herself.

But it's not true, is it? The insidious whisper inside her, whose voice wasn't quite her own, wouldn't be ignored however much she tried. *It's not true at all. You don't give a shit that Suzy's dead, do you? You can't seem to find a single sorry emotion when you think of her, no grief at all. But let me see, Little Miss Sorry, I think I can find a couple of feelings buried deep down in here somewhere. What's this? A little bit of elation. She's dead and you're very much still alive, is that it? Oh, and there's something else in the box you don't want to open, isn't there? More than a little bit of fear, wouldn't you say? They're coming. They're coming and you can't stop them.*

Feeling slightly hysterical, she crushed the inner voice, silencing it. What's the matter with me? Why am I frightened? What could Suzy's death possibly have to do with me? And Mike's right, I did know her and I should feel some kind of grief so why can't I? His hand was slowly stroking her hair, and she took comfort from his warmth, his alive warmth pressing into hers.

Her breath was still long and broken into his chest as her brain raced. Maybe I will, maybe it is just shock. Maybe tomorrow it'll hit me. That's what happens, isn't it? Grief takes time to settle in. Her lips found their way to his neck and started to kiss and nibble it, her desire from earlier resurfacing. I need not to think, she decided, trying to calm her panicking heart. I need not to think about Suzy. I need to think about me and Mike and the baby, and if I just concentrate on those, then everything is going to be *just fine*. It has to be. I haven't done all this for nothing. They won't find me. They won't take me back.

Her heart skipped a beat and her mouth paused as the chill sucked at her stomach. She had no idea what she was thinking. Oh Jesus, maybe she was going crazy, after all.

Who were "they" and what had she done? She hadn't done anything, nothing at all. How could she have? The inner voice that sounded like something she'd heard in a dream somewhere, rose up unwanted and giggled. *How do you know, Rachel Wright, the mysterious no memory girl? How can you be so sure? You don't know what you might have done. You really haven't got a clue, have you? How many answers do you really think you have? Tell me that, because I for one would like to know.*

She could still hear the giggling echoing in her head as she pushed her tongue into Mike's mouth. "Take me to bed. Please take me to bed." Hoping he couldn't see the desperation in her eyes she kissed him again, this time running her hands down his body, urgently seeking to arouse him. "Take me to bed and make everything all right again. Please Mike, please. I don't want to think anymore." It was the most truth she'd spoken to him since telling him she was pregnant, and whether he believed that or not, he responded silently, picking her up and carrying her out across the hallway and into the bedroom, after which she took total control of the situation.

At half past one, Mike slipped quietly out of bed and got himself a beer having given up on sleep. There was too big a jumble of thoughts rushing around his head for that and he needed to sort them out. Rachel had fallen into a near coma over an hour ago after she was finally satisfied, and looking at her, he had known that she probably wouldn't even move before morning, the only sign that she was alive being the tiny rise and fall of her torso as she breathed.

Pulling the top off the bottle he took a long swallow and then lit a cigarette from the packet on the table. Congratulations, here's to fatherhood. He held the beer up in salute and then took another gulp. Sitting alone in the lounge in the middle of the night, the celebration seemed hollow and he wasn't sure that was the only reason. He was happy about it, he knew he was, I mean it was a dream come true,

Rachel and a baby, but Jesus, maybe she was right, maybe it was all happening so goddamn fast. He needed to slow down for a minute and think about things. He wished he could shift the vague feeling of disquiet that had been nibbling at him since Rachel had drifted off to wherever she went when she slept, leaving him alone.

The sex hadn't helped, he knew that. For once in his sorry male life, he really hadn't been in the mood, it didn't seem right, not after the news about Suzy. The most he'd felt up to was some gentle lovemaking, something emotional. Something to put the badness of the world away and celebrate their love and their baby, hiding and growing inside her body. But not Rachel, she'd been like an animal, demanding and unforgiving, not letting him have a moment's rest. It was as if *he* wasn't really there, as if he didn't really matter and she was just using him as she would anybody to fulfill her need. And if tonight was anything to go by, her needs were getting harder to satisfy.

He smiled wryly. I sound like a woman. She's just using me for sex, what about my emotional needs? Sometimes I just want a cuddle. The slight humor did little to rouse his mood. It's just been one of those days, Flynn. Too much has happened. It'll all look different in the morning. How do you expect to feel? Your aunt's flipped out, your girlfriend's pregnant, and Suzy's been murdered. A little bit of emotional unrest is hardly surprising. He stretched his legs out and rested them on the coffee table.

The dreams stopped and then Suzy died.

Not just died. Murdered.

He wondered if Rachel had thought about that. Probably not. There wasn't really anything to think about, there wasn't any connection, the two things were miles apart from each other, separate incidents in separate lives. He sucked hard on the cigarette. So why am I thinking about it? Why am I looking for parallels? The answer came back at him in his aunt's voice, replaying words spoken to him earlier this evening.

And I think bad things are going to happen to people around her, I really do.

He wasn't really surprised. The confrontation with his aunt had probably upset him more than the news of Suzy's death. He rubbed his tired eyes.

Damn you, Ruby, you're jinxing me with your mumbo jumbo. His thoughts were angry. So the dreams stopped and then Suzy died. Big fucking deal. He didn't want to think of what Ruby had said about Rachel and he sure as hell didn't want it invading his thought processes. He knew her words were influencing his mood and tried to push them aside. It was all ridiculous anyway. There was nothing wrong with Rachel. As far as he was concerned, everything was pretty much right with Rachel. He loved her and she was going to have their baby.

Boy, telling Ruby that one was going to be fun. He figured it could wait for a while. It could wait until she'd got used to the idea of the two of them as a couple, and if she couldn't, then well, she'd be the one who lost out. It hurt his heart, though. It hurt a lot. Shit, why couldn't his life just be simple?

Draining his beer, he stood up, feeling an urge to go and watch Rachel sleeping, to remind himself of how beautiful she was and how lucky he was and to damn the rest of the world. They can all go hang, he decided. Screw them all. He wasn't really sure who "they all" might be other than Ruby, but the sentiment made him feel better, and as he eased himself back under the duvet, careful not to disturb his sleeping beauty, he felt close to his normal levelheaded self again. Maybe sleep would come, after all.

CHAPTER SEVENTEEN

The old lady's body lay still as she slept, giving no external indication of the frantic images assaulting her psyche and soul, as if her spirit were truly detached from the physical world. But then, she knew more than most, knew how the thin line between this life and the next could shimmer and dissipate into nothingness as the conscious mind drifted abandoned in the dream state. Even those with little or no perception of the things that can't be seen could have moments of psychic clarity during the dark hours that the subconscious ruled, warnings and messages laughed off and forgotten in the sobering light of day. But those were people unlike this woman, who over the years had distilled her abilities and honed her instincts, and who this evening, after quietly sipping a large sherry to ease her to sleep, had opened her mind, seeking out anyone who could help her, inviting them in.

She knew she was afraid, she had been for over a week now, the sensation covering her like an itchy blanket ever since the girl had come and she had submerged herself in the black world of the occult whose enticements she had rejected so long ago. From waking until falling into bed, she pored over books unopened for forty years, pausing to occasionally make quiet telephone calls to others more knowledgeable than she. Forgetting to eat, and even on some days bathe, she knew she was looking old, looking her age, and more than that, she was feeling it, the darkness on those pages aging her more than any amount of years could.

There was so much she didn't understand, needed to understand, and she had the overwhelming feeling that time was running out, in many ways, had run out. Whatever was happening had already begun, and she was caught in a terrible game of catch-up. And so here she was, in a dream that wasn't a dream.

She had unlocked herself and they had swarmed in: the mad, the dispossessed, the lonely, the curious, and for a few moments she let them have their way, relishing in her living flesh, her mind a racing, jumble of memories, emotive images, moments of death and confusion, none of them her own. After a while she subdued the chaos, gently forcing a channel through those competing for her attention like too many excited children, and it shone like a tube of cool, fluorescent blue reaching outward from her third eye.

Feeling her confidence rising, she pulled the information required from her conscious, and like a Buddhist deep in meditation, started to chant the words over and over again, watching as they disappeared before her into the glowing azure strip. She chanted for hours, repeated the words without thought, "Rachel Wright, Rachel Wright, Rachel Wright, Rachel Wright," her focus on maintaining the channel, using all her mental strength to send the visualization of the words as far into it as she could. Endless amounts of time passed that had no meaning here as she chanted and waited, remaining undistracted by the shapes that waited with her, their inquisitiveness, like itchy needles in her mind.

Eventually, when true sleep had almost claimed her, something came. She felt the deep chill momentarily before she heard the giggle, lilting and feminine, echoing in the void, her senses full of flashes and emotions, the smell of everything that had ever rotted surrounding this spirit, unpleasant to even the silent observers, who drew away, no longer interested in this old living lady who could commune with them.

Her sleeping face twitched with disgust. Oh dear Lord, this one was mad, this woman who had lived without ever really living, driven mad by her manner of death, probably driven mad before her moment of death, and I think she has no eyes, and she's so bitter, and so angry that her bitch mother is still with her, trapped together, murdered by the same hand, unable to let go because it isn't over, it's so far from over.

She squeezed the dead woman's mind out of hers and into the opening of the tunnel, which then closed into a sphere around it, hovering in blackness, holding it there until such time as she chose to release it. The bright prison didn't bother the spirit though, who continued to giggle to herself. She sang the words like a child would a nursery rhyme.

"Rachel Wright, Rachel Wright,
was stolen away in the middle of the night."

Although the sphere allowed some protection from the broken spirit, the old woman was still filled with revulsion and so spoke quickly, wanting this meeting across the planes over as soon as possible.

"I want to speak with her. Call her for me." The voice was hers but not hers, stronger, deeper, more masculine, and the glowing ball rippled as the power of her words reached it.

"Oh no, no, no, you can't do that. She can't come to the phone right now. She's busy. She's trying to stop them from talking to the doctor. She's screaming. She seems to scream a lot these days." Again that little private titter. "They're telling him the answer is in the file. He thinks they're her, but it's all tricks, tricks, tricks, trick or treating time is here." The voice dropped to a secretive whisper. "But he can't hear her. Not from so far away. Anyway, no pain, no gain, isn't that what

they say? And we all have to suffer in the end. Suffer the little children."

Her head was throbbing, an explosion building in her veins and she knew she couldn't keep this up for much longer. "Who are they?" Some of the strength had gone, the words like feathers instead of bullets.

The thing in the sphere released a long sigh of exasperation, breath rattling in clogged-up lungs that no longer existed. "Don't you know anything? The Soulcatchers, of course. The Soulcatchers are coming. And they're going to put everything right. That's what they do. Everything in its place and a place for everything." There was a pause, and then, quizzically, "Have you seen my mother? He killed her but the bitch just won't die." The next words were afraid. "She moves faster without her wheelchair. She'll be looking for me now. If I don't stay alert, she'll find me, and that won't do, no, no, no. It's hide and seek, please don't peek."

Having had enough, Ruby released the channel, the sphere exploding into a thousand colors, filling the void with sparkling brightness before sucking back in on itself, imploding to nothing, sending it's passenger back the way it came. Quickly, she sealed herself up before any new visitors arrived. Her bleary eyes opened long enough for her to scribble a few words onto the notepad she'd left with the pen on the side of the bed. "The Soulcatchers are coming" and then she fell thankfully into an exhausted sleep, blissfully uninterrupted by dreams or nightmares, carried away by the reassuring beat of her heart.

Unlocking the front door to his Wimpole Street consulting rooms at four thirty in the morning, Peter Hanson told himself it was because he knew he wasn't going to get any sleep and so he may as well get some work done. He didn't believe it but it sounded a hell of a lot better than the truth. Punching in the key code on the box to his left, he silenced the alarm that had started beeping and then flicked on the light switch illuminating the hallway with a soft yellow glow. Ignoring the door to his left that led to the reception area, he walked to the end of the corridor and around the corner to his office, his shoes making gentle crunching sounds on the thick carpet, echoing in the silence when he stopped at the mahogany door.

As he looked down to turn the large brass key, allowing him access, he felt the heaviness of his eyelids. I am completely exhausted. What am I doing? I must be crazy to have come here when I could have been in bed, asleep with a beautiful woman who for some reason still loves me after all these years. It's the middle of the night and I'm at work and all because of a dream.

Ludicrous as he felt, he didn't turn back. He was here now so what would be the point, and anyway, it wasn't just any dream, it was so vivid and strange, and she had been so insistent in it that as soon as he was fully awake curiosity began nibbling hungrily at his brain and there was only one way to satisfy it. Get himself out of bed and go to the office. So here he was. Still in the doorway he could just about make out his desk in the gloom, a hulking beast hunched over on thick sturdy legs, almost alive in the darkness.

Rather than turn on the overhead light, he headed toward it and then clicked the switch on the black cord running down the side. The gold and green desk lamp sprang to life, filling a surprisingly large amount of space with white halogen light, but still, he couldn't help looking at it with distaste. It, like most of the other furnishings in this rented building, was a little too ostentatious for his tastes. He preferred the modern no-nonsense feel of his office at the hospital, but as his colleagues who shared 48 Wimpole Street were quick to point out, private patients in London expected a little more for their money, with regards to decor, than your average GP's clinic.

Silly as it seemed to him, after a couple weeks of being viewed with mild distaste and distrust by exceedingly wealthy middle-aged ladies, he'd given in and conformed to the status quo, investing in plush red carpets and gilded mahogany furniture. He even found he dressed differently on his private surgery days, much to the amusement of his wife. She had a point but he figured that everyone prostituted themselves in one way or another and at least he'd sold out in a way that benefited the majority, and even though she didn't really approve of the private practice, he noticed with amusement that her morals didn't stop her spending the extra money.

He'd often wished himself that he could give it up and just concentrate on his NHS work at the hospital where he felt much more at home, but financially, that had never become viable, and now the two days a week he spent here were an inherent part of his routine, and he had to admit, it was nice to have a workplace that was entirely his own. Somewhere to store and study his files without fear of being interrupted by some other overworked doctor needing a spare pair of professional hands. Yes, he couldn't really fight it, there were definite benefits to spending a couple of days in the private sector.

Pulling open the top drawer of the desk, he took out the pair of reading glasses and put them on. He tried to keep a pair in each office and one in his briefcase so he would never be caught without. With a tinge of sadness he remembered the days when his sight had been twenty-twenty, even at the end of an eighteen-hour shift in casualty. That was all a long time past now. Just where did all those years go?

He went over to the filing cabinet and unlocked it, seeking out the Ws. It didn't take long to find what he was looking for and taking Rachel Wright's file out, he slammed the drawer shut and headed back to his desk. As he sat in the large leather chair, he tilted his head, sure for a moment that he'd heard a sound coming though the wall. Something like the tinkling of breaking glass. Listening intently he heard nothing else, and shrugged it off. Probably his imagination, or even a drunk staggering along the street outside back to his favorite doorway to sleep away the rest of the night, dropping an empty bottle as he went. The surgery hadn't had a break-in during the ten years he'd been resident here, and it would be mighty unlikely for that to occur on the one night he happened to be here at some ungodly hour in the morning.

Stifling a yawn, he turned his mind back to the task at hand and opened the buff folder. Okay, Ms. Wright, here I am. So what am I going to find in here that I haven't seen before? No answer came to him as he glanced over the top sheet of paper, and he wondered if he'd perhaps overreacted to the strength of the dream.

Not that he'd thought for a second that he'd been getting a message from Rachel while he slept; he'd never been into hocus-pocus like that, but he had thought that his subconscious had maybe been trying to get a message through to him, to point out some obvious cause for her amnesia that his conscious hadn't noticed. Those kind of things he did believe in. And it wasn't as if this case hadn't been bothering him. He was a man that was used to getting results, he was a specialist in several fields of medicine and had always, but always, come top of the class in exams. Sure, he knew he was a fallible human, no chance of a God complex with him; but it was rare he couldn't find the cause of something, even if he had no chance of finding the cure. However, as far as he was concerned, the lovely Rachel Wright's amnesia was still a mystery. And although she didn't seem at all bothered by that, it frustrated the hell out of him.

And then tonight he'd had the dream, the dream with Rachel in, where she'd been sitting on the other side of this desk and adamantly telling him that the answer was in the file. Over and over again. "That's where you'll find it, Doctor. The answer's in the file. You just have to look. The answer's in the file." It had been like a scratched record, her looking at him so earnestly, saying those lines repetitively, each time as if it were the first, her inflection and tone identical time and time again. He'd never had a dream like that, with no action, no movement of any kind, just one person speaking the same sentences at him, like a clip of a video that won't stop showing.

Drumming his fingers on the large old-fashioned ink blotter, he bit back his irritation. He'd been positive that it had to mean something, it was so weird that it just had to, but now he was here it seemed his mind had duped him. The familiar words in his handwriting looking back at him from the sheet of paper weren't offering any moments of revelation, and the sinking feeling in his stomach was telling him that that was the way it was probably going to stay.

Sighing, he rubbed his hands over his face, lamenting the loss of a good night's sleep and closed the file. Despite Ms. Wright's nocturnal protestations, there were no answers to be found here tonight and he was feeling a bit stupid for having believed otherwise and dragging himself out of bed and across town in the process. He allowed himself a small wry smile. Oh well, he was here now with the busy day approaching so he may as well give himself a head start. Leaving Rachel's file forgotten where it lay, he opened the large diary on the desk to check what appointments were coming up this morning.

The unexpected knock at the silent door made him jump out of his skin, his heart stopping completely for the length of a few beats, before starting to race as quickly as if he'd been running a marathon. The sound echoed in his ears as he stared at the solid mahogany in disbelief. He couldn't have heard it. He couldn't.

"Sweetheart, are you in there?"

Relief flooded through his veins. Caroline. It was Caroline. Of course it was. She must have woken up and realized he was here and followed him. Still staring at the door, he didn't get up. His body felt glued to the chair. But how the hell did she get in? His keys were in his pocket, he could feel the weight of them there and there wasn't another set at home. Why would she have got up and come after him? It didn't make sense. How would she know he wasn't at the hospital? She would have called before leaving, surely. The door handle started to turn and he shivered with an unease he couldn't explain.

Her voice slipped through the opening gap, and he realized with horror that it wasn't her at all.

"I brought the children, Peter. All the children. They wanted to see you. There's something they want from you." The voice changed, as if unable to maintain the impersonation and became deep and gravelly and he knew more than anything that he didn't want to meet whoever owned that voice. "Something you owe them. It's time to give them what they want, Dr. Hanson. Give them back what you took."

Frozen in his chair, the guilt of years gone past rose like bile in his chest. No, it couldn't be, it couldn't be. He hadn't done anything illegal, abortion was legal, and after they'd found out Caroline couldn't have children, he'd quit, he couldn't work at the clinic anymore, and it was all such a goddamn long time ago, he'd done *good* things with his life, good things, he'd saved lives for Christ's sake. *I'm still in my bed at home. Or I've fallen asleep at my desk. I'm still dreaming, that's what it is. I'll wake up soon. It's just a dream.*

"But you didn't save these lives, did you?" The words cut through his thoughts, and behind them he could hear hundreds of chattering sounds, distorted noises from things that had never learned to speak, but they were eager, eager and excited, he could hear that. Oh God, he could hear that.

As the door opened wider, the smell hit him, the smell of blood, black blood, and he moaned as he saw the first deformed shapes slithering toward him. *I don't want this dream anymore. It's too real, it's too real.* It wasn't possible that he was seeing them, but he knew what they were. He'd seen enough of them in his time. Watching in denial, knowing that although this was a dream, a terrible horrible dream, he probably should be *doing* something, at least getting out of this goddamn chair would be a start, a start to *getting away*, he saw that the fetuses that couldn't really be coming his way, ranged from six weeks to sixteen, some no more than revolting red clumps sliding impossibly on his thick carpet, others dragging themselves with small stumpy limbs and bulging heads, tiny mouths open, insanely gurgling.

He could sense that something had come through the door behind them, something terrible, but he knew that if he looked up, if he *saw* it, then he would have to acknowledge that this wasn't a dream at all, and he couldn't do that, no way.

"They want their flesh, Doctor. They want their living flesh."

The door slammed shut, and he could hear that terrible laugh filling the corridor outside. Inside the room, the awful chattering had stopped, and the silence spurred him into movement. Maybe if he was very careful, he could make his way slowly to the door, he could get away, he could get home.

His breath felt loud and real in his chest as he eased back the chair and raised himself up on shaky legs, trying to keep his eyes fixed on the door ahead of him, and not the sea of madness and unborn life that covered the carpet. In the periphery of his vision he could see the proudly framed certificates that covered the walls, proclaiming his excellence to everyone who entered. *I've worked too hard. I've worked too hard and I'm having a breakdown.* Having crept round the side of the desk, he hesitated as he lifted his foot and heard a ripple of excited, wet murmuring coming from beneath him. He almost let out a giggle himself. *I'm trapped. I'm trapped in my office by a gang of fetuses wanting revenge. They want their living flesh. It is insane. I am insane. But there's nothing to worry about, because I know something that thing outside doesn't. They have no teeth. Dead babies have no teeth. All bark and no bite. Ha ha.*

Somewhere between sanity and madness, he confidently lowered his foot onto the pulp below him, crushing it. The screech of pain coming from beneath his sole, was taken up and echoed by those hundreds of others around him as they surged forward, saliva dripping from their unformed mouths, the larger, *the older* among them reaching him first, climbing over the rest to start clambering up his trouser legs in a mockery of infant attention, clinging to him, demanding and needy.

Trying to haul himself across the room, the weight of his passengers increasing every second as more and more reached for him, knocking him off balance, the doctor felt his panic rise almost as he felt the first exquisite stab of pain in his ankle. *I'm not going to make it,* he thought with disbelief, as he saw how impossibly far away the door seemed, and how impossibly many of these things were reaching him, pulling him to the ground. *I'm really not going to make it.* Falling to his knees, he felt searing, hot pain engulf both his legs, and with eyes wide looked down and realized his terrible mistake. *Dead babies have no teeth. But dead babies don't come in search of living flesh. They don't come to get what's owed to them.*

The babies were eating him all right, teeth or no teeth, there was no doubt about that, he could see them, he could *feel* them, their saliva like acid dissolving his flesh to liquid greedily sucked up. He noticed with mild disdain that his blood was staining the expensive red carpet in large expanding dark patches, and momentarily wondered if he would ever get it out. It was only a matter of seconds before reality set in and he began to scream.

CHAPTER EIGHTEEN

"Daddy, Daddy, come and get in the water!"

Sebastian had his hands on his hips, just above the waistline of last year's Postman Pat swimming trunks as he called out excitedly. Janet had only just started filling the paddling pool with water from the hose, but both kids had immediately jumped in, eager to start splashing. Squinting in the sunshine, Murray laughed and shook his head from his seat on the steps leading down to the garden from the back door.

"I think I'll wait till it warms up a bit, thanks all the same! Anyway, there's no room for three in there!" It had taken him almost half an hour to blow the thing up with the bicycle pump and he was enjoying the rest, letting the sweat cool between his skin and T-shirt. Samantha's now untidy ponytail bobbed up above the rim of the blue rubber, where she was lying on her belly. "Pleeeease, Daddy!" She coughed and giggled as water from the hose splashed her face.

Watching them, he couldn't help but smile. It was amazing the resilience that children had. It was his day off and so this morning they'd gone to put fresh flowers on Emily's grave; him, Janet and the kids, solemn-faced talking to the cold white stone. Was it really three months since she'd died? Sometimes it seemed like yesterday, and others it seemed like she'd been gone forever. What he realized, sitting here on this glorious summer's day, was that whether he liked it or not, and a big part of him didn't, they were starting to heal.

The twins' dark moods lifted almost as soon as they'd left the cemetery, and if he was honest, his had followed after they suggested getting the paddling pool out. His heart still ached, that was for sure, and he wasn't beyond the odd private bout of midnight tears, but he knew that they'd reached the stage of acceptance. They were now quietly going about the business of getting their lives back together, and although in his heart that felt like a betrayal, he also knew it was just nature running its course. It was the way things had to be. It sucked, that he couldn't deny, but it was natural. Why beat himself up about something he could do nothing about? He had enough to get angry with himself about in Suzy Jenner's as yet unsolved murder and Elizabeth Ray's crazy, disjointed rambling journals.

When she'd left them under the floorboards for him to find, she'd done a pretty good editing job on them first, tearing out pages, cutting out names, so really all he was left with were details of this insane ritual, that apparently Callum Burnett and Helen Holmes were integral parts of. There was enough in the rest, however, to know that she'd done a lot of harm to a lot of innocent people from the death of her father, right up to her own death or suicide or whatever you'd want to call it. He wasn't sure if psychopathic was a big enough word to cover it. He shivered, despite the heat. Enough of that. This was precious time off. Not to be spent thinking about work.

There were more screeches and squeals from the lawn.

Janet, face protected from the sun by a tatty blue baseball cap and wearing a pair of denim cutoff shorts had stepped into the paddling pool and was spraying the kids with the hose, holding her thumb over the hole so that the water emerged in a spray. She moved it from Sam to Sebastian, backward and forward, hitting them equally, but careful not to get their eyes. "Do you promise to tidy up your rooms and put all your toys away?"

The twins were choking with laughter as they slid over the rubber trying to escape the hose. Somewhere in all the excited chatter were shrieks of "Yes, yes, yes!"

Still standing in the center of the pool, Janet fought back her own laughter as she attempted to maintain her stern voice. "Do you promise to do everything I say?" For a moment she held back the hose, and the two children huddled together, giggling. After a few seconds' pause, they shouted out together, "No!" and braced themselves for the watery attack they knew was to come.

"Wrong answer!" Janet yelled before moving in close and spraying their balled-up figures, shouting for surrender, not caring about the fact she was getting almost as much water on herself as on them.

"Get Daddy! Get Daddy!" It was Sam who started the cry, but it was only a fraction of a second longer before Sebastian had joined in, his voice louder and stronger than hers. "Get Daddy, get Daddy!"

Jim laughed, until he saw Janet straighten up, her smile mischievous beneath her hat. "What a good idea. Let's get Daddy!" She stepped out of the rubber pool, her bare legs and feet dripping on the grass and started to walk slowly toward him. The kids were side by side in the water, two peas in a pod watching with glee.

Murray stood up amused, cautiously watching her. "You wouldn't dare, Janet Bryce."

Twirling the end of the hose so that the water flew in a circle in front of her, Janet stood with her spare hand resting on one slim jutting hip. She raised an eyebrow. "What are you scared of, you big brave policeman. It's just water." Taking another step forward, her smile stretched into a cheeky grin, and Jim caught a glimpse of the woman she could be without the weight of all her grief. "Very cold water, I'll give you that, but just water all the same." She paused as their eyes met. "Don't tell me you're a chicken. More chicken than a couple of kids?"

He heard the twins giggling, enjoying this play between the grown-ups, and then heard Sebastian shouting. "Daddy's a chicken! Daddy's a chicken! Get him Nana Janet, Get him!"

Laughing to himself, he turned to look at his kids. "Look you two—" That was as far as he got before the shock of the cold water hit him, filling his right ear and covering the side of his body. He let out a shriek of his own, goddamn that was cold, and from the corner of his eye caught a glimpse of the twins clapping their hands and bouncing up and down with glee.

Holding his hands up against the spray, he turned toward his attacker, his whole body soaked now, and moved toward her, turning his head to one side so he could open his eyes. "That was a big mistake!" He called over the sound of the spray that was filling his ears. "Assaulting a police officer is a very serious offense!" He heard Janet laughing and then her surprised squeal as he leaped toward her, feeling the dampness of her T-shirt as it slipped through his fingers.

"Run, run, he's going to get you! Run, Nana Janet!" Murray had a feeling Janet didn't need the encouragement of the midget chorus, as he saw her sprinting away to the far side of the garden, face flushed and excited, still clinging to the hose. She waved it at him triumphantly. "You'll have to be quicker than that, old man!" She tried to spray him again to reinforce her point, but the water wouldn't reach that far and instead she gave the twins a shower.

Glancing at the ground, Murray noticed that the length of hose was running past his feet. He gave Janet a sly smile before dropping to a crouch and gripping it tightly. "Ah, but as old Chinese proverb says, there are many ways to skin a cat. And sometimes strength is a better advantage than speed." Standing up, still holding the hose firmly, he gave a sharp tug. Janet's victorious smile dropped as the weapon slipped through her grasp, and Jim quickly reeled it in. It was his turn to twirl it like a baton. "Now what was that about being a chicken?" Thumb over the end, ready for his launch, he moved toward her.

Janet backed away, around to the other side of the paddling pool, her hands up in supplication, eyes wide and innocent. "Come on Jim. Think seriously about this. Would you really attack a poor old grandmother?"

Looking at her, he let out a laugh. Standing there, she looked more like a teenager than a grandmother, her legs slim and toned beneath the frayed edges of her shorts, the dampness of her pink T-shirt, clinging to her trim torso. For a moment he felt a stirring of attraction, and quickly squashed it, shocked by himself. That was a place he had no right to go. He brought his eyes back up to her face and raised the hose. "What do you think?"

She screamed as the water hit her, feet dancing on the spot as she jumped around, trying desperately but in vain to get out of the range of the jet. Jim waited until she was completely soaked before lowering the hose. Laughing, Janet wiped her face and coughed. "You bastard!" She spluttered. "You utter bastard!"

Samantha looked up at her father inqusitively. "What's a bastard, Daddy?" The two adults exchanged a look and then burst into laughter. Murray squatted at the side of the paddling pool and kissed his daughter's forehead. "I am apparently."

Janet stepped over the side of the rubber and sat down, submerging her shorts. She looked at Sam conspiratorially. "Suffice it to say, it's something all men have a tendency toward." Sam looked more confused than she had at the beginning, and Janet smiled. "I'll explain when you're older."

Sebastian cocked his head. "Phone ringing." Turning toward the open back door, Murray realized his son was right. Ignoring the sinking feeling in his stomach, he trotted back inside hoping it would be something other than work dragging him away from this sunny afternoon's fun. He didn't get his wish.

The shadow fell across the doorway as he put the phone down, and he turned to see Janet standing there. Obviously, his expression said everything she needed to know. "Have you got to go to work?"

He sighed and nodded. They'd been planning to finish the day with a barbecue, but that was going to have to go on hold. He looked for some sign of reproach in Janet's face, but found none. She shrugged. "Don't worry. I'll tell them you've got to go and save the world again. I'll give them hot dogs and ice cream for tea, that should soften the blow."

He nodded at her, not ready for humor, however well-intentioned. Not after what he'd just heard. Another dead body. More broken mirrors. Maybe there'll be a goddamn clue there this time. "I'd better go and get changed." He started to walk away when he felt her hand on his wet shirt.

"If you ever want to talk about it Jim, I'm here. I'm tougher than I look you know." He looked into her earnest face, the face that he now saw as an entity in its own right, rather than a pale imitation of Emily's, and leaned forward to kiss her on the cheek. "Janet, you're the toughest woman I've ever met." His naturally soft voice was so gentle tears formed at the corner of her eyes. "And thank you. I may well take you up on your offer." He could feel her watching him as he turned to head upstairs for his clean clothes and got the feeling that Janet understood him better than he'd figured.

Just over an hour later all thoughts of his family were gone as he stood in the reception room at 48 Wimpole Street idly studying the fragments of glass that were all that was left of the large somewhat ornate mirror that hung behind the secretary's desk. Behind him, he could hear the scurryings of the forensics team as they finished taking fingerprint samples from the wooden door that looked as if it had been broken outward, the lock hanging uselessly from the splintered mahogany. He felt tired already, which wasn't a good sign. Just what the hell had gone on here? And where the hell was Carter? He tried to subdue his impatience. It had been his sergeant's day off too, and he knew the man well enough to know that wherever he was, he was on his way here. Not that they could do much until the lab boys had finished. God, he was itching to get into the doctor's office. All he knew so far was that the body had been discovered by one of the man's colleagues first thing this morning. None of the other doctors who worked here knew of any reason why anyone would want to harm him. Apparently he was a brilliant man whose life revolved around his work, but wasn't involved in anything groundbreaking, no research or anything worth killing for. Not like *that* at any rate. He could almost feel the ghost of Suzy Jenner, there were so many parallels between the two. He heard a rustling behind him and turned around.

"Sorry to keep you waiting, Inspector. They're just taking the body out now, so his consulting room will be all yours soon." In his white, thin plastic suit, Andrew Mitchell, the coroner, was looking somewhat older than his forty-two years and Murray wasn't surprised. He was the same man who was struggling to explain Helen Holmes's cause of death and still hadn't been able to find a trace of any known sedatives in what was left of Suzy Jenner's blood.

Murray took small comfort in the fact that he wasn't the only one working on this bizarre case who felt as if they were floundering out of their depth. He didn't blame Mitchell for not coming up with the answers he so desperately needed. He didn't know the man well, but he knew enough of his reputation to know that if anyone could find them, Mitchell could. His brown eyes met the green of the other man's. "So what can you tell me? Cause of death? Time?"

Mitchell's thin smile was wry. "Thankfully, these things I can give you. I'm only glad that finding out the whys and wherefores is your department." He leaned back on the receptionist's desk and sighed. "Okay. Time of death somewhere between four and six this morning. I'll be able to be more precise when I've got him back to the lab. Cause of death I'd have to put down to some kind of acid. It's the only thing that could have dissolved the lower half of his body like that. We've taken some samples from the surrounding carpet so we should find out exactly what from those and the body."

Murray nodded, trying to hold his stomach together, glad he hadn't had time to eat before leaving home. He credited himself with being pretty hardened to death by this stage in his career but seeing what was left of the doctor face down on the carpet, arms outstretched as if trying to reach the door, had been like walking into Elizabeth Ray's attic. These things just weren't fucking normal, there was no other way to put it, and they reminded him that no one was that tough.

Mitchell looked as disturbed as he felt. "Oh, and one more thing. The damage wasn't just confined to the lower part of his body. When we turned him over we discovered that his tongue had been removed. That'd explain why his screams weren't heard."

Murray's brow furrowed. Out of the corner of his eye he saw John Carter enter the room, slightly out of breath, and he held one hand up to keep him at bay while he finished his conversation with Mitchell. "Any idea how it was removed?" This time it was Mitchell that seemed to be hanging on to his stomach and Murray felt sorry for him. It was all right for detectives to get queasy at the sight of bodies, but a coroner would never live it down throwing his lunch up at a crime scene.

"Oh, you're going to like this one. It was bitten off. Judging by the burns around the insides of the mouth I'd say there was acid involved too, but if you want my opinion, his tongue was eaten away. The bite marks are small, like a child's or an animal's. Not a big radius."

Murray wasn't convinced. "A child or an animal?"

Mitchell's laugh was mirthless. "Yes, I know it makes no sense." He looked around him. "I know as well as you do that neither child nor beast could do all this damage, but I'm just responsible for giving you the medical facts. It's your job to make sense of them." He put one arm on Murray's. "And I've got to tell you, with the deaths we've been getting recently I don't envy your part of the deal." He glanced over his shoulder and saw Carter hovering in the doorway. "I see your sergeant's here." Carter gave the man a nod of recognition, before the coroner turned his attention back to Murray.

"Well, as much as I'd like to help more, anything else at this time is purely conjecture. I'll be serving you better when I get back to my scalpels and test tubes. I'll let you or Carter know when the report is ready. Needless to say we'll be putting the hours in to get it done as soon as possible."

Murray shook the man's gloved hand. "Thanks Andrew." Mitchell waved his thanks away and headed for the door. Carter waited for the man to get past him before going to join his boss.

"Sorry it took me so long to get here, sir. I was at a barbecue in Richmond of all places and the traffic coming into town's a nightmare in this weather."

Now that his sergeant was here, Murray's irritation had dissipated and he was just eager to get on with his job. "Don't worry about it. Luckily, you've missed the body. If you've eaten today, then it probably wasn't something you'd really want to see."

"That bad?"

He raised an eyebrow at his young colleague. "Well, whoever this mirror-breaking lunatic is, we can safely say he's not lacking in imagination. This man Hanson's lower half was completely dissolved by acid. A few bones still there, but nothing you'd recognize. And to top it all, Mitchell thinks his tongue was eaten. Whatever happened to it, it's no longer in the good doctor's mouth. Charming, isn't it?"

Carter couldn't really think of anything to say to that, the mental image defying words apart from those that were obvious. "Sick bastard."

Murray let out a mirthless laugh. "I'd say that pretty much covered it." Watching the forensics team passing the doorway, he stepped out into the hall, avoiding the broken glass. "Come on, then. Let's go and see what we find in his office."

Empty of police, the only sign of the terrible events of the early hours of this morning in the doctor's office was the large dark stain, a deeper burgundy than the rest of the carpet, where his mutilated body had been found. Carter's eyes lingered on it a moment, before moving upward to the walls, examining the multitude of framed certificates hanging there. He let out a low whistle. "He liked to learn, didn't he?"

Murray, who had been lingering in the doorway trying to picture the scene, nodded, and joined his sergeant. "Oh yeah. He was a brilliant man. No dodgy African universities up there. I think the way they would put it in the medical world would be: widely respected among his colleagues."

Carter frowned slightly. "Any of them jealous enough to kill him?"

Murray shook his head. "I doubt it. Anyway, that wouldn't explain all the similarities with the Ray and Jenner cases."

He moved over to the desk where the diary was open at today's date, and glanced through the unfamiliar names and appointment times. Rolling his bottom lip between his fingers, he mused aloud.

"So what made him get up and come here in the middle of the night? He didn't have an emergency call, that much we do know, so what was on that clever mind of his?" He looked up at Carter. "Get in that filing cabinet and get the files for all these patients. You never know, we might get lucky." He didn't feel convinced. All of these people had been contacted to prevent them turning up at the surgery, and none of them had left the country or seemed at all suspicious in their responses, but they had nothing else to go on and they had to start somewhere.

His sergeant nodded and started to move toward the tall wooden unit against the wall when a section of brown paper sticking out from under the diary caught his eye. "What about that one? Are they on today's appointments?"

Murray looked down at where Carter was pointing and pulled the file out from under the oversized diary, cursing himself for not spotting it first. Carter, who knew what a perfectionist his boss was, smiled. "One of the advantages of youth, sir. Twenty-twenty vision."

Murray didn't respond, turning the loose pages over on the desk in front of him. Forgetting the filing cabinet, Carter stood next to him. "Sir?"

There was a long pause before Murray spoke. "Sergeant, I think I might just recommend you for promotion, smart alec remarks or not." His heart was pounding in his chest as the information he'd been so desperate for flooded out at him from the paper, and when he looked up at Carter, his eyes were shining with excitement. Closing the file, he held it up to the other man. "It's the link. It's the fucking link!"

Carter was looking confused. "Sir?"

Murray let out a short laugh. "Rachel Wright. The name started ringing bells the minute I saw it, but I wasn't sure why. Not until I looked at the first page. Adoptive parents, Douglas and Margaret Wright, died in car crash last year. You see it?"

Carter, who had the paper in front of him, nodded. "Yeah, but I don't get it."

Murray stood up, his foot tapping, the excitement reaching his extremities.

"Ah, but you didn't read Elizabeth Ray's diaries, did you?

If you had, you'd know that when she was twelve she had a baby. Apparently it was the result of rape by her father." He paused for a second. "The child, a daughter, was adopted by Doug and Peggy Wright, friends of her mother. Peggy's an abbreviation of Margaret." He gave Carter a second to let the information sink in. "And I bet if we did the maths, the year Rachel Wright was born would be the year that Ms. Ray was twelve years old. It's sure as hell got to be worth looking at."

Murray's mind was racing as his sergeant browsed through the file. Elizabeth Ray's daughter, alive and well, and a patient of Dr. Hanson. For the first time, since all this business had begun, his gut was telling him that they were finally on the right track. They had a lead, and a damn good one at that.

"Holy shit."

Carter's exclamation brought Murray's attention back. "What is it?"

The young man was still staring at the paper in his hands, but slowly brought his eyes up. "What was the name of the publisher Suzy Jenner worked for?"

"Jackson and Brown. Why?"

"That's what I thought." Carter's eyes met Murray's, his voice calm, only the erratic movement of his adam's apple betraying his rising elation. "No prizes for guessing where Rachel Wright worked until recently. Jackson and fucking Brown."

Murray stared at his colleague. Like a jigsaw, the mess they had started with was slowly taking shape as distinct pieces. The puzzle wasn't ready to put together yet, not by a long chalk, but at least they were getting the border of the picture connected, ready to fill in at a later date.

"There's more. This is going to interest you. Dr. Hanson treated Rachel Wright when she was brought into casualty after being discovered in the bathroom of her flat, collapsed and unconscious just over two months ago. When she came around, he discovered she was suffering from amnesia. She doesn't remember anything about herself or her life from before that night. But this is the good bit. The night she was found, a neighbor called the police because he heard her screaming. When the police got there, although she was unconscious there was no sign of a struggle or a break in. But there was one odd thing. The mirror in her bathroom cabinet was smashed."

Murray looked at Carter for a long time before he spoke. "Is there a pub near here?"

Carter nodded. "There's one on New Cavendish Street, just around the corner. Quiet place."

"Good. Let's go then. And bring that file and a notebook and pen. We've got some figuring out to do."

Tempted as they were to take their pints out to one of the tables on the pavement, what they had to discuss required privacy, and the early finishing workers were consuming that area, determined to enjoy whatever sunshine the temperamental British weather allowed, making it a little crowded. Still, it was warm enough inside, and as they sat in a booth at the farthest corner from the old-fashioned bar, Murray took off his suit jacket and hung it over the back of his chair before loosening his tie and undoing the top button of his white shirt. He felt better immediately, hating the restrictive feeling of the clothes he was required to wear. It could have been worse. He could have been in uniform division. Thankfully those days were but a dim and distant memory. He took a long and grateful sip of the cool, dark beer before starting to speak.

"Okay. So this is what we've got. We'll take it as read that Rachel Wright is Elizabeth Ray's daughter." Carter had called into the incident room on their walk down here and a PC there was checking the birth details, but both men were believers that coincidences rarely happened in real life and that the records would just confirm what they already knew. He leaned his elbows on the table. "So, Ms. Wright collapses in her bathroom suffering convenient amnesia and her bathroom mirror is broken. What difference between her and the victims Suzy Jenner and the doctor?"

Carter exhaled smoke. "She's very much alive, and apart from the memory sustained no visible injuries."

"Right. Does anything else strike you about her collapse?"

Putting his cigarette in the ashtray, the sergeant scanned the pages of the file, muttering the details to himself as he read them. Murray prompted him. "Look at the date."

A dimple appeared in John Carter's left cheek as he smiled. "February the second. Three days before the discovery of the bodies at Elizabeth Ray's house."

"Exactly. And given Mitchell's albeit hazy conclusions on the death of Helen Holmes, what does that tell you?"

The two men's eyes met in a moment of mutual understanding. "He figured she'd been dead two or three days. The same for Burnett."

Murray's eyebrow raised. "She collapses on the night that those two in all probability died. Interestingly coincidental, wouldn't you say?"

Carter's eyes were drawn back down to the file, as if to confirm their thoughts. "So you think this girl could be the one? Our killer? Do you think she could be capable of doing those things?"

Murray shrugged behind his pint glass. "That's what we've got to ascertain. Maybe she did it alone, they say a madman has the strength of ten men and given the things I've seen over the past two decades, I wouldn't disagree. Maybe she's got an accomplice. The mother managed to rope one in, so why not the daughter? Maybe she didn't do it at all, but she's definitely connected one way or another." The two men clinked their pint glasses in agreement. Putting his down, Murray leaned back against the worn padding of the red velvet seat. "What did the profiler make of the broken mirrors?"

Carter raised both blue eyes heavenward into his freckled forehead. "The usual stuff. The perp could have smashed them for one of two reasons. The first, and least likely, is that he was revolted by his actions. Kills the victims and then breaks the mirrors out of remorse for his deeds. The second—"

Murray held up a hand to interrupt him. "Why is that least likely?" The soft voice was in direct contrast to the sharpness of those brown eyes.

"Apparently, that kind of self-loathing, the loathing of your deeds rather than your self tends to occur mainly where there has been some kind of sexual motivation behind the murder. And although the deaths we've got are plenty bizarre, he couldn't find any evidence of anything kinky. His second idea seems more fitting to our boy or girl. That is that the mirrors were broken by someone who was revolted by their very existence. Unable to stand the sight of themself to such a degree that you have to destroy the very object that reflects your image. So still a revulsion kick, but not by what they'd done, not a remorse thing. He seems to think our killer was beyond feeling guilt at what he'd done."

Murray's smile was small. "After seeing the bodies of Suzy Jenner and Hanson, I could have confidently told him that without the help of a fistful of degrees."

They sat in silence for a couple seconds before Carter let out a long sigh. "So what could cause something like that? What could make a person hate themselves that much?"

Murray drained his pint glass and handed it to his sergeant. "You fill those up and then when you get back from the bar, I'll run my theory by you."

Carter stood up, holding his own empty glass. "Are you sure, sir? Aren't you driving?"

The other man grinned. "Nope. You are. So you better make yours a shandy." Still smiling, he watched the slim young man muttering his way to the bar and enjoyed the few minutes to himself, gathering his jumble of racing thoughts into something coherent that he could share. God, it felt good to have something in this case that he could sink his mental teeth into. At last he had a lead that his gut told him was a good one, and the more he thought about it, the more right it felt. He waited until Carter had returned and was settled into his seat with a lit cigarette before he started.

"Okay. This is the way I see it. Last year, after the sudden death of the Wrights in that car crash, Rachel decides to seek out her natural mother and succeeds. I shouldn't imagine it would have been too difficult, after all, her adoptive parents had been friends of the family and they might have even told her her mother's name when she was growing up, or she may have come across it somewhere in their papers. Anyway, however it happened, let's say she is reunited with Elizabeth. What if Ms. Ray, who we know was probably not the sweetest of motherly figures, tells her newly recovered daughter that her father is also her grandfather. Elizabeth would probably have enjoyed seeing the pain that caused Rachel, and that kind of information alone could seriously damage someone's mental health."

Carter was nodding as he waited for Murray to light a cigarette of his own. "Yeah, that makes sense, but I don't think that would be enough to bring on this kind of insanity."

Murray ran his hand through his dark fringe. "I agree. Now remember that this is all just ideas, but what if Rachel suddenly realized that Elizabeth was an insane deadly woman? She would have probably spent some time watching her mother's house before getting up the guts to introduce herself. She would more than likely have seen several people going into the house who *never came out*, but didn't put two and two together until later when she found out what a fruitcake her mother was. Maybe she found the bodies in the cellar. Maybe Elizabeth decided to share her secrets with her daughter. I wouldn't put it past her. However it happened, let's presume she discovers that her mother's hobby is serial murder, on top of the fact that she came into the world, completely unwanted as a result of incestuous child rape, born to a young girl who then killed both her parents as revenge."

He chewed his bottom lip as he watched his sergeant slowly picturing the scene. "Now call me old-fashioned, but I think that if you were a young woman out searching for your fairy tale ending, and you found all this, it would probably be enough to make you revolted by your very genetic structure, wouldn't it?"

Carter's eyes were serious. "It works for me, sir."

"I thought it might."

"But there is one thing that's bugging me. Elizabeth Ray was dead for several months before Rachel's collapse and the death of Callum Burnett. Surely if she was going to snap, she'd have done it when her mother died if not before?"

That's why Murray liked Carter so much. He might not always come up with the right answer, but he would always get stuck into the detail, and it was details that solved crimes, little details so often overlooked. And he made Murray work his mind, which he had to now.

"Right, to try and answer that we need to go back a step. What did we know about Elizabeth's death before Rachel came into the equation? Mostly what she told us herself in her diaries. And before you say anything, I know we've only got her word for any of it being true, but I'm inclined to go along with it because it's the only thing that makes sense in an insane kind of way." He paused to stub out his cigarette smiling at his colleague. "Now I hope you're paying attention because I'm going to now give your criminal profiler a run for his money."

Carter grinned. "Fire away."

"Elizabeth was very into the occult. Apart from the bookshop, she'd spent a lifetime of study on the subject. As well as this she has the unshakable belief from childhood that she's different, special. She seems to think she can see inside people's minds, that kind of crazy stuff. Anyway, at some time in this life of murder and madness, she comes across a book. A very old book in which she finds a ritual that allows you to come back from the dead by taking over someone else's body."

Carter rested his elbows on the table. "Is that what she wanted Helen Holmes for? To take over her body?"

Murray shrugged the question away. "Who knows? She didn't really go into detail in her diaries. She was very secretive about it. Anyway, you and I and every sane man in London would know it was a load of rubbish, but she's a very deluded individual with a massive ego and sense of importance and she falls for it—hook, line, and sinker. She spends weeks studying every chapter, every word, until she can probably recite every page from heart."

"Sounds like a good book to have. I don't suppose we found it in the house did we?

Murray picked up on the sarcasm in the younger man's voice. "No such luck. Apparently she burned it so we've got no chance of seeing it, and I don't really think it's the kind of thing we're going to find on the library shelves. Thankfully we don't need it; it's enough to know that she believed in it, she was fascinated by the concept, and when the day came where she finds lumps in her breasts, rather than go to her GP, like a sane person, she thinks, 'This is it! My destiny!' Not for her the rotting and inconsequential deaths that the rest of us mere mortals have to suffer. No, not her. She will return, rising up like Lazarus, stronger and more powerful than she was before. She would conquer death and make him her plaything."

"Very poetic, sir."

Murray laughed. "I do have my moments. But credit where it's due, most of those phrases came straight from Ms. Ray's diary.

"So, she wrongly diagnoses herself with cancer, one blessing for the rest of us, and goes about the business of preparing herself for taking her own life, albeit with Callum Burnett's help. He slits her throat and drains her blood. According to the lab, Helen Holmes had some in what was left of her stomach, so he must have stored it and been feeding it to her for weeks before she died. It must have been part of the ritual. All of this we know, right?"

Carter nodded, and Murray leaned forward. "So maybe when Rachel turned up she shared her plans with her. Maybe she thought that when she came back from the dead, they'd continue to forge their relationship."

"Surely Rachel would have seen how crazy it was and tried to talk her out of it. Make her go to the doctor at least."

Murray smiled and shook his head knowingly. "Not if she wanted her mother to die. If she hated her that much this would seem like a godsend and she'd go along with it, claiming to believe, encouraging Elizabeth. Helen was probably installed in the attic by the time Elizabeth died and maybe watching her mother die gave her a thrill she hadn't been expecting. Maybe it was then that she started to enjoy watching people's suffering. Whatever she felt, she could hardly let Helen go. As far as that girl was concerned Rachel was as bad as the others, she was hardly going to listen to Rachel's version of events, was she? No, I think Rachel waited until Callum had killed Helen and then she killed Callum by slipping him some as yet undetected heart attack-inducing drug. I presume she must have done that while at her mother's house."

"Why?" Always Carter with the questions.

"Because there were no mirrors smashed at Burnett's flat, but there were at Elizabeth's house." He was starting to think out loud now, just letting the thoughts have free rein. "So maybe Callum was the first person she'd actually killed and then she goes home and collapses with the strain of what she's done, smashing the mirror, not wanting to feel that she's become like her mother, and then claims amnesia at the hospital as there's no way she can explain the truth."

Having finally finished, he leaned back and took a long drink of his beer. Carter remained silent, and he gave the man a few moments before impatience took over. "So, what do you think?"

Carter's young face looked as if it couldn't decide

whether to laugh or not. "Well, you've got my vote. That's certainly some theory. The question is: do you think it'll check out?"

Murray laughed out loud. Of course he didn't expect it to check out, there were holes in it a mile wide and they hadn't been that lucky with this investigation, why should things change now? His answer was nothing if not honest. "Who the fuck knows? But there's only one way to find out. Has that file got an address on it?" He nodded at the brown folder in front of Carter, who opened it and scanned the first page before looking up smiling.

"Certainly has. And guess what? She lives only a ten-minute walk from here. Luxborough Street off Paddington Street. The gods must be smiling on us."

Standing up and stretching, Murray picked up his jacket and slapped his sergeant gently on the back. "I wouldn't count your chickens just yet."

Dusk was settling in around them as they started their walk down to Marylebone High Street, but the air was still warm and the breeze felt good in Murray's hair, revitalizing his brain. He'd taken three of four steps before he realized Carter had stopped behind him.

"What is it, Sergeant? Forgotten something?"

Carter shook his head and caught his superior officer up. "No. Something just struck me. If Rachel Wright's our killer then that would explain something else."

Murray slowed down his pace, interested to hear what his sergeant had to say.

"What's that?"

"It would explain why Suzy Jenner opened her door in her underwear when we can find no trace of a mystery lover. She wasn't opening the door to a man at all. She was opening the door to a woman, a friend."

This time it was Murray who stopped walking. Of course, of course. They had never once until today considered that Suzy's killer could be anything other than a man, but now it seemed obvious. Carter was right. If Rachel Wright was a friend, then Suzy would let her in half naked, it wouldn't matter, would it?

He could see it now, Suzy pulling the door open, her head peering round in case her neighbors were on the stairs, smiling at her friend before saying, "Come in, come in. I'm just jumping in the bath. Help yourself to a glass of wine and then come and talk to me." And then she'd innocently turn her back and Rachel would strike with another as yet untraceable drug, immobilizing the terrified Suzy before killing her. He could feel the excitement rising in his stomach. If only those lab boys could come back with something, something concrete, then he'd probably feel confident enough to go for an arrest, but without that . . . Frustrated, he let the thought trail away. Concentrate on what you've got, he told himself. It's enough to be thinking about for the moment, and at least you've got a suspect.

He smiled at Carter. "One day young man, with clever thinking like that, you'll be in danger of promoting yourself into a desk job. That was one angle that hadn't even crossed my mind."

A flush spread up the pale Scottish skin, betraying the young man's pride in his boss's praise, and he covered it with his usual dry humor. "Oh, I have plenty of clever thoughts, sir. You just never let me get a word in edgeways."

Laughing, Murray lit a cigarette for both of them, and they strolled silently toward their destination.

CHAPTER NINETEEN

Murray took the lead as they walked two at a time up the narrow stairs inside the mansion block, eager to get to Rachel's flat. One of the other inhabitants had been leaving as they arrived so they hadn't had to buzz in from the outside entry phone and Murray was pleased that this would give them the advantage of surprise. He smiled grimly to himself. Maybe God was looking down on them, after all. Waiting for Carter to catch up, he pulled his police badge from his inside pocket before knocking on the door.

It was opened by a good-looking man in jeans and a T-shirt, probably in his early thirties, with light brown hair flopping slightly over his face reminiscent of that look made famous by Hugh Grant. His smile was open, if slightly puzzled. Murray showed him his badge.

"Sorry to disturb you. I'm Detective Inspector Murray and this is Sergeant Carter. We're looking for Rachel Wright."

A very slim and pretty girl appeared in the hallway behind her companion. "I'm Rachel Wright. Has something happened?"

Both the young faces were showing concern as the strains of gentle flamenco music blended with the smells of a just cooked roast dinner and wafted toward him, Murray felt a sinking sensation in his stomach. It all seemed a bit too goddamned normal for his liking. He smiled briefly. "Is it all right if we come in?"

They were led into the cozy sitting room and the young man hovered in the doorway. "Can I get you anything? Tea? Coffee?"

The two officers shook their heads. "We really wanted to speak to Ms. Wright alone." He registered the look of panic that flashed across both faces as if it were nothing out of the ordinary. That was how most people reacted to the police. *Especially if they don't have a clue what you're doing here*, his internal voice added

Rachel had sat down on the edge of the sofa, looking slightly pale. "I want Mike to stay. Will you tell me what's going on now?"

Ignoring her question, Murray turned to look at the young man. "Mike?" The man's brown eyes were only slightly lighter than his own but they had none of his own dark cunning and were instead gentle and caring. He held his hand out toward Murray.

"Mike Flynn. I'm Rachel's boyfriend. Well, boyfriend and neighbor. I live in the flat across the hall." He indicated with his arm. "I'm a schoolteacher."

Murray nodded, his unreadable expression giving nothing away as he mentally summed Mike up. The man was doing what most innocent people did when approached by the police. Giving them too much information. Answering questions that hadn't yet been asked. He wondered if this was the neighbor who called the police when Rachel collapsed. More than likely. There were only two flats on this floor. Putting his hands into his pockets, he nodded.

"Okay, you can stay. But I think you'd better sit down. What I've got to tell you isn't very pleasant."

Mike took a seat next to Rachel and held her hand.

"Doctor Peter Hanson was murdered in the early hours of this morning at his offices in Wimpole Street." He watched as the words hit the couple like a hard slap in the face. Rachel's eyes were wide as saucers as she gasped and clutched her mouth with her hands, trapping some of her loose dark hair, her eyes filling with tears of shock.

The blood drained from Mike's face as he muttered, "Jesus Christ, first Suzy and now this. What the hell's going on here?"

Carter had found the power switch to the stereo and silenced the Spanish guitarist before returning to an unobtrusive corner of the room with his notebook and pen.

Mike looked up at Murray, his face aghast. "He was definitely murdered? It couldn't have been an accident?"

The image of the doctor's body was still fresh in his mind and it made his voice almost sharp. "No. It was murder." He wondered how this schoolteacher would react to seeing a man who had been dissolved from the waist down and realized that he was already thinking of Flynn as innocent.

Rachel was rocking slightly, her arms protectively wrapped around her slight torso. "Could someone get me a glass of water, please? I feel a bit sick." Her voice was as small as she seemed and he couldn't help but wonder if she could have done these terrible things, before reminding himself that the fragile-looking, beautiful woman was also Elizabeth Ray's daughter, and so who knew what she was capable of? He waited for Carter to return with the drink and gave her a few minutes to sip the cool liquid.

"Thank you. I feel better now. It's such a horrible shock. Who would want to kill Dr. Hanson?" She asked this question as much to herself as to the police and Murray noticed with surprise that she did look better, the color returning to her face and her hands becoming steady again. She was back in control, unlike the teacher who looked like he was about to lose his lunch.

"That's what we intend to find out." His voice was at it's softest, as gentle and lilting as Mike Flynn's eyes. "Mike mentioned Suzy Jenner. How well did you know her?"

Rachel sighed and shrugged her shoulders, still looking at some faraway space. Eventually she brought her eyes around to meet those of the detective. Murray didn't think he'd ever seen such clear gray irises. They were startling, like looking into the faceted colors in a diamond, the cool sharpness of them turned a pretty girl into a beauty.

"It's hard to say really. Apparently I used to know her quite well, go out for a few drinks together, that kind of thing, but after my accident I never really felt we clicked. Her or my job." She glanced at him again. "I presume you know about my collapse and amnesia?" He nodded.

"We read your file in Dr. Hanson's office. It was on his desk, which surprised me slightly as you weren't on his list of patients for the day." He scanned her for some sign of acknowledgment or fear, but there was none. Instead, she smiled slightly.

"No, I saw him briefly at the hospital last week. My next appointment's not due for ten days or so, but I think he was very fond of me. Determined to get me my memory back, or at least find out what caused my collapse in the first place. Sometimes I think he is . . . sorry, he *was*, more eager than I am to find out what's behind the black wall in my mind."

"When did you last see Suzy Jenner?" Carter, who'd been almost invisible, silent against the far wall cut in, his Scottish accent making the question seem more abrupt. Murray wondered if it was intentional, an effort to unsettle the composed young woman. If it was, then it didn't work.

"I met her for lunch a couple weeks after I got out of the hospital. I don't remember the exact date, but it was after one of my appointments with Dr. Hanson. We had lunch in Soho and I told her I wasn't going to come back to work. I wanted to take some time out, rethink what I wanted out of my life. She was okay about it. It was nice." She paused and Murray thought he saw a shadow of something in her face, as if something about that lunch hadn't been very nice at all but she wasn't going to share it with them. Maybe the two women had exchanged unpleasant words. Maybe Suzy was upset at being cut out of her friend's life. Who knows?

"Anyway, that was it. That was the last time I saw her."

She waited until Carter had finished scribbling in his notebook before she spoke to Murray. "Is that it? Is there anything else you want to know?"

He wondered if there was just the hint of impatience in that voice and decided not to pull any punches with his next question.

"That's just about it for the moment. If you could just tell us where you were in the early hours of this morning, and also the night Suzy was murdered then we'll be on our way."

Rachel said nothing and just sat there staring at him, but then she didn't have much of a chance before Mike Flynn leaped to his feet, his face still pale and body shaking with emotion. "Look, just what the hell is this? Are you trying to say Rachel's a suspect or something? Because if so, then that's just bloody ridiculous! I mean, Jesus Christ, these people were her friends!" The young man ran a hand through his hair and looked from one policeman to the other with his desperate expression. Murray smiled at him gently.

"Please calm down Mr. Flynn, I'm not saying anything of the sort. But this is a very complicated case and we need to eliminate everyone who knew the victims from our enquiries. More important, Rachel is the only person we've come across so far that knew both Suzy Jenner and Peter Hanson." He watched as the information sank into the teacher. Yeah, that was a big one to swallow. The only person who knew both victims is your girlfriend. Think about that for a minute.

Mike flopped back onto the sofa, his anger and shock dissipating, and rested his head in his hands. It was Rachel who spoke, quietly but firmly. "Last night we were in Mike's flat asleep. We went to bed quite early and I didn't move until this morning." She raised an eyebrow teasingly at Murray. "I didn't even get up to go to the toilet."

Mike had raised his head and saw the look that flitted between the inspector and his sergeant.

"In case you were wondering," his voice sounded exhausted, the anger of moments ago completely vanished as if it had never been, "whether she snuck out in the night and murdered the good doctor while I was sleeping, I'm happy to tell you that she didn't."

"How can you be so sure?"

Flynn gave Carter a withering look. "Because ever since her collapse Rachel's been getting these bad dreams. Really bad dreams. They stopped for a while, but they've come back in the past couple weeks. Anyway, she woke me up at quarter to three this morning with her tossing and turning and I couldn't get back to sleep, so I got up and marked some essays." He lit a cigarette and inhaled hard.

Looking at him, Murray could see the dark circles around both their eyes and the slight hollows in their cheeks. Yeah, these were people who weren't getting enough proper sleep; he knew that well enough because it was a look his own face had had in the first weeks following Emily's death, a haunted look. Still, maybe they were looking tired because they were up all night burning the doctor away with acid. He glanced at their hands and exposed skin for any sign of burning. There wasn't any and he wasn't surprised. Rachel was a definite enigma, a cool fish, but the teacher seemed as straight up as a person could get. And if he wasn't involved then the odds were on that Rachel Wright really did spend the night in bed in the throes of a nightmare. Great, just what he needed. A dead end. None of this showed on his face.

"And the night of Suzy Jenner's death?"

Mike answered quickly. "We stayed in and had Chinese food."

Carter's scribbling stopped for a moment. "How can you be so sure of what you were doing over a month ago?

Rachel looked like she was having to think about it quite hard. How come you knew straightaway?" The sergeant was making no effort to hide the suspicion in his voice and it dawned on Murray that Carter still thought these two were in it together.

It was Mike's turn to smile, the creases in his cheeks making him seem like a man nearer forty than thirty. Something's aging him, Murray thought. Something's really wearing him out. I wonder if he even realizes?

"I've just got one of those morbid imaginations. We found out she was dead the Tuesday afterward. One of Rachel's old colleagues left a message on her answerphone while we were out visiting my aunt. I remember thinking, 'My God, we were happily tucking into Chinese while Suzy was fighting for her life somewhere.' I felt quite bad about it. It sent a shiver down my spine."

"Just the two of you then, sir?"

Murray could see what Carter was driving at, and had to admit the man had a point. On both nights this couple only had each other for an alibi. That would be enough to make any policeman's mouth water, and he wondered why his wasn't. It should be. It really should be.

It seemed that Flynn realized what Carter was implying because he let out a small laugh. "Yes, just the two of us. Again." His eyes narrowed. "But maybe the Chinese takeaway will have a record of the order. I paid for it with a cheque and guarantee card. They know me pretty well in there. They might even remember me coming in."

Carter was like a terrier with his teeth snapped round a wriggling rat. "For a young couple you two seem to spend an awful lot of evenings in."

Rachel gave the young sergeant an icy glare. "Yes, we do Sergeant. And that's because we love each other and we don't really need to go out clubbing and hanging around bars. Maybe you'll realize that one day if anyone is ever foolish enough to feel that way about you."

Carter looked taken aback, and smiling to himself Mur-

ray stepped in to calm things down before his sergeant got
involved in a slanging match with his suspect. Having seen
the composure of this young woman, he figured his colleague would probably lose.

"I'm sorry, Ms. Wright. I'm sure Sergeant Carter didn't
mean to offend you. He doesn't always have the best way
with words."

Rachel was still staring at Carter as if she hadn't heard a
word Murray had said. "Anyway, I'm supposed to be cutting
down on late nights and alcohol. I've just found out that
we're having a baby and somehow partying doesn't seem
that important anymore. We'd rather stay in and think
about names and schools and all that stuff."

Mike slid his hand back into hers and gave it a squeeze.
She turned to look at him and when she smiled all that
anger dissolved, in such a way that it made Murray's heart
ache. She was looking at Flynn the way Emily used to look
at him and the memory of it hurt him deep inside. It was
time to leave.

"Well, congratulations on your good news and I hope we
haven't taken up too much of your time."

Mike looked up, almost surprised that the interview was
over. "Is that it?" Murray nodded. "Oh, there was just one
more thing. I don't suppose the name Elizabeth means anything to either of you, does it?"

Behind their soft darkness, his eyes studied Rachel for a
reaction. There was none. She shook her head immediately, her face a blank. Mike, however, seemed slightly
more puzzled, but still replied in the negative before standing up and thrusting his hands awkwardly into his jean
pockets.

"I'll show you out then."

He led them out into the hallway and opened the front
door, chewing his bottom lip, as if unsure of whether to
speak or not. Murray held back, letting Carter go down the
stairs ahead of him, leaving him behind with the teacher

standing outside the flat. He looked into the worried face, and when he spoke his voice was a gentle as a lullaby.

"Look Flynn, I know an innocent man when I see one, and I see one when I look at you, so if there's something bothering you just tell me about it." He waited while Mike seemed to go through some kind of internal debate and then let out a sigh himself.

"There's two dead people out there that need me to lay them to rest. Two good people. Now if you don't want to help then that's up to you, but personally, I like to sleep at night."

He turned to walk away and Mike grabbed his sleeve. "It's stupid really, that's why I didn't know whether to mention it. It was about this Elizabeth thing."

Murray tried to look nonchalant. "What about it?"

Mike blushed slightly. "Well, this is really silly, but when I took Rachel to meet my aunt, that's what she called her. Elizabeth. I know it's nothing but it just felt a bit weird when you mentioned the name as well. Who is she, anyway?"

"Just another lead we're following up." Murray lingered for a second. "Do you think I could take your aunt's address? I know it's going to be nothing but I want to cover all the angles on this one." He pulled his own rarely used notebook and pen out of his inside suit pocket.

Looking uncomfortable, like a man who wished he hadn't opened his big mouth, Flynn gave him the address. "But look, she can't possibly know anything about any of this business. It was just one of those freaky coincidences."

Murray smiled and shook Flynn's hand before heading down the stairs to join his sergeant. Yeah, it probably was one of those freaky coincidences but what the hell, any lead was better than none at all.

Murray made the sergeant walk around the corner to the High Street before letting him talk about the interview. The last thing he wanted was that young couple looking out their window and seeing the police talking animatedly about their guilt or innocence, and anyway, he wanted a few moments in the warm, evening breeze to collect his own thoughts.

As soon as they turned out of Paddington Street, Carter lit a cigarette and beamed at his boss, almost hopping from one foot to the other. "Jesus H, what a pair of loonies! It's got to be them, sir, it's got to be. They haven't got an alibi for either night apart from each other and she knew both victims, which would account for the lack of forced entry at either location. It fits. It all fits. The teacher's her patsy, just like Callum Burnett was for her mother." He paused for a second, oblivious to Murray's reserved silence. "Do you want me to organize some surveillance on them? Just in case they decide to try and make a break?"

Lighting a cigarette of his own, Murray wasn't in the mood to share his doubts with the sergeant, but neither did he want the young man getting carried away. He shook his head. "No. I don't think that's necessary just yet. Baker'll do his nut if we waste money like that and don't get a result. We'll see whether we get any results back from the lab before we move. We need a presentable case." He saw the disappointment sink into Carter's face but it couldn't be helped. "What I need you to do now is go and dig up everything you can find on Flynn and Wright. I want you to know more about their lives than they do, do you understand?" Carter nodded, looking slightly appeased.

"Oh, and chase up Mitchell. I know he's doing his best, but we need some results from him soon." Murray started to walk away. "I'll catch up with you in the morning."

"Don't you want a lift?" Carter was calling after him, but he waved him away without even turning round.

Walking down to Bond Street tube station, he could see the sense in what Carter was saying but couldn't bring himself to agree. Even disregarding the teacher, that girl was too slim to have done those things. She wouldn't have the upper body strength to destroy the door in the surgery reception never mind restrain the doctor while soaking his lower body in acid. His smile was wry. I mean, who the fuck would be capable of something like that? And then there's the tongue, chewed away and probably eaten. He pushed the image away, not ready to think about that yet.

It was probably easier for Carter to be convinced about Rachel having not had the pleasure of seeing that particular corpse. Maybe I should send him down to the lab to take a look at it, he mused. That might make him a little less certain, even if he is still sure that Mitchell is going to find some kind of mysterious sedative floating around in the corpses. Having had the thought, he suddenly realized that he personally had given up hope on the lab solving this one for them. He wasn't sure when, but it was probably just about the time he'd laid eyes on what was left of that poor bastard Hanson.

He stopped outside the tube station and lit a cigarette, leaning back against a wall to get out of the way of the crowds. It was a long journey home, and he didn't want to make it without one last smoke.

Right, he thought dragging the nicotine deep into his lungs. What am I sure of in this whole mess of shit? It was only a second before the answer flashed in his brain. I'm sure that Mike Flynn is no killer. The man's in his thirties, old enough for any psycho tendencies to have emerged, but I'll bet this month's salary that all Carter's going to find on him is a clean sheet and glowing references. Yes, there'd been plenty of good men that had done terrible things out of love, but you'd have to be fucking insane in the first place to become an accomplice in this case, and Flynn might be bothered by something, but it's not a trail of dead bodies.

He sighed and rubbed his forehead. So if Flynn wasn't involved, then how the hell could Rachel Wright be? Christ, it seemed that for every answer he got, another ten questions sprang up to taunt him.

Throwing the cigarette to the ground, he pulled out his notebook and studied the address Flynn had given him.

Yes, it was probably going to be nothing, but somehow this little old lady had picked up the connection between Rachel and Elizabeth. Maybe her inadvertent name slip was to let Rachel know that she knew about her little secret? Maybe she was blackmailing her? Yeah right, he thought as he slid his change into the ticket machine. So, if she was blackmailing her then why the hell is she still alive?

Still, as many holes as he could find in the link with the old woman, he knew that her house was where he'd be going tomorrow morning. He didn't have that many options, but perhaps he wouldn't tell Carter about this tenuous lead unless it turned out to be something a little more concrete. He didn't want his sergeant thinking he was cracking under the strain. As he stepped onto the long, full escalator, breathing in the damp, odorous sweat of thousands of Londoners, he couldn't wait to get home.

CHAPTER TWENTY

Mike wasn't sure if he was going to be able to get to sleep, no matter how tired he was. God, his head was a mess. Rachel hadn't stopped sobbing after the police had left and even now as she slept, curled up like the baby inside her, he could see the red blotches on her cheeks left behind like some kind of temporary emotional scars. The news about the doctor had really upset her and he knew she'd cared about him, but he wondered how many of the tears were actually for him. It seemed, crazy as it sounded, as if she was terrified by his death, mortally terrified. She'd kept muttering, "What do you think they did to him? What do you think they did to him?" over and over until he wanted to shake her to make her stop. And who were "they"? Why hadn't she said "he"? That would have been more normal, surely?

Now you sound crazy, he told himself as he lit a cigarette in the darkness. What's your point? You know she couldn't know anything about it because she was here with you having another one of her dreams. It was the dreams, that's what it was. It was the dreams that were making him so goddamn edgy. Two blissful weeks without them and then wham bam, they were back with a vengeance. Only this time she'd taken to sleepwalking. Twice he'd caught her now as she was getting out of bed and the thought of that terrified both of them. What if she falls and hurts herself? What if she hurts the baby?

He wished he hadn't fallen out with Ruby because it was definitely time to get to the bottom of whatever was causing this, whatever memories were buried deep inside, and if it wasn't for their argument, he'd be dragging Rachel there by her hair if he had to. The end of the cigarette burned angrily as he sucked in. He felt a twinge of guilt at having mentioned the Elizabeth thing to that inspector, as if he'd betrayed Rachel somehow even if that was ridiculous. Smiling a little, he imagined what the police were going to make of Ruby. If they didn't think he was insane already, they would after meeting her.

Stubbing the unfinished cigarette out, he lay down and wrapped himself protectively round the warm female figure. What he needed was a good night's sleep he told himself for what seemed like the thousandth time since he'd fallen in love with this mysterious dark beauty. A good night's sleep and it'll all be better in the morning.

His eyelids slid shut like they'd been wanting to do ever since they'd opened this morning and as the weight flooded into his limbs he realized sleep might come more easily than expected.

"I think bad things are going to happen to people around her, I really do."

Ruby's prophetic words danced in his head, trying to get his attention, but he was already floating into sleep, and although his mouth twitched with the thought his brain didn't respond, choosing pleasanter subconscious pastures in which to drift.

He woke with a start and a gasp of breath from a nightmare of his own. He been drowning, drowning in some sticky substance he was sure was blood and no one would help him. Feeling the cool trickle of sweat running down his chest it took all his willpower not to turn the light on and check that the sheen on his skin didn't have a red hue. Slowly calming down, he leaned against the pillows feeling no movement from the side of him. Well, at least you didn't wake Rachel, he thought as he let out a long breath, even if it would have been fair. He put one hand down gently in the blackness to where her head should be and felt nothing. Just the coolness of the cotton pillowcase under his damp palm. He froze, his eyes searching her out in the darkness.

"Rachel?"

No answer. His hand felt farther down the bed and there was still nothing. "Oh no," he muttered as he pushed the covers away and stood up. The bed was empty in the gloom.

"Oh shit! Rachel?" He ran naked into the living room but from the glow of the streetlights outside, he could see she wasn't there. His heart beat rapidly in his chest. Where the hell was she? A high-pitched scratching sound caught his attention and he turned around to face the hall. He heard it again, like nails on a chalkboard. It was coming from the bathroom. What the hell was she doing in there? Cautiously, he padded barefoot out of the lounge and into the bathroom doorway. Even without the lights, he could see her, standing in front of the mirror concentrating on doing something that was causing that terrible noise. There was another sound too, and it took him a couple of seconds to realize what it was. She was humming to herself, humming some discordant tune. He caught a flash of steel in her hand and then there was that scraping sound that hurt his teeth.

Nail scissors, he thought stupidly. She's digging at the mirror with nail scissors.

"Rachel?" His voice sounded uncertain as he slowly stepped toward her. "Rachel honey, what are you doing?"

He rested one hand gently on her shoulder, hoping it would bring her out of her dream, but still she went on humming. *Whistle while you work, da da, da da da da da.* With horror, he noticed that her eyes were wide open, concentrating hard on her task as the scissors in her clenched hand scratched at the glass. Her face pulled back into a smile that wasn't hers.

"She's in there you know." She hissed at him. "I can feel her watching me. I can feel her hate. But she's in there and I'm out here and they won't take me back. I won't let them. The Catchers. The Soulcatchers." He face was twisted with anger and loathing, her eyes shining with madness in the night. "I'll cut them out!" She raised her arm back to stab the mirror and Mike grabbed her wrist, prying the scissors from her grip. She howled like a banshee, trying to break herself free of him as he tried to pull her in closer.

"Rachel, for fuck's sake, wake up! Wake up!" Pulling back his arm he slapped her hard around the face. The screaming's stopped, he thought as she slumped against him. Oh thank the Lord, the screaming's stopped because I don't know just how much more of this stuff I'm supposed to be able to take. He felt a sob building up in his chest and swallowed it down. "Oh Jesus, Rachel," he whispered into her hair, and slowly she lifted her face to his, her eyes, eyes he recognized, bleary and fearful.

"Where am I?" Her voice was hesitant as she glanced around her. "What am I doing in here, Mike? What am I doing here?"

He pulled her close and rocked her in his arms, feeling her unsteady heart beating against his own. "It was a bad dream. You were sleepwalking. Just a bad dream." Unable to find any more words, unable to explain, he just stood there holding her, feeling her cry into his chest.

What the fuck is going on here? He thought to himself. And when is it going to stop? Resting his head on top of hers, he caught sight of their distorted reflection in the damaged mirror and felt a chill settle in his stomach. We look like a monster. I don't recognize us at all. Staring into the glass for a few more moments, desperate to find some recognizable element of self there, he eventually turned away and led Rachel back to bed.

CHAPTER
TWENTY-ONE

It was ten o'clock in the morning by the time Murray pulled his car up outside Mike Flynn's aunt's house. As with most of London's suburbs these days, parking was a nightmare and he was having to block the entrance to her drive, but as the little Polo in residence there wouldn't be going out until he'd left, he'd ignored the NO PARKING sign nailed to the wall and did it anyway.

It was going to be another hot day, the stiff collar of his white shirt itching his neck already, and he let out a long sigh. Let's hope today brings *something*, he thought to himself. God knows, they'd earned it. He'd already spoken to Carter this morning who confirmed what they already knew. Rachel Wright was definitely Elizabeth Ray's daughter. But so far his sergeant hadn't come up with anything against either the girl or the teacher, nor had the lab got anything for them to go on yet. Now there was a surprise.

Still, he'd told Carter to keep on digging and that he'd catch up with him later in the day. He'd kept back that he was going to see Ruby Mulligan. He hadn't even told his colleague about his conversation with Flynn outside the flat last night; somehow he thought Carter would take it for the coincidence, that in all probability, it was. Never mind, he was here now so he might as well get on with it.

Getting out of the car, he opened the small gate and walked up the path to the front door where he got his badge out before ringing the bell. Old people were rightly cautious these days, and in his experience it was unlikely she'd take the chain off before she'd had a thorough examination of his ID.

In this case his experience proved wrong and the door was pulled confidently open from the other side by a short, well-preserved woman in her early sixties, dressed in jeans and a black T-shirt with no shoes on. For a moment he was slightly taken aback. She wasn't the frail old woman he'd been expecting, but then weren't they always saying that your sixties were the new forties? Her voice was as confident as her look.

"Can I help you?"

Smiling, he showed her his badge. "I'm sorry to disturb you Miss Mulligan. My name's Detective Inspector Murray, and I wondered if I could just have a few minutes of your time."

Her face had paled when she'd realized he was a policeman, and they were frightened eyes that met his. "Has something happened to Mike?"

Shaking his head, he quickly reassured her. "No, no. Nothing like that, I just wanted to ask you a few questions. Really, it's nothing to worry about. Is is okay if I come in?"

Nodding absently, she stepped aside and then shut the door behind him and leading him to the smart and modern lounge. "I was just making a pot of tea. Would you like a cup?"

Murray smiled a yes and then let his professional eye stroll around the room as she busied herself in the kitchen. There was a photo of Mike in a silver frame on the TV and pictures of other relatives spread around the various shelves and ledges. There were none of Mike and Rachel together though, which meant one of two things. Either they hadn't been a couple long enough for joint pictures to become the norm, or Mike's aunt Ruby wasn't keen on sharing her nephew. Not with Rachel at any rate.

He sat on the small sofa and then noticed the large tan folder overflowing with bits of scribbled-on paper and photocopied news clippings that was under the coffee table. The rest of the room was pretty much as neat as a pin, as Emily used to say, and it seemed strange that Ruby wouldn't have put it away somewhere. Maybe she'd been working on it when he arrived and then shoved it out of the way, somewhere she thought it couldn't be seen. But why? Why not just leave it on top of the coffee table? It wasn't as if she had been *expecting* a stranger, and most friends wouldn't care about a thing like that. And what kind of academic project would a little old lady be working on, anyway?

Suddenly, he felt very curious about the contents of that file and wished that he could make out some of the untidy writing from where he was sitting. It's probably just her Christmas jumper knitting patterns, he thought to himself. But then, she hadn't really looked like the kind of old girl that was into that kind of thing. Knowing he didn't have time to pull the folder out and have a look, he quickly got up and browsed the room for more tucked-away items. It didn't take long before he found the pile of large hardbacks between the armchair and the wall. Whatever their subject matter, they were very old; the gold leaf titles having worn away with age, only slight shadows remaining to indicate they were ever there. He was about to pick one up for a closer examination when he heard the rattle of crockery on a tray, and cursing under his breath, quickly retook his place on the settee.

The books and the folder aside, there was something else unsettling him a little about Ruby Mulligan. He'd been in her house at least four or five minutes by now and she hadn't yet asked him what he was doing here. Most people left the offer of a cup of tea until they knew what was going on. And why had she been so instantly concerned about Mike? If something had happened to him, the police would notify his parents, who were both alive and well, not his aunt. So what made her think a policeman at her door had anything to do with Mike Flynn? He twisted his wedding band around and around as he thought. More questions, more puzzles. Maybe this visit was going to turn out to be more worthwhile that he'd reckoned.

Ruby came in and set the tray down on the table, passing one tea cup to Murray and taking one for herself. She smiled at him as she took a seat in the armchair, her composure regained.

"I took the liberty of getting an ashtray out for you. I don't smoke any more myself, but I know how terrible that craving can be, so feel free to have one if you feel like it."

Murray looked at the small glass bowl on the tray. His suit was fresh on and he hadn't even had one today so he knew he couldn't smell of cigarettes. How the hell could she have known he was a smoker?

She must have been able to see his thoughts on his expression, because her face broke into a cheeky grin. "I just have a knack with reading people. I am right, aren't I?" He pulled his box of Marlboros out of his pocket and held it up to her like an admission of guilt. "I think you should come and join the force. We could use people like you."

She laughed, her eyes sparkling, and Murray suddenly saw how bloodshot they were, the tiny red veins standing out beside the sharp green. It seems Mr. Flynn's not the only one missing out on a good night's sleep in the family, he mused as he flicked on his lighter and took in the first lungful of pollution for the day. I wonder what's keeping the observant Ruby Mulligan awake at night?

They watched each other for a few moments while they sipped their tea, and it was Murray that spoke first. This game, or whatever it was, had gone on long enough.

"If you don't mind me saying, you don't seem very surprised to see me. After your initial shock on the doorstep, that is."

Ruby shrugged. "I've been expecting you. You're the man who investigated the Hampstead house case, aren't you? I recognized your face from the photos in the papers." She smiled gently. "They don't do you justice."

Murray was glad his tea cup was covering most of his face so she couldn't see his shock. His voice didn't betray him. "You've got a good memory."

Ruby put her own cup back in its saucer. "Not really. I've been reading up about it at the library. Very interesting."

Thinking of the stuffed file under the table, Murray decided to let her comments slide for the moment, even though his heart had started to beat rapidly in his chest. This woman knew something, knew or suspected something, of that much he was now certain. He took another puff on his cigarette.

"Well recognition is always nice, but I'm not here about that case."

Ruby didn't give him time to continue. "Of course not. You're here about Rachel Wright. Something bad's happened to someone she knows, hasn't it? Something terrible."

This time Murray couldn't contain his surprise. "How the hell did you know that?"

As she leaned forward in her chair, he could see how fiercely intelligent her tired eyes were. "I will explain, but that can wait for a moment. Please tell me, Inspector, I need to know. Am I right?"

Her question was so aggressive, so needy, that for a confused moment, Murray wasn't sure who was interviewing whom. He stubbed his cigarette out. Hell, it was hardly confidential information and the woman intrigued him.

"There have actually been two unexplained deaths"—oh, that was a nice way of putting it, he thought to himself—"of people who knew Ms. Wright. At the moment we're just trying to eliminate her"—he chose not to add "her boyfriend"—"from our enquiries." He leaned forward resting his elbows on his knees, his fingers interlocked, so that their faces were only a foot from each other, and silently cursed the tie knot that dug into his adam's apple.

"But I was curious. Your nephew told me that when you met Rachel, you called her Elizabeth. Why was that?"

The smile was wide and relieved, even as she ignored the question. "Mike told you that? He must have been at least half-listening, after all. He must have been if he sent you to me." She let out a small sigh, as if part of the heavy load she was carrying had been lifted from her and then looked sharply at Murray. "They're related, aren't they? Rachel Wright and Elizabeth Ray?"

She didn't wait for an answer. "I guess you know that already or else you wouldn't be here. I haven't figured the relationship out yet, but it's got to be close. Closer than normal people at any rate, or I doubt it would have worked."

Murray's head was spinning as he poured himself another cup of tea. He only wished it was something stronger. How the hell did this woman know the two were related? Suddenly he felt like he'd missed a turning somewhere. She was confusing him and that was something he didn't like. He didn't like at all. His eyes were hard.

"Or else what wouldn't have worked?"

Again, she answered his question with one of her own. "Those deaths in Hampstead. Did you find anything ritualistic about them? Did Elizabeth's seem more like suicide than murder?"

"Tell me how you know all this, and then please try and concentrate on answering my questions." His voice was cold, as he tried desperately to remember exactly what details the papers had released. Damn those blasted reporters!

Ruby placed a hand on his knee. "Don't worry, I'll tell you everything but I need to know the situation before I can help you."

Murray's short laugh was more like a bark. "Who says you can help me? Who says I need your help?" Knowing he was losing some of his professionalism, he tried to bite back the aggressiveness in his voice, but he couldn't help himself. This interview was not the run-of-the-mill dead-ender he'd been expecting.

"I think I'm the only one who can help you." Her voice had softened, and she finally removed her hand from his knee. "I can help you a lot more than those well-educated buggers in your squad that are no doubt floundering around without a clue. So, I've got a deal for you. You tell me what you think is going on, and then I'll tell you how wrong you are. Okay?"

Murray shook his head, a small smile playing on his lips. As if he didn't have enough on his plate to think about, he'd just gone and got himself snarled up with a modern-day Miss Marple. "I'm sorry Miss Mulligan, but I really can't divulge that kind of information."

"Why not? What have you got to lose? Are you worried I'm going to go running to the press?" She shrugged. "Even if I did, I doubt they'd be interested. The Ray case is old news. All neatly tied up as far as they're concerned." She raised a plucked eyebrow at him. "But you and I know better, don't we? We both know that if nothing's done about Rachel Wright, there's going to be a lot more killing. Killings that I bet you can't explain, and I'm damned if I'll let my nephew be one of them. I'm afraid, I'll admit that. I'm more afraid than I've been in my entire life, but if you won't stop her, then I sure as well will. So tell me about the relationship between Elizabeth and Rachel and then tell me about the ritual at the Ray house."

Murray lit a second cigarette and rolled the smoke around in his mouth for a few moments. Something was going on here, Ruby knew something and she sure as hell wasn't going to tell him without an exchange of information. He'd seen women with those ramrod straight backs before, his mother had been one, and they played by their rules and their rules only. Plus, this spinster had a vested interest in the case. She was worried about her nephew and he figured she might be right to be. More irritatingly, she'd also managed to figure out more from her damned armchair than the police had with all their running around and examining dead bodies.

He took another inhale as they sat there in silence. His brain was tired of thinking, tired of protocols. He needed this woman's information and if that meant bending the rules then that was what he was going to have to do. There was no time for cat-and-mouse games. He said a silent prayer that Baker would never hear the name Ruby Mulligan, and with a sigh, started to speak.

"Okay, I'm going to give you some of what we've got. We found some diaries in Elizabeth's bedroom under the floorboards. She wanted us to find them. They were pretty heavily edited but all the stuff we needed to know was there. Rachel is her daughter. She was only twelve when she became pregnant. Raped by her father."

Ruby let out a small exclamation. "Of course! It would have to be something like that!"

Wearily Murray wondered what she was talking about for what seemed like the hundredth time that morning, but decided his own questions could wait. "According to the diaries, after the rape she murdered her parents by setting the house on fire. It all checks out. Of course, no one suspected her and once her pregnancy was discovered her aunt sent her to a childless couple who wanted to adopt the baby."

"Rachel's parents." Ruby spoke aloud, but she was gazing away from Murray, as if putting the scene together in her head.

"That's right. After Rachel was born, Elizabeth ran away. Nobody tried to look for her, which wasn't surprising really. She'd been suffering from some sort of psychosis from an early age." His voice took on a slightly sarcastic tone. "She thought she could see into people's minds. See all the bad

things that went on in there." He let out a short laugh, but
Ruby didn't join in. Instead she sat there, shaking her head,
staring into space. "What a terrible gift. What a terrible terrible gift. No wonder she turned out so bad. Between that
and the father she didn't really stand much of a chance,
did she?" Her voice was full of the sympathy that echoed in
her face.

Quizzically, Murray studied her. "Come on, you don't believe that stuff, do you?" Please God, don't let her be a
crazy, not now, not now he was halfway through telling her
pretty much everything about this case. That would just
about finish off his week.

Looking perfectly sane, Ruby frowned slightly. "There's
plenty of things people choose not to believe in or see, it
doesn't necessarily mean they don't exist."

That hadn't exactly answered his question and he decided maybe that was for the best if he was going to finish
this story. He didn't want to knowingly share his information with a lunatic.

"Anyway, after she ran away, her killing was pretty much
of a serial nature. It's going to take years to find all the bodies, but given the way she ended up, I doubt she exagger-
ated too much. She also owned an occult bookshop. Her
interest in that field was pretty much lifelong. So to cut a
long story short, one day she finds this book that tells her
she can come back from the dead by taking over someone else's body. The details she gives are vague but it's all
pretty crazy psycho stuff. She believes it though. When she
finds lumps in her breasts, she thinks this is it, this is the
big one and decides it's her destiny to try this ritual. That
accounts for some of the deaths in her house, including
her own."

Ruby had got up and started to pace the room slowly as
she listened. She didn't seem interested in any of the gory
details and Murray was glad. Those were the bits the papers
would be interested in and he had no intention of sharing
them.

"Somewhere in the middle of all this, Rachel appears in the picture. I think that after the death of her adoptive parents last year, she went looking for her real mother with some fairy-tale fantasy in her head, and instead found Elizabeth with the truth about the way she came into the world, and also discovered what a psycho her mother was. I should imagine Elizabeth would have enjoyed telling her. I think Rachel encouraged Elizabeth to go through with the ritual because she wanted her dead. And then I think she's become a killer herself, starting by disposing of her mother's accomplice. The amnesia thing's got to be a cover. Or maybe her conscious mind believes she's lost her memory so she doesn't have to think about what she is and what she's become. That's for the psychologists to decide." He looked up at Ruby. "But if I was you, I'd be worried about your nephew too."

Ruby had stood still and was listening with a vague smile. "And what about the mirrors, Inspector? You haven't mentioned those. There were broken mirrrors at the crime scenes, weren't there?"

The chill settled in the pit of Murray's stomach. She couldn't have known about the mirrors. No one knew about the mirrors apart from those people unfortunate enough to have seen the bodies. No reporter had ever got hold of that piece of information. Jesus Christ, she had to be involved somewhere, but how the fuck would she have teamed up with Rachel, unless through Mike, and he was sure that that man was innocent. His blood began to heat with his confusion.

Unaware of his inner anger, Ruby chewed her bottom lip. "I know there was a broken mirror when Rachel collapsed. My nephew told me. When he was still speaking to me, that is." Murray saw the flash of pain across her face before she continued. "I should have picked up the warning signals then, but I didn't. These other two deaths, there were broken mirrors involved?"

Murray nodded, watching her warily. "Yes. And the Ray

house, too. That's why it has to be Rachel. She's linked to all of them."

Ruby sat back down on the edge of the armchair, her body taut as she looked at him. "The Ray house is different. They would have come through there after everyone was dead, when they began the hunt. It was the point of origin." She was looking at him as if he should understand what she was saying, and he was beginning to lose patience. Ruby drummed her fingers against the china of the tea cup. "They weren't responsible for any of the deaths there. Not directly at any rate."

Taking a cigarette out of his packet, Murray lit it and pointed it at her. His voice remained soft, but there was no mistaking the seriousness in it. "Okay. I want you to tell me exactly what it is you're talking about, exactly how you know so much about the Ray case, and exactly how you knew about the broken mirrors. And I'll tell you this for nothing. If I don't like your explanation then I'm going to take you down to the station and charge you with the deaths of Suzy Jenner and Peter Hanson and God help you, you can sweat in there until a lawyer can persuade me to let you out. Do you understand?"

Ruby nodded. "Perfectly. And with regards to what you've just told me, your theory is all very plausible and I commend your reasoning, but it's entirely incorrect."

Sighing, Murray rubbed his face. "Really? How so?"

"There's one possibility you haven't considered." Ruby paused for a second. "That the ritual may have worked."

Murray looked up, completely surprised. "You must be joking!" Her face was deadpan. "Tell me you're joking."

"I wish I was. Elizabeth Ray did come back from the dead. And she did it by taking over the body of her daughter."

Jesus Christ, and he'd thought he was going to get something useful out of this woman. "So let me get this straight. You think Elizabeth Ray is killing these people in the possessed body of Rachel Wright." His disbelief was all too apparent but Ruby didn't seem to notice.

"No, Elizabeth Ray hasn't hurt a fly since she came back from the dead. But then she's got no reason to. She doesn't even know who she is; maybe somewhere deep down she knows something's wrong, but as far as she's concerned, she *is* Rachel Wright. That's why she has the amnesia. She doesn't have her own memories, those would have been wiped away in the process of coming over, and she doesn't have Rachel's because those will be with her poor soul wherever it is." She spoke as if she was explaining the simplest thing in the world.

"You see, the irony is that without the memories of her previous life, of the terrible power she was cursed with to see the badness inside people, all the badness and none of the good; and without the memory of her abusive father, she is no more evil than you or I. Not really. I mean, yes, she chose the life she led, and like all of us should pay for it, but you've got to admit from what you said of those diaries, she was dealt a pretty awful hand."

Murray couldn't believe what he was hearing. "Okay, so if Rachel or Elizabeth didn't kill those people, then forgive me for asking, but who the hell did?"

Ruby looked him straight in the eye. "Oh, they were killed by entities far more terrifying than any human being. The Soulcatchers murdered them. And that's pretty much what they do. Catch souls. In fact, I think they orchestrated the whole thing and you're not going to be able to lock *them* away in your jail and throw away the key. They crossed over by coming through the mirrors, exactly like Elizabeth did in poor Rachel's bathroom." She tutted to herself. "People treat mirrors with such disregard, but they're objects of mighty power, anyone with even a vague interest in the occult knows that. They're gateways, you see. Gateways between the planes." She looked at Murray. "I've had an interest in the occult myself, years ago. Not any more, well at least not until this business came up. I'm sorry, I didn't mention I was a medium, did I?"

Murray leaned back against the sofa and laughed. He

couldn't have laughed any harder if his life had depended on it, but it was a hollow, emotionally exhausted sound that revolved around his head. The woman was clearly barking mad. People returning from the dead, catchers of souls. God, what a story. And she believed it!

As the laughter subsided, he knew what he had to do. At least it hadn't been an entirely wasted morning. Ruby definitely knew things that no one could have learned from reading the papers and that meant that either Mike or Rachel or both of them had been indiscreet around her. His gut instinct must have been wrong. Once he got outside, he'd ring Carter and tell him to get them picked up. At least that'd make his sergeant's day. Christ, what kind of witness was this aunt going to make? The prosecution were going to love her.

His hands slapped down hard against his thighs and he pressed against the solid muscle to propel his weary body out of the sofa. There was no point in staying any longer. If this was the way the teacher's aunt thought, then it would no longer be any surprise to find out Flynn was in it with Wright. But then, he wasn't really sure how much was left in life that could surprise him.

"Look, I hate to disappoint you, but I'm just not buying any of this crazy stuff. I'm sorry I've wasted my time and yours. I'll see myself out." Not looking at Ruby, he held one arm up in a half-hearted wave as he walked toward the door. God, Carter was going to love this one. Maybe it was his turn to do an editing job on this morning's events. He was in the hallway when Ruby's clear calm voice stopped him in his tracks.

"Emily says that you should stay and listen. She's afraid for you. For you, her mother, and the twins. She also says that I'm waffling, which is something you can't stand, and if I want to have a chance of you listening, then I should be a little more precise." There was a hint of pique in her next words. "I thought that given the nature of our conversation I was being concise enough, but she knows you best and I don't think this is the time to argue with her."

Murray could see his hand outstretched in front of him, reaching for the latch, frozen like the rest of him as all his blood rushed to his core, stopping all actions, preventing him even from turning around. The words came out like dry ice. "How do you know about Emily?"

"She's here with me. Like I said, she's worried about you."

He felt a wave of nausea as the wounds reopened, stabbing at him, reminding him that they could never go away. Not really. How could she know about Emily? Emily was sacred. Emily was *his*. He breathed deeply, pins and needles threatening his limbs.

The newspapers, that's what it was, that's where she'd got it from. It would be in one of the cuttings in the fucking crazy woman's folder. Recently bereaved officer takes charge of enquiry. The tabloids had loved it almost as much as he had hated it. Slowly, he twisted round, his grief and pain exploding inside him, his eyes full of hate.

"Don't push me lady, don't push me." His voice was raw as if it was taking layers of skin from his lungs. "Jesus Christ, I don't know what your problem is but you need locking away in some mental hospital somewhere. I'm sorry I bothered you. I really am. Good-bye."

How dare she try and use his grief against him? How dare she? Just when he thought he was coming to terms with things, something would come along and knock him for six. His heart ached the blood that it sent around his body. Shaking fingers grasped the latch and then he felt her hand, *her crazy woman's hand* touch his shoulder.

"I know where the St. Christopher is."

The shock of the words unlocked his limbs and he turned slowly to face her.

"What did you say?"

"I said I know where the St. Christopher is. Emily's telling me." Her voice was a river of soft calm in his torrent of racing emotion. "You bought it for her on your first anniversary. You knew she wanted one to replace the one she'd lost that was a childhood gift from her father. You went to Hatton Garden and got the most delicate, feminine one you could find because that would suit her best. Do you remember?"

Murray's heart was pounding as he allowed Ruby to lead him back to the sofa, where he sat reliving the memory. The sweaty heat of a small jewelry shop in central London during high summer, the look of joy on Emily's face, the sweet smell of her neck as he did up the clasp and kissed her. No one could know about that, no one. They were private things, just his and hers. He could hear Ruby talking above the rough sound of his breath in his ears.

"It was beautiful. She loved it very much. She says that after she died, on the day before her funeral, you ripped the house apart trying to find it. You wanted it around her neck so that it would always be with her, as if you were always with her, keeping her company in the dark."

Murray looked into the green, tired eyes, so full of compassion, and whispered. "How could you know this? How could you know?" He was no longer sure if she was mad or he was mad, he just knew he didn't want her to stop talking, painful as it was, and oh God it was so painful, and if this turned out to be a hoax then he was going to rip her body apart with his bare hands and damn the consequences, but these were things that *nobody* knew, so maybe, just maybe. He left the question unspoken even to himself, and turned his hollow dark eyes to Ruby.

Her smile was sweet. "I know because she's telling me. Anyway, she wants me to tell you that it slipped down the back of her dressing table. It's down there between your skirting board and the carpet." Her hand once again rested on Murray's knee, and he felt the warmth emanating from it through his trousers.

"She's laughing. She says if you vacuumed more often then you'd probably have found it by now. She was a very happy lady, wasn't she?"

Murray nodded, unable to trust his voice as he swallowed the tears that were making his throat ache, his vision blurring. Ruby moved closer to him, comforting him and he felt the strength that resided in that small body as she carried on speaking.

"She's pleased you didn't find it. She wants you to give it to Sam when she's older. Emily doesn't need it where she is, and she doesn't need it to remember you. She has so much love for you I can feel it tingling in my toes. But Sam might need it to remember her. Is this making sense to you?"

The best reply he could make was the sob that escaped him as he covered his face with his hands so she couldn't see his contortions of grief. Could this be true, could Emily really be speaking to him from beyond the grave? Angrily, he wiped away the tears that burned his face and looked up, surprised to see that Ruby's face was wet too. Well, if she was a fake, then she didn't know it, and he found that he didn't believe she was either. No one knew about the St. Christopher, no one, and his policeman's brain told him that if he hadn't told Ruby, then the only person that could was Emily. The vulnerability of hope was threatening to crush him.

The old woman's face echoed his pain as she talked. "She doesn't want you to be unhappy. She doesn't want to make you unhappy. She's not unhappy. She thinks that given time, you and the kids will be just fine. She's not gone forever, she's just moved to a different place. Everything is as it should be. She wouldn't have come back now if it wasn't so important. She says she knows you're an old cynical sea dog." Murray barked out a bittersweet laugh. That was what she used to call him whenever they ended up on the subject of religion or politics, her old cynical sea dog.

Sometimes, late at night, when she lay sweaty in his arms, their passion spent, she would raise one eyebrow and lick her lips suggestively and call him her old cynical *salty* sea dog, before giggling into her pillow like a teenager. Such a short time and so many memories away.

"But she says you should listen to me. Hear me out. And then after hearing my crazy tale, you can go home and look behind the dressing table. Okay?"

Heavy-headed, Murray pulled his mobile phone from his inside pocket and turned it off. He didn't know what was going on here, and he didn't know if he'd ever understand it, but he knew he wasn't leaving until he'd heard everything this woman had to say. His voice was husky but controlled. "It's a deal."

Running her hands through her short hair, Ruby stood up and let out a long sigh. "Well, I don't know about you Inspector, tea may be all very well but I think before we go any further, I might pour myself a brandy. Want one?"

Nodding as he reached for a cigarette, he couldn't think of anything that would go down better.

CHAPTER
TWENTY-TWO

•

"Come on then, your sandwiches are ready. But you've got to get those wet suits off before we eat!" Squinting under the shade of her hand, Janet called the shrieking five-year-olds in from the paddling pool. God, did they never run out of energy? Smiling, she handed out towels to the two wet bundles who ran in dripping through the back door. "Easy tiger." She grabbed onto Sebastian's shoulder as he tore past her. "That floor will be slippy for wet feet."

"Sorry, Nana," he called, as he trotted only slightly slower over to the kitchen table, pulling off his wet trunks as he went, ready to put on the dry shorts and T-shirt she'd laid over the back of the chair. Samantha, cautious as ever, heeded her warning and followed slowly with tiny steps, so that Sebastian was already changed and biting into his first ham sandwich by the time she reached her chair and started taking her wet costume off.

Picking the damp clothes up and taking them back outside to hang on the line, Janet felt exhausted. Happy, but exhausted. Catching sight of her reflection in the glass of the door, she had to laugh at the irony. How come when she finally gives up on trying to look younger, she actually manages it? When was the last time I actually wore makeup, she wondered. No rephrase that. When was the last time I actually had *time* to put on makeup?

Still, makeup or not, her skin was looking tanned and fresh and for all the years she'd spent with curlers in her hair, she now discovered the straight, untidy ponytail looked best. Well, how about that? Peter would probably be laughing in his grave. A light twinkled in her eyes at the thought of her husband. He'd certainly be laughing at her reliving the mother experience. Had she got this tired first time round? Maybe he and Emily were watching and giggling at her together. The stabbing pain in her stomach let her know that she wasn't ready to think about Emily yet. She wasn't ready to remember her without the pain. And as much as people told her otherwise, she wasn't sure she ever would be.

Still, she had the babies to think of. The babies and Jim, and she had to be strong for them. And although God knows, there had been times when the blackness had just seemed too much and she would stand for anything up to hours staring at that bottle of sleeping pills in the bathroom cupboard, just standing and staring until her feet were numb and cold from stillness; those days seemed to have passed. She doubted she would have done it, much as she wanted to. Emily wouldn't have wanted it, she wouldn't have wanted her to leave the children, and so here she was. And if she was honest, she was glad she stayed. She had a tentative feeling that the worst times had passed, and maybe, just maybe, she was starting to heal.

Stepping back into the coolness of the house, she saw with amazement that the twins had nearly demolished the pile of sandwiches she'd put out for them.

Munching happily, Sebastian swallowed before speaking. "Can we go back in the paddling pool after lunch? Can we?"

Their energy amazed her. Just where did they get it from? Idly, she wondered if there was a way she could bottle it and make her fortune.

"Uh, uh. You know the rules. No running around on a full stomach, you'll get a tummyache. Anyway, it's getting really hot out there now and Sam's starting to burn already." It wasn't a lie. In spite of the sunblock the tops of the little girl's shoulders were definitely getting a bit pink, unlike Sebastian's, which were brown as a nut. In many ways, they were exactly as twins should be, ying and yang, complimenting each other perfectly. Looking at the two, small disappointed faces, she sighed. "But, if you're really good, then we can go out again at about four when the sun's not quite so fierce. What do you say?"

They were never very miserable for long, and they beamed at her as she took the plates, laden with crusts, away. Why was it that kids never ate those anyway?

Sam sipped her orange juice through a straw, her pretty face, so like Emily's, deadly serious. "So, what can we do till then? Inside's boring."

Taking the plastic Woolworth's bag from the top of the microwave, Janet sat it down between them. "Well, you know how I'm such an old lady," she raised an eyebrow at their giggling and nodding, "and I like to sit down a lot and do boring things like reading the newspapers." Sebastian pulled a face making Sam snort into her drink, choking herself slightly. "Well, I thought we could go into the sitting room and while I'm doing boring grown-up stuff, you can watch this!" With a dramatic flourish, she pulled the video from the bag. Sam's face lit up, the orange juice forgotten as she bounced in her seat. "*The Little Mermaid!* Oh cool, Nana, thanks! Can we watch it now, can we?"

Feeling slightly victorious, obviously she'd learned something first time round, she nodded, knowing that the paddling pool was, for now at least, forgotten. Thank God for that. Right this minute she could think of nothing better than sinking into the armchair with a cup of tea, a biscuit, and the *Telegraph*. Hallelujah for the invention of the video! She handed the colorful plastic container over to the small girl who took it in both hands. "Okay, you guys go and get it all set up, and I'll be there in a minute." They scrambled down from their seats and were gone in a cloud of excited chatter before she'd even turned the tap on to fill the kettle. God, she did love them, she couldn't deny that.

By the time she thankfully fell into the armchair, her steaming mug of tea on the table beside her, the two little bodies were sitting cross-legged on the carpet, eyes wide as a variety of sea creatures sang to them from the screen. They were bright kids and as she opened the paper, she knew the film would hold their attention for the whole hour and a half. The heat of the sun coming through the window behind her felt good on her shoulders and the back of her neck, and as she browsed the headlines, her eyes slipped shut. Just five minutes, she thought, enjoying the relaxing warmth. I'll just shut my eyes for five minutes and then I'll read the paper. Her untouched tea slowly went cold, forgotten on the table.

Sebastian had been holding on for twenty minutes or more and he couldn't do it any longer. He had to pee, no matter how exciting the adventure was that Ariel and her friends were having. If he didn't go now then he was going to burst or wet himself and he hadn't done that since he was a baby and that was a long time ago. Pulling himself upward, he padded quickly across the carpet to the hallway. Samantha's eyes didn't move from the screen. "Where ya going?"

"Toilet." He whispered back as he disappeared from view. He knew Nana Janet was sleeping and didn't want to wake her up. Old people got tired quickly as Daddy was always saying when he wanted to stop playing football in the garden, and Nana Janet was older than Daddy and that was older than he could imagine. Not bothering to shut the downstairs toilet door, he lifted the seat and carefully peed into the bowl, enjoying the tingling feeling of relief. When he finally finished he made sure he hadn't left any drips and then pushed the handle, watching as the new water sucked the old away. Pulling up his shorts, he stepped back into the hall and his breath caught in his throat.

In front of him, screwed to the wall next to the front door, was the hallway mirror. He should have been able to see his head and shoulders in it, unlike Daddy who was so tall he could see his whole self; but he couldn't. He couldn't see anything. Nothing at all. Something had happened to the mirror, something beautiful, and he moved forward unafraid to take a closer look, his mouth slightly open with confusion.

The wooden frame was exactly the same as always, light pine like the small dresser next to it but the mirror itself, the *shiny glass*, as Sam still called it, was gone. Instead, everything inside the frame was glowing turquoise blue and the surface was rippling like water, sparkling here and there as if somewhere in its magical world there was a huge great sun shining down on it. Oh, it looked so pretty he couldn't stop his hand from reaching out to touch it, his small fingers dipping into the surface. He let out a small, fascinated giggle as he pulled his hand back, amazed to find it dry, and then after only a moment's pause slipped both arms right up to the elbows into what used to be the mirror, stretching to his fingertips.

It was warm and like water but thicker, maybe more like those chocolate milkshakes from McDonald's after they've melted just a little bit, and he could feel the liquid sucking at his skin like the tides of an ocean and he imagined it was just like where Ariel lived, far far beneath a fantastic sea. For a moment, he thought he could smell salt in the air like he had when they'd gone to Brighton for the day last year before Mummy left to go to the place she couldn't get back from, but he knew that this sea, this sea in the mirror would be far more wonderful than anything Brighton had offered them. In this sea there would be shells that sang and danced and beautiful mermaids to take them on all manner of adventures with pirates and dancing crabs and funny food and probably lots of chocolate.

His heart was pounding with excitement, and he longed to push his small frame into the flourescent blue and wherever it may take him, but mesmerized as he was, something stopped him. Samantha. He couldn't leave Sammy behind, because they were twins and he loved her more than anyone in the world even if she was a girl, and he couldn't imagine ever going off and having adventures without her. Pulling his hands back into this world, smiling at the tickling, tingling sensation as they reappeared, he whispered, "Don't go away," at his treasure and then trotted back to the sitting room.

Nana Janet's head was lolling forward as she slept in the armchair and Sam was still staring at the screen. Glancing at it, the cartoon images now looked dull and lifeless to him, boring and unreal. "S'manfa! S'manfa!" He whispered urgently across the room, as he danced from foot to foot, eager to get back in the hall. His twin dragged her eyes from the screen with mild irritation. "What?"

"Come here. Come and see what's happened to the shiny glass!"

Her little brow furrowed with mild irritation. "But the film—"

Sebastian was jumping up and down now, bouncing easily as if the carpet was a trampoline. "No but you have to see before it goes away. It's wonderful! Better than a stupid video! Come on!"

Samantha paused for only a moment and then, letting out a small sigh, gave in to her brother's enthusiasm. Crawling forward on her hands and knees, she carefully pressed the pause button on the video, freezing Ariel mid-song, and then stood up and followed her brother as she eventually always did. He was the oldest, after all, even if only by ten minutes, and anyway, it would have to be something good to get Sebastian this excited.

Back in the hall, standing in the doorway to the downstairs toilet, Sebastian watched the look of disbelief spread over his sister's face as she gazed at the glorious blue. They stood in awed silence for a few moments before Sam spoke. "What is it?" She whispered at him, her face glowing a funny color in the reflected light. Sebastian wondered if his looked like that as well, and figured it must. "I think it's the ocean. Can't you smell it? It smells like the sea, and look, it's moving."

He watched with pride at his discovery as Sam's eyes followed the sparkling ripples right up to the pine edge. He smiled at her. "Put your hand in and touch it."

Sam shook her head, fear flashing across her face. "Don't want to." Her brother smiled at her. "Go on. It feels really funny."

Still Sam shook her head, her face darkening as it always did when her twin was pushing her cautious nature to do something it didn't want to. Stepping forward, ignoring Sam's pleas to stop, Sebastian dipped his own hand into the surface, enjoying his twin's gasp of surprise as his fingers disappeared. "See? It's not scary. It's warm. I bet it's like where the mermaid lives in there." He could see Sam wavering, and pulled his hand out, wiggling it in front of her, impatient for her to have a go. "Go on. You're not chicken are you, S'manfa?"

Her little face hardened as she stepped forward. "I'm not chicken!" she said so loudly that Sebastian had to shush her so she didn't wake Nana Janet. "Well, go on then!" He whispered back.

Samantha gave her brother a long doubtful look before blowing her golden fringe away with a long huff of air and holding her arm out tentatively inches from the mirror. "Okay. I'll do it."

Sebastian beamed excitedly, as she slowly edged her fingertips in until her small nails were no longer visible, and then her wrist disappeared, until finally it looked as if her lower arm had been amputated a few inches below the elbow. She smiled uncertainly at her brother. "You're right. It feels funny." They giggled together as she moved her invisible arm up and down as far as she could reach, and then suddenly she stopped, a look of confused alarm fracturing the childish happiness on her face.

"Something's got my—!" Her breath caught in her throat, and for a split-second their young eyes met and Sebastian saw the hopeless fear in his sister's eyes, as if she'd known all along that something like this was going to happen, something terrible, and then they both couldn't help but stare at the mirror as the dream of adventure turned into a nightmare and the blue started to boil in front of them, the air smelling like rotting eggs, but all Sebastian could hear was the sound of Sam sobbing and he knew he should try and pull her arm out like she was begging him to do but just when he found the nerve to reach for her, it happened. *The thing came out and pulled her in.*

Those few moments lasted forever in Sebastian's head as he watched in slow motion. Out of the bubbling surface a head and shoulders appeared like a diver breaking the surface gasping for breath; at least he thought it was a head and shoulders as he started to shake because it had eyes, eager sharp eyes fixed firmly on Sam, but it had no skin, no skin at all, only a slimy red exterior, throbbing veins running down over the bones where the cheeks should be, and a lipless mouth stretched wide to show so many teeth, brown and rotting. Suddenly a hand appeared bursting through the liquid, a scarred and mangled hand, that grabbed Samantha's mouth as she prepared to scream, silencing her with that revolting flesh, *only Sebastian could see that his sister's eyes were still screaming, screaming at him to do something*, and then as the thing hissed an exclamation of satisfaction, its deformed face grinning hungrily, it yanked her into the mirror, her body disappearing in less than a second, bare feet waving in the air, desperate to find purchase, before vanishing helplessly into the void with the monster.

Sebastian stood there frighteningly alone and breathless,

as the mirror turned black, blacker than any night he'd ever seen, starting with a small inklike spot at the center of the churning surface and spreading outward until the mirror looked like a frozen stretched black canvas hanging there against the ordinary cream wall that Mummy had painted. Even though he'd just been to the toilet, he really needed to go again, really badly, but he couldn't get his eyes to move away from the darkness in front of him. "S'manfa?" He whispered pleadingly. Silence answered him. "S'manfa?"

And then the mirror was back to being just plain old shiny glass again and as he looked at his pale face looking guiltily back at him he found that that scared him more than anything. And as the tears welled up, he started to scream.

CHAPTER
TWENTY-THREE

By the time he'd finished eating the quick lunch of cheese and biscuits Ruby had mustered together in the kitchen, Murray's suit jacket was abandoned at the other end of the sofa along with his tie and he'd undone the top two buttons of his shirt. It was hardly turning out to be a run-of-the-mill police interview so the formalities may as well be thrown out of the window. He sipped his brandy slowly, enjoying the warmth it sent down to his stomach, and although he was still undecided as to whether he'd joined the crazy brigade, he'd calmed down and got his emotions under control. Ruby was munching on a water biscuit as she knelt down on the other side of the coffee table, looking at him frankly. "So are you ready to hear what I've got to say?"

Giving her a wry smile, he shrugged. "Ready as I'll ever be. Fire away."

Swallowing her food, she settled down on her haunches before starting to speak. "Well, I knew there was something desperately wrong when I met her. First off, Mike had told me her name was Rachel but I called her Elizabeth, and the minute I'd said it, I *knew* her name was Elizabeth as well as I knew what my own name was. And then I touched her." She shivered at the memory. "It was the most revolting feeling I think I've ever had. It was like she was filled with darkness, surrounded by badness. The best way I can think to describe it is that she was *unnatural*. I tried to tell Mike but I botched it a bit, and apart from the fact he's completely in love with her, he's a cynic like you so I really didn't stand much of a chance.

"Anyway, after they'd gone I had a look through some of the old occult books I keep upstairs to try and get a feel for what was so wrong with her. Most of the symptoms I'd experienced were synonymous with possession, so I decided to contact the spirit world and see if I could locate her there. What I *did* find was the spirit of Helen Holmes, although I didn't know it was her then, not until I'd started studying the Ray case. Quite mad, poor soul. Quite, quite mad."

Watching as she paused and shook her head slightly, Murray tried hard to keep his natural disbelief at bay. Hear the old woman out, he reminded himself. And when you get home, if that St. Christopher isn't where she said it was, then you can be as cynical as you like. Just thinking about that necklace made his heart tighten, and he concentrated hard on Ruby's words.

"It was she who told me about the Soulcatchers. The Soulcatchers are coming, that's what she said. I wrote it down before I went to sleep in case I forgot it. Some things are meant to be forgotten, they try and make themselves slip out of your mind. It's hard to explain." She shook herself. "Anyway, that's not important. It's the Soulcatchers that matter.

"It took me a long time before I found any information on them. I had to dig around in places and people I thought, *I'd hoped* I'd left behind forever many, many years ago. Still, eventually I found what I was looking for and then everything made perfect sense."

Murray was intrigued despite himself. "Found what?"

Ruby's voice was soft but strong, and a sad smile toyed with her lips. "The irony of the ritual. Oh, Elizabeth Ray did everything right, no doubt about that. After all, she was the perfect candidate. You see, from what I could gather the ritual did more than just bring you back from the dead, from hell or whatever you want to call it. It promised to negate hell completely because the soul whose body you had stolen would remain there in your place, and when that stolen body died you just passed on to the next plane without having to suffer for your sins, and the soul of your victim would have, in your parlance officer, to do your time for you."

She paused to let Murray get to grips with what she was saying. "A very appealing prospect for someone like Elizabeth Ray, wouldn't you say? A life of crime and absolutely no punishment. Although I think that maybe for her it was the idea of doing something so powerful and nature-altering that was the lure, rather than the escaping from punishment. Of all the things I think that woman is, I don't think she's a coward."

She pulled the full folder out from under the table. "It's all in here. You can take it with you and have a look if you like. The ritual's called The Passage of Shar Neigamur. A pretty-sounding name for something so terrible, don't you think? In order for the ritual to have any chance of working, the person whose body you are intent on stealing has to be a blood relative, but not a natural one."

Picking up on the policeman's confusion, she elaborated further. "An ordinary child and parent wouldn't have a strong enough link. It would be risky to try it; there's no guarantee that both souls wouldn't end up in hell. But for Elizabeth, the situation was perfect. After all, Rachel's blood was almost pure. Her father was her grandfather. How much closer a blood relative could you get? Plus, she had the added bonus of having no emotional ties to Rachel, having never known her. If anything, I should imagine she hated her for being the product of her father's obscenities. By the way, I meant to ask earlier, what happened to the book? The book with the ritual in it?"

Ignoring the tightness in his throat telling him he'd smoke too many cigarettes today, Murray lit another one, inhaling hard. He needed something with a solid grip on this world to cling to and a cigarette was as good a thing as any. His voice felt raw. "The diary says she burnt it. We can't find it anyway."

Ruby nodded. "That would make sense. As with all these things a sacrifice is required and while she was alive, Elizabeth would have persuaded that bank manager man—"

"Burnett."

"Yes, she would have persuaded Burnett that Helen Holmes was the sacrifice. And he wouldn't have any problem believing her. After all, it was Helen who was being fed Elizabeth's blood, keeping her link to the living world strong until she could summon the strength to take Rachel's body; and it was Helen who would come to an awful end at the precise moment that Elizabeth came through Rachel's bathroom mirror and took over her body."

She sipped her brandy. "But the ritual demanded more than that. It demanded the obliteration of a soul, and as much as Elizabeth knew Burnett adored her, I doubt she thought he was ready to relinquish his soul for her. So, she would have burned the book before her death by her own hand, another stipulation of this ritual not designed for the faint-hearted; and he would still believe that when she came back they would live happily ever after. He was unwittingly the ultimate sacrifice.

"Still, he must have been a daft old bugger because he should have figured out she wouldn't want to leave any links to her old life, nothing the Soulcatchers could follow, because the book would have made it very clear that follow they certainly would, and the best way not to get caught is to hide well. Perhaps that's got something to do with the loss of memory. The easiest way to stay hidden is to not know who you actually are. To have no thoughts that can be tracked down. Who knows? All I know is that whatever she believed she was on a hiding to nothing."

Fantastic story or not, Murray policeman's brain was still working. "But you said 'the irony of the ritual.' What did you mean by that?"

Stretching her legs to relieve the pins and needles that had settled in, Ruby met his eyes. "Ah yes, I was just coming to that. This is where, highly intelligent as she no doubt was, Elizabeth Ray's arrogance let her down. She didn't do her homework properly, and she didn't see the glaringly obvious. Maybe she didn't want to see the obvious. If she had then she might have reconsidered her options. You see, the Soulcatchers must have orchestrated the book. They created it. Anyone with any sense would know that you can't really escape between the planes and get away with it. The laws of nature are fundamental. They *can't* be broken. They're what keep the universe held together."

Murray felt out of his depth. "So why would they create a book, a ritual, that makes work for themselves?" It didn't make any sense.

Ruby laughed. "Well, that's the funny part if you've got a sick sense of humor. The Soulcatchers are like the policemen of Hell for want of a better word. They're creatures that have never existed as living, breathing things. I think they created the book out of curiosity. You see they're bound by the same laws of nature as we are, and the only way they can visit our plane is if they're retrieving a soul that's out of its place. They are fascinated by life, or to be more precise, *they're fascinated by death.* They have no sense of it. After all, if they've never lived, then they've never died. They enjoy watching things die. They're fascinated by the transition, by *our fear* of the transition.

"I think they could take Elizabeth back any time they want. They're just making the most of their freedom. While they're still here they can have contact with anyone connected to her. Of course, they will stop and take her back. They have to. But when? How many more people have to die? We have to find a way to stop them. To *make them* take her back."

Murray's head was starting to ache, and he wasn't sure whether it was the nicotine, the brandy, or just the craziness of what he was hearing. Hearing and almost believing, and that was the most frightening part. "So you're saying these Soulcatchers killed Suzy Jenner and Dr. Hanson?"

"Sure. They would have come through the mirrors. And I don't want to know the details but I bet they died in inventive ways."

Remembering their bodies, he grimaced. "The coroner hasn't been able to come up with any explanations yet."

"Now there's a surprise." Looking into her sharp eyes under the raised eyebrow, Murray was glad to see that Ruby was capable of being as droll as he was. The madness of the situation aside, he was starting to like this woman.

Out of the blue, Ruby suddenly let out a yelp of pain and clutched her head with both hands. Jesus, what was going on now?

"Are you okay?"

Her face was pinched, her eyes almost squeezed shut. "It's Emily." Her voice was raw through gritted teeth. "She's screaming in my head. It's like a knife going through me." Her head twisted to one side a little, and her next words made Murray's stomach lurch. "Something's not right. Oh God, something's happened to the kids. Something's happened to one of the kids." She looked directly at Murray, his fears reflecting in her eyes. "She says she's got to go and find her baby. Oh, I've never heard anyone that distraught. Never."

His whole body shaking, Murray pulled out the slim black mobile phone and turned it on. It started ringing immediately. Like a zombie, he pressed the answer button and held it to his ear. It was Janet. She was crying, her panic echoing through her voice.

"Oh Jim, thank God, I've been trying to get hold of you, Carter's on his way. Samantha's gone missing, I can't find her anywhere, I only fell asleep for a few minutes and then Sebastian was screaming and she was gone. Oh God, I'm sorry, I'm so sorry . . ."

Getting to his feet, Murray tried to get his trembling body under control. Missing. She said missing. Missing doesn't mean—

He couldn't finish the sentence in his head. "Calm down, Janet. I'm on my way. We'll find her. Don't worry. We'll find her." He was amazed at how confident he sounded. There was a distant sound of his doorbell ringing. "That'll be Carter. Explain to him what happened and I'll be there as fast as I can." Still sobbing, Janet hung up at the other end.

In the silence of the lounge the two people looked at each other. "My daughter's gone missing." His voice was as empty as he felt, the sickness rising in his stomach. I can't lose anyone else. I can't. I just can't do it. I'm not strong enough.

Ruby had torn a peice of paper from her file and scribbled her phone number on it. She gave Murray a piece and made him do the same. On her feet, she gave the numb policeman's hand a firm squeeze. "You go back to your family. I'm going to go and find a way we can end this once and for all. We're going to get your baby back." Her determination gave him strength and he realized they were both thinking the same thing. The Soulcatchers. They'd done this, how and why he didn't know, but they were behind his missing child, and the thought filled him with a terror he didn't know he was capable of. How can I fight enemies I can't see? How?

Ruby was walking with him to the door.

"I can still hear her, you know. Emily. She's very distant, but I can hear her. I think she's singing a lullaby." Murray didn't know what was filling him more, anger or grief. Ruby kissed him on the cheek. "I think she'll look after Samantha until we get her back where she belongs. You have to trust her to do that, like she trusts you to end this mess. Between us, we'll get there. I"ll call you when I've got some answers."

Murray was through the door before Ruby could see his tears.

As he screeched to a halt outside his house, he saw

Carter's red Granada in the driveway and a marked patrol car on the street. Oh shit, it was real. It really was real. The front door was open and he rushed in, bursting past the WPC who had come to greet him, and went straight to the kitchen where Carter was talking to a weepy Janet sitting at the kitchen table and cradling Sebastian on her knee, clutching him tightly as if afraid to let him go. She looked up at him, her face full of pain and guilt.

"I'm so sorry, Jim. I'm so sorry. It's all my fault." Her voice was no more than a whisper, and feeling his own emotions welling up, he crouched down and hugged them both, squeezing them to him until the tears had subsided a little. He felt Sebastian's chubby arms around his neck and when he stood up, the boy was clinging to him like a limpet.

He looked at Carter. "Any idea what happened?"

His sergeant shook his head. "She must have slipped out while Janet wasn't looking. We've searched the house and garden but there's no sign of her. Has she ever gone out the front door on her own?"

Murray ran a hand soothingly over Sebastian's hair. "No. She can't even reach the latch as far as I'm aware. Anyway, she's a cautious child. She wouldn't go off on her own. Not without Sebastian."

"Well, she can't have gone far. We've got people out there looking, but if you could try searching the house again she may be asleep in some nook and cranny that I couldn't find."

Murray's eyes met those of his calm sergeant. "Thanks John." He meant it, too. Even though the police always gave their utmost in the search for a missing child, he knew that this team would be giving more than they thought possible to help him get his daughter back. And now that he was here, in his own house, surrounded by normalcy, he was beginning to think that it *was* possible that Sam may have jsut wandered off. Maybe Ruby was just crazy.

Thinking of Ruby made him think of the St. Christopher necklace. He tried to hand Sebastian over. "Look, stay here with Janet. I'll only be a second, there's something I want to check upstairs." Janet reached to take the boy, but he started screaming, clinging to his father even tighter. Murray pulled him back to his chest. "It's okay, big fella," he said, shushing him. "It's okay. You can come with me."

Climbing the stairs, he found himself hoping beyond hope that the necklace wouldn't be there, that he wouldn't find it, because if the St. Christopher wasn't there then that would make Ruby just another crazy old lady, and none of the stuff about the Soulcatchers would be true, and Sam would probably just be hiding in a cupboard somewhere waiting for all the fuss to die down before she came out. And he could cope with losing Emily all over again for that. Oh God, yes he could.

Going into his bedroom, *their* bedroom, Sebastian's breath hot against his neck, he made his way over to the white dressing table they'd bought in John Lewis that was pushed against the wall on the other side of the bed. It looked bare without Emily's clutter, but it wasn't completely empty. Standing alone on the surface was her bottle of favorite Chanel perfume, that sometimes, in the nights where he couldn't sleep, he would take and spray on the pillow next to him. It didn't smell the same away from the warmth of her skin, but at those desperate times, it was close enough.

Getting down on his knees, as his wife used to do in front of an alter, he stood Sebastian next to him, and with one hand still holding his son's, he stretched his other arm, long and taut under the dressing table. Groping against the far wall, his face gripped with concentration, he could feel the furry edge of the carpet where it met the smoothness of the wall. Edging his hand along the length, exploring between the fibers, for a few seconds he found nothing, his hopes beginning to rise. It's not there, he thought for a wild moment. It's not there. And then suddenly there was the coolness of metal between his sweaty fingertips, stopping all thought and all feeling in his brain, his heart constricting in his chest with the shock.

Slowly and shakily he pulled the delicate silver out, until resting back on his heels, he could see it, right there in front of him, just as Ruby said he would. The image blurred, his hand and the lost jewelry becoming one.

"Oh Emily," He whispered through his tears. "Oh Jesus Christ, Emily."

With the discovery of the necklace, everything had changed and he sat there, terrified and confused, as the rocks that he'd built his whole system of belief on crumbled to dust around him.

He did up the clasp around his own neck, tucking the small medal inside his shirt, needing it near him. Reality, if there was such a thing—and right at that minute he wasn't so sure—had altered beyond all recognition. Nothing made sense, not to him at any rate. After a minute or two, he became aware of a sound outside of his own breathing, and realized that Sebastian was sobbing, sobbing in a way that no child of his age should know how to.

Looking at his child, he felt reality settle in around him. Some things, the *important* things, hadn't changed at all.

"Hey, hey, it's not your fault. Everything's going to be all right. We'll find Samantha." He gently wiped the tears away from the bowed face. "She's probably just playing a joke on us or wandered off somewhere." The boy let out another heart-wrenching sob, and Murray took both the small arms firmly in his hands, and tried to make eye contact. "Are you saying that you don't think that Carter and I can find her? But we're the best policemen in the world, isn't that what you're always telling people?" He pushed the thought of those *other* policemen away. "Carter and I'll get her back. You know that."

Sebastian shook his head, his face screwed up, spitting the words out between choking tears. "But you can't get her back, not from in there." He stamped one tiny foot in exasperation. "I told them where she was, but they wouldn't listen. No one will listen to me and it's all my fault. I made her put her hand in there. She didn't want to but I made her and now she's gone!" He clung to his father, a new flood of tears overwhelming him, and behind the heat of his son, Murray felt his blood settle cold in his veins. He waited until the little body stopped twitching.

"I'll listen to you, big guy. Tell me what you told them. I promise I'll listen."

Pulling his head back so he could see his father, Sebastian rubbed his eyes with tiny balled-up fists, making Murray's tired heart ache even more. "She's in the mirror. The monster took her in the mirror." Murray said nothing, just staring ahead of him, and Sebastian started crying again. "I knew you wouldn't believe me, but I'm not making it up. She's in the mirror and we'll never get her back. Never!"

"I believe you," Murray soothed him, "I believe you." And God help him, he did. "Which mirror?"

Sebastian hiccuped slightly. "By the front door."

Scooping his son up in his arms, he went back downstairs to the hall. The glass glinted innocuously at him. "This one?"

Sebastian nodded, scared to look at it. "It looked so pretty, like the ocean, and I touched it and it felt nice and then I got S'manfa and made her touch it even though she didn't want to and then the monster man with no skin came out and grabbed her and then it all went black and then it was just a shiny mirror again. It's all my fault, Daddy, it should have tooken me. Why didn't it take me, why did it take S'manfa?" His voice was tiny as he watched Murray with wide blue eyes. "Are you angry with me, Daddy?"

Murray kissed his hot forehead. "No, I'm not angry, not with you. I'm angry with the monster man and I'm going to make sure he brings Samantha back. Okay?"

Sebastian nodded as Murray placed him on the ground. "Now I need you to go and look after Nana Janet for me.

Just for a little while. I've got some policeman thinking to do. Are you okay with that?"

The small face was fearful as he stepped away. "You promise you won't touch it?"

"I promise."

As Sebastian wandered away, the weight of the world on his young shoulders, Carter appeared in the hallway, giving the small blond head a gentle tousle as it passed. "Sounds like he had a pretty bad dream this afternoon too, some of the stuff he was saying when I got here." He brought his focus around to his boss. "Don't go mad at me, but I had a couple of the guys watching Wright and Flynn today, so I know neither of them took her." He shrugged slightly. "I know it doesn't rule out that they might have arranged it, but I think that's pretty unlikely. I think Sam going missing during this investigation is probably just one of those coincidences you don't believe in. I'm sure we'll find her before bedtime. Maybe she heard an ice-cream van and went looking for it. You know what kids are like."

Not having listened to a thing his sergeant had said, Murray was studying the mirror, rubbing his chin and muttering aloud. "But why did they take her? Why didn't they just kill her like all the rest?" Stepping forward, he ran a finger around the pine frame as if seeking a clue there. "They could have done, so why didn't they?"

Tutting to himself, he tried to get his thoughts in some kind of rational order, which was difficult since his brain was suffering from information overload. He let out a long sigh. *Don't think about the supernatural. It's just a crime like all the others you've ever seen. Treat it like that. Think like you always do.*

"Sir?" Carter was looking puzzled, but Murray raised one hand, silencing him. He didn't need any interruptions, not now, not when things were starting to take shape in his head. "I'm too close, that's what it is. With Ruby's help I'm forcing them to take Elizabeth Ray back and they don't

want to." He laughed aloud at the absurdity of it as the revelation hit him. "They're blackmailing me. Holding her
hostage to make me back off and let them enjoy their fun.
I'm being fucking blackmailed by the policemen of hell!"

Suddenly, he felt overwhelmed by anger. Anger at his own
fragile mortality and anger at these beings who had no understanding of what that meant. Face flushing, he pointed a
finger at the mirror as if speaking directly to his foe.

"Well, Ruby was right, you really don't know shit about
human nature. This is going to end. I'm going to make it
motherfucking end. I may not be able to lock you up but
you're going to take Elizabeth Ray whether you want to or
not, and you're going to give me back my daughter and
Rachel Wright, and you're going to do it on my fucking
terms! Can you hear me? Have I made myself clear?"

He glared at the mirror, challenging it to answer. There
was only silence and his own reflection staring angrily
back at him. He let out a long rattling sigh, and watched
the strength deflating out of his own broad shoulders as
Carter stepped into the frame.

"Are you okay, Jim?"

Turning to look into the freckled face of his friend and
colleague, he could see that Carter thought he definitely
was not okay. Great. My sergeant thinks I've flipped, he
thought wryly. And he's probably right. Feeling the St.
Christopher against his skin, he took strength from it. What
was a career in the great scheme of things anyway? He met
Carter's gaze with his own tired eyes. "You may as well call
off the search. You're not going to find Samantha out there,
it's just a waste of man hours, however well-intentioned."

Laughing in disbelief, Carter glanced sideways at the
mirror. "You are joking, right? This is your daughter we're
talking about here. You want me to call off the search?"

Murray's voice was calm. "That's what I said. You're not
going to find her, so there's no point." He stared at himself
in the glass. "I know where she is."

Carter ran one hand through his short red hair. "You

think she's gone into the mirror. Jesus, Jim." He looked at Murray as if begging him to say something that was going to make some sense. The other man leaned back against the wall and folded his arms across his chest, a small smile playing on his serious face.

"I know she's gone into the mirror. You want to know why?" He didn't wait for an answer. "I know because I've had one of those days you just would not believe. This morning I had a conversation with my dead wife who told me where I could find this"—he pulled the small medallion out from under his shirt—"and then a little old lady told me who'd been killing all these people and I can tell you now that they're not the kind of creatures that you or I would like to meet, although I have a feeling I'm going to have that pleasure before long. And if Sebastian says Samantha's gone into the mirror, well guess what? I believe that too." He stared at the confused and angry face of the younger man and wished for his innocence. How nice it was when there was just solid earth beneath your feet, and good guys and bad guys, and dead people that were just rotting meat. All that was only a day and aeons ago for him.

Carter's clenched fists were thrust deep in his suit trouser pockets. "Well, whatever you want, as far as I'm concerned this is a missing child case and I'm not going to call off the search until Samantha turns up." He half turned away and shook his head. "I don't know what the hell's got into you, but I thought you were tougher than this. You must have been under too much strain since losing Emily and I really think you need to take some time off. I'm sorry, but I'm going to speak to Baker tomorrow. Shit, you're talking like a crazy person. You need a holiday, Jim."

Murray laughed. He knew what Carter was saying. No more work for you and a one-way ticket to the funny farm. He pushed away from the wall and drew himself up to his full height.

"Oh yeah, do I need a holiday, and when this is all over I intend to take it." Not that you're going to have any choice,

his inner voice added quietly. Suddenly he felt tired. Tired
and without the energy to face the friendship that was dis-
integrating in front of him. He pulled open the front door.
"Now do what you want with the search and with Baker for
all I care, but for the moment just get out of my house. I
want some quiet time with what's left of my family."

The hurt was clear on the young Scotsman's face as he
called the WPC to leave and then stormed out after her to
the car. Gratefully, Murray shut the door behind them, resting his head on the wood for a second. He wasn't a fool. By
this time tomorrow he knew he'd be off the case, but found
that he didn't care that much. Not really. It wasn't as if
Carter would ever believe what he had to say, and there
wasn't the time to play the game and act as if everything
was normal. His job wasn't important. Samantha was important. Rachel Wright was important. Putting things right
was important. Wasn't that what being a policeman was
about in the end?

Turning round he saw Janet, pale and wan, in the hall
doorway leading to the lounge.

"Did I hear you say you spoke to Emily today?" God, there
was so much fragile hope in her voice. He looked at her
with gentle eyes.

"Look. Forget I said it. I didn't realize I was talking so
loudly. There's enough people around here who are going
to think I'm crazy by the end of today without adding you
to the list."

Raising her eyebrows, she gave him a soft smile. "Well,
that may be, but I know you better than that. I don't think
anything could drive you crazy even if you wanted it to. I've
made some fresh coffee, so why don't you come into the
kitchen and tell me about it?"

Fingering the necklace, he looked at her thoughtfully.
Her hysteria had passed and once again he was amazed by
how much this woman could cope with. "I don't think
you're going to have heard anything like this before."

She shrugged. "You're probably right, but I've been close

to madness myself not so long ago and I know how that looks and it's not like you. So come and tell me about Emily. And tell me about Samantha. Let me worry about the craziness, okay?"

He smiled as he started to follow her to the kitchen. "It's a deal. But I've got to warn you, this is going to take some swallowing." Frustrated as he was, there was nothing he could do until he'd heard from Ruby and baring his soul might do him some good. And so would that coffee.

CHAPTER
TWENTY-FOUR

Ruby parked the Polo outside the large red-brick house in the leafy suburb of Muswell Hill forty minutes after saying good-bye to Murray. Clutching the stuffed file under one arm, she paused for a moment while locking the car. My, my, Marjorie had done well. But then, her family always did have money, and given the passing of years most of it would be in her coffers by now. She felt a twinge of nervousness as she crossed the road, and cursed God for leaving her no choice but to come here.

She and Marjorie Pettigrew had been very close when they were in their twenties, but that was forty years ago now, and Ruby wasn't sure if time would have done anything to heal the rift between them. But then Marjorie shouldn't have anything to be bitter about. As Ruby had pointed out at the time, her friend had ridden a long way up the ladder of the occult society on the back of her talents before she'd pulled out. Marjorie had never forgiven her for that, since to her own chagrin, she'd never shown any psychic abilities of her own and enjoyed basking in the reflected glory of Ruby's.

Still, due to her own gifts, ones that Ruby didn't share, such as back-stabbing and politicking, Marjorie had carried on her rise all by herself, and done quite nicely, thank you. By day, she had been an archivist in the British Library, but by night she was *the* Librarian, and that was a position of power and trust. Now that she was retired, she could give the collection and her position in that other culture her full attention. Her old friend should be pretty smug all things considered.

God, it was all such a long time ago. Had they really been that young and passionate? She could use a little of that energy right now, she grumbled to herself as she pressed the brass buzzer. But never mind, there was nothing to be gained by wishing for things that couldn't be, however much you wanted them.

There was the sound of heels clicking on wood and the door opened and there was Marjorie, the glamour of her youth still visible on her aged but perfectly made-up face, clothed in a timeless suit that must have come straight from Bond Street. Looking down at her jeans and worn plimsoles, for a nanosecond Ruby wished she'd at least put on some lipstick, before putting her vanity into perspective with the current situation. Lipstick most definitely wasn't going to help her with what she had to do.

Marjorie covered her initial shock with a small supercilious smile. "Ruby, what a pleasant surprise, it's been a long time. I heard through the grapevine that you've been re-opening a few doors recently, but I didn't think anything could bring you to knock on mine."

Ruby glared at her, the false clipped tones irritating her already. "I need to use the library."

One delicate eyebrow arched on that pinched face. "Oh, you do, do you? Well, I'm sorry but you revoked your right to that privilege quite some time ago. The library is only available to a select few. My instructions are to not let you in. I'm so sorry."

Marjorie was obviously not very sorry at all, and Ruby's patience with the game ran out. "Cut the crap, Marjorie." Snapping, she stormed inside, barging past the other woman like a small tornado. "And get your glasses on," she called over her shoulder, "because this is a job for two."

Sebastian had been asleep on his father's knee since the two adults sat down at the kitchen table, his small body exhausted by the events of the day, and Murray had taken comfort from his warmth while telling Janet his extraordinary tale. He'd been more truthful than he'd set out to be, but in order for her to at least partly believe him, he'd decided she needed all the gory details, the manner of Suzy and Dr. Hanson's deaths included. And those of Elizabeth's parents. Now that he'd finished, he watched her as she twirled the St. Christopher between her fingers opposite him, her coffee cold and forgotten on the pine table. Frankly, he was amazed that she hadn't run out of the room calling for men in white coats to come and take him away. Letting her mull it over, he waited for a few minutes before speaking.

"You seem to be taking all this remarkably well."

Tilting her head, she smiled, her voice quiet and calm. "Ah, but I'm a good Catholic girl remember? We're brought up to believe in heaven and hell and have a healthy fear of eternal damnation. Although I have to say all this goes a little bit further than what they taught us at Sunday School." Her brow furrowing, she looked down at the necklace again. "But if you believe this woman is genuine, then I'll go along with you." Her frank eyes met his. "I can't say that I believe it all one hundred percent, but there's nothing to be lost by giving her the benefit of the doubt." Reluctantly, she handed the necklace back to him, and he reclasped it safely round his neck. "I think I'm afraid to believe it. Do you understand?"

Murray nodded and took one of her hands in his across the table. He knew only too well what she meant. They were only just getting over the loss of Emily and now they had this message from beyond the grave and they were left in limbo, somewhere between grief and joy, not knowing quite which way to turn.

Janet stretched her slim body upward and then slumped down in the chair. "So what happens now?"

"To be honest I can't say for sure. I'm a little bit out of my depth on this one." They both gave a small laugh at the understatement. "Ruby thinks she can find a way to force these Soulcatcher creatures to take Elizabeth back and return Sam and Rachel. But if I haven't heard from her in an hour or so, then I'm going to have to arrest Rachel or Elizabeth or whatever her damned name is, and see if I can force the issue somehow. I'm working on borrowed time. If I'm going to do something in any kind of official capacity then it's got to be tonight." He rubbed his face, the constant pumping of adrenaline through his body wearing him out. "I shouldn't have kicked off at Carter like that. It was stupid. After he's spoken to Baker tomorrow, there's no way I'll still be on this case, or any other for that matter. and I can't say I blame them for thinking I've cracked."

He drummed his fingers on the table as he watched the silent mobile phone. "God, this waiting around is killing me. Those bastards have got Samantha and there's bloody nothing I can do about it. Jesus, I've never felt so helpless!" If his son wasn't settled on his knee he would have been pacing the room, wearing down the linoleum, fists clenched deep in his pockets.

Janet pushed her chair back and stood up. "I know something you can do. Something useful."

"What?"

She opened the fridge and pulled out a large dish topped with mashed potato. "I made this fish pie for dinner. We may as well warm it up and eat it now."

Murray shook his head. "I really don't think I could eat anything." He wasn't lying. Just the thought of putting anything in his churning stomach made him ready to vomit.

Sliding the pie into the oven, Janet turned on the heat. "Whether you want to or not is irrelevant." Her voice was firm. "You haven't eaten all day, and you're going to need as much energy as possible for whatever this Ruby needs you to do tonight. Sam's my granddaughter and I want her back, safe and well. Therefore, if I have to tie you down and force-feed you this dinner, then believe me, I will." Turning round to face him, she confronted him with that logic that only women have. "And anyway, it's not as if you've got anything better to do, is it?"

Ruby's knees were hurting from kneeling on the cold stone floor of the cellar, and her eyes ached from straining in the dim yellow light that oozed lethargically from the electric lanterns hanging along the ceiling above the rows and rows of books that lined the walls for the length of the house and probably halfway under the garden. Her old friend obviously took her position very seriously indeed. You couldn't really call the room a cellar anymore; it was more like an enormous sacred vault, the floor one enormous piece of dark marble, the ornate bookshelves plated with what she was pretty sure was gold. It must have cost thousands to do all the work down here and get that gothic feel just right.

Sitting back on her heels, taking her attention away from the mass of open books that surrounded her, she shut her eyes for a few moments, giving them a well needed rest. They'd only been at it for two hours but it felt like days, and so far they'd come up with nothing. God, she wished she could see better. "Jesus Marjorie, couldn't you have put in some halogen bulbs or something? This light is killing my eyes." A comfy sofa or two would have gone down a treat with my old bones as well, she grumbled to herself as her right ankle clicked.

Marjorie's head popped out from the doorway of the cool room where all the ancient texts and parchments were preserved. Without the smart suit jacket and with her glasses perched on the end of her nose she looked a little more like the Marjorie of old, before they'd got into all this crap. The serious, studious girl whom Ruby had first met all those years ago. The Marjorie who had been her best friend. "Some of these books are very old you know, they need dim lighting to keep them."

"That's bollocks, Marje and you know it." Marjorie's natural prudishness had always brought out the bad language in her. "You just like that clichéd occult look. You always did. Everytime I smell that awful patchouli oil I think of you."

Marjorie looked decidedly put out. "Well, I'm surprised you spared the time from all your good works to think of me at all. And anyway, may I remind you that I have let you in and helped you much against my better judgement, so a little thanks and appreciation wouldn't go amiss."

Her head disappeared again, and Ruby let out a long sigh before gazing down again at the large pages filled with ridiculously small print. She had to admit, Marjorie had a point. Without her help, it would have taken years to find her way to all the literature that was relevant, let alone get the information she needed. Plus, she'd have had no chance at translating all the old works in the cool room, which were mainly written in some kind of old Latin. The classics had never been her forte at school.

But still, she thought, turning a page, if we pull this off, good old Marje will have a story she can live off for years, and no doubt she's thought of that as well. And dear God, she added looking at the hopelessly large amount of books she still had to work through, if we ever pull this off, I'll kiss her feet and help her tell it. Looking at her watch, she saw it was twenty to three. They had to find something and they had to find it soon. Time was running out. Pulling the next heavy tome from the pile, she started to read.

It was only about ten minutes later that her work was interrupted.

"Ruby. This shit really is real, isn't it?" Marjorie was standing in the doorway, a magnifying glass in one hand. Her voice sounded strange and then it clicked that she wasn't using that ridiculous upper-class accent that she'd obviously adopted at some time over the past forty years. "I mean, that crazy bitch from the bookshop really has come back from the dead, hasn't she?"

Ruby looked at her, not sure why the other woman was wasting precious time going over something they'd already covered. "I've explained all that to you already. Weren't you listening?"

Marjorie put her spare hand on one hip and raised her eyes to the dim ceiling. "Yes, I know you *explained* it all to me, but it doesn't necessarily follow that I believed it, does it? I mean that kind of stuff just doesn't really happen. Not in this day and age. Believe me, I've been in this business for forty years and to be honest I've yet to find even a measly love potion that I can guarantee will work. And if they're honest, the same can be said for most of the others in the network."

Ruby resisted the urge to point out that no matter how much of an obsessive interest in the occult a person had, all those years of dedication and study were worth zip without natural power. And from what she could gather, Elizabeth Ray had had enough natural power for Marjorie and all her cronies. Instead, she let out an exasperated sigh. "So what you're saying is that you didn't believe me when I got here, but you believe me now?"

Marjorie nodded.

"So what changed your mind?"

Marjorie grinned like a teenager, her eyes sparkling. "I changed my mind because I think I've found what you're looking for."

Ruby's heart froze in her throat. "What did you say?" If this was Marjorie's idea of a joke, then it would be the last one she ever played.

"I said I think I may have found it."

"Really?"

"Really."

There was a second or two's silent pause during which Ruby got to her feet without realizing she was doing it, and then the somber room was filled with the sound of the two old women whooping and screaming like teenagers, their old bitternesses forgotten forever. "Thank God for you, Marjorie." Ruby whispered into her friend's neck, thinking of that little girl lost in the darkness. "Thank God for you."

As was invariably the case with these things, Murray found that when Janet put his plate in front of him, his stomach started to growl in anticipation of being filled. He placed the still sleeping Sebastian on the sofa in the lounge and covered him with a coat to keep him warm, before rejoining his mother-in-law at the table. They ate in relative silence, the enormity of what they faced slowly sinking in, fear settling in the dry lines around Janet's mouth as she considered the things he had told her, trying not to picture Samantha trapped in some place more terrible than her imagination would allow. In the end it was she who completely lost her appetite and pushed her plate away, the food barely touched while Murray scraped up the last forkful of his.

When the mobile phone rang, the sharp loudness of it made them both visibly jump in their seats, Murray's fork clattering to the floor beneath him as he reached to take the call. Janet leaned forward and watched him with wide eyes.

"Ruby?" God, yes it was her, and her voice was clear and excited on the other of the line, making him want to cry with relief.

"I've got something." There was an indignant sound in the background that he couldn't make out and an exasperated gasp from Ruby. "I mean *we've* got something. We found it in some old scripts in a kind of encoded Latin so I'm not sure if the translation is entirely accurate but it's going to have to do."

Standing up, Murray started to pace. At last, at fucking last. "Brilliant, Ruby. What do we have to do?"

"Don't get too excited, there may be a slight problem. Well, there will be if any of those bodies have been buried yet. Have they?"

Her worry came at him through his ear, but his own excitement was starting to rise. "No. They're being kept at the morgue."

"Great. Do you have access to them?"

Murray's head was suddenly filled with the revolting image of filling up his car with decaying corpses. "What exactly do you need?"

"A little bit from each one. It doesn't have to be a part of the body as such," Thank the lord for small mercies, he thought to himself as he listened intently, "but either some bodily fluid or nail clippings. Even hair should do it. You're going to have to get something from Helen, Burnett, Suzy, the doctor, and of course, Elizabeth. The more the merrier. Do you think you can do that?"

Running through it in his head, he knew he could. Mitchell would have preserved samples of all of them, and if not then he was just going to have to go and get something from the bodies himself. It was going to be the death of his career, but then what the hell, there weren't many policemen that got to play with justice on this kind of level. "No problem." He hoped.

Ruby was getting excited at the other end, her words speeding up, as eager as he was to get on with things. "Good. Then that's what you have to do first. Without those samples there's nothing we can do. When you've got them I need you to mix them up in a small container with a little oil. Baby oil or vegetable oil will do, but mix them up well. Then we have to speak to Mike. You'll have to call his school, St. Margaret's Secondary, and arrange to meet him after work, somewhere Rachel won't be. Maybe a pub. Yes, a pub will be good, he'll probably need a drink. Don't for

God's sake tell him I'll be there. I'll give you half an hour with him and then I'll join you."

"We need him to get Rachel and meet us at Elizabeth Ray's house. You're going to have to be honest with him, tell him everything because when we get there he's going to have the pleasant job of smearing that stuff on her."

Murray was confused. He didn't think he had it in him to convince another person of all this wild stuff, let alone Mike Flynn. "Can't I just pick her up and take her to the house? I can't see Mike getting involved in this too easily."

"Believe me, I wish you could do that too, but it has to be him." There was a weight of sadness in her voice, and Murray wondered, not for the first time that day, just how damaged they were all going to be if they ever got through this alive.

"From what we can translate, she has to be betrayed by a lover. A lover who knows he's sending her back and doing it willingly. That's why I need you to talk to him before I do. If he thinks you believe this stuff he might just give it a go, if only to get you to leave them alone once and for all."

He should have guessed that none of this was going to be easy. "Okay, I'll call and arrange to see him at five." Looking at the clock on the wall, he saw it was ten past three. "That should give me enough time to get the things we need. I'll call you back when I've got a location."

"Fine."

Murray's voice caught in his throat a little as he spoke the next words. "Ruby, do you know how Samantha is? Sebastian says she went into the mirror. They've got her, haven't they?"

"Yes, they have." Even though she was just confirming what he already knew, his stomach turned. Her voice was soft. "I'm trying to keep all my channels open, but she's not in a place I can reach. I can hear Emily faintly though. She's singing and soothing her. She can't reach her either but she's close enough for Sam to hear her. They can't keep her there forever, but for her sake we have to get her back, and we have to do it soon. I think there's only so much of that a person could take."

Murray clicked the phone off, unable to speak. Ruby hadn't pulled her punches and he was glad about that. He'd had just about enough of platitudes when Emily died. He didn't need any more. Janet was touching his arm.

"What's happening?"

Pulling himself together, he gave her a squeeze. "I've got to go out. Ruby's found a way to end this mess. I don't know what time I'll be back, but if Carter or anyone should be looking for me tell them I've gone out for a few hours looking for Sam, okay?"

Nodding, she chewed on her bottom lip. "Is there anything I can do?"

The idea of putting any more of his family in danger was more than he could bear. He kissed her forehead, enjoying the smell of her hair. "No. Not out there at any rate. I need you to look after the pair of you. I'll have my mobile on if you need me and try not to worry." As he opened the back door her face was awash with fear, as if she truly believed she would never see him again. Giving her his best grin, he winked fondly at her. "I'll be back before you know it. And I'll have Samantha with me too, just you wait and see." He shut the door quickly behind him before she caught a glimpse of his own terror lurking under his mask.

CHAPTER
TWENTY-FIVE

On his way into town he'd rung the school and arranged to meet Mike Flynn in The Cricketers, the closest pub to the school. The young man hadn't sounded too pleased about it, but Murray knew he'd turn up alone as requested. First, he was a law-abiding citizen with a natural fear of what the police would do if he started flouting them, and second, he'd be curious to find out this information about Rachel that Murray had told him he wanted to share. He'd then called Ruby and got her up to date.

The soft soles of his shoes still managed to echo as he walked quickly down the blandly decorated stairs to the morgue. Quickly, but not too quickly. He could feel the sweat building up in the palms of his hands, and hoped his nervousness wasn't too apparent on his face. Pushing open the swing doors, he strode confidently, at least he hoped it was confidently, into the cool silence of the large brightly lit room within. A young woman, no more than twenty-five, sat behind the bland office desk to his left, her dark hair pushed away from her face in an alice band that seemed a little old-fashioned for someone of her age. She was concentrating hard on taking notes on some A4 paper from a large medical journal.

Pulling out his badge, he approached her. So far there was no sign of Mitchell, but he couldn't rely on it staying that way. The man was a dedicated professional and had been known to sleep on one of the trolleys usually reserved for less lively people when he hadn't wanted to waste the traveling time getting to and from home to get a little rest.

"Hello, I'm DI Murray. I don't believe we've met before. I'm the officer in charge of the Ray, Jenner, and Hanson cases. Is Dr. Mitchell around?" He hoped his soft voice was working its charms, wanting to find a balance between authoritative and casual. Putting her chewed biro down, she smiled at him.

"No, I'm afraid they've all gone to a meeting. He should be back in about forty-five minutes. I'm Dr. Jones. But please call me Claire. I'm hoping to specialize in criminal pathology, so I've come in to assist Dr. Mitchell for a few weeks. Well, assist his assistants at any rate." She almost blushed. "I've heard a lot about you though. You seem to be something of a legend around here."

He gave her his best disarming smile, although it felt like more of a grimace on his face. "Flattery will take you far, young lady." He glanced around and then at your watch. "Did Andrew mention that I was coming by to pick up those samples? I told him this morning that it was urgent."

Her pretty face became concerned as she scrambled around in the papers that covered her desk. "No, I don't think so. Not that I can remember. What were they for?"

He felt bad that he was going to get this girl into trouble but there were bigger things at stake than a little hurt pride after a telling-off. And anyway, she'd definitely learn a lesson about procedure.

"I need samples from Ray, Burnett, Jenner, Dr. Hanson,

and Helen Holmes. I'm taking them for some secondary DNA testing." It was a pretty flimsy excuse but the best he could come up with in the short time he'd had. Mitchell wouldn't have fallen for it in a million years, but this girl probably would. "Are you sure he hasn't got them ready? I'm supposed to have them there within the hour."

Standing up, she chewed her bottom lip. "What hospital are they going to? Maybe I can get Dr. Mitchell to Medex them straight after the meeting."

He shook his head, feigning irritation. "No, that'll be too late." Looking her in the eyes, he let out a soft sigh and he could see her sympathy for his plight. "Couldn't you go and get them for me? Ones that he's already used will be fine. I'll sign for them. It's just that this really is a matter of urgency, and if I want to make an arrest then I need the tests done ASAP. I know he's busy, but I can't believe Andrew overlooked this. There are innocent lives hanging in the balance." Turning away, he shoved one hand deep into his pocket and ran the other through his hair, praying that he wasn't overacting. From the corner of his eye, he watched her mental battle. Come on, Claire, he thought, come on.

In the end, her TV diet of Inspector Morse and P.D. James thrillers won out. After all, he was a detective inspector, so of course, she could trust him with the medical evidence. It would be silly to think otherwise.

She gave him a large smile, filled with the naïveté of youth. "I'll go and get them now for you, sir. Just give me five minutes," and then vanished into one of the side rooms, busying herself with her important task. Those few minutes seemed to last an eternity, as he paced the room with one eye on the door. All he needed now was for Carter or another of his colleagues to turn up and he'd be left with no samples and an awful lot of explaining to do. But he had to give Claire her dues, she was bloody efficient. It was barely over the stated five minutes that he heard the swish of her skirt and she was standing in front of him with the sealed container. He took it, enjoying the feel of its solidity in his grasp.

"There you go. I hope you get them to the hospital on time, and good luck with the arrest." She gave him a conspiratorial wink. "I'll tell Dr. Mitchell off for you when he gets back."

"Thank you, Claire. Thank you very much." Eager to get away, he gave her a quick kiss on the cheek and was gone, leaving her standing there pleasantly surprised and touching her face.

She was still humming to herself when Andrew Mitchell got back from his meeting half an hour later. "Anything happen while I was away?"

She shook her head. "Nothing much. But DI Murray came by and picked up those samples he asked you for this morning. He's a lovely man, isn't he?"

Mitchell looked at her, his eyes narrowed. She must be mistaken, that didn't make any sense. "He never asked me for anything. I haven't spoken to him today, although I was meaning to call. The poor man's daughter went missing this morning. Are you sure it was him?"

He perched on the edge of her desk while she gave a description. Yes, that certainly sounded like Murray. He was getting an unsettled feeling in his stomach. "Did he say what he wanted them for?"

Claire was starting to feel distinctly stupid. "He said he was taking them for secondary DNA testing. Have I done the wrong thing?"

Andrew looked at the nervous woman who was really little more than a girl and didn't have the energy to tell her off. "No samples leave here unless you have precise instructions from me, okay?"

Claire's bottom lip was beginning to tremble, and he sighed.

"But don't worry about it, maybe it did just slip my mind. Now why don't you pop upstairs to the cafeteria and get us

each a cappuccino and a pastry." Nodding, it was her turn
to flee the room.

Waiting until he was sure she was out of earshot, Andrew
Mitchell picked up the phone and dialed Carter's number.
Murray knew the procedures and he definitely hadn't
asked for samples of any kind. And secondary DNA testing? Only someone straight out of med school would believe that one. All their testing was done in-house unless it
was specialist specific. Whatever was going on, he hoped
Carter was going to be able to shed some light on it. The
number began to ring.

Murray pulled his car into a bay of the underground car
park and killed the engine. He couldn't believe how
smoothly that had gone, although by now he was sure that
Mitchell would be screaming blue murder. But never mind,
that couldn't be helped. Just one more nail in the coffin of
his career. Taking a quick look around to check there was
no one watching him, he opened the dashboard and
pulled out the baby oil and the small childproof medicine
container that he'd just purchased in Boots. Opening it, he
half-filled it with the pleasantly scented liquid and held it
between his knees, while he unclasped the chilled medical box.

The petrie dishes were carefully placed inside, and taking them out one by one he scraped their contents into the
tub using the lid of a pen to make sure he'd got as much as
possible out of them. He didn't look at the lids to see which
unrecognizable substance had come from which body, but
instead threw them untidily back into the icebox, not really
wanting to know. Once they were all in, he closed the lid of
the small container and started shaking hard. God, he
couldn't believe he was doing this.

The ringing of his mobile phone almost made him drop
his precious cargo and he picked the source of the unwelcome noise up from the well next to him. Don't let it be

Janet. Please don't let anything else have gone wrong for
my family today God. I'm out on a limb for you here.

The green face of the screen read CARTER MOB, and as he
let it ring out he allowed himself a small, sad smile. And so
the game begins. The hunter has become the hunted. Taking the original samples carrier, he got out of the car and
dropped it into the nearby dustbin, making sure the tub of
mixture was sitting tightly in the small confines of his top
pocket.

Starting the car again, his face was set in grim determination. Let's just hope they didn't track him down before
the end of the night. Screeching back out onto the street,
he had half an hour to get to his meeting with Flynn, and
he was damned if he was going to be late.

CHAPTER TWENTY-SIX

Watching the policeman setting down the two pint glasses, Mike raised a weary eyebrow. He hoped their thus far idle chitchat was over. He didn't have time for this, he hadn't slept in days, and he didn't think there was anything this inspector could tell him about Rachel that he really wanted to know.

"I asked for an orange juice."

Murray's smile was grim as he sat down on his worn burgundy stool. "I know you did, but believe me, you'll thank me later."

Taking a sip of the lager, Mike pulled a packet of cigarettes from the pocket of his cream chinos and lit one. "Well, let's make this quick shall we, because to tell the truth I'm exhausted and all I want to do is go home, have some dinner, and go to bed. And on top of that I'm bored of telling you that Rachel and I didn't kill those people."

His sarcastic tone didn't seem to ruffle the policeman. Why did he have the feeling that this man wanted to be his friend? And why didn't he want Rachel here? All the questions hanging in the air were starting to make him feel uncomfortable. What made him more nervous was that Murray seemed a little on edge as well. A bit jumpy as if he was eager to get on with something. Maybe just a touch afraid, too. At their last meeting, he'd been as cool as a cucumber so what could have happened to shake him up?

"I know you didn't. I also know who did, but we've got a bit of stuff to go through before we get there. Just agree that you'll hear me out, okay?"

The policeman's gaze was intense and Mike couldn't help his curiosity. "Fire away."

Even though they were sitting at the back of the pub, which was nearly empty, Murray leaned forward, resting on his forearms. "What do you know about Rachel's parents?"

He shrugged. "They were killed in a car crash last year. Why?"

"Wrong. They were her adopted parents. Do you know anything about her biological parents?"

Shaking his head, Mike was puzzled. He vaguely recalled the Rachel of old mentioning something about being adopted but it had gone straight out of his mind. She hadn't made a big deal out of it. Murray wasn't looking surprised.

"I don't think she does either. Do you remember the Ray case? Multiple murders? It was all over the papers a couple months ago."

Unsure of where this was leading, Mike felt himself waking up. "Sure, how could I forget? Hampstead House of Horrors, isn't that what the tabloids were calling it?"

Murray nodded. "That's the one. I hate to break it to you like this, but Elizabeth Ray was Rachel's mother." Dumbfounded, Mike sat on the other side of the table waiting for the punchline, while the policeman's soft voice continued. "Elizabeth was raped by her father when she was twelve. Rachel was the result and was adopted by the Wrights, who were old friends of the family. Elizabeth ran away shortly after the birth so Rachel would never have known about her unless Doug and Peggy told her, which they obviously didn't."

Sleep suddenly seemed a distant dream to Mike. This man definitely wasn't wasting any time by pulling his punches. Jesus Christ, how was he going to break this one to Rachel? *Hi, honey. I've been thinking about names for our baby. How about Elizabeth after your mother? You know, that psycho woman from Hampstead. Yeah, that's right, she's your mother.* Oh yeah, that would go down well. He took a long sip of his beer. No, he wouldn't do it. He couldn't do it. She seemed to be on the edge as it was, and this could just push her over. This was one little burden he was going to have to bear by himself. Even though he'd just put one out, with shaking hands he took the cigarette the policeman was offering.

"So you think that maybe Rachel's father is doing all this stuff? His way of trying to get back in touch with his daughter, or should I say, his granddaughter?" The thought of this unknown old man was making him feel sick, and he wished his expression could have some of the hardness that was evident in Murray's.

"No. He died a long time ago. Shortly after the rape Elizabeth set fire to her parents' house after locking them in the bedroom. They both died."

"Jesus Christ." It was all he could manage to say. He didn't know what he'd been expecting the policeman to tell him, but it was nothing like this. For an awful moment he wondered whether this kind of evil could be passed down in the genes. Was his child going to turn out like that? Was he going to be father to a monster? Suddenly his old blue sweatshirt wasn't keeping him warm anymore. As the shiver ran visibly down his spine, he squashed the thought. No. Not his child and not Rachel's. Their child may not turn out to be a little angel, but it was definitely going to be normal. They'd make sure of that. "How do you know all this stuff?"

Murray had almost finished his drink, just one or two

mouthfuls left in the glass. "We found Elizabeth Ray's diaries at her house. She left them there on purpose. She wanted us to know exactly what she was up to. I think she thought of all this as a kind of game."

Mike leaned back in his chair. "I haven't got a clue what you're talking about."

The policeman glanced at his watch before continuing. What was he waiting for?

"I'm going to tell you a few things about the Ray case that very few people know, and what you decide to do with that information is up to you, but I hope you keep it to yourself. Elizabeth Ray thought she had cancer. She thought she was dying and she decided that she wanted to come back from the dead. You probably know she was very into the occult, had an occult bookshop? Well, she'd found this ritual, it's got some weird name that isn't important right now, and she went through with it. She killed herself and then her blood was fed by Callum Burnett to Helen Holmes until Elizabeth's spirit was strong enough to come back. At that point poor Helen virtually exploded and Callum died shortly afterward."

Mike's smile was uncertain as he glanced around at the solid familiarity of the tatty but welcoming pub. "You sound as if you half believe this stuff."

Murray pushed his empty glass to one side. "Just hear me out. For this ritual to work, the blood tie between the person coming back and the person whose body they were intending to steal had to be stronger than normal. Elizabeth and Rachel have got such a link. After all, they both have the same father. And Rachel collapsed on the same night that Helen Holmes died. Elizabeth also left a letter with her diaries addressed to the officer in charge in which she says she looks forward to meeting me in the future, even though she won't remember anything. Doesn't all of that strike you as a bit odd?"

Rubbing his face, Mike knew what he found odd, oh yes indeed he did, and it was this crazy policeman. "I don't know what's going on here but I know you need to go and see a doctor. You're cracked! Are you trying to tell me that Elizabeth Ray has taken over Rachel's body and is killing these people? You're off your head."

"I believe she's come back from the dead, yes, but I know she didn't kill Suzy Jenner or Dr. Hanson even though that's what I thought until Ruby—"

Mike sat bolt upright in his chair. "Ruby? My aunt Ruby? She filled your head with this shit?" He started to laugh. "Oh it's all beginning to make sense now."

His laughing stopped as Murray's thick hand gripped his arm, pulling him forward, his face contorted with restrained fury. "You know I don't give a shit whether you believe me or not, but God help me, you're going to help me send Elizabeth back whether you like it or not, and if it doesn't work then tomorrow you can start suing my ass for millions and you and Rachel can go and live in the Bahamas for all I care, but these Soulcatcher creatures have got my baby girl and I'm going to get her back if it's the last thing I do. Do you understand?"

The two men stared at each other for a few seconds before Murray relaxed his grip. He looked into the shocked face of the teacher. "I'm sorry, I'm sorry." His voice was soft again, the anger gone. "I know this sounds crazy. I know. I thought it was crazy when I first heard it from your aunt, but then, then. . ." He hesitated for a moment, before meeting Mike's eyes, the pain in his soul written on his weathered face.

"I spoke to my dead wife through your aunt, you know? Really I did. She told me things that no one else could've known. *No one*. Things that were private. You know the kind of things I mean." He let out a long sigh. "God, I wish you could see those bodies. Nothing human could've done those things. The doctor was dissolved below the waist by an acid we can find no trace of. And Suzy? Well, there's no explanation for what happened to her or Helen." Mike was still staring at him, shocked, and he shook his head, gather-

ing his cigarettes and lighter together getting ready to
leave. The heaviness in his soul seemed to weigh down his
whole body. "I'm not making any sense at all, am I? I'm just
going to have to try and do this myself. I'm sorry to have
mucked you around. I just don't have the time to break this
to you gently."

"Wait!" Finally Mike had found the use of his voice, and it
was quiet and terrified. The policeman had said something
that had shaken him. Shaken him to the core. He'd mentioned something he couldn't know anything about, not if
it was just in her dreams. How could he know? "Did you
say the Soulcatchers had your daughter? Is that what you
said, 'the Soulcatchers'?"

Slowly sitting back down, Murray nodded. His voice was
slow and controlled. "Why? Have you heard of them?"

Mike Flynn shook his head and squeezed the words out
in a whisper. "Rachel dreams about them. I know because
she screams it out loud. The Soulcatchers are coming.
They're something in her head, something that haunts her."
He stared incredulously at the other man. "How could you
know about that? How?"

"Because they're real."

The strong female voice made both men jump, and Mike
looked up to see Ruby standing by the table. He didn't
know whether to laugh or cry, but he did know he loved
her and was glad to see her, deluded or not. Oh what the
fuck was going on here? Could Ruby and this normally ice-
cool policeman really both have gone insane? He felt his
aunt's warm hand on his.

"Well, I think we could all use a drink, so while Mr. Murray goes and gets us one, why don't we talk about Rachel?
She has changed, hasn't she? And the dreams are getting
worse, aren't they?" She gave his hand a squeeze. "And
when you've got all that off your chest, then I'll tell you
about the Soulcatchers, and what we've got to do to put
things right."

Mike nodded, his throat choked with more emotions

than he could isolate, and wondered for a second if you could catch craziness by touch, and then thought about Rachel and the way she'd changed. Suddenly, he didn't know where to start.

Two drinks later and he'd told them about the new and improved Rachel Wright, as she liked to call herself, and Ruby had just finished imparting the somewhat more bizarre information about the Soulcatchers, which was somewhat harder to swallow. Dead women walking? Demons? But if some small part of him didn't believe it was true, then why was he feeling so terrified?

"So they come through the mirrors? And that's how Elizabeth stole Rachel's body, by coming through her bathroom mirror?" It felt weird just saying this stuff, and spoken aloud sounded even more ludicrous.

Murray didn't look ludicrous though, he looked deadly serious. "Yes. There were smashed mirrors at the murder scenes and they took my daughter through our hall mirror. My son was there. He saw it."

Biting his lower lip, Mike shook his head. "So you want me to take Rachel to this address," he held up the scribbled peice of paper that Murray had given him, "where you two will be waiting, and then I have to smear some oil on her, and we all wait and see what happens. Have I got that right?"

Ruby and Murray nodded.

"Do you know how ridiculous that sounds?" He leaned forward. "And one other thing. Let's say you two are right. Let's agree, just for the sake of argument that Elizabeth has come back and taken over Rachel's body. How could I have fallen in love with a woman like that? I mean, Jesus, we're having a baby together. Don't you think I would have noticed if she was a homicidal maniac?" He heard Ruby's sharp intake of breath. "Yeah, that's right. She's having my baby. There's something you didn't know."

Ruby paused to collect her thoughts. "Elizabeth was a very disturbed lady. A lot of terrible things went on in her early life that helped turn her into the monster she became. Without the memory of any of that, there's no reason for her to resort to murder any more. The impetus has gone."

Mike laughed. "You really have got it all worked out, haven't you? But whatever you tell me, I don't think I can go along with this. I don't believe it." *Brave words, Flynn,* he thought to himself, *but not entirely true are they? Little things are bugging you. The way Ruby called her Elizabeth that time. The way she knew bad things were going to happen to people. The way Rachel's changed, and all those fucking bad dreams about these Soulcatchers. Maybe if it was just the policeman then you could put it down to insanity, but Ruby? She's the sanest person you know. It's not that you don't believe it, is it? It's that you don't want to believe it.*

Murray pointed the end of his lit cigarette at Mike. "Well, if that's the way you feel about it, then you've got nothing to lose. If nothing happens tonight except a confused Rachel gets moisturizer on her skin, then you can start suing the police tomorrow morning and neither of you will ever want for anything again. You'll certainly never get any police harassment. Not after something like this. So what are you worried about?"

Mike's bravado oozed away from him. "But what if something does happen? What then? I love her, you know. I love her more than I could ever imagine. I don't want to lose her. I can't lose her. I couldn't cope."

"Yes, you could cope. We all learn to cope." The soft voice didn't detract from the hardness of the words.

Ruby looked her nephew in the eye, and he could see her own love shining there. "This isn't going to be much consolation, but if we're right, then you're going to lose her anyway. They will come for her, there's no doubt about that, the only question is how many more people have to die before they do? It might be any of us next and in the mean time they've got the real Rachel and little Samantha. We have to get them back." She paused as he hesitated.

"You know it's not often a person gets the chance in life to do a right thing. A really right thing. This is our chance. And we have to take it. If we don't, then we're as bad as Elizabeth Ray was."

Mike stood up. "Okay, I'll do it. I don't like it but I'll do it." He knew he didn't really have any choice. It was time to put those nagging doubts to rest once and for all, otherwise, crazy as it sounded, he'd spend the rest of his life wondering if they were right. "I'll see you there in an hour and a half." He glared at both of them. "But once you've finished wasting my time with this, I want you to promise you'll leave us both the hell alone!" He stormed out of the pub, scared and confused before they had a chance to answer. Nothing was going to happen. Nothing could happen.

CHAPTER
TWENTY-SEVEN

Murray's car pulled up on Hampstead Road a few feet away from the entrance to the driveway of Elizabeth's house, and checking in his rearview mirror, he saw the Polo behind him. They were on double yellows but a clamp was the least of their worries tonight. Although it was still early evening, the sky was filling with ominously black clouds and the air was heavy and hot when he stepped out onto the silent pavement, his shirt sticking to him instantly in the muggy warmth.

"Well, I think that went all right, all things considered." Ruby was opening the boot of her car and trying to pull out the three large bubble-wrapped packages that filled the rear of the folded down passenger section and had protruded dangerously over the top of the front seats. "Give us a hand with these." Her voice was straining with the awkwardness of her tiny body trying to carry them.

Moving quickly, Murray easily managed to take two. "What are they?" Ruby's sharp eyes appeared above the rim of the object that was almost her height. "Well, we're not going to get very far without any mirrors. You said the three here were already smashed when the bodies were found and I doubt that anyone's replaced them. So I picked these up from Days Gone Bye. They were cheap, but we don't need anything fancy. It's not as if they're going to last long, is it?"

The gravel of the drive crunched under their feet. "Good thinking." Silently, Murray cursed his own lack of thought, a reminder once again that he really was out of his depth with all this supernatural shit. Jesus, how was this night going to end? They only had one shot at this and if he'd been doing it on his own then he'd have blown it already. But then, he added to himself, if I'd been doing this on my own I'd still be prowling around looking for a flesh-and-blood killer. Feeling a pang of loss for that innocent life, he put the mirrors down and took his jacket off, wrapping it round his arm.

"You wait here. I'll go round the back and smash a window to get in."

Ruby nodded and watched him disappear round the side of the house before resting her own package against his. With her hands on her hips, she looked up at the large house that seemed to loom threateningly over her, angry at having its secrets disturbed, and felt a ripple of the fear that had lived with her since all this began.

Part of her wished she'd given in to Marjorie's whining requests to come, wanting safety in numbers, but the majority of her knew she'd done the right thing by leaving her old friend firmly behind. The rest of them were *involved* in this, whether they liked it or not and knew the risks they were taking, but for all her protestations to the contrary, Ruby knew this situation was out of Marjorie's league. Hell, it was out of all their leagues, and there was no need to involve anyone who didn't really need to be there. She'd left Marje surrounded by candles on the library floor chanting a protection rite. She was probably still there now and the thought gave Ruby some small comfort. Any help they could get would be better than none.

There was the sound of locks being undone, the noise deadened by the humidity, and she was relieved to see the policeman pulling open the door. He had an air about him that kept her feeling solidly rooted to reality, and boy, did she need that now.

Picking up the mirrors, they silently crossed the threshold into the coolness of the house, the drop in temperature making her shiver slightly for a second. Although the broken glass had been cleared up, the ornate frame still hung emptily on the wall above the mahogany dresser, and for a moment Ruby could almost see those creatures from beyond breaking through to rage their anger against this empty, deadly house, full of the bodies of the unfortunate, the scene of a terrible crime against nature. She pushed the image away. She had no doubt she'd be seeing them in all their awful glory soon enough, so there was no need to torment herself unneccessarily? God, she could be such an old fool sometimes.

"Where shall we put these?" She whispered in the gloom. "And could we possibly turn a light on?"

Murray looked at the small elderly woman and grinned. "Upstairs. And we'll put a light on when we get there if the electricity's still connected. And why are you whispering? Do I detect a touch of the jitters?" His own voice was loud, echoing in the stillness as he climbed the stairway.

"Enough of your cheek, young man." Her words were firm but she was smiling as she followed him up the three flights and into the dusty wooden attic room, grateful to at last put her burden down. Murray flicked the switch by the door and watery yellow light surrounded them from the single bulb hanging from the center of the tired-looking ceiling. "Well, thank the Lord for small mercies," she panted, relieved to be able to see clearly at last. Her joy was short-lived, however, when she noticed the large, brown stain that wept through the floorboards, oozing outward from the middle of the room.

"Helen?" The distaste was evident in her voice. Murray was busy unwrapping the mirrors and peered over his shoulder, following the path of her gaze. "Oh. Yeah." He looked up at her. "Sorry, I should have warned you but I didn't think. I guess things like that stopped affecting me years ago. A hazard of the job."

Turning her attention away from the floor, Ruby gathered together the large sheets of torn bubble wrap and bundled them into a corner, while Murray positioned the mirrors against three of the walls, reflections of their legs catching their eyes everywhere the two people looked. Standing back, he admired his handiwork. "Well, let's just hope that nephew of yours turns up."

"Oh, he'll turn up. He may think we've flipped, but he'll turn up all the same. I know him well enough to be sure of that." She looked up at the policeman. "So what do we do now?"

Pulling a cigarette from the packet that was looking frighteningly close to empty, Murray lit it and inhaled hard before shrugging. "Now we wait."

CHAPTER
TWENTY-EIGHT

"But I've got a chicken roasting in the oven." Rachel complained at him as she stood up from the sofa.

"It doesn't matter, turn the oven off and get your coat. The taxi's waiting downstairs. You haven't been outside all day so the fresh air will do you good, and there's something I want to show you."

His voice sounded light despite the nerves that were eating at his stomach. He'd ordered the cab on his way home from the pub knowing that if he hadn't, then he'd lose his resolve to go through with this crazy plan as soon as he'd stepped through the front door. As it was, his heart tightened with a pang of painful guilt when he looked into those gray eyes, still beautiful, even surrounded by dark circles.

"You know I haven't felt much like going out recently."

Watching her, Mike felt the hopelessness of someone knowing they were doing the right thing against their own will. To say she hadn't felt much like going out was a bit of an understatement. She didn't go out, full stop. It was like she was afraid of something out there, her devil-may-care confidence slipping away from her over the past few weeks.

Often he came home from school to find her standing by the window looking out, watchful, eyes darting backward and forward as if there was someone out there, someone she couldn't quite see, eager to *get her*. For all he knew, she might have been standing there all afternoon. Watching her nervous indecision, he knew it had to stop. All of this had to stop, and if that meant taking her on a trip down memory lane to her natural mother's house, then that's what he'd do. Maybe she did know about Elizabeth Ray, maybe that's what this amnesia and nightmares were all about, and maybe a trip there would put all this madness away and they could get back to normal.

He held up her black jacket. "I won't take no for an answer. Now get your cute ass down into that cab. It's costing me a fortune already and we haven't even left yet!"

Giving him a tired smile, she took the coat and put it on over her slim fitting T-shirt. "Okay, okay. I didn't realize you were such a nag!" She kissed him softly on the lips and he felt his heart bleeding inside. "I'm only going because I love you. And you better let me have a glass of wine as a reward when we get home."

She was moving away from him toward the door and he pulled her back, overwhelmed by the urge to feel her next to him, wondering if he'd ever have the chance again, and knowing how crazy that sounded. He kissed her slowly and gently, exploring her with his tongue, savoring the flavor of her. "I love you more than I thought I was capable, you know that don't you? I'll always love you, no matter what."

Pulling back slightly, Rachel looked at him. "That's always nice to hear. Especially as I feel the same. I love you, Mike Flynn. You and your baby."

Suddenly he didn't want to go out at all, just wanting to take his beautiful woman to bed and hold her and protect her from all the demons in her mysterious head. To leave his aunt and that policeman to their delusions. To surrender to all the unanswered questions, to do his best to keep her safe. There was nothing the matter with her that his love couldn't cure, nothing, and he had the terrible feeling that after this was all over, once the two people waiting at that awful house had been proved wrong, he'd lose her trust forever for taking her there. For listening to them. For half believing their crazy stories.

She tugged on his hand, smiling at him. "Come on then, slowcoach. You've got me intrigued now." And then, against his will, his feet were moving. He shut the door behind them and said a silent prayer.

Carter knocked gently on Murray's door, the drizzle that was finally falling from the heavy sky settling on his suit like a mist. Shit, this had been a long day. None of the search teams had found any sign of Samantha and his throat was sore from speaking. He'd spent the past few hours knocking on as many doors as he could asking people if they'd seen the little girl, all to no avail. And he hadn't needed the phone call from Mitchell. Just what the hell was Jim up to? He didn't like it. He didn't like it one bit, not given the insane way his boss had been speaking when he'd last seen him. His daughter going into a mirror? I mean, come on.

Janet opened the door to him and for a moment he saw something flash across her face. Was it panic or fear? But then that was to be expected. After all this woman had been through, now her granddaughter was missing. The look was gone in a second, replaced by a wan smile.

"Hello John. I would invite you in but I've just got Sebastian off to sleep on the sofa and I don't want to wake him up."

"That's okay. I understand. I just thought I'd come and update you on the search." Janet looked at him, waiting for him to continue, and he wondered why she wasn't more eager, more panic-stricken.

"We haven't found her yet, but the team will search for as

long as they can tonight, and if we haven't found her by then, we'll be out at first light tomorrow. I just want you to know we're doing everything we can to get her back to you as quickly as possible. I know this can't be easy for you, not after everything else you've suffered recently and if there's anything I can do for you just call me, day or night."

Still smiling, Janet nodded and Carter got the unsettling feeling that she was trying to get rid of him. This wasn't what he'd been expecting, tears, yes, hysteria, yes, but this calm collected detachment? No. It was as if she hadn't been expecting him to bring Samantha back at all. What the hell was going on with the people in this house? Surely they couldn't have all gone crazy?

He looked at Janet's quiet smile again and realized what it might be. Sedatives. Maybe she'd taken a couple sedatives to calm her down. That would explain it. Relieved to have sorted one thing out, he turned his attention to another.

"Is Jim in? I've been trying to get hold of him but his mobile seems to have been turned off."

Janet shook her head and he noticed that her eyes were just a little too alert for the sedative theory. "No, he went out a little while ago. Said he wanted to be on his own for a while. To think about where Samantha might have hidden herself. He said he wouldn't be home late though, so if you want to call back in a couple hours he should be back."

She's lying, Carter realized. *She knows exactly where he is, she just doesn't want to tell me. Those lines were just a little bit too well rehearsed. Well, damn them both, I'll just have to find him on my own. He's gone too far for me to ignore.* He wondered for a second whether Janet knew her son-in-law had been stealing samples from dead bodies, and decided, improbable as it sounded, that she probably did.

"Okay, I'll do that. If he gets back sooner though, can you ask him to give me a ring?"

Janet nodded. "Of course I will. And thanks for everything."

He had barely said his own good-bye before she'd shut the door on him. Getting into the dryness of his car, he felt dumbfounded. What could Jim have told Janet that would make her lie for him? Turning the engine on, he pulled away. He would come back in a couple of hours, and he might just have to bring social services with him. Who knew whether that house was a safe place for little Sebastian to be in? In the meantime, he'd just have to try and find the detective inspector by himself.

Rachel's nerves had started kicking in about ten minutes into the cab journey, her breath coming quickly, heat leaving her hands and filling her head. Why did she feel like this? What was she so afraid of? She glanced warily at Mike, his handsome face turned away from her as he gazed thoughtfully out the window. "You wouldn't take me anywhere I don't want to go, would you?"

He looked at her quizzically. "What kind of question is that?" Although he was smiling, it wasn't his normal open grin, and his soft eyes slipped away from her uncomfortably.

It's the kind of question you're not answering, she thought to herself, as they turned into a long beautiful Hampstead Boulevard. It should have been a soothing sight, but something made her heart beat faster. She swallowed the tears that threatened to rise. What's the matter with me these days? Why is everything frightening me? Do all pregnant women feel this way? She pressed herself back into the leather seat of the black Hanson seeking comfort by making herself small.

"Just here'll do mate." Mike had leaned forward and was talking to the driver through the open part of the glass divider. The car came to rest at the pavement's edge and Rachel got out on shaky legs while Mike gave the driver twenty pounds, waving away the change. God, it seemed like a lifetime ago since they'd got out of a similar taxi after she'd left the hospital. Then, he'd been her knight in shining armor, but now, now she had an inexplicable feeling that someone had offered him thirty pieces of silver and he'd accepted. A wave of unreality swept over her. If only she didn't feel so tired and confused all the time then maybe she'd have a chance of understanding some of these thoughts she had. Ever since the doctor died, things had gotten worse and she'd sometimes find that she'd lost hours of the day, with no idea of what she'd been doing or thinking.

Slipping one arm around her shoulders, Mike led the way up a gravel drive to a large detached house. Blowing away the first drops of rain, she buried her head against his neck, sucking in the familiar smell. Of course she could trust Mike. What wasn't to trust about him? He was a good man. Inside her head she tried to squeeze out the hard female voice that was hers but not hers.

Don't kid yourself, princess. There's no such thing as a good man. There's just men, weak and disgusting. They're all the same. Monsters under the skin. Can't you see its scales rippling there, eager to get out? Take a closer look next time you let him lay on you. If there is a next time, you stupid bitch!

Sighing, she wished the angry voice away. These weren't her thoughts, even if they were inside her head. *Schizophrenia.* She pushed that word away too. She was just hormonal, that was all. The voice would go once she'd had the baby.

Still, she couldn't lose the sense of foreboding that swallowed her when Mike knocked on the imposing door. "I want to go home," she whispered, looking pleadingly at the man she loved. "Please take me home."

Squeezing her tight, Mike kissed her hair. "I love you, Rachel. Just remember that. I love you." His voice was choking slightly and that scared her more than the sight of Ruby and that policeman on the other side of the door. What was he afraid of? What had he done? Before she knew it, he had swept her inside and the door was closed behind them. Trapping them.

Pushing Mike away, she turned on the three of them, her panic rising. "Just what the hell is going on here? What am I doing here?" Her voice was little more than a growl and her flesh seemed to be tingling from the inside. Oh, this was a bad place. She shouldn't be here, she really shouldn't be here.

Ruby was smiling at her, trying to calm her down. "We thought if Mike was honest then you wouldn't come. I just want to try and get your memory back, dear. I think it's time. Why don't we go upstairs and I can hypnotize you."

As the old woman reached for her, she swiped the hand away, scratching the other woman's skin with her nails. *"Stay away from me you old bitch!"* Her dark hair had fallen into her eyes as she spun round looking for an exit she could get to in the eerie hallway, but just before the police-man grabbed her firmly from behind, lifting her off the floor and pinning her arms down in his strong hold, she was sure she saw him handing something to Mike. What was it? What was it?

There was a grunt from behind her ear as she kicked Murray's shin, but still his grip on her was firm. "Let's get her upstairs and get this done."

"Nooo!" She screamed, as she was carried struggling up the steep flight of stairs into the gloom, *"Nooo, please, please!"*

"Don't hurt her, Jim." Mike's voice was full of pain and the sound of it made her twist her head painfully far around on her neck to catch a glimpse of him. Tears were silently run-ning down his face as their eyes met, his full of hopeless love, hers full of fear and betrayal.

"What have you done to me, Mike? What have you done? I thought you loved me? Why are you letting them do this to me?"

Mike paused on the stairs, her words like knives cutting through him, his limbs heavy. "Because I have to know." He whispered back at her, before Murray turned the corner ahead of him, taking her out of sight. "Because I have to know." Part of him wanted to turn and run, and perhaps he would have stayed there, frozen on the stairs until it was all over, if Ruby hadn't given him a gentle prod in the back.

"Come on. You have to be strong. You owe it to them, to Rachel, Elizabeth, and your baby. We can't do it without you." She couldn't bear the pain that was on her nephew's face. "I wish we could. I really wish we could. But we can't." They stood there silently regarding each other for a few seconds.

"God, I hate you Ruby. It must be terrible to always be so right." Mike's eyes were almost soulless as he spoke, and then he turned and took the stairs two at a time, eager to be back with Rachel for what little time they had left.

Murray was struggling to hold onto Rachel in the middle of the attic room by the time Mike and Ruby got there, shutting the door behind them. Ruby turned the key in the lock and slipped it into her pocket. With relief, the policeman put his burden down. "God, she's got a kick on her." Groaning, he rubbed his shin and went and stood by Ruby near the door, leaving the center space to the two lovers. The rest was up to Mike now. They'd done all they could for now. Watching the two young people, he slipped his hand into Ruby's and they squeezed tight. He didn't think he'd been this scared in all his life.

Rachel's eyes were darting around the room, as she shook uncontrollably. "What are the mirrors for? What are the mirrors for?" Her face was wild as she stared at Mike. "*Will someone tell me what the fucking mirrors are for?*"

Even in the midst of all this fear, all this terrible mortal fear, she still knew she loved the gentle face in front of her. Tears were flowing down her pale cheeks. "Hold me, Mike," she whispered pleadingly at him, her anger replaced with despair. "Hold me. I'm so frightened and I don't understand. Why am I so frightened?"

Taking her into his arms, Mike felt his heart rip apart irreparably. "I don't know, my darling. That's what we're here to find out." He held her tight for a few moments, needing to remember the feel of her forever. As she softened against him, her muscles relaxing slightly, he slowly unscrewed the lid of the small tub that he held in one hand, scooping out some of the oil with the other. "I love you, whoever you are. God help me, I love you. And please God, I hope you can forgive me."

Shutting his eyes, he rubbed the oil-laden hand down the back of her hair as if stroking it. *Please God, don't let anything happen. I'd do anything, just don't let anything happen to her.*

It was a hopeless prayer and he knew it, because even behind his closed eyes something definitely was happening. At first it felt like a small cool breeze was blowing, gently lifting his hair away from his face although he knew there couldn't be a breeze because they were *inside*, and there couldn't be a breeze inside. Rachel squirmed against him, pulling herself free, and he opened his eyes to see her staring up at him in horror as she touched the back of her hair. The breeze dropped as quickly as it had come, and all he could hear was his own ragged breathing.

"I'm sorry," he whispered. "I'm so sorry."

Rachel's scream started low in her chest, rising and rising until it reached such a high pitch that Ruby had to cover her ears to try and block it out. *"Get back here, Mike!"* She shouted over the noise. *"Get away from the mirrors. Quickly!"* Mike stared at his aunt and then at Rachel, feeling the pressure that was building around her. Underneath her tormented scream he could hear another sound. A distant whistling that was getting louder, compressing the air, as if something was pressing down hard above him. Rachel's hair was rising with static, floating around her horrified face as she stood frozen on the stain from Helen Holmes's blood. Oh, there was so much anger around them, anger that was so palpable he could almost taste it and he could feel a scream rising in his own throat when the lightbulb exploded, sending him diving toward Ruby and the policeman, as Rachel curled up in a ball, her scream turning to a helpless moaning. His own panic taking over, he reached for his aunt, wanting human contact, but it was as if they were each surrounded by a magnetic field pushing them away every time they got close, keeping them spread out along the back wall. In the gloom he could see Murray watching the distorted mirrors, *Oh shit, the mirrors were rippling red*, his intelligent face looking stupified with disbelief.

Oh God, it was starting. It was starting and there was no going back. The Soulcatchers were coming. Raising his head against the awful pressure he looked up at the small skylight above and saw the ice crystals that were forming against the glass, spreading outward at an unnatural speed, like mad creepers breeding across the walls and ceiling, bringing a terrible wind with them. It hit him so hard, he thought his breath had frozen in his lungs, unable to expel it, making ice form on his eyelids. Through blurred vision, he saw Rachel sitting silently in the middle of the floor unaffected by the madness going on around her, untouched by the crazy weather in the attic, like the small core of stillness in the center of a tornado. Twisting his head sideways, he watched helplessly as Ruby's old fragile tiny body was pressed flat against the door by the onslaught, her lips blue with cold, eyes shut tight with pain.

In the far corner Murray was fighting forward but getting nowhere, like a man in a wind tunnel, his clothes like a second skin at the front and billowing out behind, his face contorted with the effort of trying to move. Gazing at the scene, Mike felt a kind of serene calmness settling inside him. *We are never going to survive this*, he thought quietly. *We betrayed her, and that betrayal is going to cost us our lives*. There was a justice in the thought that gave him a moment's peace before the mirrors exploded, sending his head back hard against the wall. *This is it*, he thought, as the darkness spread across his vision, his consciousness fading. *Well, if this is it, then it's not so bad*. And then there was nothing.

CHAPTER TWENTY-NINE

Janet was screaming in the darkness of what until moments ago had been their sitting room, the only light coming from the hard flashes of lightning from the storm outside. The glass from the imploded windows covered the floor around her, cutting her legs and hands as she crawled toward the small bundle that was Sebastian, curled up on the sofa, racing the thick tentacles that were coming impossibly fast from the hallway covering the carpet and walls, seeking him out.

Grimacing, she ignored the pain, calling instead to her sobbing grandchild. "Nana's coming, Nana's coming," hoping her voice had more calm than she felt. Oh, Mary mother of God, where had this thing come from? She moaned as one thick boneless limb brushed over her leg, it's suckers clutching her for only a second, scenting her, before she felt the sliminess slip away. *It wants Sebastian. Oh Jesus, it wants Sebastian.*

She didn't know what she had expected when their

world had suddenly exploded, the foul smell filling the
room, the creature escaping from the mirror. Something
terrible, yes, but not this *thing*, this monster of her own cre-
ation that she hadn't seen since her childhood nightmares,
where it used to live, clutching at her, suffocating her in her
dreams.

*They're using my fears, they're using my own fears against
me. And oh shit, it's working.* Letting out a wail she
clutched Sebastian just as one long limb of the unseen oc-
topus monster slid around his ankle, tightening and pulling
him away from her with impossible strength. *Oh God, I
can't hold on*, she panicked as she felt his small limbs
grasping desperately for her, unable to get a grip as he
screamed, the blood pouring from her cuts and gashes acting as a lubricant. Taking a deep, angry breath she bit
down hard against the rubbery surface, bitter fluid filling
her mouth. *"JUST FUCK OFF AND LEAVE US ALONE, YOU
FUCKING SHITHEAD!"* She screamed, spitting the black liquid out of her mouth, knowing how futile it was, knowing
that Sebastian was still being pulled from her pathetically
weak arms, and she couldn't hold on, she couldn't hold
on. *"IT'S NOT FAIR! IT'S NOT FUCKING FAIR!"* As she was
dragged to the hallway, still trying to hold on to her grandchild, the only part of her daughter left, she grabbed a
shard of glass and stabbed it into the tentacle of the beast.

A fraction of a second later, Sebastian was blown free of
the limb as the monster screamed, a scream of rage and
disappointment, landing safely on the slime-covered sofa
from which he had just been sucked away. Still clinging to
the slithery sucker that writhed in her grasp, Janet looked
around in amazement at the several others that were re-
treating so fast it was as if a vacuum in the mirror were
yanking them back at an impossible speed.

Did I do that? She thought for a second as they thrashed
against the walls, breaking the plaster as they went back
from where they came, to the cause of that terrible howl-
ing. *Did I really do that?* And then the thing in her hands

exloded, the thick fluid sticking to her eyes, burning her, blinding her, in a final gesture of contempt.

It was a few minutes before she'd stopped screaming, and just lay there sobbing in the blackness, her heart broken, her spirit destroyed. They had beaten her, beaten her and taken the last of her precious children. It was as if there were a distance between her and the terrible pain in her eyes as she moaned and waited and wished to die.

When the small hand touched her shoulder, her terrified instinct was to swat it away, thinking the monster was back—*had it ever really gone away?*—was back to finish the job it had started in her dreams so long ago.

"Nana Janet? Nana Janet?" The small voice was full of tears, but just hearing it made her force herself up on painful hands and reach for him in the darkness. Was he still there? Was he really still there?

"Where are you, Sebastian? I can't see you?" She felt his arms around her neck and his sweet hot breath, his alive breath, dampening her face, stinging the agony of her eyes.

"But I'm right here. The lights are back on. Why can't you see me?"

Somewhere outside she heard the distant rumble of thunder, and ran her fingers over the face so very close to hers. "The monster hurt my eyes." She whispered to him gently, not wanting to spread her numb fear. "Is the monster gone now?" Her hand still touching his face, leaving smears of blood she couldn't see, she felt him nod.

They sat there, holding each other in the wreckage, until the storm had passed.

The small candles that surrounded her were almost completely burned out, but Marjorie didn't notice as she started her third hour of chanting, her spirit separated from the agonizing ache in her limbs caused by sitting on the cold marble for so long. She knew that when this was over it would take days of resting in a long hot aromatherapy bath to cure the stiffening in her lower back and legs. But this she could deal with, years of meditation giving her an advantage over her aging body. She had learned a long time ago to switch off the mind from the restrictions of the physical, if only for a few hours. Ruby may have thought her friend lacking in powers, but Marjorie had always thought she'd underestimated the power of will. Willpower was one thing she had never lacked.

She softly chanted the ancient words, words she wasn't even sure she understood properly, quietly and evenly so as not to tire her voice more than was necessary. Interspersed between the Latin she spoke the names Ruby had given her, Michael, James, Ruby; Michael, James, Ruby. These were the ones who needed protecting.

The panic she had felt when Ruby had gone, her sense of uselessness and lack of ability, had faded when her chant had begun; a calm stillness filling her, flowing out from her like an aura. But still, when the surge ran through her, blowing her hair out behind her, filling her with fear and cold, their fear and cold, the three of them slipping out of consciousness far from her but yet inside her; her breath caught in her throat with sheer surprise. Without skipping a word, she flashed her eyes open for a moment, verifying that despite the sensations she was still in the sanctity of her library, in the sanctity of her own skin. It's working, she thought somewhere in her distant conscious mind. It's working. I'm doing fucking magic! While part of her reeled with the glory of power, the rest sank back into the trance and danced on the flow of the words.

CHAPTER THIRTY

Murray came to with a groan, for a moment unsure of where he was or what had happened. All he knew was that he had been desperately cold and now he was warm, the wonderful heat surrounding him, covering him with a golden hue, wrapping itself like a blanket around him. What a wonderfully strange dream this was. Through the haze of yellow, he saw Ruby and Mike struggling to their feet, each giving off the glow that he realized was the cause of the warmth he was feeling, and the reality of their situation sank back into his bones.

"What is it?" He called to Ruby who was staring incongruously at her luminous hands, his voice deadened by the light that seemed to be a force around him. She looked over to him, smiling, her laugh a sweet tinkle in his ears, and despite how strange his own voice had sounded, he could hear her as clearly as normal.

"It's Marjorie's protection spell! It's working!" She laughed again, shaking her head in disbelief.

"Oh shit. Oh, holy, holy shit." Following the dull voice, Murray's eyes found Mike Flynn, standing in the corner,

staring ahead of him, his mouth open with horror. Turning
to see what he was looking at, Murray thought the teacher's
words were as apt as any. Hearing Ruby's gasp beside him,
his own eyes widened as his stomach turned to water. "Oh
shit." He whispered in agreement.

The room in front of them was glowing blue, the air
sparking with electricity, cracking and spitting as it flashed,
reflecting on the broken shards of mirror that littered the
room. The empty frames still leaning against the walls were
oceans of blackness, true blackness, darker than any created by paint or pen, darker than the night, sucking in the
light surrounding them.

Rachel stood sobbing and hugging herself as her hair
blew wildly in a wind that only she could feel, her body
wrapped in shimmering threads of black and red, from
which she couldn't break free, like a fly trapped in a web,
waiting for the spider.

"What's happening to me? What's happening to me?" She
whispered as she squirmed in front of them, trying to twist
around to see them. Screaming her name, Mike tried to
move toward her, but this time it was the barrier of yellow
that stopped him, gently pushing him back, matching his
strength with one of its own, protecting him from himself.

Ruby moaned as the three figures surfaced in the blackness that only hours ago had been mirrors on a shelf in a
warehouse, first a head or a hand reaching into the air
from nowhere, and then pulling themselves free from the
confines of the cheap frames and sliding with a series of
disgusting thumps into the attic, where they stood victorious. The Soulcatchers had arrived in all their terrible glory.

Glancing at Murray, she saw by the confused horror on
his face that the policeman had recognized two of the new
arrivals, *who they were pretending to be*, just as she had.
The crimson-crusted burnt shell of a man, if you could call
him that, grinned fleshlessly at Rachel, his white, lidless
eyes full of hate and lust. Harry Ray was back.

"Remember me, princess? It's been a long time. I've

come back to light your fire. It's time to go, baby. Time to start reliving the good times." The voice was raw and harsh, the vocal chords singed beyond use so many years ago, and the smell of barbecued meat hit Ruby so hard she thought she would vomit. She wasn't strong enough for this. What had she thought she was doing? Her eyes fell to the dead man's torso that was distended beyond all belief, the huge swelling stretching down so that his stomach covered what was left of his legs almost to the floor. What was in there? What was inside him?

Rachel moaned as the thing ran his black tongue down her face and she could hear Mike screaming her name behind her, sounding so far away; and in that instant, she knew that he was lost to her forever, the pain in her heart caused by that realization overwhelming the fear of these awful creatures that surrounded her.

"I don't know you. I don't know any of you."

She looked from the dead man in front of her to the fat, rotting girl, whose mousy hair was matted to her face with the gel that used to be her eyes, who giggled as she stroked the belly that seemed to wriggle under her fingers, and knew somewhere inside her that that wasn't entirely true. Somewhere in her memory these terrible things had a place, but she just couldn't get there, didn't want to get there because that might mean that all this was really happening, that it had meaning, that it made sense.

The fat girl tilted her head and giggled, the hollows in her face fixing on Rachel as if she could truly see. "After all we did for her. After all she did to us, she says she doesn't know us." She twirled a strand of Rachel's hair between her fingers, her singsong voice high and shrill. "But then Elizabeth doesn't remember, does she? Elizabeth will never remember, never, never, never, never remember."

Something in Rachel's head snapped. *"DON'T CALL ME THAT! DON'T CALL ME THAT! MY NAME IS RACHEL! IT'S FUCKING RACHEL! YOU'VE GOT THE WRONG GIRL!"* And for a small moment she believed it herself, her anger mak-

ing her spirits soar, until the third thing spoke and as she
looked at him, *at it*, her heart froze with the finality, the
eternity of his being.

He was tall, the tallest man she had ever seen, could
ever see, and for a fraction of a second she thought he was
clothed entirely in burgundy red, although she couldn't
quite make out what he was wearing, because it seemed to
be running, flowing over him, blending into his face as her
eyes followed it, his features constantly shifting, changing,
his mouth a hole into which the liquid that covered him
was sucked. *He's made of blood.* She thought dimly as she
stared. *He's made entirely from blood. Dark blood. Bad
blood.* This one filled her with fear. This was the thing she
had dreamed about. When he spoke, the depth of his voice
was like a knife in her ears and she felt a warm trickle of
blood oozing down her left cheek.

"We have come to take you back. We have been sum-
moned. Your name is Elizabeth Ray and you will return with
us. You have broken the laws of life and death, for you there
in no hope of redemption. You shall stay with us forever."

The name hit her and as she reeled, her head was filled
with images of newspaper covers, pictures of Helen Holmes,
Helen Holmes when she had eyes, when she was alive and
suddenly she realized whose house this was, whose house
Mike had brought her to, Elizabeth Ray's house, but not *her*
house, not hers.

The creature stepped closer to her and she screamed at
it. "Then why don't I remember? Why don't I remember being her? I'm Rachel! Rachel!" Suddenly her own name felt
unfamiliar on her tongue, and then the redness of that fluid
face was leaning down from its impossible height, the slit
that was its mouth stretching into a parody of a smile.

"You will never remember. All of eternity with its exquisite suffering is waiting for you and you will never remember your life, your crimes. Your punishment is that you will
suffer forever in innocence with no hope of transcending
to a better place. Through your pain you will forever be ask-

ing why." The voice had such power it made her whole body resonate. "You would have been better to have just let yourself die."

She could feel her sanity cracking. "But I'm Rachel." She whispered to herself, the tears flowing down her face. "I'm Rachel."

The thing, the Soulcatcher, laughed, and it was the most terrible sound she had ever heard. "No. No you are not. Rachel is your daughter." He lifted his hands and she felt the warm wetness as they held her face. Shutting her eyes, the strength sapping away, her legs like water threatening to collapse and take her to blessed unconsciousness, she prepared herself for her fate.

"Nooo!" Mike was screaming, struggling against the warm restraint that held him. "Take your fucking hands off her, you bastard! It isn't fair, she doesn't remember! It isn't fair! That's not justice. You're sick! You're sick!" This wasn't right, it wasn't right, he couldn't let them take her like this, not like this.

Oh Mike, Rachel thought softy with what was left of her mind, Oh Mike, it could have been so good, it was so good. If only you'd let us have a little more time.

The creature roared at the man she'd loved, the power of the sound sending him sprawling to the floor, and he had a feeling that without this shield or whatever it was that coated him, it might have been enough to kill him. His head spun as he struggled to sit up.

"We have no sense of your human justice. It is too frail, too full of flaws for us to comprehend. Our justice is final. Do not dare to question us!" Tentacles of blood were separating from him and wrapping themselves around Rachel, drawing her to him, pulling her closer, eager to get on with his task, while the creatures in the guises of Harry Ray and Helen Holmes giggled slyly and caressed each other, watching the show with hungry eyes.

"Wait a second!" This time it was Murray that was shouting, waving an arm angrily at the creature he couldn't

reach. "You don't get to take her until I get my daughter
back! I want Samantha back now! Do you understand?" His
voice sounded pathetic and infinitesimally small, unable
to carry the weight of his emotion.

The screeching demon sent electricity flying at Murray,
raging its disapproval at another interruption, its tendrils
lashing out at him with such strength that the yellow
around him winked out for a second, leaving Murray
winded against the wall. Its opposition taken care of, it lowered its head in a mockery of a kiss over Rachel's mouth.
Mike pressed his face into his hands, unable to watch, and
it was then that the door burst open from the other side.

"What the fuck?" Carter looked at the madness around
him with disbelief.

It had taken him an hour or so after seeing Janet to figure
out that Murray may have gone to the Ray house. He
couldn't think of a good reason why, but then he couldn't
think of a good reason why he would have stolen the samples from those bodies either, and at least there was a link
between that and Elizabeth Ray's house. Heading toward
Hampstead, his windscreen wipers working overtime in
the approaching thunderstorm, he felt exhausted. Shit, it
had been one hell of a long and emotionally draining day,
and he decided that this was going to be the last place he
looked for Murray before heading back. If he wasn't there,
then his erstwhile boss could stay on the missing list till tomorrow when he'd speak to Baker and sort the matter out
at a higher level. He didn't have the energy to deal with this
shit.

Even through the gloomy rain he spotted Murray's car
parked ahead of him to the left, just a little before the driveway of Elizabeth Ray's house. "Bingo." He muttered under
his breath and wondered why Jim hadn't driven up to the
front door. Surely, he had enough respect to know that
Carter or any other officer looking for him would see his
vehicle wherever on the street it was parked? As he turned

in he heard the gravel hitting the underside of his car, and cursed quietly, not wanting any chips in his paintwork. The department was notoriously stingy about that kind of thing and like most young men, he was proud of his wheels.

Turning his collar up against the onslaught of water, he stepped out and gave the front door a push. It didn't budge. Okay, so maybe Jim had got in around the back. Ignoring the rain that trickled down the back of his neck and under his shirt, he jogged down the path at the side of the house and through the small gate leading to the back door and the garden. He smiled to himself. There it was, one large pane of glass smashed cleanly above the handle. The door wasn't locked and he quietly let himself in. So far, so good.

Moving through the kitchen, he padded into the hall and poked his head slowly into the dim, empty lounge. Okay, so where was Murray? Standing at the bottom of the stairs he heard a scream coming from above him. A woman's scream, the kind that made your mouth go instantly dry with fear. Oh shit, what was Jim doing up there? There was no time to call for backup, and not stopping to think, he ran up the stairs two at a time, the noise getting louder the closer he got to the source. It was when he reached the second landing that he knew where it was coming from. The attic room. The room where they'd found what was left of Helen Holmes, and now it sounded like his boss was murdering someone else in there.

His heart pounding in his chest, adrenaline killing off his tiredness in an instant, he flew up the final flight of stairs and rattled the door handle. Oh motherfucker, it was locked. What the fuck was going on in there? The screaming had stopped but he could hear a man shouting over what sounded like a storm going on in there. That couldn't be right. It couldn't. Surely, even with the skylight open, the thunderous rain outside couldn't cause that much noise *inside* a house could it?

Well, there was only one way to find out. Taking a deep breath, he moved as far back as the narrow landing would allow and then ran at the door, shoulder forward. Grunting on impact, he felt the old wood give way, and then he was falling into the room, stumbling to keep his legs upright as his mind tried to comprehend what his eyes were seeing. "What the fuck?" he muttered as he looked at the huge red thing, *just what kind of a thing was that?* that was spreading itself like a fungus over Rachel Wright. *Oh Jesus Christ, what is that?* He thought as his stomach turned to water, the heat of panic making his brain feel as if it were about to explode in his skull. *Oh Jesus, it's looking at me, it's looking at me, Oh Jesus motherfucking Christ, what am I doing here?* The terrible thing in front of him started to howl, the cold wind hitting him, burning his face and then he heard a woman shouting to the right of him, an old woman in jeans, glowing yellow in the unnatural blue light.

"*He hasn't got any protection! He hasn't got any protection!*" The woman's eyes were wide with fear looking slightly beyond him, and tearing his eyes away from the monstrosities in front of him, *was that Helen Holmes, Oh God, that's Helen Holmes, what the hell is she doing with her hands?*, he turned to look at Murray who was screaming at him, screaming and gesturing frantically, but he couldn't make out what he was saying, the rushing cold in his ears was too loud, and his eyes were dragged back to the dead woman whose hands were spinning round and round on her wrists, faster and faster until they broke free, separating into two spinning flat disks, whirling in the air between them as she laughed and spun, and then they, Oh God they . . . Oh shit . . . I should run . . . I should move . . . they're . . .

"*GET OUT JOHN, GET OUT!*" Murray screamed at his young colleague who stood staring stupidly, uncomprehending at the insanity of the attic room. "*GET THE FUCK OUT NOW!*" For a moment their eyes met and Murray felt a small glimmer of hope, urging Carter to run, to get away, not to look back, and then the young man's gaze was drawn back in front of him. Murray shouted at him incomprehensibly, but it was as if he wasn't listening, as if he was beyond listening. Oh God, he had no protection, Ruby was right and he strained against the light that held him in place, willing to sacrifice himself in order to save his friend. And then, as he let out a wail of grief, he watched his friends eyes widen in a moment of dawning understanding and the spinning disks that had been the Helen creature's hands shot across the room in an instant, one decapitating him, the other slicing through his torso. Without even a murmur, John Carter was dead.

Somewhere in the distance he heard Ruby and Mike screaming, but all he could see was his friend's body, for a moment still standing as if in disbelief of how quickly death could come, and then that young shocked head toppled slowly to the ground, the movement making his torso slide away, blood soaking the floor around them as the divided body crumpled.

Gagging on his vomit, Murray leaned into the corner and collapsed onto the floor, his friend's blood soaking into his trousers. *I can't fight any more. I can't fight anymore*, he thought dimly behind his numb mind. *I just can't take any more of this*.

All that could be seen of Rachel was her dark hair, showing in patches through the crimson bindings around her as her face was upturned to the creature who had been lowering himself, as if ready to devour her. Drained and exhausted, Murray willed it to take her. To finish this thing. The wall of redness paused and stared with eyes that were merely patches of darkness and shadow in its shimmering visage at Murray's collapsed form, and for a moment seemed thoughtful, before speaking. "Give back the child."

Ruby understood now why Harry Ray's body had been so terribly distended. As the three of them watched, no longer able to feel any fresh horror, not after Carter, not after all this, the monster dug his burnt and clawed hands into his charred flesh, ripping himself open. At first, all they could see was a flash of golden hair, and then as he tore himself apart, wider and wider, there she was, complete, eyes numb. Samantha stepped out of the body as if it could have been a cupboard she'd been hiding in, and walked slowly to her father who was crying out her name between his sobs, and sat next to him.

Grabbing her, needing to be certain she was really there, he hugged her unresponsive small body. "Are you all right, baby? Are you all right?" She didn't answer, but leaned her head against his shoulder and went to sleep. Kissing her hair again and again between his tears, he held her tight and waited for the madness to be over. His baby was back, the rest could go to hell for all he cared, and he decided he'd seen enough. Shutting his own eyes, he hummed gently to his child.

At the other side of the room Mike watched, numb of all emotion as the red monster embraced Rachel, kissing her as gently as he himself had done only an achingly short time ago. "I love you." He whispered as she began to shake and convulse, her body trapped in the unnatural caress. "I love you, Elizabeth Ray." Silence had fallen, and out of the corner of his eye he could see Ruby weeping silently beside him, and Murray curled up with his daughter, no longer interested in the game being played out around them, only a dark shadow in the gloom.

The dealthy kiss finally over, Elizabeth absorbed into its mass, the red creature passed the limp body over to Helen Holmes as if it weighed no more than a feather, and she placed her rotting lips over the mouth, the wriggling mass in her belly, rising upward, up into her unbreathing chest, transferring it into the flaccid flesh to which it belonged. With a gasp of air, Rachel Wright collapsed to the floor.

Stepping backward, the three creatures spoke in unison. *"WE ARE DONE."* The room exploded into a thousand colors never seen in a rainbow and then there was only blissful nothingness as unconsciousness claimed Mike for the second time in an hour. It was all over.

EPILOGUE

The summer long gone, Murray could feel the autumn chill seeping into him from the cold wood of the bench beneath his coat and trousers as he looked out over the calm water of the lake in the peaceful secure hospital unit's grounds. They had met here once before, months ago after Rachel was deemed mentally unfit to stand trial; and absorbing the tranquility around him, he waited for Mike Flynn's gaunt figure to appear around the bend in the path.

As the man approached, his appearance was a painful reminder of how much he had changed. Gone was the youthful grin, the handsome face having lined prematurely, and the mid-brown hair was now heavily flecked with silver. But the eyes were always the window of the soul, and as he looked at the teacher, it hurt to see how much hardness lived there now. But then, he thought, as the weight sank down next to him, this had changed them all, changed them all for life, and they were just going to have to do their best to live with it.

Side by side, they smoked silently for a few minutes before speaking.

"How is she?"

Mike let out a long sigh, the lungful of smoke hanging in the air in front of them. "They have to keep her arms tied down." His voice was soft and laden with so much emotion it almost seemed devoid of it. "She keeps trying to hurt the baby. Punching herself in the stomach. That kind of thing." He didn't look at Murray, but gazed at some distant spot out on the lake. "The doctors don't think she has any chance of recovering her sanity. They call it a complete mental collapse."

He paused, his cigarette burning forgotten between his cold fingers, and his breath hitched slightly. "They don't think I should visit anymore. They don't think it's doing her any good." He frowned. "I could have told them that. She fucking hates me, I can see it blazing in her eyes. She hates me and the baby. I think she's sane enough to understand what I did to her body. With Elizabeth."

Looking at the young man's tired profile, Murray sucked on his own cigarette, feeling its warmth against his lips. He was back up to twenty a day, but what the hell, he figured he'd earned it. "But what about you? What are you going to do?"

Mike flicked the butt away, and gazed down at his dark shoes. "I'm okay. The baby keeps me going. As soon as it's born, I'm thinking of taking a job in America. Take the kid and try and start myself a new life. Away from London. That's the plan so far, anyway." For the first time since he'd sat down, he turned that stony expression to Murray. "And what about you, Jim? How's the family? Have you got a job yet?"

Murray leaned back, enjoying the almost painful feel of the rough slats behind him. It distracted him from the weight inside. "I think I might go private investigator when Janet's eyes are better. My record before all this happened should stand me in good enough stead to get some clients. Ruby's going to work with me, maybe. You haven't seen her yet, have you?"

Mike shook his head, his face closed down. "Not ready for that yet. Sorry. How's Sam?"

It was Murray's turn to grimace. "Getting better. The child psychologist says she coming on well, but she's still getting the nightmares. Doesn't talk much. I'm hoping she's young enough for it to fade as she grows. We'll have to wait and see. Maybe now we're a proper family, it'll help." He hesitated, unsure of how to continue. "Me and Janet, well, we've kind of got it together recently. Taking it slowly, but it's good for all of us." He smiled slightly. "I don't think Emily would mind. I think she feels life is for the living. I still miss her though. We all do." He stood up, getting ready to leave, sensing Mike wanted to be on his own, but the other man spoke, his voice barely audible above the rustling of the leaves.

"You know what I heard Rachel muttering last time I was here? She was talking about Suzy. She said she'd seen her there, in hell or wherever. It made me think. We all sin, you know, in little ways or big. We've all got to pass through there, to make whatever atonement is required, just the same as we all have to die. It's just the length of stay that varies. Not for Elizabeth though, she's going to be there forever." He paused and Murray wondered what his point was, and then Mike looked at him with all the hopelessness of the world.

"I wonder if that's what my hell will be. Seeing her again and then having to leave her in that insanity for all eternity. I don't think I can do that. I really don't."

Murray pushed his hands deep in his pockets as he looked at the other man. There was no answer for his questions. No answer that he had anyway.

"My advice is worry about that when you're dead. But if you really want to know what I think, I think we've already served our time. We're serving it now and damn any God that thinks otherwise."

Turning away, leaving the young man alone with the breeze, he strolled toward the gates and his car beyond, toward whatever life that waited for him.

THE WIND CALLER
P. D. CACEK

Listen to the leaves rustling. Hear the wind building. These could be the first signs that Gideon Berlander has found you. They could be the last sounds you hear. Gideon hasn't been the same since that terrifying night in the cave, the night he changed forever—the night he became a Wind Caller. But the power to call upon and control the unimaginable force of the wind in all its fury has warped him, twisted his mind, and unleashed a virtually unstoppable monster. Those who oppose Gideon are destroyed . . . horribly. No one can escape the wind. And no one—not even Gideon—knows what nightmarish secrets wait in its swirling grasp.

IN THIS SKIN
SIMON CLARK

The Luxor Dance Hall has seen a lot over the past hundred years. From Vaudeville, through the big bands and up to the hottest rock acts, the Luxor had them all. It's closed now, a boarded-up relic, standing alone in a run down industrial part of town. But the old dance hall isn't empty. A hideous presence lives there, a monstrous evil that has the ability to invade people's fantasies and nightmares...and bring them to life. Three strangers will soon learn the extent of the dance hall's power. As their lives become more and more entangled in its inescapable web, they will come to see that what haunts the Luxor is far worse than any ghost.

Dorchester Publishing Co., Inc.
P.O. Box 6640
Wayne, PA 19087-8640   ___5157-5
                                                         $6.99 US/$8.99 CAN

Please add $2.50 for shipping and handling for the first book and $.75 for each additional book. NY and PA residents, add appropriate sales tax. No cash, stamps, or CODs. Canadian orders require an extra $2.00 for shipping and handling and must be paid in U.S. dollars. Prices and availability subject to change. **Payment must accompany all orders.**

Name: _____

Address: _____

City: _____ State: _____ Zip: _____

E-mail: _____

I have enclosed $_____ in payment for the checked book(s).

CHECK OUT OUR WEBSITE! _www.dorchesterpub.com_
_____ Please send me a free catalog.

STRANGER
SIMON CLARK

The small town of Sullivan has barricaded itself against the outside world. It is one of the last enclaves of civilization and the residents are determined that their town remain free from the strange and terrifying plague that is sweeping the land—a plague that transforms ordinary people into murderous, bloodthirsty madmen. But the transformation is only the beginning. With the shocking realization that mankind is evolving into something different, something horrifying, the struggle for survival becomes a battle to save humanity.

JAMES A. MOORE
POSSESSIONS

Chris Corin has the unshakable feeling that he's being followed. And he's right. But he doesn't know what's after him, what waits in the shadows. He doesn't know that what his late mother left him in her will is the source of inconceivable power. Power that something hideous wants very badly indeed.

By the time Chris realizes what's happening it may already be too late. Who would believe him? Who could imagine the otherworldly forces that will stop at nothing to possess what Chris has? No, Chris will have to confront the darkness that has crept into his life, threatening his very sanity. And unless he can convince someone that he's not crazy, he'll have to confront it alone.

JAMES A. MOORE
FIREWORKS

It begins on a happy day. The small town of Collier gathers on the Fourth of July to watch the fireworks. But in the middle of the celebration, the shocked spectators witness something almost beyond comprehension, something too horrifying to believe. The lucky ones are killed immediately. They escape the true terror that is yet to come, terror that will come from an even more surprising source. . . .

It's quiet now in Collier. The townspeople are waiting, resting, gathering their strength. They know the quiet will soon be shattered. They know the screaming will soon begin. But they don't know what will be left when the screaming stops.

DOUGLAS CLEGG
NIGHTMARE HOUSE

There are places that hold in the traces of evil, houses that become legendary for the mysteries and secrets within their walls. Harrow is one such house. Psychic manifestations, poltergeist activity, hallucinations, and other residue of terror have all been documented in Harrow. It has been called Nightmare House. It is a nest for the restless spirits of the dead.

When Ethan Gravesend arrives to inherit Nightmare House, he does not suspect the horror that awaits him—the nightmare of the woman trapped within the walls of the house, or the endless crying of an unseen child.

Also includes the bonus novella *Purity*!
